SNOW BIRDS

Book 2 of the **GRAND-MAFIA** series

Sandy W Robson

ISBN (eBook): 978-1-7381904-9-2
ISBN (Paperback): 978-1-7381904-8-5

PUBLISHED BY: Sandy Robson Books
Original cover design by Sandy Robson
For a deeper dive into Sandy Robson's writing visit:
www.sandyrobsonbooks.com
Or
Scan the QR code below for more!

Those who fail to plan—plan to fail.

This one's for the original

1

Back on Track

Her body was cold. Lips a deep purple and her eyes were a wash of white. Death looks the same on everyone. It knows no prejudice, has no favorites and makes no bargains. Death is the business partner of the devil, and Bernie was in business with them both.

"I thought you had this under control?" Bernie shouted from the door of the trailer.

"She did—I have—I thought she was doing better!" Ruby got down on the ground beside the frail frame of Natalie.

The sirens outside kept getting louder and so did Bernie's cell phone.

"Yes?" Bernie said answering the call, while staring blankly into the empty eyes of the dead girl on Ruby's red carpet.

Ruby started to pound on Natalie's chest, over and over, with precise placement and strength—a paramedic of the streets. This is the kind of triage learned from experience, not Ivy League and usually is far more effective.

"It's us. There's two—no, three, but one needs

handling immediately," Bernie spoke broken, calm sentences to whoever was on the other end, until whatever they were saying jarred her out of her corpse coma. "Then you make sure you're first! Do you understand?! That's what you're being paid for!" Bernie jammed her index finger into the END button on the phone, like she was stabbing it into the eye of the caller.

"Wake up!" Ruby screamed. Down on her knees— raising her clasped hands in a united fist above her head— readying for another cardiac blow.

"Poob. Stop," Bernie told her little sister, knowing the repeated effort was in vain. "Stop!"

Ruby stopped. It was just a husk. Just a shadow left of the light that was Natalie. The girl that was in her care, that she cared so deeply for, was no longer there. Ruby looked up from the stiff 18-year-old lying on the floor in front of her. The whites of Ruby's eyes were full of red cracks that warned of the ensuing tidal wave. This was Benny all over again, but this time it could be worse. If the dike between Ruby and her bottomless pit of sadness broke, there might be no stopping the deluge.

Bernie knew what was behind Ruby's eyes and she knew what had to be done. She walked over and pulled Ruby up from the ground, quickly, but gently. "Poob. Poob! Look at me. She's gone. You know she is—but we are still here. I know you can hear those sirens outside. Those aren't ambulances, they're cops, and they are on their way here—for us. I know this is hard, but she'll have to wait. I need you to pull yourself together and do what you need to do. You need to call Kurt right now. RIGHT NOW! Turn your air on high, call Kurt, then go sit outside, catch your breath and get your shit and your story straight."

Instantly Ruby sucked her emotions inside, as if her raw nerves were Raman noodles dangling from her lips.

2

She wasn't soulless, this was just the way it was for them now. They had stepped far beyond the shoes they wore here. Out of the pumps and into blood-covered sandals. They were no longer Buffalo Girls, or Three Dames' Dinner Delivery—they were players, they were feared, they were the Grand-mafia.

This story had grown too. So far from the Lincoln and the tussle with Connie by the shuffleboard courts. The bodies were piling up and so were the problems. The woman that wanted to fly below the radar was suddenly in the crosshairs. I started telling you this story with the promise of showing you the how of it all. This is it—such an important part of that how. A point on the map of this story that would forever have a pin in it. Not because they broke or because Natalie had joined her brother in that great gallery in the sky, but because it's the moment she made the decision. The moment Bernie knew it was time to make good on her promise.

But I'm getting ahead of myself. This is an important juncture, but it is one pearl on the necklace that made the strand. One important bead that aligned with the others and began to tighten around her neck. There is so much that led to here. Each of the pieces that built this legendary puzzle are important, and if I don't tell you all of them, then no one will. Because no one else can. So, let's go back a little. To the fall of 1991.

By the time most of the snowbirds had returned to winter in Cicada Hollow, the women were in full swing. Bernie, Ruby and Opal were making runs every week between the drugstore on the outskirts of Miami and the warehouse in Georgia. The drops had changed locations though. They were now being made at the safe house. The apartment that Hellsa had set up for them to rest at before returning to New Smyrna. The change was made because it looked better having the boxes of adult undergarments going into a dwelling, instead of an industrial building. More believable and less suspicious to possible prying eyes. This new plan was working wonderfully. Hellsa was very happy with the movement of goods and the women were happy with the piling stacks of money that kept coming in.

The delivery of money had a new system too. Instead of tiny black duffle bags of it—it was now delivered by dead drop. Paid upon each of their return to the park. It was paid every time, on time, with no banter or parking lot exchanges. It was delivered close, but not too close—left in a hiding spot, just outside of the trailer park grounds. It was hidden behind the first thing Ruby saw when they arrived at the retirement ranch all those months ago. Hidden in the right side of the curved, white-painted cinder blocks that flanked the entrance gate. More specifically, it was hidden behind the sign. The thing that got stuck in her craw immediately. The one that made her feel old, the bronze plaque that said, 'A 55+ Community'.

The sign had been pried loose and the wall hollowed out, so that the money could be tucked behind it. The bronze sign was the obvious difference in an all-white wall, but that's the best place to hide things—in plain sight. This kept their payroll close and the amount of suspicious traffic coming and going in and out of the park to a minimum. It also made sure that no money was being exchanged anywhere along the run. No bands of cash to be found on any old ladies moving diapers down the I-95. The plan was good, and the good times had begun to roll.

Ruby wasted no time in putting her dollars to use, but even with stacks of money it wasn't easy. She had the dream and the money, but not the papers. She was dying to get the transformation of the old Quonset hut in the woods underway, but there are gatekeepers of dreams and Ruby's were made of paper. Not dollar bills, she had stacks and stacks of those now, her paper gatekeepers were red tape. Permits. Building permits were mandatory for her to hire a professional crew. Skilled trades people who could make her vision come to life, get it done right and in a timely fashion. The Quonset hut, however, was going to be an illegal 'booze can' in the middle of the woods, whose title was put into the name of an old, vegetative woman. This was not going to check the boxes on the county application. So, Ruby worked around the permits. She did what all folks who run with the devil do, she stuck to her people. She called someone she knew might be able to get a crew that didn't need permits. Someone she had history with. Someone who had stared down the barrel of the gun beside her. Someone she could trust—and that's how this someone came back into the picture.

"Ruby?" Daz called over to the self-proclaimed forewoman, from the other side of the hut. "Why are we putting the stage all the way out here?"

Ruby stormed over to the shirtless, ponytailed biker, with the tool belt hanging off of his hip, "Because the dressing room will be behind it. My word, I know you have been to a strip bar before, Daz." She pointed to the right and left of where he was standing. "DJ booth there and door to the dressing room there."

"This would be so much easier if I had plans," Daz grumbled.

"And life would be so much easier if I were a house cat, but we can't always have what we want, pumpkin."

5

Ruby turned to Natalie who was enjoying the barb, as Daz shook his head and rejoined his rag tag construction crew made up of bikers.

"Every time? It's a thousand questions a day when you're here. And when you're gone, they barely do anything at all. Why didn't you just hire real construction workers?" Natalie asked, perturbed.

"I heard that!" Daz shouted.

"I wanted you to!" Natalie fired back.

"Hey, lay off him." Ruby got in front of Natalie's line of sight. "They are real builders, some are better than others, but they are all trustworthy—and that is worth more than a little down time. You know what we're doing here. I can't go out and hire just anybody—they are on the same side of the tracks as us. And you better get used to them, because they are going be around long after the build is finished."

"You're serious? You're still set on that? I thought that was just an idea, not a 'for certain'."

"We need them. Just like the Rolling Stones did. We need security, outside and in."

"You mean the Altamont Speedway concert?"

"My word, how'd you know about that?"

"Mom was a big fan and if I remember, that didn't work out too well." Natalie was not buying the comparison.

"Fair enough, but the truth is that nowadays no one shits where these guys live. If their club has an interest in this place, a financial interest, then all of our interests can be protected. Speaking of interests—don't you have some-where to be?" Ruby pulled her phone out of her purse and checked the time.

"I don't know why you're making me go. Don't people go to school so they can have this? A business? We already have it." Natalie glared at Daz. "Well, we will if these animals ever finish the work."

"We have it, but we need to keep it. That's why you need to go. You need to know more than anyone else. More than me and anyone who would try and take this from me. I was swindled by men my whole life who knew more than I did. Not street smarts, you and I have those in spades, but their smarts. The jargon they throw around to confuse us and make us feel small. They let me build it all just to take it all—but that won't be you. You are going to know both sides of the tracks. Both sides of the coin so no matter which side it lands on, you will have already called it. It's not just me who wanted this for you. Ben worked his ass off so you could make more of yourself. So go make more. Perfect the perfection that is you, Natalie. Your claws are sharp enough, now is the time to sharpen your mind and turn both your strengths into weapons."

Natalie relented in a small, defiant huff. Although the speech was inspiring, she was still an 18-year-old girl, being told to go to school. She reluctantly retrieved her knapsack from behind the partially constructed bar and headed for the door.

"You need a ride?" Daz stopped hammering and stood up.

Ruby shouted, "You keep your eyes on the nails, Daz, or I'll be the one hammering the last two into your pine box." After giving Daz the evil eye, she handed Natalie a ring with a single key on it. "Do the speed limit, no passengers and—"

"I know, I know. It's my grandma's car."

Ruby raised her eyebrow, "Which grandma?"

Natalie thought for a second. "Dalia? It's Grandma Dalia now, isn't it?"

"No, that was last week. It's Grandma Mary this week. Mary Dunford."

"Mary Dunford. Got it," Natalie flippantly assured her with all the sincerity of an omnipotent youth and left the hut.

Ruby turned back to face Daz. "Whatever it is you've got going on in your little head—or your other little head —forget it. Natalie is off limits. I wasn't joking about the pine box."

"Got it!" Daz scoffed.

Ruby stayed fixed on him. "And put a shirt on!"

She had the corner all set up. A pseudo-living room of sorts. The large, stiff armchair was lined with pillows and crocheted blankets, making it bearable for old bones and flat asses to endure it for longer than an hour at a time. A smaller chair that was in the far corner had been enlisted to contribute to the nook. It was brought over and adorned with throw pillows stolen from the lobby to act as a footrest. The table between the chair and the bed was now the home for a stack of books she had been meaning to read, and an 8"x10" picture of the two of them. It was a colorized black and white photo of their wedding, dramatically lit up by the dim bulb of the extra floor lamp she'd brought from the trailer to read by. Ceiling lights would have worked, but she didn't want to disturb him—even though he couldn't be disturbed. Reg looked so young in the photograph, so smooth and handsome, you could almost smell the Brylcreem in his combed hair. Freda was a vision in white. Her bouquet was a dome of blue hydrangeas, her favorite color, which satisfied both her and one of the wedding rhyme requirements. Reg always joked that she was one of the other three rhyme requirements, the 'something old', because she was two years older than him. He also always followed up that punchline by stating his insatiable desire for older women.

That was the joke and the flirt, but it was also the truth. She was older. Freda was supposed to go first. That's what was fair, it's what she'd always thought would happen. She never had envisioned sitting by his hospital bed, day in and day out. It was supposed to be the reverse. He was supposed to be holding her hand, adoring her no matter how withered she became. He was good at that, she wasn't. Empathy wasn't on her traits list—she was no Florence Nightingale. This was a reality she could never have conceived of. The reality where she sat bedside, wondering when the other woman would show up and if she'd ever get the chance to ask Reg the big question—how? How could he possibly love the two of them? How could he make babies with her and just walk away from them? How could he be the man she loved and be something else, someone else entirely? Freda was there every day alone with her thoughts. Every day spent by his side with her hows and every night she spent in the lanai, crunching numbers for the crew. Money was a blessing and a curse for Freda. It always is for those who run with the devil. It's not the making of it that's hard, it's the using it.

The door opened to Reg's newly appointed, private room. Freda looked up from her hardcover of Great Expectations to find the doctor entering. It was Doctor Noth, the same doctor who, just over a month ago, had tried to talk her out of long-term care for Reg.

"Good afternoon, Mrs. Hall," he said, cheerfully. "Hope the new room is working out for you."

Freda went back to her book. "It's sufficient."

The doctor picked up the chart hanging off of the end

of Reg's bed. "I see that Sylvia is keeping up on his washes and Jennifer has been diligent with the monitor stats."

"Uh, huh," Freda said, keeping her eyes on the pages of her classic.

"Well, everything looks consistent." Dr. Noth scanned the front page of the clipboard.

"Still a vegetable. Same as last week," Freda grumbled.

Uncomfortable with the jab, he placed the clipboard back on the hook at the end of the bed. "While I'm here is there anything else you need?"

"Uh, uh." She continued to ignore him.

"Right. Well then, I'm off," he stated but didn't move, standing there as fidgety as a child at an opera.

"Oh shit, Noth!" Freda slammed her hardcover closed and looked up at him. "Are you blind? How the hell do you do surgery if you can't see what's right under your nose? It's on the clipboard—under the chart you so diligently looked over."

Dr. Noth looked around, worried. "You left it there?"

"Calm your stethoscope, I put it there a few minutes ago. You arrive at the same time on the same day, every week. I'm not the weak link in this chain—did you figure out the funnel like I told you?"

"Funnel?" Dr. Noth responded as if he'd been asked a question he didn't know was going to be on the exam.

"Oh Christ—the money. Did you figure out how to wash the money?"

"Yes," the doctor said, clueing in. "It's being spread out. Small charges. A little on each on my rounds. Like you said," he stated, in a whisper, unclipping the envelope from the clipboard and quickly stuffing it into the large lower pocket of his lab coat.

"How about that, huh? You learned that from little old me—and to think, I never went to college." Freda hit him with the insult before returning to her hardcover. "I'm sure you have less salad-like patients to attend to. See you next week."

The doctor was given his cue but was still standing there. "He's not going to wake up, Mrs. Hall."

"I know," Freda said, softly, free of jabs or insults.

Dr. Noth took a step towards her. "Is it worth it? I don't know where your money is coming from, but you came in here with no insurance and no idea how to pay the initial bill. This is a lot of money and wherever it's coming from, it can't be good. I've gotten myself into a few corners before with gambling and I know how these people work. At this point in your life, you shouldn't be risking yourself and wasting your money like—"

"It's not a waste and it's none of your business. So, unless you learned how to make miracles happen— goodbye—take your money and I'll see you next week."

The phone had been ringing twice a day since she ran out. The calls came in like clockwork, 9:00am and 2:00pm. It was a problem that she couldn't go to Bernie for. Bernie would just pick up the phone and tell the person off, but Opal wouldn't hear of it, so she opted for the alternative. She figured out where the line came into the trailer—the junction box attached to the side of her house where the phone wire from the pole led to. She opened it up and found that it was surprisingly simple in its design—simple to disconnect it. All it came down to was two screws and a flathead driver. This lineman act was a part of Opal's routine now. Twice a day. At 7:45am she would go outside, open the box and undo the screws and she would reverse the task every day just after 2:00pm. She was pretty proud of herself for handling this on her own. For not needing Stan or Bernie. But the truth was, she never told Bernie who really was calling, because she knew that Bernie would go right to the source and Opal could not have the leader of the Grand-mafia meeting Reverend Kind.

The Reverend wasn't calling because of the first donations she had made or the stage fright she had at the show, he was calling about her continuing support. Opal had been sending the Reverend envelopes of money every week since they started up again. Not all of it. She was also sending some home to her three kids, keeping Stan on a steady allowance and socking a little bit away for herself. But the runs had increased along with the money, so the portion she was sending to the Ministry was enough to have the good Reverend salivating.

"Opal? Did George call?" Stan was already sipping on a beer, and it was just after 8:00am.

Opal shook her head. She didn't speak for fear of the twitches that took over her with untruths. Technically it wasn't a lie, because he hadn't called, but she really didn't want to mince words as to why.

"I'm going to be off soon," Opal said, cheerfully.

"Alright then. Where's my play money?" Stan asked, looking around the main room.

Opal pointed to the small kitchen table where she had set out a fan of bills. "Two hundred and fifty. Like you asked."

Stan snatched the cash from the table before wrapping his arms around her and giving her a big, beer-soaked kiss. "Thank you, Bunny."

Opal lit up like a Christmas tree. She could only see the was in Stan, not the is.

"You drive safe. That Corolla is special order."

"Champagne," she said with a nod and a smile.

"That's right, Bunny. Champagne." He then did a horrible Robin Leach impression. "Champagne wishes and caviar dreams." Opal giggled on cue, clearly being the solo audience to this deplorable act before. "Well, I'm going to go see what's cooking on the courts," Stan said getting a new beer from the fridge.

"Oh, alright, Stan, I'll see you when I get home then."

"Bunny, you have a memory like a sieve. It's boys' night remember. George is still mourning, so I may be late. You just make yourself something to eat when you get back. I'll get food at the bar—don't wait up," he said with a wink as he left out the carport door.

Don't wait up? More like see you tomorrow. The new runs the women were doing included an overnight stay in Georgia. Which would have been a big issue if Stan was waiting for her to come home, so Bernie helped her work the magic. Like everything Opal's inebriated husband did, it was secretly managed from the sidelines, so Bernie gave her a new play to run. Stan loved to be the big shot at his bar and buying drinks for the low-lifes that frequented the place was how he held his title. Bernie convinced Opal to up his allowance, giving him more to play with and to consume. Opal then orchestrated a chance meeting between him and George—the newest widower in the park, who liked to drown his loss in liquor. This was something that Stan and George quickly bonded over. The glue was not the loss, it was the burying of daily life under a sea of ethanol that fused these two booze hounds together. Once Opal told Bernie that the 'chance' meeting had gone well, Bernie made sure to bump into George in the park. After condolences and niceties, she then hit him with brilliant idea of a boys' night out. It was a welcome concept to George, but Bernie had to explain to him that Stan had a bit of an issue with alcohol and that if Stan got too drunk, it was probably best if he slept it off at George's place. This ticked off a huge box on the alcoholic's check list. The one right under denial. There's nothing a drunk loves more than feeling superior, in control and not as bad off as one of their buddies. Bernie told him that Opal was sensitive to that sort of thing, that she just hated to see Stan drunk and with George still being so sensitive about his dearly departed, he was more than happy to be the gentleman and oblige. Stan always got blind drunk, every boys' night out started at 8:00am and week after week George obliged. This was good management. Stan was out of the picture for a clear day and night once a week, every week, with a babysitter and Opal didn't have to lie to make it happen.

Looking out through the back bedroom window, Opal made sure that Stan was all the way over at the shuffleboard courts before she got her things together. Her 'go' bag was simple, just like the run Bernie and Hellsa had designed. All Opal had to take with her was her purse and a change of undergarments. Carrying around a pair of underwear in her purse made her feel like a woman of the night. It felt dangerous and saucy—and she loved it. It was all part of the allure, that first brought her into this and still had not gotten old for her. If anything, it had gotten better. Fresher, more titillating and addictive. A pair of loose panties in her purse was the uniform of her alter ego—the knee-high boots and golden lasso of her superhero, her road ego, the one that she called Bernadette. A bitch who took names, threw hands, made moves and never apologized or felt guilt for any of it. Bernadette was a bad-ass and once a week Opal got to slip into her panties. The underwear wasn't the only thing she brought, there was also the brown paper bag. The other women didn't pack anything really on these runs and usually bought food at gas stations along the way, but like she did for Stan, Opal always packed a lunch for Bernadette. Forever the caretaker, even Opal's alter ego was to be mothered by her and apparently, Bernadette liked egg salad sandwiches, something that had turned Opal's stomach ever since her first pregnancy.

With the panties stuffed in the purse, the top of the lunch bag perfectly rolled down and Stan affectively bothering everyone at the shuffleboard courts, Bernadette set out on her run. First, she put her handbag and packed lunch into the champagne-colored Corolla, then she went over to the junction box to reattach the phone line. The heads of the screws were getting so worn from the constant use, that the driver kept slipping out of the slots. It was frustrating and just as she finished putting the last one back in its place, something even more frustrating happened— the phone inside the trailer rang. It was well past 8:00am, past the time the Reverend had been calling, so her mind started to worry. Stan and Opal didn't receive a lot of calls. None really that they weren't expecting. What if it was one of the kids? The fantasy had been put on hold, forcing Bernadette to take a time out and for Opal to rush back into the trailer.

Opal picked up the receiver on the wall mounted phone. "Oh, hi, this is—"

"Opal Rose?!" A woman cut her off excitedly.

"Yes?"

"Opal, this is Paula. The Reverend's assistant. I'm so glad to catch you. Are you alright? We've been calling for over a month now. Have you been away?"

This was a double-edged sword. It wasn't just lying; it was also lying to the assistant of the self-proclaimed direct line of God. Opal was in a corner and with only a rock and a hard place as exits, she chose to hide under the cover of silence.

"Opal? Are you there? Opal?"

"Oh—this really isn't a good time."

"Opal, I need to speak with you about your donations. They have been very generous but—"

"This isn't a good time."

"But Opal, I need to confirm a few things—for taxes. Uncle Sam is sure to ask questions about our new bene-factor and the Reverend needs me to get all the—"

"This is not a good time."

"I realize that, but with our quarterlies due, we really need—"

"I said, it's not a good time." Opal hung up—again.

She hadn't thought through the workings of her kind-ness. All the red tape that's tied around illegal money. She was trying to do some good, by giving away some of Bernadette's money, to offset the bad, but all it was creating was headaches and questions. The phone rang again. Opal looked to the wall mounted rotary, but the ring wasn't coming from there, it was a different kind of ring, and it was coming from outside.

Opal made her way to the carport and dug her pink-painted cell phone out of her purse. Ever since Bernie told her that phones cause cancer, she's treated the modern convenience like Chernobyl.

"Is there something wrong? If it's Stan, I can go talk to him," Bernie said on the other end, loud enough for Opal to hear without bringing the phone to her ear.

"Nothing's wrong. Stan's out at the court."

"Alright, then why aren't you on your way?"

"I was just leaving," Opal said, holding the phone out in front of her and speaking into it like it was possessed.

"Safe travels," Bernie wished.

Opal ended the call with a press of the button and looked up from her phone. Bernie was standing out on her front lawn. Opal waved to her then got into her car and turned it on. As the air-conditioning kicked in, she opened the glove box, and she pulled out a tape. A single, white cassette tape with no case. The writing on the tape was completely faded, smudged from the ample handling of sweaty thumbs, making it impossible to see who the band was, but she didn't care. She knew who it was. She jammed the tape into the open mouth of the factory-mounted cassette deck in the dash and hit the rewind button. As the motor of the tape player spun backwards, making a whining sound, Opal backed the car out of her driveway. Just as she righted her direction, the tape player clunked, and the motor stopped spinning. Opal pressed play and dug a pair of sunglasses out of her purse. They were fancy sunglasses. Too fancy and not pink enough for Opal. She pressed play on the stereo and turned the volume up. Way up. 'Gloria' by Laura Branigan suddenly blasted through the speakers of the air-conditioned sedan, she put the car in drive and stepped on the gas. Opal had left the car and someone else had taken the wheel. Those were Bernadette's sunglasses and 'Gloria' was Bernadette's song.

Bernie and Freda sat across the street from the bar, like a couple of old-timey cops on a stakeout. Their seats were reclined back, sunglasses on, windows rolled down, sipping shitty coffee from paper cups as they watched the parking lot closely. Well Freda watched it more closely than Bernie did, because she loved this stuff. She was gonna be Starsky whether Bernie wanted to be Hutch or not.

"You really watched me every day?" Bernie was still grappling with the notion.

"And night. The best evidence came at night. I had enough juice in just one of my notebooks to guarantee you a tattooed girlfriend named Cherise."

"Doesn't sound so bad. Especially if Cherise makes good jailhouse hooch." Freda didn't laugh, so Bernie pulled the binoculars away from Freda's eyes. "Why were you watching me?"

"Because I knew who you were."

"You recognized me?"

"No. I had a brother who was like you. He didn't last long, but he was in it long enough for me to catch his scent. You smelled the same. My gut was doing circles and I needed to quiet it."

"Scent huh? Look at you now. Guess we're wearing the same perfume," Bernie smirked.

Freda raised the binoculars back to her eyes. "It was a waste. I should have spent that time with Reg, instead of watching you."

"How is he?"

"Same. And don't ask—because the answer is no."

"I wasn't going to." Bernie looked back to the parking lot. "We've been here a while, Freda. You sure he's here?"

"Believe you me, he is. I saw him peel out of here on my way back from the hospital more than once. Trust me, he's in there and he's the one."

"If he is the one, the only way to flip someone like him is to have leverage."

"That's why I brought you here. I found the sod, that's my department, the flipping however is up to you."

Across the street, there was movement. Bernie followed suit and lifted her binoculars up to her eyes. They both watched as a portly man left the bar and staggered around to the back of the building.

Bernie sounded surprised, "He's drunk. You were right."

From the back of the bar a car appeared. It was a two-toned one, a black and white, Ford Crown Victoria, with blue and red lights on top. The portly man was behind the wheel.

Freda looked over to Bernie. "You wanted leverage?"

"That's leverage, but we just need to play it right."

Freda opened the door and started to get out.

"Where the hell are you going? I said I need to figure out a plan."

"I know. But he's leaving and that coffee is going straight through me—and not in the convenient way either. So, come on," Freda snarled, motioning with her head towards the bar. "Call it reconnaissance!"

At this pace, the club would be open by the end of November. Darcy, Nola and Cathy were all in. What they couldn't contribute financially to the dream, they were investing in sweat equity, and it was paying off. Ben's paintings were being lovingly protected by Cathy, who spent her time up on scaffolding preserving his brushstrokes and sprays, on the walls and arched ceiling, under a thick layer of varnish. Nola was working her magic on the booths. She was stretching plush, crushed velvet over the bench seats they'd acquired and covering the tables in a collection of their vintage flyers—turning every table into a scrap book of stripper advertising under glass. Darcy was a one-woman painting machine, painting anything and everything that Daz's boys finished building, working right behind them, keeping them moving, like a pit bull at their heels. And their tireless leader, Ruby, was at her sewing machine, making massive, red-velvet curtains for the stage. She and the girls decided that even though this place would be under the radar, it had to be over the top. They wanted it to ooze class and nostalgia and they wanted a stage that demanded respect.

"Who's going to get the first dance?" Ruby threw out to the room, pausing the whir of her Singer for a moment.

"You!" was the unanimous answer that came back.

"My word, ladies. Thank you, but I was thinking that maybe we could all come out together."

"Oh, I love that idea." Cathy was excited.

"But not for the first dance. No offense, Cath, but all of this is because of Ruby, she should be first." Nola picked her ground.

"What if we all came out at the end together, every night?" Darcy was onto something.

"Like a curtain call?" Ruby asked.

"Yes. But we do a number first, then the bows," Darcy kept riffing.

"That would make it more like a show than a strip." Nola was not sure.

"It is a show." Ruby stood up from her sewing table. "It's what we talked about. Something new, but also old. Most young people have no idea about pageantry. It's all tits and ass for them. Well not here, we are going to bring Burlesque to the Bush."

"So, no nipples?" Nola seemed upset.

"Not if you don't want. We can tease or please, it's up to us. We make our own routines. Anything goes as long as it's dazzling!"

"Does that mean my 'Pinto' can park out back?" Nola winked. "You know, for 'Very VIP' customers?"

Ruby laughed, "Lady, it has its own reserved spot."

"So, we've decided? It's a curtain call then?!" Darcy was ecstatic.

Nola was strutting around the room shouting, "Honey, we will have them on their feet, before we have them on their knees!"

Natalie was far from the Bone Park and in her element, surrounded by youth, big brains and big dreams. It was only a community college, Daytona State—Edgewater Campus—but it was Harvard to her. She loved the lectures and the murmur of the other students in the common areas. The exchange and defense of ideas, the pursuit of knowledge and the underlying hunger to change destinies. Business major. That's what Natalie was. She could have rumbled with anyone at any of the big universities, but she insisted on staying close. Ruby had offered and it wasn't a money issue, it was a family issue. She had a role model now. Someone she wanted to live up to and impress. She didn't want to be alone anymore and that was worth more than the Ivy League certificate.

She did originally have other intentions, another path of passion to pursue, but this practicum was translatable. Natalie could see its practical use in every facet of Ruby's business. She could picture herself one day building a dream like Ruby. She was her little protégé and had a million ideas on how to improve it all.

"What are you working on?" the boy with long curly surfer hair asked and Natalie slammed her binder closed.

"Nothing." She was angry he had walked up on her. "Do I know you?" she asked, even though she knew she did. He sat a couple of rows down from her in Biz 102. It was an easy class for her, so she spent most of her time in it staring at his hair. It was blonde, but it wasn't bleached by the bottle, it was bleached by the sun. His eyes were blue, his skin was deeply tanned, and you could smell the ocean on him from two rows back. He was so different from her. Alien almost in comparison, but that's what she found so interesting.

"You're in my Biz class," he stated honestly, with that lackadaisical drawl that seems to come with every surfboard.

"Your Biz class?" Natalie shot down his plane before it ever left the runway.

"Our class," he corrected himself. "What was that you were doodling?" He pointed to the binder that she was desperately holding closed, as if it were a clam that might open suddenly and scream out all her secrets into the common area.

"What's it to you?" She was on the defensive.

"Nothing. Sorry. Forget I asked." The boy backed off, raising his hands in surrender and walking away. "I just thought it looked cool. That's all."

"A gallery," she blurted out, causing the boy to stop.

"A gallery?" He turned and cautiously walked back towards her, unsure if this was some kind of feminine trap.

"Yeah." She opened her binder, reluctantly, and turned it around on the table for him to see. "It's an art gallery. Sort of. Just some ideas."

The picture was crude, but visionary. It was like a Gehry building, angled and jarring, with energetic lines and curves that demanded attention and were totally awe-inspiring.

"I'd go to that gallery," he said with a smile.

"Have you ever been to a gallery?"

"Nope. But I'd go to that one, for sure."

"Thanks."

He tilted his head. "Why are you in Biz?"

The question seemed out of place. "I just showed you. So I can open a gallery like this someday."

"Open? You should be designing them, not running them."

Natalie slammed the binder closed again. "Right. Thanks, but I'm not the artist in the family."

"It's no Mona Lisa, but that building was dope. Seriously you should be an architect not a manager."

Natalie got up, hurriedly grabbing her things. "Thanks for the advice."

"Hey, I didn't mean to insult you, straight up. I like your drawing. I was just giving you my opinion."

Natalie threw her bag over her shoulder. "Well I didn't ask for it."

As the month's end drew closer, Bernie made her run to Miami. Even though she had been making this run for months now, Bernie and the clerk of the drugstore still pretended they'd never seen each other. He did the same with all of them—it was part of the plan, and it was being followed to a T. The framed picture on the wall behind the cash register showed that the clerk was employee of the month, yet again. No doubt for his high sales on the adult undergarments that were flying off the shelves.

Everyone was benefiting, especially Hellsa. Her product was moving at an unprecedented rate, without interruption—profits had never been higher, and she had a trustworthy partner. A partner she liked to deal with face to face. Once a week, every week, Hellsa waited for Bernie in the safe house at the Georgia end of her run.

"On time, as usual," Hellsa said in the same way as the week before, with that slight Norwegian lilt to her words, sitting at the small table in the tiny kitchen of the rented apartment.

"Vergil used to say the same thing." Bernie set down her purse on the spotless counter, just inside the door.

"He was a good man." Hellsa gave a genuine pause—a moment of silence that spoke as highly about her as she had about him.

"What is all this?" Bernie asked, referring to the wrapped present and large bottle of champagne on the tiny table.

"It's our dozen! Today marks your twelfth run." Hellsa was beaming.

"Okay?" Bernie said, sitting down across from her. "Twelve doesn't seem like the number most people celebrate at. Fifty or a hundred maybe, but twelve?"

"You and I are not most people, Verna," Hellsa announced as she popped the cork on the bottle and scrambled to catch the explosion of foam in one of the flutes. "Twelve uninterrupted, untarnished, undetected, full-load runs. That is unheard of along the I-95 and you did it."

"My girls and I did it—with your help, of course."

"Verna, this is just the beginning. The moment I heard that you were in Florida, I knew that we were going to make waves." She poured Bernie a full, but less foamy, glass of bubbles.

"I don't like celebrating until it's over."

"Over?" Hellsa seemed a little perplexed. "When would we be over? Why would we be?"

"You and I both know that someday this will come to an end." Bernie wasn't being cryptic, just factual.

"That is correct—someday. But someday is not today. Not today, devil, not today!" Hellsa raised her glass.

Bernie sighed. One of her big, breathy tells, that thankfully Hellsa was yet to pick up on. "Someday is not today!" she cheered, clinking glasses and drowning her subtext under the nose-tickling fizz of the champagne. "Be honest," Bernie said, following her swallow. "Why do you come here every week? There's no need. It's more hassle and heat for you to come all the way here. If there was a problem I could understand, but there isn't, so why? Are you checking up on me?"

"Heavens no. You are right, there is no need to check up on you. You are like Swiss clockwork. Precision. Clean movement, consistent and reliable. Verna, I come because we are partners. Partners work together, not for each other. But in all honesty, I come because I enjoy your company. We are cut from the same cloth."

"I enjoy your banter too, Hellsa, but we are not from the same cloth, not even the same material or factory. I'm polyester and you're silk."

"Is that so? Foolish of me. I clearly know far more about you than you about me. It's funny how we do that. When we know facts about another, we feel akin to them. That our knowing bonds us and they somehow know us as well. Like movie stars or musicians. But that is not true, is it? You don't know me."

"No. So, tell me. Tell me how you and I are the same?"

Hellsa sat back into the bench seat. "Contrary to what you may believe, I was not always sailing on yachts and moving mountains of white. Back in Norway, I grew up on a farm. It was a beautiful farm. Stunning green fields sitting under the sheer rock faces, that towered over the fjord. It was a magical place when I was very little but as I grew, I began to see that we were poor. Goats and greens were our only means of food and income. My father was not much of a fisherman, so we were stuck working the land. We worked it, very hard—the kind of hard labor that does not lead to long lives. My father and mother both fell ill at the same time one year. I was 11 years old. I did my best to take care of them, but I was only 11 and they died within a week. I spent the next seven years alone on that farm. Tending to the goats and greens—the best I knew how, surviving—barely. One day a man showed up and promised me a better life. Starvation and isolation make bitter tongues sound sweet, so I left the farm. Walked away from my troubles with him, only to endure the worst ten years of my life. It was not life. No winter on the farm could ever compare to the hell he led me to. I was trafficked and used, bought and sold. Your sister and I have a lot in common as well. I may not have been sharpened on the same stone as you, Verna, but our grinding rocks are from the same pile. We climbed out of our pits before the dirt could be stacked on top of us. That's why I come. Because we are the tattered sheets. Only women like us can understand women like us. And women like us who stick together, can take over the world."

Bernie took it all in. Swirling Hellsa's story around her mind, like a sommelier of trauma. The brief, tragic overview of Hellsa's past was not what she was expecting. There was no silver spoon, just ashes and no words to follow it, just a gesture—a raising of Bernie's flute, in salute to her fellow phoenix.

The ladies gathered at the front of the hut, because the men had made good on their word. In fact, they had done better than good, they had finished ahead of schedule.

November 28, 1991 would be the date engraved on the plaque. The official day that a dream came true and there was nothing left to do but name it. The outside of the Quonset hut was left just as Ruby had found it. Rusty and raw, with the exception of the front door, that had been painted red. This was to preserve the charm of the weathered hut, allowing it to keep blending into its surroundings, slowly disappearing into the forest that was trying to take it over. It was a natural layer of camouflage that was necessary as it was an illegal booze can after all. Ruby had decided on a name, but she hadn't told anyone yet. The only other living soul that knew what she wanted to christen the speakeasy with, was the man hired to make the sign. One of Daz's friends who was sworn to secrecy. That's who they were all waiting for. A former biker in a big, old pickup truck to come down the dirt path with the hut's handle in the bed.

"Ruby's," Darcy said confidently, but the other women were not in agreeance.

"There is no way in hell she is naming the place Ruby's, it not only puts a target on her head— it's too pedestrian." Nola shut that down.

"My word, Nola. I have been called a lot of things, but pedestrian?" Ruby was comically insulted.

"You know what I mean." Nola blew it off. "I bet you went for something metaphorical. Spectacular and theatrical, like...The Looking Glass?"

The bikers and the ladies liked the sound of that one, taking a moment to ponder it.

"No, but now I wish I had called it that." Ruby was having second thoughts. "That does sound spectacular and theatrical, my word."

Cathy was eager to contribute. "Or The Orange Peel. Get it? Double meaning."

"I get it," Ruby chuckled. "But I think it might be a little too on the nose."

"Well, it looks like Jeopardy is over ladies, you can all stop guessing," Daz said, pointing to the dirt tracks that led out from the clearing, into the woods. "He's here."

The beat-up old truck bounced its way down the rough tracks, into the clearing, then swung around the group to back up to the door. On the front of the Quonset hut, above the newly painted entrance, high up at the top of the flat wall near the arch, Daz's guys had installed two L-shaped brackets. They were bolted to the metal hut, waiting to be graced with their new, massive placard. A couple of bearded men got out of the truck's cab and walked around to the back. They undid the straps from either side of the bed, then pulled out the large sign, still hidden under a drop cloth.

"You want us to hoist it up or are you going to do it?" the driver of the truck called out to Daz.

"I believe that question was for me?" Ruby spoke up. "We talked on the phone. And no, I am not the secretary. This is my place. I'd appreciate it if you could hoist it up for me but leave the tarp on it."

"Yes ma'am," the driver of the truck replied, respectfully.

The men proceeded to sling ropes up and over the brackets and attached the end of the ropes to the rings on the top of the sign. They then pulled it up, hoisting it into the air like circus folk erecting the Big Top and tied it off. With the covered sign dangling in the air, they hustled up separate ladders and connected the sign's rings to their waiting, permanent fixtures.

Once the two bearded workmen came down, Ruby walked up to the bottom of ladder on the left. "Well, this is it. All our blood, sweat and tears have come down to this."

Ruby started to climb the ladder, rung by rung. "When I first saw this place, I knew it was special. It was more than what met the eye, more than what the world saw from the outside—just like the person who brought me here. The one who made a pearl inside of this shell. While this place is a dream for us four old tassel twirlers, it's also a living gallery—for the artist that was here." Ruby reached the top of the ladder and pointed to her heart. "And still is here."

Ruby reached out from the ladder and pulled the tarp off. It was a hand carved, hand painted, wooden sign, with a crescent moon at the top, a heart at the bottom and in between the two, in a cursive font was the name. A single word that meant so very much—Moonlight.

Everyone gazed up at the sign in silence—everyone but Natalie, whose head was hung down. She and Ruby were the only two who knew what Moonlight meant and that meant a lot to both of them. Ruby climbed down from the ladder and went right over to Natalie, pulling her under her arm and kissing her head. Natalie looked up and saw the charm that Benny had put on layaway, hanging at the end of a thin gold chain around Ruby's neck. He was close, she could feel him, and she loved that Ruby kept him there.

The drive back from Georgia was always pleasant. There was no contraband in the car, no pick-up or drop-off waiting and there was always OJ. This had always been a tradition for Bernie, one she shared with me, and I shared with mine. It was a staple on any road trip. A pop off the I-95 and into the Florida Welcome Center—a rest stop just inside the Florida State line. There was a small kiosk just inside the building where they gave everyone a small paper cup of free orange juice. It was touristy and cheesy, and Bernie loved it. Opal and Ruby never stopped here on their runs, but Bernie did every time. She had acquired a 'handicap' sticker recently from Daryl and was loving its use in finding front row parking. At her age, only other people her age questioned the sticker's validity. It was kind of a 'parking lot free pass', so she put it in the front window of every car Daryl gave her now. Besides giving her rockstar parking, it added an extra layer of invisibility to her highway image. Blue hair, white skin, lame sedan and handicap sticker was not the profile that Dade or New Smyrna County were looking for.

Bernie steered the borrowed Toyota Tercel towards the main building and parked it smack dab in front of the rest stop, right beside the walking ramp. She had a seasoned road bladder. Always able to hold it, never needing the facilities, that is until she came to a stop. That's when the bubble gut kicked in. The metamorphosis of menopause has many delights that it bestows upon its congregation and being on the constant edge of flatulating or diarrhea is just two of those blessings—a miracle that manifested in Bernie's innards as soon as she turned off the ignition.

Being a Welcome Center, it was high traffic and high profile, which meant that the facilities were usually kept clean. Unlike a lot of roadside rest stops, the hover ratio of the women's toilets at the arrival to orange country was one to one. 50/50. For every toilet that had been visited by a constant chain of inconsiderate sprayers, there was one commode that was spared, blessed by civilized, polite potty-trained adults. Bernie walked the line of soaked stalls until she found the latter. She was no longer embarrassed about her functions, like she was when this hormonal body snatcher first showed up and set up shop in her body, like an uninvited squatter. Back then, it felt like a flu that she couldn't kick or predict. It was hard enough to keep the reins tight on her organization, to earn their respect and loyalty without the constant threat of blameless smells, random chin hairs and spontaneous combustion. But now she could care less. She was owning her changes. She prepared for those she could predict and accepted the surprises. It was all part of the bigger breakdown of women anyhow. She got wise to that early on. The fear, shyness and secrecy of this stage in life was clearly written and driven by men. Most doctors were men. Men who saw this incredible morphing into the next stage of a woman's divinity as being useless. Barren. That a woman's purpose was tied only to her womb and without a fertile one they were valueless. The truth, however, is that it is another stage in their power. It is a season armed with experience, a lack of patience and open eyes. Men fear it because they have only one stage, childhood. Boys become men who become boys and all of those stages are focused on wanting to return to the womb—in one way or another—whereas women are magical. They have three distinct lives and in those lives a thousand others. Men chase their mothers until they die, while women reconcile their place in creation. The last stage of their lives is one that is filled with grace and wisdom and is quite possibly the most powerful of them all.

Power—that was one word for it. It was a wild one. No rhyme or reason to the demons that had chosen to escape her, there never was anymore. To the sensitive male world, it was unladylike, but this was the women's washroom. Supposedly a safe place, however she had heard a few of her own gender cough and gag as they passed her closed stall. She took no offense, in fact, she found it quite humorous. Both because their reactions to the spell she was casting in the porcelain cauldron were so precious and

31

because she knew this curse would fall on them as well in time. Washing up, she caught the eye of a young woman who seemed to be watching her in the mirror. The woman was maybe in her early 30s, olive-skinned, jet-black straight hair with all the curves that make Latin dancing so sultry. The woman looked away as she walked up and took the sink next to Bernie. She was wearing a beautiful floral sundress. Something Bernie wished her pale skin could pull off.

"I like your dress," Bernie said into the mirror, catching the woman off guard.

"Oh, thank you," she said startled, in a thick Hispanic accent. "I just got it."

"Well, it's very nice," Bernie said as she left the sink and went over to the hand dryer.

"Where are you from?" the woman asked, following her over to the wall.

"Up north originally, but I'm here now."

"Me too. Down south, but I'm here now too."

Bernie shook off the last of the dampness from her hands and headed for the door. "Welcome then."

"Welcome to you as well," she said following her out the door.

Bernie felt something jab into her side.

"Keep walking. Don't say a word," the woman whispered into Bernie's ear, taking her by the arm and walking beside her, leading her out of the center.

This was exactly why she didn't want to 'cheers' Hellsa —the reason she never celebrated before a job was done. The jinx that came with gloating, with counting your chickens, was real and it was at the other end of what was jammed into her side.

As they passed by the crowded kiosk of free orange juice, Bernie was able to look down and catch a peek at what she was being threatened with. It did make a difference. If it were a knife, the likelihood of her surviving was good. In a crowd of people, being stabbed to death was unusual. Too violent and a high chance of being caught. If it were a .22, it would hurt, but with its current trajectory, shooting right into her kidney, it also would not be life threatening. But it was neither. It was a gun though, a .45 —smaller than her stubby.38 Ruger, but just as deadly.

"Over there, the white van. Walk," the woman said, rushing Bernie towards the friendly-looking family van.

It was the kind you'd see in a campground. Double doors on the side, ladder on the back and rails on the roof. As they reached the pleasure cruiser, the side door opened, and a young man climbed out. He took Bernie by the arm and guided her up into it.

"You sure this is her?" The young man was amped.

"Yes, it's her. I've seen her before."

The door to the van slammed shut and an older, white-haired Hispanic man in the front passenger seat spun his captain's chair around to face Bernie.

"Where the hell have you been?" he snarled.

"I'm sorry, I don't haven't the foggiest idea who you are," Bernie said plainly. "And I am not in the habit of talking to strangers."

The older man was not amused and suddenly a fist collided with her face. As Bernie pulled herself back up, she saw the young woman in the floral dress beside her rubbing her knuckles.

"That just went on your bill," Bernie said to her, running her fingers across her lips, checking for blood. She looked to the old man in the front seat. "I am afraid you are way out of your depth. I don't know who you are, but you know me apparently and therefore you should know that I am untouchable."

"Untouchable?" the man scoffed. "Who would give you a crazy idea like that? You sound just like Vergil."

Bernie was instantly fuming, but she also realized that these people had no idea about her and Hellsa. "So it was you. You're the ones he was working for."

"We are indeed."

"You already got your pound of flesh, so what the hell do you want?"

The old man laughed. "You. We are not done doing business with you and you have cost us a lot of business."

Bernie shook her head. "Is that so. Well, as far as I'm concerned, our business was done the moment you killed my friend."

Before the woman beside her could react, Bernie shot the heels of her feet out, stretching the reach of her long legs into the front, connecting with the old man's jaw, spinning his chair around and knocking him into the windshield. With her feet in flight, she thrust her hand in her purse and squeezed the trigger of her revolver, sending a slightly muffled bullet out through the faux leather and into the woman beside her. As the woman fell into the side door, Bernie pulled the gun from her hands and jammed the barrel of it into the back of the front passenger seat. At the same time, she freed her own gun from her purse, and she pressed it into the back of the driver's seat as well. She launched two shells through each seat. Two bangs in each hand, muffled slightly through the quieting layers of the cushioned seat backs. Two bangs that tore into both the young man behind the wheel and the old man beside him. Three down.

Not waiting for signs of life or a chance they had backup, she pushed the gurgling woman between her and the door aside and climbed over her blood-spitting body. As Bernie stepped out into the sun-soaked parking lot, she closed the sliding door of the van behind her and suddenly it was like she had never been in there. Like she hadn't been held hostage or taken the lives of three Cartel. Aside from her racing heart, swollen lip and the micro dots of blood splatter on her yellow blouse, everything was normal. The packed parking lot was littered with out-of-state tourists, who were just going about their day, sipping their free OJ and stretching their legs. It was a blind of Bush supporters. A forest of sun-starved skin that she was able to fade into and make her way back to her car that was parked beside the ramp, in the coveted handicapped spot.

With just over a month to go until the new year, the sun was setting so early that the Dames were forced to pedal their trikes around the park after dark. They were the last pack around the horn ever since they went out on their own. Keeping to themselves, and riding under cover of night, made them seem even more bad-ass. Rebels prowling the grounds, with limited reflectors and no lights. It was their daily show of defiance over the park's gossip machines as well as their stress relief and mobile conference room.

"How did they find you?" Ruby asked pedaling in unison with the three others.

"I was made," Bernie said over her right shoulder, so Ruby who was beside her and the other two could hear.

"Oh, my, made? What does that mean?" Opal, who was right behind her was playing catch up.

"It means they found me. I know it wasn't Vergil. But somehow, they know who I am and that I'm here."

"In the park?" Freda was immediately on guard.

"No. If they knew that, I'd already be gone. They have been looking for me on the highway. I spoke with Hellsa, she's on it, but I can't make any more runs until we know they are all taken care of."

"But you just said you shot the three of them." Ruby let her mouth get ahead of her head. "Sorry, Opal, what I meant was, that you…canceled…their deliveries?"

Opal nodded, approving of her 'God friendly' adjustment.

"Both men yes, but the woman? I only…canceled…her once. She could still…request another delivery?" Bernie was working hard to make the analogy fit. "Jesus, Opal, you know what's going on, must we do this?"

Freda jumped in, "But there is a possibility she's still above ground?" She turned to Opal. "Not dead? There, I said it—grow up."

"Yes," Bernie answered, relieved to be dropping the charade. "She very well might not be dead, so we need someone else to take my runs until this is settled. They think they just caught me out and about. They don't know about our business or about you all, so—"

"I'll do it." Freda was in faster than water in a foundation crack.

"What about Reg?"

Freda looked forward. "He's not going anywhere and honestly, I could use the break."

"You sure?"

"Believe you me, I love bean counting and hiding your funds, but ever since you brought me in on this, I have been dying to get my hands dirty. And don't you worry, if I do cross paths with those Cubans, they best not pick on me, because I have a lot of pent-up anger that's desperate to find a home."

Bernie shook her head. "Alright but you keep a lid on

it, Freda. What happened in that parking lot was survival. I didn't go looking for it. If there had been another way out of that van, I'd have taken it. We make our mark by making no mark, remember? This world isn't kind to our kind. We are invisible to everyone under 65. That's our armor. Being invisible makes us—"

Ruby, Opal and Freda answered at the same time, "Invincible."

Bernie seemed satisfied with their impromptu reciting of the credo. The one that had become their mission statement, that would have been stitched across the back of jackets and printed on bumper stickers, if it weren't the secret words of a secret society. They were the 'Masons of Menopause' whose deeds and rituals were never to leave the confines of their rolling tricycle lodge.

With Freda's promotion established, it was on to other business. "The sign went up on the hut today," Ruby put forward to the group.

"Oh, my, that's right," Opal was excited. "What did you name it?"

"Moonlight," Ruby said proudly, and Opal cooed.

"Moonlight?" Freda was not as impressed. "What the hell kind of name is that for a bar?"

Ruby tried to let the poison arrows bounce off her. "My word, you really did miss the manners meeting, didn't you. First of all, it is not a bar, it's a club and second—the name came from Ben."

Nothing like the dead to humble a blowhard. "Christ, my apologies." Freda wished she could chew on her flip flop.

"Keep them. I have a feeling you'll need them soon enough." Ruby was not accepting the backpedaled apology.

"Moonlight? Like a second job. That's a wonderful

name because you are moonlighting." Opal was extremely impressed with herself.

"Yes, Opal, that is true, but Moonlight is something Ben used to call me."

"He called you Moonlight?" Freda couldn't help it—it was in her nature to be cantankerous.

"He said that I was Moonlight because I lit up his dark world." Ruby recited the words as if they were Keats. "The sign was made to look like the charm he bought me." Ruby fished the charm out from her cleavage and flashed it from side to side like an Olympic medal.

The crew knew he hadn't actually bought it for her. She had told them about going to the mall and picking it up after Natalie had shown her the receipt, but no one was interested in being that petty. They joked, they traded barbs, but underneath it all, they loved each other. Ruby had come so far since she lost Benny, they all had, so there was no point in breaking this part of her fantasy. The charm was, after all, the entire reason he wasn't with her anymore. Wanting to buy her that bauble was the reason he'd got behind the wheel that day—the reason he was shot. So, if she wanted to change the truth, to make that run not completely in vain, then they were going to let her.

"When does it open?" Bernie asked, making sure to keep the conversation moving.

"Friday night! I hope you all are coming," Ruby was buzzing.

"Absolutely," Bernie was first.

"Open bar, right?" Freda followed.

"Yes, but just for the first few hours," Ruby warned.

"Then that's when I will be there," Freda claimed her spot, "for the first few hours."

"Stan and I will be there too. I just don't know for how

long. He gets a little foolish as the night gets longer." Opal was a mix of emotions.

"Five minutes or five hours, all that matters is that you show your pretty face," Ruby said with love in her eyes. "You're family and that's what we do."

Opal nodded in agreeance.

"Just remember, Opal, I will be dancing," Ruby was quick to add a disclaimer.

Opal nodded again.

"On the stage."

Opal nodded.

"Naked."

Opal's trike swerved. "Oh, my. I forgot about that."

"I thought you might have." Ruby raised a brow.

Opal regained her composure and her bike's course. "On second thought then, I believe I will leave Stan at home."

There were thousands of students at Daytona State, so she couldn't understand why he picked her. Every day since their first altercation, he had come up and talked to her. Sometimes he talked so long that she was late for her next class. She didn't get it. He was a white surfer, and she was a proud black woman. What was his deal? They had nothing in common. It was all him chasing her down, she never went looking for him. Even their conversations were one-sided. Not a back and forth, an exchange of ideas, most of the time it was just him asking her questions about things she liked and her replying—no. But there was something else to his barrage of words, something she was not used to hearing—compliments. He was big on giving her compliments, even when they weren't quite right.

"I like your hair," he said, pointing to Natalie's braids. "My mom had that done, they call it cornrows, don't they?"

"They? Who's they?"

Natalie was always gruff with him, so he didn't pick up on her immediate disdain. "People. Don't people call it that? That's what my mom said it was anyway."

"Is that so. Is your mom a big Africa enthusiast?" Natalie was not having it.

"Africa? I don't know. I mean the song's alright, but it's like ten years old." He was truly clueless.

"Lemme guess, your mom had her hair done on the beach?"

"Yeah, in Jamaica. Some old woman came up to her, kept bugging her and she finally gave in. Took a while, but it cost her nothing."

"I bet it did. You seem proud of that. It takes a very long time to do this. Your mom must have gotten a hell of a deal."

"She's a lawyer, so she knows how to haggle. She's taught me a thing or two."

"Haggle? Wow. Nothing like beating down the price of someone's art, when you're on vacation in their country. Gotta be careful though, right? Those people are always hounding tourists."

"Yeah, that's right."

"Funny. Their home is your free time. You get to stay right on the ocean. The best beaches and views and she lives in a shanty. A nice little shithole away from your blue eyes. As a guest in their reality, you either ignore them or beat them down on price. The woman who did your mother's hair probably makes less in a month than your mother makes in an hour. Haggle? More like rob. That is a hell of skill she has."

The boy finally keyed in on her discontent. "Hey, I wasn't saying—"

"Yes, you were. You said every word. Why are you talking to me? Those people, as you and your mommy dearest called them, are most likely related to me. We are both descendants of slaves, we just landed in different prisons. Every day you come down here, right where you know I eat my lunch and you bug me. You haven't got a clue who I am, or what I am. You say the dumbest things and ask the dumbest questions. If you're trying to build up the courage to ask me to do your hair, don't. Trust me, I cost a lot more than your momma paid and I don't haggle."

The boy sat, stunned for a moment, feeling the wounds carved into him by her words. The air was heavy and hung between the two of them like LA smog, until he finally spoke. "You know, it was rude of me to say that about my mom's hair. I hear what you're saying. I don't know shit about what it's like to be you. I'm sorry, but I think you're the one with the issues. I was just being friendly. I was trying to get to know you. I have been trying for days. That's why I ask you so many questions but the only answer you ever give me is, no. My mom's hair was a reach, but I was just trying to crack your shell. Trying to relate—somehow. Find out who you are, but it doesn't matter because now I know why you never respond to me. You don't need me to get to know you because it sounds like you already know everything about me. I'm just another dumb surfer, right? A rich, white bigot, with a racist mom and a life of entitlement. You never asked me a single question, you just told me who you think I am. Put me in my place based on others who look like me. Judged me on my appearance and lack of knowledge about your culture." The boy stood up from the table. "I won't bug you anymore." With that, he just walked away, leaving

Natalie to sit in the middle of her own negativity that was pooling around her.

As he walked away, she was able to drop her guard a little and let his words in. She knew she had been harsh. She wasn't wrong, but she was able to acknowledge that he didn't know any better. It didn't make it right, most people with his complexion said and did the same things, but she was supposed to be trying to rise above. That's what Benny had always told her to do. He said that just because the world had low expectations didn't mean she was supposed to live up to them. That surfer boy's heart was in the right place, even if it was misguided. But that's what made her angry. That she was always the one to educate, to 'rise above' and turn the other cheek. If she had to stretch, then so did he. His intentions may have been good, but she was too young and too tired of giving out lectures for free.

Moonlight was still putting on her lipstick for the big debut as the sun was setting above the trees. A few of Daz's bikers were tidying up outside and getting the clearing ready to welcome all the cars that would be arriving soon. Inside, the girls were practicing—their last 'undress' rehearsal before the night's big reveal. Darcy and Nola had just killed it up on the stage, but now Cathy was having issues. It had been a long time since Cathy Cutie worked the boards and her head was getting in the way of her feet.

"Cutie, you're so hot!" Ruby shouted out and the other girls joined in, supporting their comrade as she stumbled a bit in her very high heels.

Cathy was doing a pure burlesque routine, keeping it all on at the end—by all, she meant pasties and bottoms. It was a very sexy number, slow and sultry with feathered fan work. It had peek-a-boo moments woven into the performance that made you feel like you were getting away with something. Like you were sneaking a glance over the screen as she was undressing. Overall, the dance was great, it was just the confidence and the wobbly heels that were hindering her.

"Stop the music!" Ruby shouted over to the right of the stage, to the biker in the DJ booth and the song came to an abrupt halt.

Ruby approached the foot of the thrust stage, standing between two of the chairs in the newly named 'Admirer's Alley'. 'Perverts Row' was low brow. It reeked of seediness and shame, not the kind of message they wanted to bring into the velvet gallery of Moonlight.

"I know. I know..." Cathy was muttering apologetically. "Maybe I'm just not ready for tonight. Maybe next week. Yeah, by then I should be good. Next week."

"My word, Cathy. You are selling yourself far too short. You are a goddess. A moving sculpture of sex and power. Your fan work and body are exquisite. You're ready, it's the heels that aren't. So, lose them."

Cathy looked down at her feet. "Lose them? You mean go barefoot?"

"Yes, I mean barefoot. It's sensual. Grounding. Art deco. All those old pictures of the feathered flappers had bare feet. Just try it, will ya?"

Cathy looked to her like she was treading water and Ruby was the only one with a life jacket. "Okay," she said hesitantly to Ruby.

"You heard her. Start the music again, once she's ready!" Ruby shouted to the DJ.

Cathy undid the straps on her sparkling shoes and kicked them to the side. She ran to the back of the stage, standing against the red velvet curtains and gathered her large, feathered fans, placing one in front and one behind, before nodding to the DJ booth. 'Sweet Dream' by the Eurythmics came on and she began her number again. Within the first two bars of the song, she went from fumbling to fluid and the arousing routine bloomed, flowing together in a moving stream of titillation.

"Woooohoooo!" Ruby shouted like a cowboy at a brothel and the girls joined right in. But they weren't pretending, they weren't boosting up a friend or blowing smoke, they were cheering with excitement over the rebirth of a long-lost icon.

"Ruby!" Daz called out over the music, waving Ruby over from the front of the club.

"Just a second," she said to Nola and Darcy. "I'll be right back." Ruby put her two fingers into her mouth and let out an ear-splitting wolf whistle for Cathy as she made her way back to Daz. "Whatever it is, can't it wait? We're almost done the run through."

"There's a guy outside that says he works here," Daz stated with concern.

"What guy?"

"A very big guy," Daz said a little shaken. "I tried to get him to leave, but it's going to take more than me to move him."

"Kurt!" Ruby screamed as she pushed past Daz and burst out the small, red, front door of the hut.

Outside of Moonlight, standing in the middle of the gravel clearing, was Kurt. The enormous, tattooed bouncer from Shakers.

"You came!" Ruby ran right up to him.

"Damn right I came. I wouldn't miss this for the world, Ms. Ruby." Kurt looked up at the Quonset hut, impressed. "This it?"

"Yes, it is. My word, I am so glad you are here," Ruby

said and behind her Daz cleared his throat. Ruby turned her head to address him, "Right, Kurt this is Daz. Daz this is Kurt, my Head of Security."

"What?" This was obviously news to Daz. "Ruby, could I talk to you for a minute please?"

Ruby rolled her eyes and patted Kurt on the arm, "Everyone wants a minute with me today." She walked back to a very unhappy Daz.

"What the fuck is this? Head of Security? Ruby, me and the guys are security. That's the arrangement. The one my organization agreed to. We aren't in the business of breaking contracts."

Ruby nodded. "I know. That is the arrangement. And it stands."

"But you just said that giant is Head of Security."

"My word, Daz, listen to you. Are you jealous?"

"This isn't a joke, Ruby. My organization has a lot invested in this place and its future."

Ruby sighed. "Relax, Daz, you and your boys are the security for the club. Kurt is my Head of Security. His interests are me and my interests."

"Like a bodyguard?"

Ruby smiled. "Sure. He guards my body and my money." She called over to Kurt, "Come on, Kurt, let me show you around the place."

Ruby turned away from Daz and went back into the club. Kurt followed her, making sure to rub shoulders with Daz on his way up to the door. This didn't sit well with Daz at all, no matter what Ruby was calling him.

Once inside, Ruby introduced her bodyguard to the girls and gave him the grand tour, starting at the front tables and working their way around to the bar that ran along the right side of the hut. The long bar with the front covered in black tufted vinyl, that sat directly underneath the massive nude painting Benny did of Ruby.

"Ms. Ruby, this sure is something." Kurt tried to avert his eyes from the unavoidable nude above him.

"It's alright, Kurt. Nothing you haven't seen before. We are all born nude and we become dirt the same way." Ruby reached down below the bar. "Now that you're here, there's only one thing missing from this place."

"What's that?" Kurt inquired.

"This." Ruby pulled out a mason jar from below the bar and placed it up on the top liquor shelf behind her. The jar was full of clear liquid, it could have been mistaken for moonshine if it weren't for the eyeball floating around in it. "This is a little reminder why you're here. Keep an eye on me," she said with a wink.

It wasn't often that Bernie got all done up. She didn't have the wardrobe or the cosmetic knowledge to make the cover of Vogue, but she did her best and put on her best for her sister. Her perm was tight, her blush was presentable, the pleats on her yellow blouse were pressed and her white jacket's shoulder pads were crisp and went on for days. She was a page right out of the 1984 Sears catalogue—only it was 1991. Bernie didn't agree with it all. The risk that the club created, the attention and the bikers Ruby had brought in, but this wasn't about her. After watching her baby sister crumble with Benny's death, anything that got her up on her feet again, she would make work. This was her sister's night, and she was going to support it. Opal and Freda had come by earlier, but she told them to go on ahead. She said she was looking for her shoes, but the truth was she wanted to be late. Not fashionably—fade-ably. She wanted a crowd of people already there that she could just mingle in and out of. No eyes directly on her. Yes, she was shy, but it was more than that. After the parking lot incident, she wasn't fully sure who was or wasn't after her. A target on your head can have many shooters, especially if the right price is set.

As she put on Vergil's big, gold, bison ring and grabbed her white purse, the one with the long gold-chain strap, she heard a car door slam outside. She went to the front bedroom and through the blinds she could see there was a car parked out front. It wasn't a car she recognized, but it wasn't a fancy car or a police cruiser either. Again, her mind went back to the parking lot at the Welcome Center. Those gangsters weren't driving a fancy car. They were using a family camper van for her intended kidnapping, so this may be another hornet from the nest.

There was a knock on the thin, metal frame of the screened lanai door.

"Verna?! Verna Hewton?!" a man's voice bellowed.

Instead of running to the bathroom, to lift the Barbie up off of the tin can and retrieve her revolver, she set her purse down and stepped down into the screened porch, unarmed.

The man on the other side of the mesh-covered door shook his stubble-covered face. "I don't believe we were done," he said, raising his hand near his face, flashing a badge.

"Agent Wallace," Bernie said as she sat down in her wicker throne. "What took you so long?"

2

Crowbar

He was what you'd expect an FBI agent to look like. He was as Caucasian as they come, in his late 40s, relatively short hair with just enough facial scruff to make you question his hygiene. Bernie sat in her chair; body relaxed as if he were just one of the park ladies joining her for tea. Agent Wallace took the chair Ruby usually sat in at the wicker table, the one under the trailer side window, keeping his eyes locked on Bernie the whole time.

"Ten months. I have been looking for you for ten months," he said with a flutter of excitement, like he'd finally found the rookie card he was obsessing over.

"Congratulations. But you're a long ways from Buffalo."

"It's the Federal Bureau—Federal—there's no juris-diction."

"Still, you're a long way from Bill's Stadium."

"So are you. I would never have looked for you this far south if it weren't for your dear old pal Vergil. Came across the wire. Heard they found him in pieces."

Bernie did her best to bury her anger.

"I'll bet you're the reason he fell apart." Wallace was relentless. "I knew he was in Miami, but then I tracked a credit card to a motel in Daytona. Not exactly a 'no-tell motel', but it got me thinking. So, I started looking around. Asking around. You should be more careful, six foot tall, 60-year-olds really stand out."

"What can I say, I make an impression on people."

"But you weren't staying in any hotels, so I had to go back to the drawing board. Where would be the best place for an old lady to hide? There are a lot of Bone Parks in the Daytona area, but eventually, your Big Bird stature pointed the way." He pulled out a small, black notebook from his suit jacket pocket. "Funny, this place isn't in your name."

"A friend's renting it to me."

"Is that so. Does this friend take sparkles and farts at par for cash? I put a lock on all your accounts, so how are you paying for it? Could it be that you're funding this little retirement fantasy on the wages of illegal activity?"

"My sister is helping me out."

"Your sister? The famous—what was her porn name again, um—oh right, Ruby Rain? Wow, is she down here too? Jackpot for Jack Wallace! I know they call it New Smyrna but it's starting to feel like Vegas." He was right back to the game. The rattling of cage bars. Just like when Bernie had spent the day across the table from him, being pelted and prodded, trying to get her to react.

"Am I under arrest?" Bernie cut to the chase because the only dancing she was interested in was happening at Ruby's club—and she was very late.

Wallace laughed, "No, but you should be."

This was news to Bernie—should? It only added to her questions, the next of which was why he'd come alone. "Where's your shadow? Pam, was it?"

"Agent Conner is on another assignment. You're all mine."

It was Bernie's time to laugh. "Another assignment? You know, Wallace, that sounds to me like she's moved on —so why haven't you? If you had anything on me, we'd be doing this behind cement walls and two-way glass."

"We both know what you did—who you really are." He tightened his eyes. "You just took off before we had a chance to get to the good stuff."

"And what's that?"

"Billy Johnson. Manny Dominguez. Pascale Falcone— you want me to go on?"

Bernie grinned, "Impressive, Jacky boy, you know all the names of friends in your kindergarten class. Good for you!"

"I know it was you. All of it. And so does someone very close to you."

"Then arrest me." She sat forward, staring down the lion. "I have somewhere to be, so unless this date includes bracelets, I want you to leave."

"Now that I know where you are, I can get back to getting you that stainless steel jewelry. You know you had me fooled too—for a bit. I almost bought it. The old lady routine. And now, wow! I have to hand it to you—this blue-hair trailer park is really selling it. You've gone all in, haven't you? I bet you even belong to the Canasta Club. But I see you, Verna. I see right through your wrinkles and your doilies and your arthritic socks. I see through it all and into the devil behind."

"You have an overactive imagination and a funny way of saying goodbye, Jack."

Agent Wallace stood up and stuffed his little black book back into his jacket, that was clearly way too hot for the heat of the New Smyrna nights. "I'm at the Ocean's Edge, if you decide to come to your senses, otherwise, I'll be seeing you around," he said, showing himself out of the lanai and sauntering back to his very plain car.

Bernie stayed seated, watching him go. The game had changed yet again. More moving pieces to juggle and more eyes on her. It's so hard to make moves in an open field. He was straight out of her past. He knew her past, the one she thought she had left behind, but past is a shadow we cannot shake. The trickster that follows us everywhere we go. You can run, but you can't escape your nature.

The gravel clearing out front of the club was bumper to bumper with cars. Inside, it was standing room only by the time Bernie made her way down the walking path; the thin rut in the woods that ran between the park and the hut. The same path she'd taken when she first found Ruby here. The day she thought she'd left or worse. She hadn't walked down it since then, but just like before, her mind was full of worry, only this time it was for herself. Bernie waited in her lanai for another hour after Agent Wallace left, then snuck out through the carport door, before making her way across the inner circle grass. This was going to be the new way of doing things. She was going to have to not only look out for the Cartel that were after her, but she was going to have to watch her comings and goings, because Wallace was watching her.

"Bernie." A massive smile came to Daz's face as she approached the small front door of the hut. They hadn't really seen each other since the night at the motel, although he had heard whispers about her reputation through his own networks. "Fashionably late?"

"Something like that," Bernie smiled back but had to

speak up because the music inside was reverberating off of the arched metal building as were the whistles and cheers. "Everything going alright?"

"Without a hitch. It's mostly our people in there tonight, but a good turn out."

There was an eruption of applause and screams inside the hut.

"That sounds like I am missing out. Time for me to see what all the fuss is about," she said, stepping up and Daz graciously opened the door for her.

It was practically shoulder to shoulder inside, which wasn't that hard for such a small club, but that was the beauty of it. Manageable. The crowd was mostly bikers, with a few older invites that the women had made, and they were all sitting up in 'Admirer's Alley'. The mostly salt-haired men in the chairs lining the stage were the friends and lovers of the women, so they were purely fixated on the show, not the intimidating 'Sturgis' gathering happening all around them.

Bernie was blown away by what they had done with the place. She hadn't seen it since she found Ruby here and it had come so far since then. It was all DIY but it worked. The wall and ceiling paintings by Benny were softly lit by dimmed floodlights that turned the artwork into a Michelangelo sky, watching over the plush playground below. Small cocktail tables and chairs, velvet booths and a raised Vaudevillian-style stage, all worked together to set the tone for the performance that had just begun.

"Alright Moonlight," the DJ shouted out over the speakers. "And now, for your viewing pleasure. The one. The only—Cathy Cutie!"

The red velvet curtain at the back of the stage parted and 58-year-old Cathy came strutting out, barefoot, confident and fluttering her feather fans. Bernie had expected strippers, but not this. The music blared, but it was Cathy that caught everyone's attention and took command of the stage. It was more class than ass and Bernie finally understood what Ruby had envisioned.

"Took you long enough," Freda said, having found her way over to Bernie. "This one's real good. It's her second time up. I never was for all this, but the woman can move."

"Oh, hi, Bernie! We were starting to get worried." Opal was right behind Freda. "This is really something, isn't it?"

"It sure is," Bernie said with full sincerity. "Have you seen my sister?"

Opal pointed to the long bar over on the right.

"I need to say hi." Bernie excused herself and made her way to the bar, weaving through the crowd of leather vests and beards.

"Poob!" Bernie shouted out over the music and her sister, who was wearing a red, velvet robe, turned her attention away from the stage.

"Bern!" Ruby was elated, reaching over the bar, trying to close the gap between them and hug her sister. "I thought maybe you didn't want—"

"Absolutely not. Just got hung up. But I'm here now. Did I miss your number?"

"You did. My first one, but I'm up again after Nola."

"So, I get a second chance."

"Always." Ruby felt and meant the double weight of the word.

"Thank you." Bernie felt it too.

"My word, where are my manners?" Ruby said, pulling over the white-bearded old man who was pouring a beer. "Bernie, this is Quincy. He's from Shakers."

Bernie extended her hand, "Thanks for being nice to my sister."

This wasn't the disheveled roadhouse drink slinger from Shakers, he had been rebranded for Moonlight. Ruby had cleaned him up a bit, putting his hair back in a ponytail, dressing him in all black and tidying up his wayward eyebrows.

"She…was nice to…me. You…reap…what you sow," he growled his choppy parable through the device pressed into his throat.

"Ms. Hewton." Bernie spun around to find Kurt towering over her.

"Kurt, you're here too?" Bernie was very surprised.

"He's my personal security," Ruby said proudly.

Kurt winked and pointed to the mason jar, sitting high up on the top shelf. The one with the clear liquid and floating eyeball in it. "I'll watch out for you too, Ms. Hewton."

Bernie turned back into the bar. "Poob, you shouldn't have poached both of these guys. Won't Sugar be asking questions?"

"To hell with Sugar. They both wanted to leave. She didn't treat anyone right, that's her fault." The music stopped, drawing Ruby's attention back to the stage. "Wooohooo!"

Bernie tried to be discreet, leaning over the bar, trying to speak just below the murmur of the room. "Ruby, I need to talk with you about something."

The DJ shouted out over the speakers, "Moonlight, put your hands together for Naughty Nola!"

"Now?" Ruby was put off by the poor timing of Bernie's desire for a meeting of the minds. "Can't it wait?"

Bernie knew it should, but it couldn't. There was every chance in the world that Wallace was watching this place right now. "Not really. It's serious. Is there somewhere we can talk, that's a little quieter?"

Ruby rolled her eyes and motioned for Bernie to follow her, walking out from behind the bar and across the club, leading Bernie to the swinging doors on the left of the stage.

The swinging doors opened up into the dressing room. But not just any dressing room, this was a dressing room designed by dancers—for dancers. It was cozy, clean and beautiful. Very bohemian. There were four vintage vanities set up along the far wall of the room. They were lit by frames of naked Edison bulbs, like the makeup tables of old Broadway. Layers of decadent fabric and lace draped down over the walls and makeup tables, giving the room more of a tent feel. There were comfortable plush couches, vintage satins and chaise lounges staged perfectly around the open area, like the master suite in a Victorian brothel. But it was not without modern conveniences, there were showers and toilets on the right and even a small kitchen near the exit. The music was still loud in here, but it was muffled a bit by the drywall, and many layers of fabric between them and the club.

"One night, Bern. One night! Is that all you can think about? Business?" Ruby was not pleased.

"This isn't about business—well actually, it is, but in a roundabout way."

"My word, I do not have time for this, just spit it out. I have a club full of customers and a dance number on deck."

Bernie took a deep breath. "An FBI agent came to my trailer tonight."

Ruby almost went dizzy. "Come again?"

"Agent Jack Wallace. He was the lead on the team that ransacked my place in Buffalo and hauled me in for questioning the day before I came and got you."

"Holy shit, Bern. What the hell does this mean? I just

opened this place—do they know? Are you going to be arrested? Am I?"

"Slow down. Like I said when we got here, if they were going to arrest me, they would have. He said as much tonight. But he followed me all the way here, so he's digging."

"The FBI is digging around? This is not good."

"I don't know that the FBI is. He came alone. He didn't come with a partner and looked like he hadn't slept in a while. He's a hound for sure, but something isn't right about it. He clearly doesn't have what he needs to pull me in, so maybe he's here to find more, digging to get what he needs, or maybe it's something else."

"Like what?"

"Alright Moonlight!" the DJ shouted. "You all have heard the rumors, but now it's time to make it rain! Put your hands together for Ruby Rain!"

"Bernie, I have to go. After. Okay, we'll talk after," Ruby said, undoing the sash on her red, velvet robe.

"After," Bernie agreed, watching her sister walk out of the dressing room looking hotter than the sun.

As the music started up and Ruby emerged from the red curtains, in her red lace corset, red silk gloves and red stilettoes, Bernie rejoined her gang.

"Everything alright?" Freda asked.

"No, but we'll talk about it tomorrow morning."

"What's going on?" Opal was sniffing around.

"We need to talk—tomorrow."

"Tomorrow?" Opal searched her mind for something she might be missing.

"Tonight, is her night." Bernie looked to the stage, where her sister was in her glory.

An icon of beauty and power was moving her way around the raised platform, gracing the eyes of the undeserving below. She was a vision. A master of her own form and flow that dazzled even the hardest bikers in the room. Ruby was the descendant of queens whose hips sunk armadas, whose calves brought castle walls down and whose lips toppled crowns. But she wasn't dancing for them. She was making love. This was the art of self-ownership, moving under the art of paint and brush. Dance and drawing. Two artists, connecting, breaking through space and time, life and death, speaking through the expressions of their purest selves. Ruby and Ben, two lovers reunited, in the backwoods of Florida, witnessed by a lucky few.

Small stomachs and large amounts of liquor do not dance well together and outside the back of the hut, Natalie was doing the tango with regurgitated mango and rum. Quincy had been generous with her, not in a creepy way. He was just being attentive to Ruby's charge. It was common practice for any bartender who wanted to keep his job, to take care of the owner's friends. So, Quincy took care of her, whatever she asked, when she asked, the only trouble was that she was underage and overpoured.

Puke never comes out the way you want, especially as a girl. It has a mind of its own and has a strange magnetic attraction to your hair, your favorite top and your new shoes. Tandem is the only way for a woman to vomit, a buddy system of sisters, but this spew fest came on fast and, in a bar full of bikers, sisters were few.

"Oh shit," Daz said, coming around the corner of the hut to find Natalie on all fours, shooting pizza and fruit cocktail out into the ferns.

"Get my hair," Natalie grunted between loud convulsions of dry heaves.

"I'll get Ruby!"

"No!" Natalie screamed. "My hair, get my hair!"

Daz was flustered, but powerless to the calls for help of the opposite sex, so he stepped up and cautiously took Natalie's braids in his hand and held them up, just in time for her to blow chunks once more. For a tough, tattooed, long-haired biker, he sure had a weak stomach and the first whiff of her regret had him gagging right with her.

"You done?" He was anxious for this horror to end.

Natalie wiped her mouth with the back of her forearm and fell over onto her side. "I think so," she said, huffing and puffing. "Just a little nap and I'll be fine."

"Oh no," Daz said, letting go of her hair to get his arms under her. "You can't lay down out here and you can't lay down inside. Ruby will kill both of us if she sees you like this. I was supposed to keep an eye on you." Daz scooped her up in his arms, one under her knees, one under her back, lifting her off the ground. He cradled her, carrying the intoxicated youth around to the front of the hut, where another biker was standing guard at the door.

"Cover for me," Daz said to him and kept on walking, heading out towards the foot path in the woods.

"Where the fuck are you going?!" A loud, dominant voice stopped him in his tracks. Daz turned around to find Kurt standing outside the front door of the club—having just pushed the biker aside.

"Relax, alright? I'm taking her home."

Kurt was leery, "No. I'll do it."

Daz stood his ground. "No. I got it. Ruby told me to watch her. I'll make sure she's safe. Let's be real. You're needed here. Those guys inside are getting more and more rowdy."

Kurt and Daz were in a silent standoff, but it wasn't ego or territory, it was based on concern for this girl's well-being. Both men searching the other's eyes for intent. Suddenly, there was the sound of glass breaking, followed by a roaring cheer from inside the club, that broke their stalemate.

Kurt growled, "If anything happens to her—"

"Oh, fuck big fella, I know," Daz nodded with exasperated understanding.

Kurt nodded, while giving him a final glare of warning, sending Daz on his way, and leaving him to deal with whatever situation was brewing behind the red door.

It only took a few steps into the overgrown forest for the sound of the club to fade and the moonlight to cast its shadows on the jungle floor. Daz's footing wasn't the best and the slick bottom of his Dayton's weren't helping. They were great for perching on the pegs of his Harley, but they slipped on the wet, forest ground and their blunt toes kept tripping over roots. Natalie was slight, not a challenge to lift off of the ground, but even a pencil weighs a ton if you hold it long enough. By the time they reached the end of the path, where it opens up onto the double dead-end lane on the edge of the park, Natalie was a small sedan.

"You sure are strong," she said wistfully, opening her eyes slightly.

"Yeah, thanks." Daz was doing his best not to gasp like he had been doing while she was out. This was around the time he started to reconsider his love for Newport's. He was gassed and his lungs felt like they had been rubbed with steel wool.

"You like me, don't you," Natalie said, smiling up at her human carriage.

Daz fumbled his words a little, because he was trying to breathe normally and because her words hit a nerve. "I think you're—a nice person—yeah."

"No, you like me. Like—like me. I know you do. I've seen you look at me. I know that look."

"Do you? Well then—there you go."

Ruby's trailer, the one with the red pinstripes, was just ahead, just past the entrance to the double dead-end lane they were on. He could see it from there, he could see the end to carrying this ever-increasing weight, and so he picked up his pace.

"If you like me, then why don't you do something about it?" Natalie asked with a bite. "You keep looking at me—undressing me with your eyes, so why don't you do something about it?"

"You're drunk, Nat." Daz tried to ignore her.

"And you're horny for me, so what? We both are something." She reached up to him. "Kiss me," she demanded, trying to pull his head down to hers.

"Stop it, Nat. You're going to make me drop you."

"Good! Then you can fall on top of me, and we can get to the good stuff."

Ruby's trailer was only a few feet away.

"Natalie, please. Ruby and that gladiator of hers would fucking kill me if I even look at you like that."

"But you do."

Daz stopped at the door to the lanai—looking down at her. She was drunk, but she was beautiful, and she was right. He did look at her like that. He couldn't control it even though there was a five-year gap between them. She did something to him every time he saw her. Something that wouldn't heed the threats of Kurt or the punishment of Ruby. His eyes were drawn to her. She was his opposite though. In his mind, she was as far away from what he wanted as she could get, but that made him want her even more.

"Sleep it off," he said looking up from her, trudging on, into the porch and straight into the trailer.

"Are you shy, Daz? Not into outdoor sex? That's alright. My room's the one at the front, Romeo. How romantic."

"Pipe down," Daz hushed her, suddenly feeling awkward, looking at the door to the front bedroom. It was a gateway of sorts. A portal to her secret world. Intimate. Somewhere he knew he shouldn't be. Daz gently opened the door with his foot, took a few steps in and set Natalie down on the bed. "Stay put," he said, walking back out through the main room and into the kitchen. He opened a few cupboards until he found the one with glasses in it. He turned on the tap and filled the glass with water, then he searched a few more of the upper cabinets until he found a box of saltines. Brandishing the two staples of a sick tummy, he headed back into the front bedroom.

"Shit!" he shouted, taking one step past the threshold, dropping the box of crackers onto the floor. "What the fuck, Nat?"

In the minute he'd been gone, she had geared down and was sprawled out on the bed—Natalie was completely naked.

"Nat?" he said cautiously. "We can't do this. I can't—"

Daz was in full panic, but her only response was a deep, nasal snore. She was out cold.

He set down the glass of water on the side table then picked up the box of crackers from the floor and put them beside it. Carefully, he gathered the sides of the top blanket that Natalie was laying on top of and folded them over her, turning her into a beautiful burrito. It was not all chivalry; he did pause a little, staring at her naked form, before covering her with each side of the comforter.

"You about done?" There was no mistaking that voice, it was Ruby.

Daz turned around to find her standing in the main room, with the human wall, Kurt, right behind her.

"Ruby, I was just putting her to bed, I swear nothing happened," Daz was speaking fast.

"What happened to her clothes?" Ruby looked past him to the swaddled girl on top of the bed.

"She did that, I went to get her some water and crackers—when I came back, she was like that. I didn't touch her."

Ruby could see the drink and snacks on the side table and the pleading honesty on his face. "I got it from here. You should go back to the club and watch your buddies. They're reaching the point of no return. I want that place to last longer than opening night."

"You got it," Daz said stepping out into the main room. "Ruby, I should have told you, but I didn't want her to get in trouble."

"No, you didn't want you to get in trouble. But no blood, no foul. You did what I asked. You looked out for her," Ruby said, walking into the front room to check on Natalie.

Kurt was standing right in front of the door to the lanai. He didn't budge, making it very hard for the long-haired biker to pass. Daz had to turn his body sideways, shuffling to slip between the mountain of a man and the door frame. As he slid past, he looked up at Kurt, and sneered, like a slighted little brother, "Snitch."

Mullet had called in sick to work. He normally did that when the surf report was stellar, but that morning it wasn't tidal, it was financially driven. It was another one of the peculiar, cash paying requests of his new favorite park resident—Bernie. Mullet was sort of on retainer these days, running errands for her at her beck and call—always eager to make the extra bucks and those bucks were adding up. The early alarm clock wasn't pleasant, but the job today was simple. Easy money that could go right into the jar he was filling to take him to Hawaii. It was a pipe dream of pipelines, a North Shore, Oahu fantasy that he never thought could come true, but now with all the extra cash from Bernie, his beach front surf shack was getting clearer by the day.

Mullet was parked across the street, just chill'n, making a cool two hundred bucks to watch the car with the New York plates. The Ocean's Edge Hotel wasn't full this time of year, with just a few weeks till Christmas, so keeping his eye on the prize was easy. Mullet never asked questions, just asked how much, where to go, what to do and was always loyal. Bernie liked it that way and liked working with a young man who could care less about the law. That's the anarchy of surfers. Those that worship mother earth and ride atop her fury. The law of nature rules their world, not the made-up laws of man.

Mullet's phone rang. The new cell phone that Bernie had bought him, the one with the Dr. Zog's sticker he'd stuck to the back. He answered it, keeping his eyes on the hotel parking lot the whole time. "Wassup?"

"Any movement?" Bernie said on the other end.

"Nah, nothing to tell. New York is still parked."

"Okay, Tony. Call the moment you see anything."

"Will do, buckaroo."

Freda was the worst of them—red eyes and a pissy frown. The other three looked relatively rested, even Ruby, although she looked antsy, like she had somewhere else to be. Somewhere better than standing out in the middle of the grassy inner circle at the crack of dawn.

Bernie ended the call on her cell phone and addressed the girls. "No movement yet. He'll call if there is."

"So, what does this mean for us?" Freda did not have the patience or electrolytes to deal with a long 'lawn conference'.

"We are still in business, I won't be making any runs, I'll be lying low, but that was already in the works because of the Cartel. I don't think he knows anything about you three or our business down here. The only thing he knows is that you're here, Ruby. I had to use you as a cover for how we're getting by."

"But if he's sniffing around, he's bound to find something." Freda was bitey.

"Nothing to find. Nothing happens here. We don't move anything in or out of the park, so as long as he doesn't tail you to Daryl's or on a run, he's got nothing. We keep our meetings to the trikes, so there is no chance of bugging our homes and we settle the cash at Moonlight from now on."

"Moonlight? You want to bring illegal money into my club?"

"Poob, all the money in your club is illegal. Which brings me to the next point. We can't have all the traffic of your club coming and going up and down Pioneer Trail, it draws too much attention. All those motorcycles and cars outside your place will only attract pigs."

"I'm not shutting down." Ruby was firm.

"You don't have to. Daryl has found us a bus. A small, decommissioned transport from a retirement community that he will be driving to and from your club. Moonlight now has a shuttle for its guests. They will leave their vehicles in the big back lot of the strip mall and take the tinted transport to your club. Daz and his guys are cutting a new trail in, one that enters from the road at the four-way stop, not off of Pioneer Trail and will be covered with foliage. A natural camouflage gate that will be guarded and only opened for Daryl's Shuttle. This is good all the way around. Cuts down on sound, makes sure you control your numbers, and no one visiting will know exactly where Moonlight is. The windows on the shuttle have been completely blacked out on the inside."

"Great. My business has now become your business." Ruby was not as excited as Bernie had hoped.

"All business is each other's business now, Ruby. We are all in this together. No weak links, no solo practitioners. To be clear, the transport only runs three nights a week. Thursday through Saturday."

"You're imposing business hours too?"

"Ruby, you can't run a shuttle every night or an illegal club for that matter. Daryl is only available those nights, so that's what it is. We can trust him, he's already deep in bed with us and trust me, this is a far better way of working. You can't have every Tom, Dick and Harry driving to and from your illegal bar, every night of the week, if you did, you'd be busted in a month."

"My word." Ruby was stunned by her sister's ability to just pull the rug out from under her. Swoop in and take control of what she had worked so hard to make a reality. "So that's that then."

"Anything from Hellsa about those people in the parking lot?" Opal raised her hand as if she were in class.

"The Cartel? No word on what's next. Other than the runs are still expected and that—" Bernie was about to say something else but noticed an odd mark on Opal's wrist. "What's that?" she asked pointing to it.

Opal quickly tucked her wrist under her other arm, crossing them in front of her, perturbed. "That path from Moonlight is very dark—and dangerous. I fell on my way back last night."

"No, you didn't," Freda jumped in. "I walked back with you—you didn't fall."

"You were very intoxicated, Freda. I doubt you'd remember if you took your teeth out or not. I was having Shirley Temples and I think I would know if I fell or not." Opal was oddly defensive.

"I was sauced," Freda relented, scratching her tight, bluish perm. "Speaking of which, are we done here? If I don't lay down soon, I will kill one of you."

"Well boss?" Ruby said to Bernie, snarky. "Are we? I have a very queasy young lady at home. Natalie got into the liquor too last night—she's not feeling well."

Bernie looked around at her crew. "Yes, we're done. For now. Opal, I believe you have a run today and Freda, I'll see you later."

"For what?" Ruby was not in the loop.

"For security," Bernie assured her, although Ruby was feeling less than secure.

Mullet called as soon as Wallace emerged from his room. It was later than expected, early evening by the time the Fed left his hotel and headed out for the park. Mullet followed him, giving Bernie reports the whole way. Wallace wasn't being very discreet, he knew he was being tailed, but didn't bother to shake him. He drove slow and steady the whole way, driving right into Cicada Hollow and setting up shop right by the Activity Center. Bernie made sure to put on a show, getting Ruby and Freda together to ride their trikes by him. They made sure to wave at the disheveled agent as they passed, and he returned the sarcastic gesture. As the sun fell into the indigo of night, Bernie walked around her trailer, turning on strategic lights as well as the TV in the main room. She then made a call to Freda, who then made a call to the park super, inquiring with great concern about the presence of a strange car in the visitors' spot out front of the Activity Center. Not long after the neighborhood watch call, Agent Wallace was encouraged to leave and he did, moving his position to just outside the park gates. Cicada Hollow was, after all, private property and with Wallace not on official business, he had no cards to play. This repositioning of Bernie's nemesis allowed her to make her way through the inner circle undetected and down the path in the forest to Moonlight, where Freda was waiting. Just like everything Bernie did, she was two steps ahead, stealthily moving like a spirit through the 'pre-graveyard' of the Hollow, through the shadows of the woods and out to freedom. As instructed, Freda had left her car at Moonlight when she came back from the hospital, earlier in the evening. It was necessary to have transportation parked away from surveillance, so the two of them could slip away in the baby-blue station wagon, while Wallace waited just outside the gates for the ghost who was long gone.

After leaving the clearing using the new trail cut through the woods for Daryl's Shuttle, they made a short pit stop at Sea Harvest, before heading out to the dark side road. There wasn't much on this strip of pavement, no shops or houses, just forest and dirt, which is what made it perfect for Bernie. This would have been difficult to pull off at any other time of the year, but with the December nights setting in early, these back roads could be treacherous.

Freda pulled the wagon over to the side of the road, just around the corner, where it jetted off the main one. She turned the lights off and the two women went around the back and opened the wagon's tailgate.

"Why couldn't we have gotten a small one?" Freda snarled at Bernie, looking into the back of the wagon.

"Small one? I don't want to see a small one. What is wrong with you, Freda?"

"Small one, big one, believe you me, once they get to this stage, they are all the same."

"No, they are not. Look at this one. It's not going to work."

"Yes, it will. It's pitch dark out here."

"Well, it's too late to change it now. Zip your lip and lift with your knees," Bernie said, reaching into the back and hoisting out the heavy load.

The moon was covered by ocean cloud that night, so it was very dark. The kind that your eyes can only adjust so much to, but through their blindness, the two old biddies shuffled their package out into the middle of the lane.

"Here," Bernie said, but before she could finish, Freda had already dropped her end. "A little notice, Freda?"

"You said here."

Bernie huffed, "Jesus. Come on, we need to move!"

Leaving their package on the road, the two women ran back to the wagon and got in.

"Go, go, go!" Bernie urged and Freda peeled out, heading down the straight road away from the main road. "Here," Bernie said, and Freda slammed on the brakes, spinning the wagon one hundred and eighty degrees so they were facing back in the direction they came from. "Christ, Freda, you are a pill today."

Freda shot her a look. "Today?"

"Turn off your lights," Bernie instructed, and Freda turned the car lights off, leaving the two of them sitting there in almost complete darkness.

"You're sure this is the way?" Bernie questioned.

"Positive. I followed him right down here."

Bernie looked down at her watch, which was useless given the lack of light. "What if someone else comes?"

"They won't," Freda said. "No one uses this road, that's why he does."

So they sat and waited. Time stretches out in the darkness, especially when it's piggybacked by quiet. It's like each is amplified by the other, making people lose their patience or fall into fear that lies in the abyss of sound. For Bernie, it was the silence of the dark road that was killing her—she would have been far calmer, far more patient, if this was her own plan entirely, but it wasn't. She had come up with the what and the how, but not the where and that was what was gnawing at her. Down at the far end of the dark road, car after car drove past on the main drag, but just as Freda said, none turned in. It was nail biting, watching the glow of headlights build on the main road, wondering if it was who they were waiting for and worrying that it was not who they wanted.

"What time do you have?" Freda asked.

"Don't know, I can't see my watch."

"Check your phone," Freda snapped, and Bernie reluctantly touched the keypad on her Motorola, bringing a green glow of life to the phone's small, square screen.

"10:15," Bernie said and as she looked up, another glow of lights was building, washing over the pavement of the main road down at the end.

"That's him," Freda smiled. Bernie couldn't see the pearly whites, but she could hear it in Freda's devilish tone.

At the end of the road, the lights got brighter and brighter until a car appeared, but unlike all the others that had flown past, this one was moving much slower, as it approached the side road. Other than the headlights, it was far too dark to make out much of the car as it made its way around the corner and started heading towards the women.

"That's him," Freda gloated.

Bang. The bright headlights bounced violently up and down, and the car suddenly screeched to a stop. Just beyond the headlights, Bernie and Freda could see the faint shadow of the driver's side door opening.

"It's time for a really big shew," Bernie said to Freda, in her best Ed Sullivan voice and Freda cranked the ignition.

Freda stepped on the gas and drove a few hundred feet before turning on her headlights. Immediately switching to high beams, the lights revealed that it was a police cruiser that had stopped in the middle of the road. Freda pulled the wagon over to the side, in perfect alignment with the stopped police car and Bernie quickly got out.

"Oh, my Lord!" Bernie shouted, running up to the rear of the cop car, where a very stunned, very portly police officer was standing over a very dead body. Freda's headlights were perfectly angled to light up the dead man lying on the road. "Why did you hit him?" Bernie got right into character. "We saw him all the way down at the end of the road—he was just walking, Officer, why did you hit him?"

The police officer started to stutter, "I...I...he came out of nowhere."

Freda suddenly appeared on the other side of him. "Is that alcohol I smell?" she said looking at his badge. "Officer...Gilroy, have you been drinking?"

The realization of their observations brought the cop

back to the surface of the very drunk man. "I have done nothing of the sort. Now, you ladies need to move along."

"Aren't you going to call an ambulance?" Bernie kept on with her concerned citizen routine.

"I told you to move along!"

There was suddenly a flash of light. Then another and another. Blinding white hot flashes of light.

As Officer Gilroy's eyes struggled to return to normal, he saw that Freda was holding a 35mm camera. "What are you doing?" he shouted at her—swiping out at her—trying to knock the camera from her hands.

"You committed a crime, Officer Gilroy. I'm making sure you are accountable." Freda was standing well enough away from him to avoid his stumbling attempts to grab her.

After a few unbalanced steps and one fall to the ground, Officer Gilroy stopped his pursuit of Freda. He did his best to gather himself, getting back to his feet and straightening his gun belt. He turned around, looking back to his cruiser, assessing the situation and the possible image that was captured on Freda's camera. The image was not good. A fully clothed, dead male was laying on the road, behind his clearly marked and numbered police cruiser, with him in uniform standing in front of it all. He knew what this looked like. He knew that the bar he frequented held no loyalties to him, that they would gladly snitch on a cop drinking there, that these two old women had witnessed his vehicular manslaughter and had photographs to verify it. It was all happening too fast, too surreal for his inebriated brain. He used to know how to handle these things, but the whiskey had taken those abilities from him. His ability to reason, to sort things out or take charge were left in the bottom of a bottle a long time ago and now— the only thing he knew how to do—was run.

Officer Gilroy let his instinct take over. He hoisted his

dangling belt and sprinted back to his car, as fast as his fat, stubby legs could take him. He threw the car into drive before the door had even closed, making Bernie have to jump out of the way. He had no plan, other than to put as much distance between this horror and himself and then drown it all with the bottle he had stashed in the cupboard under the kitchen sink at home.

As the black and white cop car disappeared into the never-ending black of the long road, Bernie and Freda walked back to the body lying on the ground.

"You were right, Freda, he must have been blitzed," Bernie said looking down at the corpse, whose face was sunken and leathery and whose eyes and mouth were clearly stitched shut. "Even if I didn't see the stitches, I would have smelled the formaldehyde right away."

Freda slung the camera over her shoulder and without prompting, the two women started dragging the body back to the rear of the wagon.

"Besides keeping my Reg around, Doctor Noth has come in handy," Freda grunted. "Now we have a doctor and a coroner on the take."

Bernie commended her, "Indeed we do, but we also now have something better—we have leverage."

She packed the tuna fish sandwiches at the bottom of the cooler, wrapped first in wax paper then placed inside a Ziploc. Mayo and relish, that was the way Stan liked them, half an inch of spread between two pieces of white Wonder Bread. Tupperware was the only way to keep them from getting squished under the weight of the dozen beer cans that sat on top them. She'd prefer to put them on top, but Stan hated that. He hated reaching into his cooler and touching anything other than his next fix. Opal liked to think that the sandwiches were the prize at the bottom of this AA cereal box. That when he'd fully filled up on buzz, he'd find her little gift, lovingly made, waiting at the bottom and that the solid sustenance might sop some of it up.

Opal handed Stan the peaked-top cooler and as he reached for it, she flinched—it was involuntary, but it didn't go unnoticed.

"What was that for?" Stan seemed strangely offended by her twitch.

"What do you mean, Stan?" she tried denial.

"Right there, you moved—when I reached for the cooler." Stan stepped towards her and she immediately, stepped back. "That—just like that."

Opal had nowhere to go, with her words or space. "Oh, my, it's just my nerves. They are a little on edge today."

"Why?" Stan's offense changed to concern.

Opal looked at her husband. The early morning version of him. The one she liked best, that liked her the best. Before the first beer of the day, he was the man she married. The one who took her to Quebec City for their honeymoon, during Carnival. The man who doted over her when she was pregnant with Kim. This was the brief slice of time when he forgot the night before and remembered who they were—the only trouble was her body couldn't forget.

"Last night," Opal trod lightly, not wanted to trigger her lying response or his memory.

"Bad dream?" Stan was genuinely worried.

Opal just smiled.

Stan set down the cooler and took her into his arms. "Oh, Bunny. Nightmares are just a way to make us appreciate how good our real life is. It wasn't real." He pulled back a little and kissed her on the head.

It wasn't everyday she got to see this side of him. The sober side. It was once a week, if that, which made it all the more devastating to watch his shaking hands reach for the cooler once again. His chattering knuckles mocking her, reminding her of the monster and teasing her with this brief morning illusion of what he once was.

"I'll be home early today. Just a shuffleboard game with Fred and a brief stop at George's. How about we go to bed early tonight? We can cuddle. I'll wrap you up in my arms so you can get a good night's rest," Stan said, heading towards the door and he meant it. He truly wanted to make her happy. To make her feel safe and take care of her. All alcoholics mean it and it terrified her.

Stan shot her a wink and blew her a kiss as he stepped down out of the trailer. As his footsteps faded away, Opal turned on the TV and sat down in the chair. The Florida winter days were too cool to sit outside, which made catching up on her show a lot more comfortable. She had already disconnected the phone lines, so the next hour or so would be just her and the Reverend, on TV that is. Just her, the preacher and the big man—no Stan, no phone solicitations, no interruptions. She really needed the Reverend's guidance today. The kind words he used on the show, speaking right into the camera, the ones that seemed to point the way to better days. It wasn't so much what he said, it was how he said it. Contrary to what Bernie and the others thought, his tone and smile made her feel safe. A hell of a lot safer than the promised cuddle of Stan's arms. The Reverend's love of the Lord made her feel like everything was going to be okay and that no matter how bad her 'nightmares' were, it was all part of a greater plan.

Right on time, the broadcast came on, but it was

strange today. The opening of the show was the same as usual. The same pictures of the glass church, the sweeping shots of the packed, handsome congregation and the obligatory slow motion of the white doves ascending into the blue sky. Opal knew the church and the people were just for effect, because she'd seen the studio firsthand. She knew that the Reverend was just using the images to make the worship feel more authentic, because that's what he'd told her. As soon as the organ music and happiness-stuffed opening came to an end, it all changed. Everything else was different. Part of the appeal of the Reverend's show was its predictability. The reliable consistency that seemed to soothe. No surprises, just segment after segment in the normal order. But not today. It was all taped interview after taped interview with no call to prayer. Just things she'd seen before with no live interaction with the Reverend. Sure, there were musical numbers and readings from the 'Good Book', but none of his words of encouragement. The words she was longing to hear.

Opal began to wonder if her messenger from God was ill. Flu season was strong that year, so maybe he had a touch of it. Her disappointment over the broadcast changed, her mind began to consider what she could send to help him feel better. Of course there was soup, but soup didn't ship well. Cookies would though, but they don't heal anything except a craving for cookies. Maybe it was money he needed? It must take a great toll on him running the Ministry. The stress of it all—maybe money would do the trick. She worried this might be her fault. She hadn't sent the Reverend a dime since the call. The one where they'd got through and Paula pushed her to confess where the money was coming from because of the 'tax' obligations. Since then, Bernadette had been calling the shots when it came to the many cans of 'No-J' that were now taking up most of the freezer. Bernadette was greedy. She wanted the money for herself and for Opal. She wanted to shower the kids with it, take Opal on a spa day and maybe even on a holiday—a solo holiday. Bernadette had no time or use for the Reverend Kind. But Opal did. Against Bernadette's protests, Opal wondered if maybe a lump sum would lift his spirits. As she considered her best course of action, the easiest way to send thousands of dollars to the preacher, something outside the window of the trailer caught her eye. At first, she thought she was seeing things, but after moving to the louvers that opened up onto the lanai, she almost fainted. It was either a ghost, or the Reverend that was walking around in her lanai!

Opal opened the door to the screened-in room, but said not a word, she was too awestruck to move her tongue.

"Opal Rose?" The Reverend, dressed in a soft pink suit and matching tie, flashed his pearly whites.

"Reverend?" Opal slurred, doing everything she could to stay upright, trying to avoid doing a face plant off the top step, down onto the AstroTurf. "What are you doing here?"

"I'm here to see you." The Reverend was earnest. "May I please come in?"

Opal remained relatively non-verbal and just used a hand gesture to signal the well-dressed cleric inside. As her idol stepped inside her humble abode, she remained stiff, unlike the Reverend who had no reservations, just waltzed right into the main room, undid the top button on his suit jacket and sat right down.

He looked over to the TV that was flashing his recorded image on the screen. "Dedicated. I am not surprised. You truly are one of the best of the flock. I will have you know that today's broadcast was for you."

Opal was trying to catch up, but was completely lost. "Me?"

"Yes, I had them tape my sermon and fill the rest of the slots with past interviews, so that I could come here and see you. It's about the time we were able to reach you last—on the phone."

"Dear me, you didn't have to do that." Opal was flattered and still a deer in the headlights.

"Oh but Opal, I did. My staff have called you. I have called you, repeatedly and when we did finally get a hold of you, you hung up. This is very concerning for me. Opal, you have sent my Ministry over a hundred thousand dollars. You are our biggest benefactor, yet you won't let me in. Your phone seems to be disconnected and you stopped writing letters. I know something is troubling you and I cannot—in good conscience or God conscience— continue my Ministry without checking on you."

"Oh, dear, Reverend, you are too kind. But I'm fine."

"Have you had a change of heart?"

"About what Reverend?"

"God?"

Opal was stunned. She never used the big guy's name and to have his messenger question her faith in him was stupefying.

He continued, "Your generosity was unexpected at first, but became a consistent light. A pillar of our Ministry, something that we have grown to count on, to spread the word, but it has stopped. Have you stopped believing in His message?"

"Oh, no, Reverend, I believe very much. I always have."

"Then what happened? Have you become destitute?" the Reverend asked, pointedly looking around the meager trailer.

"Why, no. I'm not poor at all."

"What is it then? Is it the source of your contributions? Has the well run dry?" The Reverend's questions were getting farther from the Almighty and closer to home, feeling more like an interrogation than a wellness check. "Paula told me what you had said to one of our operators a while back. About the money being from the wages of sin."

Opal panicked, she remembered right away the call and her words and regretted both.

The Reverend had hit a nerve and he knew it. "Opal Rose Murdy, I want you to be light of heart. The Lord knows you have earned it. You have earned the forgiveness you seek. If your contributions are indeed the wages of sin, there is nothing to be fearful of. In the war of good versus evil, the end sometimes justifies the means. You can take from the dark to reinforce the light."

Bernadette was screaming deep inside Opal, telling her to kick him out. Calling him a charlatan, begging her to see the real reason for this silver-tongued serpent's house call. But Bernadette was only allowed out on the road. In the face of this false idol, she had no power.

"Opal, our flock is no stranger to the converted. The ones who turn over new leaves to unburden their hearts and their wallets that are plagued with sin. We need your generosity, Opal. That is why I taped the show, put everything aside and came down here to see you. Please, Opal, uncork your heart, tell me your troubles, so you can open the dam of generosity once again and continue to be our golden dove."

That's what did it. The imagery of the white birds in the opening of his show. The doves that fly across the screen in slow motion. In one sentence the Reverend had made her one of them—the most precious of them—a golden one.

"I have done some things I am not proud of," Opal blurted out, looking down at the ground. "They were done with good intentions, but I know that the devil lives in them."

The Reverend was not prepared for this. "You? Not someone you know? A son or daughter. Maybe your husband?"

"Oh, no, Reverend, it's me. I'm the sinner."

The Reverend practically cheered, like he'd cracked the serial killer's confession in the first interview. "It's okay, Opal, I know. I was just testing you. The Lord told me as much. There are no secrets between Him and you—or you and me for that matter. Please continue."

"I don't really know exactly what the crime is, but I do it and I reap the rewards." Opal was telling the truth. She was voluntarily oblivious to what she was actually doing, but Bernadette wasn't.

"So how do you know it's a crime?" The Reverend continued to pull on his thread.

"I drive. To and from places, carrying things for people who are nice to me, but I know are bad, and they pay me more than my husband used to make in a year." Opal was loosening her truth pouch as rapidly as he was pulling on its ties.

The Reverend's eyes were bright and excited. "So, you are breaking the law then, Opal Rose?"

"I am," she responded with the bowed head of a schoolgirl in confession.

"Is anyone forcing you to do these bad deeds? This carrying of illegal things?"

"Oh, no. I do it because I want to. Because I want to help. I've helped my kids with the money, my husband and you. You said so yourself, that I helped spread God's word."

"Yes, you did. But you've stopped. So does that mean that you stopped doing the crime?"

Opal looked up at her confessor, "No, Reverend."

"Then why has the money stopped?" His tone changed as did his body language. He went from leaning forward, concerned with his hands in prayer, to standing over her. "Opal Rose, you have had the protection of the Lord, the forgiveness of His Grace because you did it for Him. If you stop now, stop helping our message, then you are no longer a Warrior of God. You are doing it for the other one. The fire and brimstone. The Lord is kind, caring and generous, but He is also vengeful. I am the Lord's messenger and I too carry His traits. I am the Hand of God. The Hand that will strike those that go against His will. I have been sent here to you, Opal, to make it abundantly clear. You must continue to grace His work, or His vengeance and wrath will fall upon you."

Opal jumped up, frightened, and move quickly over to the freezer. She pulled out a frozen paper can of OJ and tossed it onto the kitchen table in front of the Reverend.

"Thank you, Opal, but neither the Lord nor I am thirsty," the false prophet scolded like a pimp unhappy with the take.

Opal walked back to the table and peeled the thin piece of tape off the bottom of the can and opened it, revealing the healthy roll of cash inside it. "Will this do? Will this put me back in His graces? Into your graces?"

The Reverend snatched up the roll of cash and stuffed it in his pocket. "It's a start. A nice apology. I see you now understand the kind of offering your Father expects." The Reverend tilted his head back and closed his eyes briefly, like he was listening to the ether around him. "He thanks you, Opal Rose, and is asking if this means that your mail-in donations will resume?"

Opal nodded. The good, God-fearing nod of the duped, as deep inside her, Bernadette was screaming bloody murder.

Maryanne had put up a fuss at every council meeting since Natalie moved in with Ruby. She pelted the park council with motion after motion about it being a 55+ only community, but the council kept saying that the matter was in review. Sure, Maryanne and her gang were the self-proclaimed patriots of the park, but they were not the park, just a small clique within it. Behind those white walls there was a large community that felt the same about Maryanne as Ruby and the others did. They saw through her crocodile smile and passive-aggressive plays for control. Besides aligning with the women's sentiments about Maryanne, they also were benefiting from the Grand-mafia's generosity. Since the women started up with Hellsa, there had been new improvements made to the Activity Center, new gear for the courts and open bars donated for bridge nights. They were being done anonymously, but well-placed gossip had the women's names whispered around the park. So, while Natalie was not 55+, her guardian was a hell of a lot friendlier than the complainant and the gin on bridge nights was the good gin.

Natalie was standing just outside the gates of the park waiting for her ride. Benny's Sable had broken down long ago and Ruby had promised to replace it, but that hadn't happened yet. She was supposed to take the bus, that's what Nat and Ruby had agreed upon, but a better offer came up. An offer she didn't need the eyes of the park on. A louder, windier offer, that made her breath quicken.

Daz rolled down Pioneer Trail on his Harley— sunglasses, thick leather jacket and tight jeans. He'd left his vest at home. Not just because December was too cold for it, but because he didn't want the possible attention of the 'po-po' with Natalie on the back. Daz pulled around, making a U-turn in front of the curved white wall at the end of the road and stopped in front of his opposite. The cute, smart, tough girl, with a weak stomach and a backpack.

"I told you to wear jeans," Daz said irritated, looking at the short skirt and boots Natalie had on.

"They're all dirty," she said, walking up to him.

She tried to hop on, but he stopped her, holding out a helmet. "Put this on," he ordered.

"Why? You're not wearing one."

"But you are. Your legs may end up sushi, but your head will survive. You either put it on or walk. The choice is yours." He scolded her a little, and all it did was add to the fantasy of it all. On the outside she scowled, but on the inside, it was a dance of submissive joy. The excitement of getting in trouble and what this dangerous biker might do about it.

Natalie reluctantly put the helmet on, then Daz helped her kick her leg over the bike and put her hands around his waist. Folding them over each other and tapping them against the bottom of his stomach, "If I feel your hands move, at all, for any reason—I stop. You hold on the whole way, got it?"

The concerned act was killing the prior vibes, so she nodded to get him off her back and back into the naughty story that was far more enjoyable in her head. Daz twisted the right handgrip, and the bike quickly found its centered balance, pulling away from the shoulder. As the cold wind picked up force, rushing over her face, she felt the freedom of it all. The romance of the motorcycle that had gripped the rebel heart ever since the first world war. But it was more than the open road and risk, it was the very visceral, tactile interaction playing out on the tiny seat that was taking over her. The bike bounced and rumbled, moving her hips helplessly towards Daz—forcing her body to press against his. Turn after turn they leaned together, their bodies moving as one, like a rehearsal for her desires. Her hands stayed folded over each other, like she was told to do, but they did begin to drift. As they hit the I-95 and the bike hit fifty-five, she let her fingers fall, gracing the top of his fly. Daz noticed. He had been feeling everything she was, from the moment she called him and ask him for a lift. He struggled with the lie he told himself, the one about duty, about taking care of her, when all he could think about was her naked body. Her smooth skin spread out on her bed; the image burned into his mind from Moonlight's opening night. Even though he tried to tell himself that he was like a big brother to her, his body said otherwise. He should have pulled over right then and there. Put a stop to this, or at least reached down with his hand and moved hers—but he didn't—and she noticed. She let her fingers move down farther, and farther, until she was holding him in her hands. She squeezed, tightening the muscles in her hands a little, sending instant shivers up his back. He took his left hand off of the handlebars and reached back, but it wasn't to stop her—he was giving in. His rough hand gripped her hip, pulling her in tighter to him as he pushed his butt backwards, pressing the curve of his ass into her crotch. He held her there. Held her firmly in place, sliding his hand down a little, under the flapping material of her skirt and cupping the left cheek of her ass. His callused hands gripping her smooth, bare skin. She began to grind. Slowly gyrating her hips in small circles, pressing against the back seam of his jeans, with only the thin cloth of her panties as a barrier. Mating in movement, him pulling her in, her pressing forward with every thrust. There was no room left in the front of his denim—the handle that she was holding onto, pulsating in her grip, mimicking her movements behind him. She started kissing the back of his neck. Opening and closing her lips around the edge of his jugular, bringing his skin to the edge of bruising, and her to the edge of it all. Ecstasy, racing down the ocean front highway. Suddenly, her body began to shake and not from the rattling pistons of the Knucklehead. Daz felt her crumpling and squeezed her ass in his hand while she held on to him for dear life, dying a little, melting into the seat.

The offramp approached just as she was finishing—what definitely was not finished—and he uncupped his hand from her quivering cheek, returning it back to the handlebars. It had happened, but it hadn't. It was still in the world of fantasy for him, with his eyes focused on the road. He could still pretend he was above it, better than letting himself fall for a girl he was supposed to watch over. A girl who had already outgrown his intelligence and would leave him anyway for a brighter future. But she couldn't pretend. This was not a fantasy for her at all. They had done this together. He had guided her to the edge of sweet death and all it had done was leave her empty. Unsatisfied. A sample of his true feelings for her and she was ready for the next stage. The main event, where they faced each other, where there were no seams between them, and she could let go.

Freda liked the break, the run up and down the highway. It was a great time to reminisce about her Reg. A great time to be away from the chaos of the club, and the business and the clear tubes that were keeping her love alive. It was a rolling holiday, complete with a night's stay in a bachelor suite in Georgia. She had very little concern while on the run, other than pee breaks and the odd motherfucker who cut her off. Freda was a Road Warrior. Always was. From the moment she got her license, she was shouting obscenities and throwing middle fingers. It was a gift, but one she had to keep in check as she drove back from the safe house. Not only did she have trigger fingers, but her foot was also made of lead—which could lead to the cops. Old white women weren't part of the racial profiling list, but old women were the profile for bad driving. That stereotype preceded the Volusia County's foolproof bigot list. Everybody, even other old women, thought that grey hair, on top and below, meant that you suddenly lost all hand-eye coordination and the capacity to navigate. It was like the world was a reverse 'Children Of The Corn'. That as you approached the dyslexic age of 18, you were suddenly useless and should be denied the rights of life. Just having blue hair could lead to the red and blue lights, so she made sure to watch the MPH needle.

There was a lot to look at on the drive. It was another part that she liked about it, but something was distracting from the view. Something that was begging for her attention, almost as much as the speedometer—that car. The brown one in her rearview mirror. Freda had an excellent mind, even though it was full of swear words, it remembered things like the operations manual for a top-of-the-line Hewlett Packard. She could have sworn she had seen the same car yesterday. On her way to the border. It had gotten behind her somewhere around the Florida Welcome

Center—the importance of which hadn't set in, until now. The Welcome Center was where the Cartel had jumped Bernie, so this brown car could very well be the same people. Bernie had said that Hellsa was taking care of it, but Hellsa wasn't sitting beside Freda. There were no signs of backup swerving in and out of traffic, keeping pace with the car that she was now convinced was following her.

Freda picked up her cellphone that was sitting on the seat beside her and pressed the pre-programed #1 contact. It only took a couple of rings to get the voice she needed.

"Bernie, it's Freda. I think I got one. There has been a strange car following me from Georgia and before you tell me I'm crazy, I saw it yesterday."

"No one knows you are working. Other than us. Are you sure?"

"Believe you me, it's the same car. Followed me from the Welcome Center right into Georgia. I didn't see it when I got to the warehouse or at the apartment, but it showed up again, just as I passed the Welcome Center a few minutes ago."

"Don't come back here," Bernie ordered.

"I beg your pardon?"

"I'm contacting Hellsa, you try and lose it, but don't come back here. If by chance they are on to you, we can't lead them back to the park."

"I'll try but tell Hellsa to hurry up."

Freda hung up the phone and changed lanes immediately. Looking in her rearview, the brown car had matched her movements. She changed back into the slow lane and once again the brown car did as well. Freda let her lead foot set in on the pedal, chancing a speeding ticket over a bullet in the back of her head. She brought the baby-blue wagon up to a noticeable seventy miles per hour and headed back over to the passing lane. With the power of the wagon's v8, she was able to put a fair amount of distance between her and the brown car, but only for a mile or so, when it showed up again. Now there was no doubt in her mind that this was a tail. There were no more coincidences to run through, just the ever-increasing chance of sudden death.

She let her foot off the gas and steered the car hard, across three lanes of traffic, right into the offramp. She screamed and swore the whole way, a mix of curses for the other drivers and pleas for her own mortal soul. The wagon shot up the offramp and in her side mirror she saw that the brown car was still in pursuit. Freda had no idea where she was, other than somewhere between the Welcome Center and New Smyrna, so she made another hard right, down the next road. It was a miscalculation. The pavement on this side road was rough and getting rougher. She was speeding away from the familiarity and relative safety of the highway, heading deeper and deeper into wooded areas that were perfect for a shooting. Why didn't she have a piece, she contemplated with regret. She'd always wanted one, especially when Reg was away on business. She hated sleeping alone in the house. If she had a gun, she'd feel better right now, but she was without protection and losing the distance she had gained on the highway.

Freda slammed her foot into the floor, sending the engine into a loud rampage, 'sling-shotting' the family car down the pothole-pitted road, throwing herself around the front seat as she tried to make her escape. The tires pounded into the wheel wells as they crashed up and down into the asphalt pits and all she could do was pray to a God she didn't believe in that the rubber would last. One flat on the wagon and she was dead. Up ahead there was a curve, a tight one that she couldn't see the other side of, so she plowed towards it. Looking back, the brown car was falling behind, getting lost in the dust she was kicking up and losing ground trying to navigate the hazards she was going full tilt over.

The brown car weaved its way through the obstacle course left behind by the heavy Floridian fall rains. It had lost all visual on Freda's car, but there was nowhere else to go so it pushed on, knowing that the chances of the old wagon getting a flat were good. As the brown car rounded the hard curve at the end of the road, it locked its wheels, causing the car to slide sideways to a stop. It was a dead end. A finish to this rural road, with the only way forward being bush. But Freda's car was not there. It wasn't in front of the brown car where it should be. The man behind the wheel turned to the left, and in the clearing of the dust, he saw the rear of Freda's car. The nose of it was in the ditch and the driver's side door was—

There were no more observations for the man. No thoughts or ideas. Just a bright, white light. The same one we all see when it comes time to pass on. The one that was made possible by his open driver's side window and the prying end of the tire iron that Freda had driven through his skull. Temple to temple, she took his life. Murder. Freda had committed murder—that was for sure—she just didn't know whose life she'd taken.

3

The Ball Drops

Freda drove into the park, with a few branches and leaves still stuck in the grill of her wagon. Bernie saw her coming and quickly followed after her, around the inner circle to her house. This was not laying low. If Agent Wallace was outside the gates, her botanical vehicle would have definitely drawn attention. Freda had disobeyed her orders. She had ignored the twelve frantic calls Bernie had made to her since they first talked—and worse, she had come back here. To where they live. The perfect smoke screen had been cleared. Their days of fading away into the retirement landscape were over. Whatever had happened, it had better have been worth it.

"What are you doing?" Bernie snapped as Freda was slowly getting out of the wagon. "I told you not to come back here."

Freda shot her a look, an unimpressed, disobedient look. "I took care of it."

"What does that mean? Hellsa's men were on it—there was nothing for you to take care of other than to not come back here."

Freda moved towards her carport door. "I took care of it." As she reached for the doorknob, Bernie noticed the crusted blood all over her hands.

"Jesus, Freda, what did you do?"

"I told you. I took care of it." Freda stepped inside and Bernie followed.

"Cartel?"

"I don't know." Freda made her way to the kitchen sink and started to wash her hands—feverishly with Macbethian obsession.

"You don't know? How many?"

"Just one. A man."

"A man? A Hispanic man, a—"

"I don't know. He was a man."

"You killed someone, but had no idea who they were?"

"Was I supposed to be on a first name basis with my assassins?"

"Jesus Christ, Freda, you don't even know if it was Cartel or not?"

"They were following me, that much I know. And now they are not."

Bernie pulled back from the energy of the moment to assess. "How? You don't have a gun."

"I took the tire iron out of the trunk and jammed it through his skull," Freda said, drying her hands off on the baby-blue dish towel.

Bernie was dumbfounded. Both by the method and her demeanor. The sheer savagery of this tiny woman. "You're sure he's dead?" Bernie had to ask, and Freda raised her eyebrows. "Crowbar, skull. Sure—you're sure." Bernie's cellphone rang. She answered it. "Yes?"

Freda stopped her movements, waiting for what news was coming in, trying to glean some slice of solace regarding her barbaric actions. Bernie hit the end button on her phone. The look on her face wasn't promising.

"Well, now you've done it. That Cartel that was following you, wasn't Cartel. It was FBI. You put a tire iron through Agent Wallace's head."

Freda's hard exterior crumbled and the pure terror of what she had done set in. "What—I had no idea—he was right behind me—I—I."

Bernie took her hands, "Freda, look at me. Right in the eyes. That's it. What's done is done. There is no rewind in life, just play. No looking back, just forward, therefore we have some housekeeping to do. I need you to keep it together and help take care of what's next."

Freda bore down, squeezing Bernie's hands tight. "Alright—I'm here. What's next?"

"Where's the tire iron?"

"In the back of the wagon," Freda said, clean and clear, sticking to the facts.

"Did you leave anything else there? Anything at all? We can't have another Benny situation."

"No. I didn't leave anything, I'm sure of it."

"Alright then. Now we need to get rid of the wagon."

This didn't sit well with Freda. "Get rid of it…can't we just clean it? Get rid of the murder weapon and bleach the car or something?"

"No. That's television, Freda. In real life we need to make it like it never happened. We need to make your wagon disappear, from top to tires. Nowadays, tire treads are as good as shoe prints and there's a good chance that someone might have seen you leave. That old baby-blue barge outside is easy to remember. Especially with the camouflage you have sticking out of its grill."

"Reg bought it new."

Bernie could hear the sentimentality in Freda's voice,

but there was no room for emotion now that Federal attention had been drawn to them. A murdered agent was call for a manhunt and these women had a brief window to hide their scent.

It was a sweep. A professional, tidy way of doing business. Just like anything the Norse did, it was planned and precise. Hellsa had worked her magic. Her men found Agent Wallace's car and the body of the lifeless Fed not long after Freda had fled. Those men were soon met by more of Hellsa's men driving a flatbed truck with an SUV strapped onto the back of it. The men lowered the ramp on the flatbed and maneuvered the SUV into a forty-five-degree angle, blocking the road and trapping Wallace's car behind it. With paper suits and latex gloves on, they pulled the agent's gun from his holster and shot up the staged SUV. They made sure to make a mess of it all, shooting the windows, doors and the already deceased Hispanic male that had been placed behind the steering wheel. Then, they did the same to Wallace's car, but this time with another gun. After shooting up the agent's brown car, they pressed the second gun into the Hispanic driver's hand, getting good prints on it, before leaving it beside him, on the front seat of the SUV. Last, but not least, they made a drip trail of blood, from the SUV to Wallace's car and jammed a tire iron into the tight hole that Freda had left in the Fed's head. After pulling it out, they dropped it on the ground just outside of Wallace's driver's side door. It was forensic pantomime. A perfect picture that told a complete story. Once the tire tracks from the flatbed and Freda's wagon were swept away with tree branches, there was no evidence left that anyone other than these two deceased men were ever there. This was how Hellsa did business. Not sloppy or emotional. Methodical and clean.

Bernie and Freda stood well back from the crane as its ginormous magnet slapped down onto the roof of the baby-blue wagon and lifted it high into the air.

"How did you know about this place?" Freda was amazed by the scale of it all.

"I sold my Lincoln to them. It's kind of a one-stop, chop shop."

"A what?"

"They do what most garages say they aren't doing."

The crane swung around and hung the wagon over a massive metal box. Even from down on the ground, you could tell that the towering metal machine was the automotive grim reaper, the last stop for Detroit ingenuity.

"It's like I'm letting go of Reg," Freda said, open and soft, completely out of character.

"How's that?" Bernie gently inquired, following this rare lead into Freda's heart.

"That car. Reg bought it—a gift. He came home with it as a celebration."

"That's a nice birthday present."

"Not my birthday. My pregnancy. I'd kept it from him for a while, because I was unsure. But I had gone to the doctor, and he confirmed it. Reg was so excited. I remember he picked me up and spun me around so fast I threw up. Some men buy cribs, but not my Reg. That night he came home with the wagon. A step up, he called it. For our growing family."

"I didn't know you had—"

"I don't. I lost it shortly after. But he kept the car.

Miscarriage after miscarriage. He kept the car, so I wouldn't lose hope. Kept telling me every time I was huddled by the toilet in tears, that we would fill that wagon with our own, someday."

The crane dropped the wagon into the open top of the machine and the walls of the metal-mashing behemoth began to move in on it, crushing the car and Freda's memories with it.

Freda whipped an elusive tear from her eye. "He had children with that other woman. Maybe he did it, because I couldn't."

Bernie put her arm around Freda, who winced, but didn't pull away. "I don't think so, honey. I think things just happen sometimes. Whoever he was when he was with her, was not Reg. That doesn't sound like the man I met. The one you describe. The sweet, loving husband who bought you a wagon to hold your dreams in."

Freda looked up at her boss. Her partner. Her friend— and finally let go—she cried.

The Harley popped and rumbled up to the front of Daytona College. It was the last day of Natalie's exams before break. Her hands were cold, her nose burnt from the frozen wind and her ears were buzzing, but that wasn't why she was so pissed off. For the last week, Daz had driven her to and from school and each way they teased each other. They had indulged in their highway foreplay, racing down the road, bringing each other to the brink of insanity, with many close calls along the way. Daz almost lost control of the bike a few times, letting his hand that was reaching back go a little too far. A little past flirting and closer to the act, making it hard to steer and a little too obvious for the lurking eyes of the cars they passed. Natalie had gotten far too comfortable as well, going from touching her guardian, to opening his fly and reaching her entire hand inside his worn jeans. She had also graduated from kissing the back of his neck, to biting his jaw line and cheek, leaving marks and startling the pilot. They had gone as far as they could on two wheels, standing upright and moving at terminal velocity. There was only one way this could go and it occupied Daz's every thought. He wanted her so badly, with every cell in his body, begging to be pressed against her, but the next stage was complicated. It came with all sorts of hang ups. Commitments and promises, things that rely on tomorrow, and tomorrow was not something that this biker was used to planning for. There were promises made prior to his heart's calling and so today, he was ice.

Natalie got off the back, making sure to be rough with Daz, pulling on his leather jacket and kneeing him in the back as she moved her leg over the seat.

"What's up with you?" Daz snapped at her.

"What's up with you?" she threw back at him. "You moved my hands like a hundred times."

"It was distracting."

"It wasn't distracting every other day."

"Well, it was today."

"So, what's changed?" She wasn't letting this go, stepping up to him, face to face, and turning the key off on his bike.

"Fuck, Nat. Don't do that. I was in gear."

"What—the fuck—has gotten into you?" Natalie was on fire.

"Ruby. That's what."

"Ruby? Come on, Daz. You know she's cool. She has done far worse things in her life than this and there is

95

nothing wrong with this. I don't know why you're acting this way."

"I'm supposed to watch out for you, not fuck you."

"Don't you want to fuck me?" she said with a blend of anger and seduction.

Daz had to avert his eyes. "That's not the point. You're my job."

"Well, if I'm your job, then you're not doing it right. You need more follow through. How 'bout we go back to the park after my exam, and I will evaluate your performance."

"Damn it, Nat, stop. We can't do this. You're like five years younger than me."

"Again, so?"

"Look at us? I'm the kind of person you are supposed to hate, I'm supposed to hate you."

"What the fuck are you talking about?"

Daz lowered his voice, not wanting to cause more of a scene outside the school than they already were. "You go to college. I sling dope, beat people up for money, and guard illegal clubs. We are not right for each other. Trust me, I am no good for you. I know that, but I guess that's because I'm older. You're too young to get it. To see the bigger picture, how these people look at us just riding in together. Ruby wants better for you than me and she's right. That's why we can't do this."

Natalie wanted to cry, but instead she lashed out—punching him in face. "Fuck you."

Daz took the blow. She hit hard. Hard enough to trigger the natural, animal response of retaliation inside of him and his tear ducts to fill, but he took it. He took the hit and the humiliation because he deserved it. He'd let this go on for too long. He'd crossed the line the moment he pulled her into him on that first ride. He was older. He knew where flirting and teasing like that would lead, but he let it happen. He'd indulged in his fantasy, then pulled the rug. It was cruel to treat her like that, so he took the pain that was rushing into his face, pulsing from the bridge of his nose, as she stormed off into the school. Frustrated, furious and heartbroken.

It had only been a day since Bernie and Freda had turned the baby-blue wagon into a Rubik's cube, but crime waits for no one. The newly bonded duo were out in Bernie's loaner. They had left the park as soon as Freda got back from the hospital and today, she came back far more somber than usual. She had less salt in her words and more on her mind. Bernie had learned a lot in that junkyard about Freda, and one of the main things was that there was no need to pry. She learned that Freda would open, that she was capable of opening up, but she would do so in her own time. Bernie also learned that because she opened up like she did, it meant she trusted her, so Bernie returned the respect. She let silence set in, trusting Freda to sort out her emotions, knowing she'd reach out when she was ready.

The ladies parked the loaner in the gravel lot and walked right into the seedy bar. But they were all seedy. By now Freda had realized that all the bars down here, except the tourist ones on the A1A, were. It was sort of a local requirement for all the inland watering holes. They were the kind of places that ran solely on the dimes and nickels of their regulars. Barely stocked, barely running, barely living—just like most of the clientele.

Passing through the sticky door, Freda and Bernie

made a beeline straight for the bar. They bellied right up, slapped a twenty down on it and ordered.

"Tequila sunrise. Heavy on the grenadine," Bernie stated.

"And a rum and coke," Freda followed.

The two women waited patiently for their drinks while the slowest bartender in the south attempted to fulfill their orders. It was painful watching this old broad behind the counter make busy, because she looked painful doing it. Her body had a slight forward lean to it, like her hips were locked, her hands were definitely an apartment for arthritis and her throat never seemed to be able to clear. She kept making noises, somewhere between a cough and a hork the whole time she moved around behind the wood, clanging glasses together.

When the tortoise finally set down the drinks in front of the two blue-hairs, they switched their focus from the drink slinger to their mark. Actually, they were surprised that they hadn't been made the moment they walked in, but then again, seedy bars were dark inside. Almost as dark as it is on a side road at night.

Freda and Bernie grabbed their drinks and moved over two seats, so they were shoulder to shoulder with the man at the end, putting themselves on either side of him. Bernie set down her drink, purposefully, uncomfortably close to the man's tumbler of whiskey.

"I'm not interested," the man slurred, clearly bothered by the women's presence.

"You sure about that?" Bernie said, slapping down two 3"x5" photo prints in front of the man.

"What the fuck?" The man looked up from the pictures and back and forth between the women. "You?"

"Yes, us," Freda smiled.

The man started to panic. "Oh, shit. Shit!"

"You alright, Charlie?" the bartender called over— concerned, hobbling towards him.

The man snatched the pictures up and hid them under the lip of the bar. "I'm good."

Freda jumped in, "We're old friends of Charlie's. Isn't that right, Charlie?"

Charlie nodded, unconvincingly, but he nodded, just enough to make the bartender stop her approach. As the mangled mixologist moved away from the end of the bar, Charlie whispered, "How did you get these pictures?"

Bernie laughed. "Jesus, Charlie, I thought I had a drinking problem. Do you seriously not remember the camera? Freda practically blinded you with the flash."

Charlie was sweating. "I thought it was a dream. I woke up in my bed, checked my car, there was no damage. No one said anything at the station."

"The station. Oh, that's right. You're a police officer. Why aren't you in uniform?" Freda played confused.

"I'm on leave. After that night—I took some time off. Time I was owed. No one has said anything about that night."

Bernie smiled, "That's because we took care of it for you."

Charlie looked back and forth at them. "You did? But you're—"

"What? Women? Old?" Bernie leaned in close to him. "Us two old women, took care of the young man you hit. The one you killed."

"How?"

"So now you're concerned with his well-being? Don't you worry about it. Don't want to add more stress to your leave. Let's just say that he got the cremation he wanted. But not before we took more pictures. See Charlie, we helped you and now you are going to help us."

The off-duty cop was beside himself. Was this really happening to him? Realizing that it wasn't a dream was one thing but being extorted by a couple of pensioners was ridiculous. "Help you? How? What is it you want?"

Bernie chuckled. "It? Oh no, Charlie, it's not one thing, it is many things. It is an ongoing relationship that started the moment you ran over that nice young man—drunk— in your police cruiser. You are now ours. You are going to help us, like the good friends we are. And the first thing you are going to do, is go back to work."

Charlie leaned back, grabbed the pictures with both hands and tore them up.

Now it was Freda's turn to laugh, but Freda wasn't the chortling type. "Oh, Charlie, you really are a case. Those are not the only copies we have of those pictures, and they are just two of the many images we have of you doing all sorts of things. Coming to this bar, leaving this bar, driving to that other bar, parking at that wood bungalow? The one where the ladies of the night frequent. Charlie, you are ours, unless you want to lose your pension and go to jail. Do you know what they do to pigs in jail? Now, Charlie, before you wet yourself or start crying, don't think we're asking you to do this for nothing. Once we feel we're even, once you've satisfied payment for our little cover up, we are going to make your time—moving forward—worthwhile. Very worthwhile. By the time we are done with you, you'll be able to retire early and move to Key West where you can drown yourself in whiskey and die in full Jimmy Buffet style."

Drunk, tired, nerves fried and resigned to the barrel he was being bent over, Charlie gave in. "Okay. I'm yours."

Christmas at Moonlight was anything but ordinary. The club had been gaining visitors since it opened, and Daryl's Shuttle was working like a charm. Gone were the rougher edges of the biker crowd and incoming were the smoother, deeper pockets of the semi-law abiding. The clientele was rising, getting more mainstream, more manageable and even younger. Natalie had taken care of that, enlisting the help of her surfer stalker from school, together they had spread the word amongst the locals. But only the select few, the fringe of the beach crowd, not the popular kids. Popular kids had loose lips and no loyalty. They didn't understand the value of a good secret, but Moonlight's crowd did. They coveted it, keeping their dirty little secret close, feeling like it made them part of an exclusive group. It was a healthy mix now of men and women, young and old along with some guests from the park. Included in the blue-hair fray were Fred and Cecilia. They had practically become regulars. Fred had heard about it from George and the old couple followed the path through the woods. Of course, Maryanne had been left out of the loop on this. She had to be if this place were to stay open. So, just like all the rest of Moonlight's elite crowd, Cecilia kept this secret locked down.

The strip club was not a normal place to find Yuletide cheer, but the club was full of it. Nola and Darcy had worked out a fantastic number together, stripping to "The Little Drummer Boy", the duet between Bing and Bowie. Nola was dancing to Bing's part and Darcy was playing the Star Man. It was funny, sexy and perfect for the season. Cathy had done a dance to "Santa Baby" and as a Christmas surprise, had gone all the way down past pasties, ending the number like a Christmas tree, with metallic balls hanging from her nipples.

Ruby let the girls do their numbers a few times

throughout the night, saving her show for the end. Being Christmas Eve, they had decided to close early, giving last call at midnight. No one was upset, in fact it made the whole night fit into most people's schedules. Ruby took the stage, and the entire club went silent. She was wearing all white, not her usual rouge. It was a wedding dress she had altered, plunging low and cutting high, wearing it with white-lace high heels and long lacy gloves. She began her routine with her eyes closed, dancing to nothing, no music at all, just her and her outfit, slinking across the stage. Her lines, the A to B of her hands to feet were straight as a pin. Her flares, the fanning of her hands as she moved through the open space of the stage, were sharp and stern, like a tango or a flamenco dancer casting a spell on the crowd. She worked the arc of 'Admirer's Alley', sliding her gloves slowly off, one finger at a time, until she found her way back to the middle of the stage. The DJ slowly put the needle down onto the record he had already spinning, waiting for his cue and the first rolling drums and bass line of "White Rabbit" came in. It was not the Christmas song anyone expected, but lights suddenly switched from white to all red and she fell into a trance. She began to writhe, kicking legs up into the air, snaking her back and rolling her head around, a priestess enthralled in echoing vocals of Jefferson Airplane. No one moved—nothing but their eyes to follow her. No one spoke, not a sound, but their quickening breaths as Ruby's fluid body made waves in the red light. Her curvy frame undulating so beautifully, so hypnotically that they didn't even realize she had gotten completely naked. From her ruby-red hair to her white-lace heels, she was as she was born. Curvy, captivating and unwrapped, a Christmas gift for all.

The bothersome surfer was like everyone else, completely taken by Ruby's performance and that didn't sit well with Natalie. She was splitting her attention between the stage and Daz. And Daz was splitting his gaze between the door he was guarding and her. She had used him to get a few of the younger crowd here, but that was just so Ruby would let her bring him. The real reason for parading the beach bum around was because she knew that it wouldn't fly with Daz, and it hadn't for most of the night. But by the time Ruby took the stage, the level of Daz's discomfort was settling, so she chose to up the ante.

"Kiss me," Natalie said, turning to the long-haired wave rider.

"Really?" He was caught off guard, but not unhappy.

"Yes, you doorknob. Kiss me."

"Do you even know my name?"

"Do I need to? Kiss me."

The awkward, suntanned boy leaned in and kissed her. It was cautious, the boy was being respectful, but she wasn't. Natalie made sure to slowly turn, keeping their lips locked, so she could see Daz and he could see everything. He was instantly fuming, so she put her hands on the back of the surfer's head and pulled him more into her. Deepening the kiss and raising the stakes. Daz started to move towards them, so Natalie grabbed the boy's hands and guided them down to her butt. She held them there, making his suntanned palms cup each of her cheeks, a direct insult to the way Daz had held her. The boy was in absolute heaven—that is until Daz reached them and pulled the stunned surfer off Nat, by his bleach-blonde hair.

"What the fuck?!" Nat shouted at Daz, causing some of Moonlight to take notice. Now that Ruby's Christmas number had finished, Natalie had become the floorshow.

"You're out of here buddy," Daz said to the boy,

ignoring Nat's ranting and pushing the peaceful kid towards the door.

The boy wasn't putting up any fight, but Daz didn't care, using the kid's face to open the door as if he were a belligerent drunk and tossing him out into the gravel clearing.

Natalie ran out the door, pushing Daz aside, to check on the boy she'd used. "Oh God," she gasped seeing the new split down the boy's forehead. "Daz, you didn't need to do that!"

"Neither did you," he said, pointed, knowing full well what she was up to.

"You don't want me, remember? But he does."

"I have a name," the bleeding surfer muttered. "It's Buck."

Nat looked down at him. "Buck?"

Buck cracked a half smile. "Yeah, after the TV show. Buck Rogers?"

Natalie rolled her eyes.

Ruby came running out of the club, wrapped in her red robe. "Daz, explain—now!" A very 'pumped up' Kurt was right behind her.

"This kid was all over Natalie," Daz said sheepishly.

"My word. Is that true?" Ruby turned the heat on Natalie.

"All over? He kissed me, because I asked him too."

"I was just watching out for her, like you said to," Daz assured Ruby.

Ruby assessed the scene, looking over the minor damage done to Buck. "Well, show's over. We are about ready to close up anyway." Ruby continued to diffuse the situation. "Probably a good time for you both to go home, Nat.

"You're taking his side? That greasy skidder?" Nat was inflamed, pulling Buck up to his feet.

"No sides, Nat. You just need to know when enough is enough. You've both been drinking, I can tell, and it's enough."

Natalie gave Ruby a death stare while holding up two middle fingers—one for her and one for Daz, before guiding Buck towards the footpath back to the park. She wanted to kick and scream, to cause a fuss, but she knew that Ruby was right. Enough was enough. She had used this poor boy and he had suffered for it. This round was over and stumbling back through the woods was the smartest thing to do right now, before Daz took another go at Buck. The walk wasn't long, but it was long enough for Natalie to cool down a bit and for Buck to unrattle his cage. By the time they popped out of the other end of the path, his head had stopped bleeding and he wasn't dizzy anymore—just a little upset—but not at Daz.

"You did this on purpose. Why? Does that guy like you? 'Cause, if you're trying to make him mad, it worked."

"He doesn't like me. He told me himself."

"Then why? You treated me like dirt at school, then asked for my help out of the blue. You brought me here, making it very clear we were just friends, only to kiss me and get my ass kicked."

"What can I say. You've grown on me."

"Really?"

"Keep asking, Buck, and you'll grow right off me again."

They made it back to Ruby's trailer, where Buck had left his van, and he started to walk towards his 'on brand' mode of transportation, but Natalie stopped him. "Where are you going?"

"Home?"

"Don't you want to sleep with me?"

"What? Are you fucking with me?"

"Yes or no?"

"Yeah, I do—but now? I mean—"

"I'm offering…but I don't know for how long."

"Won't your—Ruby—be back soon?"

"What about your van?"

Buck was having to play catch up—hard and fast. Not just 'cause his bell got rocked, but because his blonde roots went deep—but as she stared at him, with her hand on her hip, he got it. He picked up the signals she was blatantly sending out and opened her door to his van for her. Natalie climbed up and into the passenger seat, a little put off by the thickness of her suitor and he, now fully clued in, wasted no time getting behind the wheel. As soon as he slammed his door shut, he leaned over to kiss her.

"Fuck, Buck. Not here. We're in the driveway. Take me somewhere."

Buck was not the sharpest fin on the surfboard, but he could see his chances of a home run lessening by the second, so he turned the van on and backed out of the driveway. If he was going to salvage this opportunity, he was going to need to get them somewhere fast—luckily, he knew just the place.

Buck was the first to climb into the back, moving his surfboards to the side and laying down his pile of towels and blankets. It was no Craftmatic or the Ritz, but it was comfortable, and the view was worth a million dollars. His whole life centered around this view. This kingdom of sand, and it was the only place he could think of to bring her. Down onto the beach, behind the dunes, with the nose of the van pointed at the rolling mounds and the back doors open to the ocean. After his botched attempt at kissing her back at the trailer, he made no advance. He sat patiently on his bed of beach towels and waited for her come to the back of the van. Natalie had been full steam ahead up until then, but had suddenly switched gears, taking her time moving towards this next step. She was nervous. It was all bravado and revenge until the van stopped and she realized what it was going to take to follow through on her threats. On the offer she had made. Buck was a nice guy. He was handsome, muscular and kind. But he was the opposite of Daz. There was no danger in this boy. Nothing that got her going like the man who held her life in his hands, screaming down the interstate. She wanted to give this to Daz. It was, after all, something she could only ever give once, and she respected the importance of that. But she was mad and impatient. She was a young woman with desires and needs. Needs that this handsome boy in the back of the van, overlooking the ocean, was wanting to fulfill.

Natalie thought about the look on Daz's face when he had seen Buck kiss her, the way he raged watching her butt being held in the surfer's hands. She was smart and strong, but she was still just 18 and self-sabotage was still a viable tool in her kit. It was one of the reasons Daz was trying to avoid her. He knew that she was innocent in all the ways that could hurt her. Emotional maturity only comes with time and the wounds of experience. Her age was showing. Hurting herself seemed to be a great way to hurt Daz and that misguided logic drove her out of the passenger seat and into the back of the van. She didn't want to lose her nerve, that rush of defiance that had come over her, so she took the lead, bending over and kissing him before she had even sat down. He welcomed her lips and her body onto his bed of towels. As they continued to press their lips together, Buck ran his hands over the shape of her side, on a slightly hesitant, exploratory mission. This wasn't so bad, she thought. He was a good kisser and his hands felt good running down her side, but he wasn't—Daz.

Something dug into her back. It was hard, like a brick. "Ow!" She searched around in the towels under her. "What's this?" she said, pulling out a long leather box. It was about the size of a pencil case, hard top and bottom, with a zipper that ran down the side.

Buck was quick to take it from her. Snatching it uncharacteristically from her hands, which made her all the more curious.

"Why are you being so weird? What is it?" Natalie had an idea what it might be, but it was dark in the back of the van, so she wasn't sure.

"It's stupid. Alright, just forget about it. Can we just get back to what we were doing—what we were about to do?"

Natalie pulled away from him. His reaction made it clear. "Holy shit. It's junk, isn't it?"

Buck's face dropped.

"Is it yours? Heroin? Do you—do it?"

Buck squirmed for a moment, running through all his possible answers, then shrugged. "Sometimes. Not a lot. Just sometimes."

"Why?" Natalie suddenly seemed far more interested in what was in the leather case than what was in his pants. "What's it like?"

The war in her head was raging but now it had nothing to do with losing her virginity—well, not her sexual virginity at least. She may not have been emotionally mature, but she had a lifetime of experience in other areas. Natalie knew what a Works Kit looked like. She knew from experience, because one just like it sat on their mother's bedside table for most of her life. It was a prized possession of Mama's, kept safe, out of the way, not like the glass tube that she smoked her crack out of. Crack was the everyday medicine. The stuff that made her mother twitch around like a chicken with its head cut off and stole all her teeth. But the Works Kit? It was saved for the good stuff. The treat her mother would give herself. The one that she would pour a bath for. The one that lasted a long time and made her sleepy. The special occasion that eventually took her mother away, leaving her cold body lying on the bathroom floor for Natalie to find and poke at, until her brother called the ambulance.

"What's it like?" she asked again. Softly, sadly.

Buck squirmed a little. "It's like a hug. A warm hug and the best sex mixed together. It's a hiding place. A soft fort I can go to, when I need to, that always feels like home. But I'm not sad there."

"Sad? What the fuck do you have to be sad about? You're a rich kid whose mama takes him to Caribbean islands, buys him vans and surfboards—you're spoiled, not sad."

"You just found out my name tonight. You don't know me, or what my life's like at all. I've asked you hundreds of questions—you've never asked me one— not until right now. I have problems. Everyone's got problems. My mother's mean, my stepdads' are worse. My skin and my things don't make me immune to hurt. Sad is everywhere."

"I know sad. My whole family's dead. My mom a few years ago, my brother a few months ago. Murdered by the cops. Sad is all around me." A tear fell down her cheek. "Can you take me to that fort? The one that feels like home? I don't want to be sad—not on Christmas Eve."

She wasn't bossy or pushy or mean. She was sincere and he saw himself in her eyes. The first real thing she had said to him was everything. An outpouring of the girl he wanted so badly to know, and she looked just like him on the inside. He slowly unzipped the case, revealing the needle, spoon, cotton balls, lighter and baggy of heroin. Misery loves company and the road to every grave starts somewhere.

Bernie and Opal left just after Ruby's dance. They both didn't do well with crowds for long periods of time, so they made their way back through the path before the rest were done. There were no snowflakes in New Smyrna, save the ones cut out of paper in mass crafting derbies at the Activity Center. They were the season's 'must have' and were strung inside the front window of just about every trailer in the park, turning the retirement roads into a kindergarten classroom. Bernie missed the snow. Not the cold—but definitely the snow. She remembered all the runs my sled took down Shakespeare Hill and all the times she pulled it back up to the top for me. There was something empty about a Christmas Eve where your nose wasn't cold. Where your cheeks weren't red from wind and your stomach wasn't bursting from a table packed with food. It hadn't been that long since I'd left. It was still odd for her not to have a turkey thawing in the refrigerator and to be planning the order in which the spread of sides would be prepared in. It made her lonely. Made her long to have that connection back. One she had been trying to reattach for months and months, so maybe—just maybe, one more try wouldn't hurt.

Bernie dialed the yellow phone, hoping that a wave of Christmas kindness might swoop down and travel through the line to find Marcie on the other end—but she was skeptical.

"Hello?" It was Marcie—

"Marcie, it's Bernie!"

"Bernie? What is it with you and the late calls?" It was very late, and Marcie sounded gruff.

"Merry Christmas. Just wanted to be the first to wish you one." Bernie put on her happiest persona. "Did the kids get the cards?"

Bernie could hear a lot of grumbling in the background.

"For God's sake, it's Christmas, Brent." Marcie cleared her throat and softened her tone. "Yes, Bernie, they got them, but it's too much. Those kids don't need that kind of money."

"What money?" Brent huffed in the distance.

Bernie whispered, "Brent doesn't know?"

"Uh huh." Marcie didn't put her 'no' into words.

"Probably better that way, the money's for them. It's Christmas, Marcie, let them get whatever they want with it. I would have spent it on them if I was there, so, it's all the same."

"You and I both know that Gary wouldn't want you spoiling them," Marcie whispered.

Brent snarked, "Gary?! Did she bring him up?"

Bernie took a deep breath, ignoring Brent's outburst. "Well, he's not here, so…"

There was more grumbling in the background on the other end of the phone and Marcie began to speed up her speech. "Well, it was good to hear from you, Bernie, but I better get going."

Bernie was losing her, so she blurted out, "You can't go before I give you your gift."

"My gift?" Marcie sounded uneasy.

"Yes, it's the real reason I was calling. To give it to you, well, it's actually a gift for everyone, Brent too. A family—gift—kind of thing."

Marcie's voice turned away from the phone, "Brent, she's calling to give us a gift."

Bernie kept rolling with it, "I wanted to invite you all. You, Brent and the kids down here. For spring break this year. All-expense paid—by me."

"Oh my God, Bernie, that is far too much!"

"What is it?" Brent sounded very awake now. "What's too much? Is it a pool?"

"Tell him kind of," Bernie said. "The only hitch is you have to drive. I don't like putting the kids on a plane."

"She wants us all to go to Florida on the kids' spring break," Marcie said away from the receiver.

"We can't afford that," Brent scoffed.

"On her dime."

"Wow! Thank you, Verna!" Suddenly Brent was very happy to have the late-night call.

Bernie suddenly processed what she had offered. What had slipped out of her mouth, and she would have to follow through with. It wasn't to make Brent happy, that's for sure, but it would bring Marcie and the kids to her. The connection she was dying for. "It's—my pleasure—Brent. So, Marcie, you'll come down then? I'll pay for the gas too. The drive will be fun. The same run I used to do with Gary, that we did together. Remember?"

Marcie hesitated, trying to make sense of it all in the foggy mind of the midnight hour, "Yeah. The drive down, I remember. I think the kids would love it."

"So, is that a yes?"

Marcie giggled a little. "Yes. Thank you, Bernie. It's been a while since we had something to look forward to, so yes!"

Bernie's face became the joy that is promised in all Yuletide carols. The gift she had offered was already giving back. Christmas Day felt good for the first time in years.

New Year's Eve was a record setter for Moonlight—1991 had its ups and downs but 1992 would go down in history. It was jam-packed like always, but tonight everyone in there had paid the extra hundred-dollar cover charge on top of the inflated bar prices. But the money wasn't just flowing there; Ruby, Nola, Darcy and Cathy had never had so many bills in their G-strings. Their undergarments were so loaded down with Lincolns, Hamiltons and Jacksons, that they had to keep running back to the dressing room to unload. Kurt had been moved from Ruby's side to the back room so he could guard the cash, while the four feather dancers were being run off their feet. They had started offering lap dances now, between their solos, which had been spaced farther apart. The years and miles on their money makers were catching up and the pace they originally started out with, was not sustainable. The good news was that the club, in and of itself, was entertaining. It was still new to most who were coming in on Daryl's Shuttle. Its art-plastered walls, burlesque décor and backwoods kitsch seemed to be keeping them all entertained. The shine of a new find was dazzling, but Ruby knew it wouldn't last for long.

"My word, we need new blood," Ruby said, pulling the other three girls aside, over by the bar. "Don't get me wrong, you three are the main attractions, but we need filler."

"Everyone seems happy," Cathy shrugged.

"Tonight, yes. But it's New Year's. Everyone's happy on

New Year's. The nights leading up to now, however, have been getting less and less lucrative."

"I can't do more numbers, Ruby. My dogs are barking, and my back is breaking as it is." Nola was not having it.

"I'm not suggesting we do more stage time, or floor time for that matter. We need other things to keep these people here. They'll come in for us, but we need them to keep coming back and spending more money."

"You're thinking of bringing in new dancers?" Darcy asked hesitantly.

"I am," Ruby said. "Younger ones. New ones."

Nola looked like she was ready to throw hands.

"My word, hear me out. We could scout a few of the hot little numbers from around town and give them a great opportunity. Fill the early spots of the evenings and the spaces in between our stage numbers with them. Besides more eye candy for the guests, it would give us backup if we need a night off and we could help them too."

"Help them by taking a chunk of our tips?" Nola was still not liking this.

Darcy keyed in, "Sure, we'll lose some of our tips, but it's more than that. I see where you're going with this, Ruby. It's like you and I were talking about—when we first bumped into each other again at the bar. This is our chance to be the Pepsi's!"

"Pepsi's?" Cathy was missing something

"You mean those old French dancers?" Nola remembered the offensive slang.

Darcy's eyes sparkled. "Yes, we could mentor them. Like the ones from the Eastern Townships in Magog did for us. We could help the new girls find the pride in our art form, maybe inspire them to do what we've done."

"I like it." Nola tilted her head. "Like professors."

"Like professors," Ruby agreed.

"Gambling!" Cathy shouted. It was like her two cents had blown the lid off of the pressure cooker. "We should add gambling too. Poker or blackjack. They're easy to set up. I worked for a while in Vegas as a dealer. I know the ins and outs and we could pull in a load of money from just a few tables. It would keep them drinking too."

Ruby thought about it. A couple of tables would add secondary draw to the place and like Cathy said, it would add a lot of extra money to it too. "How about over there? Where those booths are, on the back wall, would that be a good spot for tables?" Ruby was seeing the vision.

"Two or three tables would do it." Cathy was excited that Ruby was not only listening to her, but that she was into it.

"Then let's do it," Ruby said. "I have a feeling, ladies, that 1992 is our year. Look out world 'cause we are just getting started!"

Freda could hear the buildup to the countdown. Sure, it was quieter than most other places around town, but even the palliative care ward was eager to celebrate the coming year. Down the hallway, away from the murmur, it was just her and her man. Like it had been for so many New Year's before. Reg was usually away for Christmas. Back then he said it was business, but now she knew the real reason. He had kids that deserved to have a dad along with the tree. She spent every 'holy night' alone, but not New Year's— no, the rebirth of the calendar was theirs. No matter what 'business' he was attending to, no matter what 'storm' had come up or crisis he was needed for, he always made it home for the ball to drop. In the early years, the two of them went out. Paid heavy cover fees and made extravagant reservations for multi-course meals. But as the years went by, they realized that all the reservations, the champagne towers and chocolate fountains, the crowded dance floors and impossible cabs, were all just noise. That it was all just a giant waste of time because all they truly wanted when Auld Lang Syne rang out—was each other. To be holding their true love in that gap between the past and the future. The magical kiss at the stroke of midnight that should only be shared with your destiny. They had shared that kiss every year. That hopeful joining of their lips and their dreams under the twelfth gong of tomorrow.

"I know about her, Reg," Freda said out into the dark room, lit only by the soft tube above his bed and blinking lights of his monitors and respirator. "I know about her and the kids and—I'm not mad anymore."

Freda got up out of her chair and walked to the side of his bed.

"I was angry. Believe you me, I have said a swear word before your name for months now. Out loud and in my head. But not anymore. I don't know why you did what you did. I blamed myself, for losing our babies." Her breath halted, "All our babies—but that was above me. Far beyond my paygrade. I tried to give you—what she could. But I guess that wasn't my role this spin around the sun. I was just here to love you. And Reg, I did. I did with all my heart. With every beat of it and every breath in my lungs, I did. And I know you did too. I couldn't give you babies, but we had our own little family. In our own way. Just you and me—and for my side of that bargain—it was enough. More than enough. Reg, I loved being your girl. It made me the belle of every ball."

Through the closed hospital room door, Freda could hear the nurses—who had been secretly sipping Spumante Bambino all night—beginning their countdown.

"I'm not angry anymore. Now, all I think about is our love. It was not a lie. It was real. It is real." Freda reached over and unclipped the plastic clamp on one of the I.V. bags. The clamp that regulates the speed and quantity of the drips leaving the bag and going into the tube attached to Reg's arm. "I love you, Reg. I love you enough to know that I can't keep you here like this." Freda squeezed the bag hanging from the stand, the one with the morphine label on it, pushing fluid down the unclamped tube and into Reg.

"Three, Two, One!" The nurses down the hallway cheered and Freda leaned down, laying her lips down over her Reg's.

"Happy New Year," she whispered to her love, as she crawled up onto the bed, over the tubes and wires, nestling her back against him. She pulled his arm over her, turning his frail body onto his side, positioning him into a cuddle— into the Big Spoon. Freda closed her eyes and listened as his breath spaced farther and farther apart and his heart-beat faded away into the promise that their kisses always held. Eternal love.

The Albatross, as Bernie had come to call it, had left Miami shortly after she was attacked in the Welcome Center parking lot and had taken up new mooring at the Smyrna Yacht Club. It was closer to Bernie and farther from the growing heat of the Cartel and corrupt police of Miami. It dwarfed all the other boats at the club, which was a flag that Bernie didn't like being waved so close to home, but with Agent Wallace out of the picture, no one was watching so she was able to move freely once again. Hellsa and Vergil were displayers of wealth. The ones that lived in the opulence of their work, unlike Bernie who had showed up to Hellsa's private New Year's Eve bash, in a borrowed hatchback wearing an old yellow pantsuit and slightly scuffed flats.

The party was mostly Hellsa's family—the family, including Donnie and his henchmen, Kenneth—the overindulged asshole grandson—and the rest of the Norwegian clan. Hellsa had arranged for an elaborate firework display to go off at midnight, shooting out over the water, all launched from the stern of the boat. It was the most impressive thing Bernie had ever experienced at year's end and for a brief moment she enjoyed it. She was able to drop her worries about the expense and the perception of the outside world for the duration of the blasts, closing the eyes in the back of her head and only looking forward. Out into the star-studded sky that was being painted in light, celebrating the hard work she and the gals had done, and marking what was promising to be a very prosperous new year.

Once the light show was over, a lot of the guests trickled out. Most of Hellsa's family that had children left, and the ones that were staying onboard the ship had turned in. All that was left was the two Matriarchs. With white plush blankets wrapped around them, the two Donnas sat out on the open deck and took in the ocean air, mixed with a healthy dose of their accomplishments.

"A few bumps and bruises, but overall, a stellar end to the year, Verna."

"Bumps and bruises? I think bodies and bloodshed is more accurate." Bernie soured the sugar coating.

"True. But mine is more poetic." Hellsa grinned. "At this rate, with our established networks and your contributions, we will bury the Cubans and be the sole supplier for the entire east coast."

Bernie looked around at this floating Olympus. The uninhibited grandeur of it all. She had spent the night as a wallflower, watching Hellsa's family enjoy all of it. The grandkids running around, the cousins, aunts, uncles, sons and daughters, lapping up all the luxury without guilt. Without worry.

"Life is short, Verna." Hellsa was contemplating a completely different train of thought.

"It is," Bernie responded.

"None of us know when it will all end. It's a game really. Some think it's a moral pursuit. A list of rules to follow, to get into the next place. They work their nine to five's and save their pennies—have only one lover and only drink on the holidays, but they've been lied to. It's not a qualifier, it's a game. It's a movie that we are writing for ourselves every waking moment." Hellsa was a little thick in the tongue from the night's celebrations, but she wasn't drunk. This was a train of thought that only someone who was close to the destination could dictate. "If we choose to play the game or not, it only matters to the player. But there is no punishment. We all suffer the same end. I chose to play to win. To take as much as I could, because in the end, no one takes anything with them. None of this matters, only to the ones we leave it to and share it with. Oh, Verna, it's all a game. Unfortunately, most don't know they are playing."

Bernie was overtaken with an epiphany. "I do. And I want it all."

Hellsa chuckled, "We all do, Verna."

"No. I want it all. All of your product. All of your distribution. I want to be your only vein."

Hellsa sat up from the back of the couch. "Invisible, Verna, remember? Invisible, that is your invincibility."

"I can still be invisible. Keep it all unseen, while

moving it all." Bernie had this idea for a while, but it was too big, too many moving parts to put into action, but something had changed. Something that Hellsa could see in her eyes.

"What has gotten into you, Verna?"

"Family. I have spent my time, laying low. Never really profiting from the deeds I've done, hiding what I did reap. I could do so much more with more. I could have a New Year's Eve party too. With my family."

Hellsa nodded, "Higher levels bring many devils, Verna. You would need to protect yourself better. And your chain as well. You can't protect that kind of operation with tire irons."

"I know. I've thought that through too," Bernie said stoically, with the unwavering solidity of a choice already made.

Hellsa saw it too. "Alright. Let's hear it, partner. After what you've accomplished already, I'd be a fool not to hear you out. If it's feasible, I'll give you a chance. A trial. My other networks will stay in place just in case, but if it's at all as good as what you've already done, I have no doubt we'll be celebrating next year on your yacht."

It was wrong. She knew it was wrong and so did he. There was no love in the movements, in the sweat building between their bodies or in their panting breaths. Their kisses where open and wet, and the energy was aggressive. It was a rush of forgetful pleasure. A portal to a dimension where only the sensations of their skin were felt. All of the other pain and worry was left at the gate and as they grinded together, they were united in self-preservation. United in the escape, but not in each other, because both of them were thinking of someone else. They were using each other to feel what they could not feel, what was forbidden and impossible.

Ruby wrapped her legs around him, pulling his hips into her as she pulled his head down, hiding his face in the nape of her neck. She could imagine this way. No face staring down at her, let her fill in the empty space with her own images. It wasn't perfect, but she could almost pretend it was Ben, and not Daz. He felt different, but the rush of hormones and blood inside her were enough to perform this brief magic trick. The same one he was performing, conjuring up a different body than Ruby's below him. It was consensual, desperate and intense, and it was wrong.

This was nothing foreign to Ruby—falling into bed with people to fill her voids—it was the pattern she knew and in the early hours of this promising New Year, she found herself being visited by old ways. It was doing the trick and, in all fairness, the wrong wasn't on Ruby at all. She had no idea what had transpired between Daz and Natalie. If she had— actually, there is no way to know if it would have changed the drunken impulse of the two of them at all. Ruby's past was filled with all sorts of men who were spoken for. Doing the wrong thing was a form of flagellation. It was punishment to cross the line and reinforced her deep, negative self-image. But these New Year's Day fireworks weren't about shame, they were about remembering. Losing Daz's image in the darkness of her room. Letting his white skin turn red, in the ruby color cast from her bedside light, just like Ben's did. In the erotic thickness of a red silk scarf covered light, all lovers blend together. A witches brew of beaus stirred up in a crimson stew of perspiration. But all pleasure is fleeting, and as Daz turned her over, she turned her head, to bury her face into her arm, hiding the tear that accompanied her approaching orgasm. Reality had found its way in. As fast as the rush consumed her, it left. It was the same for Daz. As Ruby hid her face, he collapsed onto her back and his eyes opened. The image of his desired lover lost, instantly replaced with the relentless ache once again. They were both back where they started, unsatisfied, although Ruby had no idea that he was imagining someone else too.

But Natalie did.

It had been a week since she'd let the surfer put a needle in her arm. A week full of confusing thoughts and wants. Of regret and longing. Both heart and chemically driven. She had promised herself that she was done with the brown sugar. The syringe escape. She had told Buck as much and the two of them had spent the night, just sipping beer and watching the bonfire that the other kids had set ablaze on the beach. It was a return to innocence. A pulling back from the edge of destruction and more in line with who she was. But this wasn't. She could see the Harley tucked into the carport as Buck dropped her off.

"Wait here!" Natalie didn't wait for the van to stop. She didn't announce herself as she opened the carport door, and she didn't knock before she kicked open Ruby's bedroom door.

"Jesus!" Ruby shouted but was unable to move, to change the scene. She was pinned on her belly, with Daz on top and inside of her still. "Natalie? Knock for Christ's sake!"

Natalie ran straight for Daz and started swinging. Punching and slapping him as he struggled to get off of Ruby.

The biker cowered under the young woman's blows, crouching naked at the end of the bed. "Stop! Nat! Stop it!" Finally, he was able to get control of her hands, grabbing onto her wrists and managed to stand up.

"How could you!" she screamed.

"Natalie, calm down!" Ruby urged, wrapping herself with the sheet of the bed to cover up.

"No! I love him!" she lashed back at her mentor.

Ruby was stunned. "Daz, what is she talking about?"

Daz stuttered, "It's not what it sounds like. Nothing happened, we—"

"You basically dry humped me for a week then told me you didn't want me.'

"Daz!" Ruby was furious. "You touched her?"

"You're fucking right he did, grabbing my ass while he drove, grinding me into the back of him, letting me kiss him, and touch him."

Ruby was mortified. "Natalie, I would never have, if I knew."

Natalie ignored Ruby's plea for forgiveness. "Was this your plan, Daz? Was I just your way to get close to the boss? Is that it? You want to be the big man, but I can't do that for you, can I? You used me!" Natalie didn't wait for another word, ripping her hands free from Daz and running out of the trailer to Buck's waiting van.

Inside Ruby's bedroom, the smell of sex was overburdened by the cloud of guilt. Daz pulled on his jeans, waiting for the insults and threats to start.

"So, are they going find my body in the woods?" he asked, not sarcastically.

"Why?" Ruby asked. "I get the physical, but why me? Is Natalie right? Is this some kind of move to get in good with me? A move on my club?"

"Tonight was just what it was. You and me, getting off together. Nothing more. I swear. But Natalie was right about the rest. I do like her, and it all happened like she said. I let it go too far, for too long. I know it was wrong.

You told me to watch her, and I overstepped. So, I stopped. I backed off."

"Tonight, you were thinking about her, weren't you?"

"Were you thinking about me?" Daz asked, but Ruby didn't answer. "I'll go find her. That surfer kid's van won't be hard to track down."

"Let her go. You scorned a broken woman. You have no idea what happens when you turn a scarred girl's love into hate. She needs time. And so do you. Take some time off."

"But I—"

"No, Daz. Stay away from her and the club until this is made right. Your guys can work the door until then and I have Kurt. I'm serious. Stay away until I tell you, if I tell you or they will find your body in the woods."

It was all hands-on deck. Even Natalie, who had not been home much since her New Year's surprise. She too was pulled out of bed and put into the back of the shuttle along with the rest of them. Daryl was heading out of town, using back roads, working his way inland and down. A five-hour drive from New Smyrna, heading southwest of Fort Lauderdale. It was part of the next phase of their empire. Part of the plan that Bernie had laid out for Hellsa on her boat, the one she had yet to tell the others about. It was supposed to be all business, but it was also going to be a team building trip. A reweaving of their crew. Securing the bonds and trust between them all and it all was set to go down deep in the heart of the Everglades.

After multiple pitstops, uncontrollable smells and a lot of complaining from all parties, Bernie, Ruby, Opal, Freda and Natalie arrived at an old wooden dock. It was a hand cut, hand hammered relic that had lasted through many hurricane seasons and showed its scars. It was tilted a fair amount to the right, there were splinters and nails popping out of it everywhere, but it was still strong enough to dock the large fan boat to.

"Ms. Hewton—I mean, Bernie. How are you?" Cliff asked, but it was more of a greeting than a question.

Bernie made her way quickly over to him. "Cliff. I am so happy to see you."

"Me too," the army-fatigue-wearing bodyguard said, as gentle as a sheep.

"I am so sorry about Vergil."

"I tried Bernie, I promise I did." Cliff turned his head, revealing the still-healing scar on his neck. The round one, in the shape of a bullet wound.

"I know you did, Cliff."

"They took very good care of me at the hospital, Bernie. Thank you, for that." Cliff was overflowing with gratitude.

"It was a joint effort. My partner—your new boss, made it happen."

"I look forward to thanking her," he said, and Bernie knew he meant every word.

Bernie turned to the women that were slowly spilling out of the shuttle. "Ladies, this man here is Cliff. He is one of the toughest, smartest and most lethal man on the planet. Today I have asked my dear friend to take us on a little excursion where you all might learn something new."

"Enough with the surprises, Bernie, just tell us what the hell we are doing down here?" Freda was already at her wits end four hours ago, so this prolonged climax was too much for her.

"Just get in the boat, Freda." Bernie's smile left her face.

She didn't say much else, just pointed down to the dock and waited as the four road-worn women reluctantly made their way down to the odd-looking boat. Once they all were sitting in their seats, strapped in and wearing the large ear protection that was provided for them, Cliff took the chair at the back. The one sitting high up, above the rest, perched just in front of the massive fan, with long levers on either side of it.

"You can go get the rooms set up, Daryl," Bernie called back to their car salesman chauffeur, who was busy working hard on the white spittle in the left corner of his mouth. "We'll be back in three hours."

"Three hours?" Freda was not liking the prognosis, but before she could say another word, Cliff brought the huge engine attached to the fan to life and no one could hear a thing.

The flat, steel boat pulled away from the dock and sped off into the lily-covered water. Cliff steered the skipping craft over land and bog using the long rod on his left side that moved the fins at the back of the fan. It was a fast, exhilarating ride through the alligator-infested glades, and it injected new life into Bernie's burned-out bunch. The rushing wind and roar of the fan blades made everyone powerless to the smile coming to their face—everyone except Natalie. She was completely withdrawn and unamused, silently protesting her involvement, but at least she was there. That made Ruby very happy. They hadn't spent any time together since New Year's Eve, so every second in her presence was a win. Ruby knew broken hearts take time and maybe with Ben's death on top of it, Natalie's was just going to take a little longer.

Cliff brought the fan boat around the corner, skipping the aluminum along the edge of the bank, sending the boat into a hidden inlet. It was not the kind you find on the ocean or a lake, this was a marsh inlet, that ended in a stumpy, muddy horseshoe of land, with a small wooden cabin on it. Cliff cut the engine off, the only form of brakes that an air-propelled boat has and guided the metal boat towards the shore, where he beached it right in front of the wood shack.

Bernie took her ear protection off. "We're here."

Natalie and Freda looked very displeased. "Believe you me, there had better be a bar and a bathroom in there."

Bernie turned to Cliff, and he shrugged. "I'm afraid not, I don't drink. But the bathroom is around the back. I just go behind it."

"I beg your pardon?" Freda was livid.

"Pipe down, Freda. It's a cabin. You can pop a squat behind it," Bernie scolded her.

"Sorry, Bernie," Cliff said.

"Not a problem, Cliff. Freda likes to pretend her ass has only ever touched Boston porcelain."

"Bernie. This is an interesting place, but why are we here?" Opal had been quiet up till then, but the creepy cabin in the woods was starting to give her weird vibes.

Cliff walked over to the shed, undid the padlock on the door, opened it wide and stood to the side. Opal, Freda and Natalie took the bait, walking over to take a look at what the five-hour drive and windburn was all for. As they stepped inside the small cabin, their jaws dropped—all of the walls were lined with guns. A whole lot of guns. Hand-guns, shotguns, machine guns, grenades—if you could shoot it, it was there.

Bernie stepped up behind the women. "This is our boot camp, ladies. It's about time that you all learned how to protect our business and yourselves. This shack is Cliff's private retreat. Away from the eyes and startled ears of the public, where we can all get comfortable with our new security."

"Security?" Opal asked, as always trying to keep up.

"Yes. We can't keep relying on others. We can't keep doing this without getting our hands dirty," Bernie stated clearly enough for Opal to get the drift.

This was music to Freda's ears. She had wanted this for a while, to pack heat and she went straight for the magnum. It was a large handgun in the grip of an average sized man, but in her little paws, it was a hand cannon.

"Whoa, whoa, whoa!" Bernie got in front of her. "Just point to the ones you want to try. Cliff will bring them out to the range for us."

Freda was bummed, setting the gun down on the ledge, pouting and pointing at it as she walked back to stand alongside the other women. Natalie was next, pointing to a fully automatic rifle. Bernie pointed to a stubby Uzi, Ruby to a matching set of Colt Mustang 380s and Opal pointed to nothing. She didn't know what to make of it all, or what to do. This was not dinner delivery or diaper delivery or anything she could lie to herself about in her head. It was lining the walls of the cabin. It was what Bernie used to shoot those Cubans in the Welcome Center parking lot and what the police used to kill Benny. This was real. The money she was sending to the Reverend was worse than the wages of sin, it was the fuel for it. Money came from guns that came from money. She started to hyperventilate. Inside, the two voices of herself began arguing. Opal and Bernadette were going at it, fighting for their run of her soul. She felt faint, slipping backwards into the wood plank wall and collapsing onto the floorboards.

"Water!" Bernie shouted and Cliff ran back to the fan boat to get some from the supplies he brought. "Opal, come on. Breathe. You're having a panic attack. Just breathe."

Opal tried to catch her breath, but the war inside of her was in full swing. She had no control over her own faculties, her bladder released, and her eyes rolled back into her head.

"Opal!" Bernie gently slapped her face as Cliff returned with the large plastic bottle of cold water. Bernie poured it over Opal's head, soaking her from crown to collar and her pupils appeared. "Opal, you get this under control. You can handle this. You've been handling this. You're strong enough, so breathe. This is just part of what we do. You know what we do. Stop pretending. Stop lying to yourself. You are a good person. You are a good person who is making money off bad people. If you didn't do it, someone else would. Someone bad, who would use the money for bad things. We are out here to learn how to protect ourselves from those bad people. So, we can keep sending money home, keep building our future. It's time you owned that, Opal. You are a woman. Not an angel or little girl. People all over the state respect you and they have never even met you. They have just heard whispers of you. Of us. Take that power and own it. That's what we all are here for."

In Opal's head, the voices quieted. One no louder than the other, but both still there, leaving a space in between them for a mix of the two. A mix that was standing up, drying off her face with one hand and pointing to the shotgun with the other.

The range was only a few hundred yards away from the shack. It was an open area, surrounded by swamp overgrowth, with wooden targets set up at the water's edge. Any misses by unskilled marksmen, or markswomen, would go straight into the drink. Cliff lined up the ladies about five feet apart from each other and had them stand behind wooden tables he had built just for the occasion. On top of the tables, in front of each of them, was their firearms of choice and the corresponding ammunition. Cliff took his time, going down the line, showing each of them the ins and outs of their weapon. He showed them how to load their guns, how to hold them and how each required a different brace for recoil. He demonstrated how to clear jams, how to aim and finally how to breathe and pull the trigger. He went over it all and then instructed them to put on the ear protection they had used on the boat.

The women were nervous. Everyone is the first time they hold a gun. It's an experience that holds so much meaning. It is the tipping point for taking life, animal or human. It is the realization that in your hands you hold the power of the gods. The will to take the breath from another. It can be an empowering moment or one that makes you appreciate all life and vow to never, ever take someone else's. It's a conference with the self. The place inside where we find or give up our power and these women found the power.

The guns erupted in an assault of starburst. Blasts, both automatic and single fire, rained out over the marshy land and tore through the wooden targets like they were paper dolls. The women weren't accurate at first, but they were persistent. They loaded and reloaded over and over, righting their stances, lining up their shots and not backing down. Opal was pumping shells through her shotgun so fast that the barrels were glowing and so was she, while Natalie turned into a Bayou Rambo, holding down the trigger and spraying her vengeance all over the alligator sanctuary. It only took a half an hour to turn these pseudo-criminals, these unarmed dependents into the hellfire of the Grand-mafia.

By the end of the day, they had all tried every weapon that Cliff had, except for the grenades. Even that far out, a small mushroom cloud of smoke rising in the sky is hard to hide. After trying the lot, they found their way back to what they each had started with. Cliff packed up their respective weapons into individual cases and took the 'mercenary ma'ams' back to the slanted dock where Daryl was waiting. Once the lethal ladies boarded the shuttle, Cliff got on with them. He sat down, right next to Bernie.

As the doors closed, Ruby asked what everyone was wondering, "Is he coming with us?"

Bernie turned back to her and said, matter of fact, "He is indeed."

"Why, we know how to use the guns now." Freda wasn't satisfied. "What do you need him for?"

"We need him, to do what we are going to do." Bernie was stern.

"And what are we going to do?" Ruby asked cautiously.

Bernie turned back to face the front of the shuttle. "We are about to embark on a massive expansion of our business. We are going to take over Florida."

4

Girls' Day Out

As soon as the girls got back, the word went out and a meeting was called. The meeting would be in the usual place, Moonlight, but this was a new kind of meeting, because there were more members attending. It wasn't just the core, the fellowship of four old women who joined forces in Freda's lanai a few months back, this meeting involved Nola, Darcy and Cathy—and it didn't stop there, it also included the opposite gender—Daryl, Mullet, Cliff and Kurt. Daz was M.I.A., he was still in Ruby's doghouse and that worked well, because what she had to say wasn't meant for the ears of his motorcycle club.

"Alright everybody, take a seat," Bernie addressed the group like it was a union meeting back in Buffalo, only back then the crew was bigger, much bigger and scarier. "First of all, I want to thank Ruby for letting us meet here and also to bring to all of your attention the blackjack and poker tables that she has just added to Moonlight." Bernie motioned over to the four new tables along the wall.

"Those were Cathy's idea," Ruby corrected.

"That's right, great work, Cathy. Those are bound to

bring in a large return and on that note." Bernie motioned over to Cliff. "For those of you who don't know him yet, this gentleman is Cliff. Amongst his other duties, Cliff is bringing in three pit bosses, to watch over Cathy's dealers."

"What about Daz's guys?" Kurt had clearly not been included in this decision.

"They're still going to run security. But the tables and their take—are ours. Not a part of the original arrangement."

"You sure they are going to be okay with that?" Kurt seemed skeptical.

"You and Cliff will make sure they are. They respect you and you both know how to be persuasive." Bernie laid out the first order and Kurt nodded in agreeance. She then looked around the group, searching for someone. "Where's Natalie?"

"She's not feeling well," Ruby replied—not very convincingly.

"Is that so? She's not been feeling well a lot lately," Bernie said, with zero sympathy.

"My word, Bern, lay off her." Ruby stood up to her. "I'm on it."

Bernie sighed, one of her big sighs, letting go of the young woman's absence, picking her battles and getting back to business. "The reason I have asked you all here, isn't just to introduce you to Cliff or talk about the cards being added to Moonlight. It's to include you in our next move. You are all here, because either I or my sister trusts you. Not in the traditional sense, but in the bloodletting bond of trust. Each of you over the past few months, have proven your loyalty, never wavering in your character and for that we want to include you in the next stage of our journey. So far, our tiny crew has filled a very large void in a supply chain, that until we came along, had been practically cut off. We have done exceptionally well, but there is room for improvement. Room for us to strike while we're hot, to grow our presence and possibly seize the whole kit and kaboodle. We have been given the opportunity to prove ourselves and if we do, the keys to the kingdom will be ours. Each of you has a valuable role to play in this plan and you must all stick to it. We must stick together, back each other up, stay loyal and focused if we are to make history. But I promise you that if we do this, if we stand by each other and the plan—we will make history. Do you want to make history?"

The group all mumbled adult, under-enthused words of approval, but not Mullet. Mullet didn't march to that drummer, he was a stranger to decorum, to the opinions of others, so he shouted his inclusion with passion, "I want to make history!!!"

Bernie chuckled, "Yes, Tony. That is the enthusiasm I was hoping for. That is exactly why you are here."

"I'm ready to make history!" Nola shouted as well and the rest followed one by one, except for Kurt and Cliff— they stayed mountains—excitement was not in their DNA.

"Ruby," Bernie nodded and her sister walked over to her fellow strippers and handed them each a stack of glossy flyers.

"What are these?" Darcy asked before reading the words across the top of the thick card out loud. "Girls' Day Out?"

"That's the new plan," Bernie said with a smile. "We have moved away from single runs and are spreading out. What you are holding in your hands, ladies, is your part in our new way. You three will be advertising our new shuttle service that runs up and down the coast. But this is not just any shuttle, this one will take women from our surrounding area all the way down to Miami and back on a day trip of shopping, sightseeing and female bonding. It is a 'women only' outing, done in the air-conditioned comfort of one of Daryl's shuttles. It will pick up passengers all along the coast, Daytona, New Smyrna, West Palm Beach, Boca Raton, Fort Lauderdale and everywhere in between where you can sell a ticket. The shuttles will be run in teams of two, one of us driving and the other acting as a tour guide. We will provide beverages, lunches, a safe trip to and from —and of course fun. The kind of day out that the women will tell their friends about and want to come back for more. It will be entertaining enough to be different, but tapioca enough to make it accessible to all of our aging sisters."

"Whoa." Darcy wasn't sure if she was hearing this correctly. "So you all aren't running drugs anymore? You're moving into blue-hair guided tours?"

"Yes, Darcy, we are venturing out into 'women only' tourism—but we are most definitely still running product. My friends at the junkyard have been so kind as to customize our fleet of three shuttles with large false floors. These floors have enough empty space to carry a few million dollars' worth of cargo each trip. A few million dollars of product that will be transported under the seats of our happy, clueless, senior citizens. The shuttles will travel to Miami with empty holds, and then loaded with product once our guests have been dropped off to enjoy one of the pleasant stops on the day's itinerary. Our guests and our product will be driven all the way back on the I-95, under the noses of our fine county peace officers and state troopers. After dropping off our happy ladies, the product will be delivered to our new tour company head-quarters, right here in New Smyrna. Freda, Opal, there will be no more driving to Georgia and staying overnight."

"Oh, thank God!" Freda exclaimed, however Opal seemed a little disappointed by the news.

"No more warehouse, or apartment, just our new tour facility that's close to home. The place where we will return our shuttles to at the end of each day. Like any other company would."

"This all sounds great but what if we can't sell the tour tickets?" Cathy was concerned.

Ruby spoke up, "You can, Cath. Trust me. Women want to be you and Darcy and Nola. They want the secret to your confidence and carefree attitude. Just be yourselves and sell them the magic elixir that you can only get from a 'Girls' Day Out'. They will be begging to go. Also, just to make it more enticing, the first trip is free."

"Free?" Freda was taken aback.

"Exactly." Bernie smiled. "That is the response that you all are going to get. Come on, all of us on the hormonal roller-coaster love a freebie. Anyone over 40 does. Sale is practically a religious word and free? Well, it's blasphemous to turn away from that. The shuttles will only run on the days Moonlight is closed. That way it won't interfere with your performances or the success of this place."

Just then, the door behind the group opened and they all spun around, startled. Kurt and Cliff drew their guns, Ruby and the girls gasped, and Daryl threw his hands in the air, surrendering to the police officer who was suddenly standing inside the door.

"Everyone relax," Freda snarked. "This is Officer Gilroy."

"You brought a cop here?" Ruby was livid.

"We did, but he's our cop. Isn't that right, Charlie?" Bernie said motioning for Kurt and Cliff to lower their weapons.

Officer Gilroy nodded. "I'm here, aren't I?"

The officer looked better than the last time they'd seen him. A little less sweaty, a little less wobbly, a little less drunk.

Bernie cleared her throat, both in preparation for her next words and in condemnation of the ounce of attitude the officer had given. "Charlie is our eyes and ears in the Volusia County Sheriff's office. If there is so much as a whisper about us, he'll let me know and I will let you know."

Cliff was not buying it. "Why? What's in it for him?"

"Same as all of you. A piece of this," Bernie said. "That and our brother in blue here killed a man in a hit and run. One that we took care of for him. So, he's now on board and in bed with us."

"I don't like cops." Cliff was still on edge.

"I don't like them either," Officer Gilroy scoffed. "They're all on the take, not just me. Or running something themselves. I'm not the only sinner. Church is full of them, so why wouldn't the precinct be. At least now I'm gonna get something out of this uniform other than the shit pension."

While it didn't calm Cliff, it rang true with the rest of the crew.

Officer Gilroy addressed Bernie. "I did what you asked. They bought the Cuban story. They aren't looking anywhere else or at anything else. FBI dug around a bit, but they've moved on. Sheriff's closed the file."

Freda sighed, showing a sliver of the relief she felt.

"So, we are clear for takeoff?" Bernie asked.

"All clear, but I'll be listening to the chatter for any sign of your Cuban friends along the interstate," Charlie said with robotic enforcement to his tone.

"Maybe this is better," Opal said, in her softened,

cotton candy tone. "If this kind police officer is with us, then there will be no trouble. No craziness like before." Opal shot a look at Freda. "And we won't be alone anymore on the road. Girls' Day Out, it sounds kind of fun."

"Who cares about fun? I'm just happy to be out of the diaper business," Freda said, "it was embarrassing."

Bernie raised her brow. "Well, we aren't exactly out of it."

Mullet had his headphones on as he drove the metal-encased Grumman delivery truck down the highway. He stayed in the slow lane, not just because the speed of the truck was bad, but because the smell coming from the back was worse. Just like the new shuttles, Mullet was making stops along the I-95. He too was going around to old folks homes and Bone Parks, but his route was contained to the local area and what he was picking up was very different. He wasn't picking up old people, he was picking up their diapers. Not the boxes of disposable ones, clean and unused like the runs they were making before; no, now he was picking up bags of cloth, adult diapers. Soiled and stinky. This was the second prong of the new plan. Another vehicle customized to carry a large sum of product, only this one was transporting the drugs under burlap sacks filled with shit-smeared nappies that no traffic cop or DEA agent would ever sift through. Bernie and Hellsa had purchased the pick-up service from a man in Clearwater that was very happy with their 'all cash' offer. The truck and the route came complete with its own laundry facility that was situated near Horne Lake RV Park, just a mile or so from the Georgia State line. Mullet's daily route started with a stop at the new shuttle depot, where his hidden cargo hold would be filled with the ladies' haul from the previous day's tour. Then the goods would be driven around the area, picking up dirty diapers from multiple stops, perfect for throwing any fuzz or Cubans off the scent, before taking it all back to the laundry facility. The great thing about this business was the laundry plant. More so, where the plant was situated. It was down at the end of a secluded road, and it backed onto the St. Mary's River. That's where a small fishing boat of Hellsa's would pick up the product and take it down the river to the ocean. From there it would be distributed to inlets and small harbors down the coast, drop spots in multiple states along the way, bypassing any inland heat.

This was the perfect job for Mullet. He liked helping people and picking up their stinky laundry was just another way of doing that. It was no big deal for him. He'd been picking up after the elderly for years at Cicada Hollow, so this was an easy transition. The new promotion meant he could play his tunes, make small talk with old folks who needed it, put smiles on faces and make a killing doing it. That was the point of the new plan, make a killing, without killing. There had been enough of that.

There was hair pulling, scratching, kicking, biting and lots of it. Ruby and Sugar were going at it, right out in the middle of the parking lot, with all the strippers and clients watching. The idea was to get new talent. To fill the spots and mentor the next generation of performers, but this was not the ballet. Ruby's original proposal was idealistic, based on a memory that had gotten rose-colored by the lenses of time and didn't take into consideration that strippers were involved.

"You bitch!" Sugar shouted in her G-string and bra top, wiggling out of Ruby's headlock and squaring off with her. "You take Quincy and Kurt and now you want my girls?"

"Not all of them. Just the two nice ones. Penny and Tara. You can keep Diamond and Candy and the rest of the other trash." Ruby was fists up and ready.

Penny and Tara, two lightweight young women, looked flattered. They hadn't ever been fought over before, well at least not by two women. One of which was porn royalty.

"You calling me trash?" Diamond tried to step up, but Sugar waved her back.

"You can have her after I'm done with her," Sugar said, even though her bloody lip and swollen eye were saying that she was losing the fight.

"Sugar, don't make me hurt you more. If Penny and Tara want to go, let 'em. You're not their pimp," Ruby tried to reason.

"I fucking helped you, Ruby. I gave you a job," Sugar shouted before spitting a bloody wad onto the ground.

"You did. That's why you're still breathing. My word, Sugar, drop it. This will not end well for you."

Sugar lunged forward, all one hundred cocaine-snorting pounds of her and Ruby greeted her with a solid right hook. Knuckle to nose and the skinny Shakers' boss lady dropped like a bag of bones.

"Stay down, Sugar," Ruby warned, then looked up to Penny and Tara. "The choice is yours. We have a couple of other new girls coming from other clubs as well. We aren't like Shakers or any other of these dives. We are a family. If you want to work in a place that will respect and protect you, where you can learn from real pros and make real money, then call me."

Natalie didn't have much of a part to play in any of the new plans, and that was fine by her. She was fine with just doing the minimum, working at the club on the weekends, even though Daz had come back. She tried to ignore the biker as best as she could, but the heart wants and when it doesn't get, it seeks out something else to fill the void, so she snuck drinks where she could, to dull the ache. It was simple to sneak booze, working as a 'bar-back' for Quincy, keeping things stocked up. She could down a beer no problem between the cooler container outside and the back of the club, even take a shot while she was crouched down, restocking the fridge racks behind Quincy. Ruby wanted her to take a bigger role, to work under her, learning the business, but Natalie had pulled back. Ever since the night she caught Daz in Ruby's bed, her idolization had dissolved, as had her self-worth and pursuit of a degree. Natalie hadn't returned to class that semester. She told Ruby she had, but all she was doing was hanging out with Buck. In his van or at his house, getting wasted on junk and blocking out the sex that filled the spaces in between fixes. She lost her virginity, control of her body and count of how many times she had let him in. Conscious or unconscious. She was lost, empty and hateful.

It was her last restock of the night. Last call had been announced, the gambling tables were being settled and the patrons were being escorted out to Daryl's waiting shuttle. Natalie filled the milk crates with the few cans and bottles she needed, then closed the doors on the refrigerated shipping container and put the padlock on. The club was now under the watch of both the bikers and Bernie's crew so keeping the liquor under lock and key seemed unnecessary. But the lock wasn't there to protect the liquor, it was there to save lives. Booze stored in a container, out in the middle of the woods is tempting, and if someone was stupid enough to steal it, they most certainly wouldn't live long enough to drink it.

"You need to stop," Daz said, walking out from around the corner of the cooler container.

Natalie was startled, but she gathered herself quickly and started walking towards the club, ignoring him.

"Nat." Daz tried to stop her with words. "I know."

She kept walking, so he caught up to her and he grabbed her by the arm.

Natalie curled her lip and squinted her eyes, making her message known before even making a sound. "You were told to not bother me. Let go or I'll scream, and Kurt will fucking kill you."

Daz didn't let go and Natalie filled her lungs, readying to bury him.

He didn't look worried, he looked angry. "Smack. You're doing smack," Daz said pointedly.

Natalie let the air out but didn't make a peep.

Daz shook his head. "That kid who picks you up. He's a junkie."

"You don't know fuck all." Natalie pulled her arm free from his grasp.

"He buys from a guy I know. And he's been buying a lot lately. My guy says that he's been coming to get it with a girl. A girl that looks a lot like you."

"You're spying on me?"

"I'm worried about you."

"You don't want me—you want Ruby and God knows who else, so fuck off."

"I want you to be okay. Nat. I care about you. That's why I can't be with you. But I still care and if you're doing smack then you're not okay."

"I'm doing smack and I'm doing just fine," Natalie snarled.

"Really? You're not going to school. I checked."

"Fuck, Daz, are you working with that fat cop of Bernie's? Running tabs on me?"

Daz's voice went calm, "Nat, you have to stop."

Natalie assessed the situation. He knew it all, so there was no point in lying. "Or what?"

"I know that kid is giving it to you. Don't make me take him out. Stop fucking around with that shit. Or I'll have to tell Ruby—and you know what she'll do."

Natalie stepped up to him, "You touch him, and I kill you myself." She turned to walk away.

"Don't make me do this. There is only one way the needle points, Nat, and it's down."

"That's funny, because there is only one way my finger points." She set the milk crate down on the ground. "It's up," she said, giving him the middle finger.

Natalie picked up the crate and went inside the club, leaving Daz outside with the dilemma. She played tough but she was worried about Ruby finding out. Sure, she was mad at her free-will foster mom, but she still cared what she thought. She cared and needed her help but wouldn't reach out. Junk does that. It creates gaps and wedges in morals and relationships. It pushes your true feelings down, convincing you that your angels are devils and that the reverse is true as well. She didn't love Buck, but he didn't deserve the wrath that would come down on him if Ruby found out—if the crew knew they'd tear him apart. And there was more to it. More than his safety, it was her opinion. Natalie couldn't bear to see the look in Ruby's eyes that would follow her admission. The disappointment. The same look Natalie used to give her mother.

As she restocked the racks of the glass door fridges behind the bar, she wondered how she could have let it go this far. Why she would ever have torn the skin the first time. Let the razor-sharp tip of the needle dig into her flesh and search for the vein. She hated Daz, but he wasn't wrong. It had to stop. This had no other ending than what she had seen with her own eyes. She had to do better, she had to keep her promise to herself and be better than the woman who picked up the needle and let her down.

Opal was in her element. She might as well have been conducting the Jungle Cruise at Disney World, decked out in a fun, pink, safari jumper and pointing out all the hot spots along Miami's Ocean Drive. This was a long way from the woman who practically collapsed from dehydration and a panic attack, out front of the Marlin Hotel on Bernie's first run.

"Oh, now there's a special spot." Opal pointed to the right. "That is the home of Johnny Versace."

"I believe it's Gianni." Maryanne raised her hand, proudly correcting Opal.

"Oh, my, you're right." Opal nodded, taking the criticism, while inside her, Bernadette reveled in the notion that Maryanne would be riding home on top of a mountain of cocaine and that Opal had a shotgun stashed under the seat in front of her—and could waste the mouthy bitch any time she wanted.

Bernie looked away from the road for a second and up at Opal, checking to make sure she was okay.

Opal shot her a knowing smile and carried on. "Today

ladies, we will be dining at Lulu's on Washington Avenue. Oh, boy you are all in for a real treat, they have a Red Velvet cake that is just to die for."

"I'm going to die if you keep on with your flapping gums." Maryanne was especially snarky, even for her.

"It's my job, Maryanne. To point out the points of interest? I'm the tour guide," Opal said, trying to stay professional.

"What do I need a tour guide for? I've been to Miami before, Opal."

"Well, others may not have." Opal stood her ground. "Can I have a show of hands, how many of you have been here before?" Opal said and immediately almost every hand in the shuttle went up.

"See?" Maryanne was in full gloat.

"How many of you are enjoying Opal's delightful commentary?" Bernie asked, shouting from behind the steering wheel, and every hand stayed up.

Opal's frown turned on itself and her chest swelled a little. Bernadette was, of course, leaning towards the sawed off at her feet, but Opal saw the victory before her. She took a breath, turned and pointed to the window on the other side "Oh, over there is the Vidal Sassoon Academy." She returned to her cheerful self. "I always wanted to be a stylist. Wonder how much a cut and set would be there?"

The food at Lulu's was wonderful, but the atmosphere made the elderly women feel like hip movers and shakers. Most of them were used to the blue plate special at the local waffle house, so the mix of indoor and outdoor dining, under umbrellas and rounded brown awnings, surrounded by hot young socialites and pseudo-celebrities, was enough to keep them talking for weeks. The restaurant, however, was not overly happy to see the approaching cluster of white hair. But Bernie changed their tune immediately with a hefty tip—pre-service—and the promise of much more to follow if the seniors were given the VIP treatment. It was like this everywhere the Girls' Day Out tours went. It was part of the reason it had become so popular, so fast. Cheap trips to and from Miami, and memorable moments in places their husbands would never take them, and they most certainly would never go to by themselves.

Once the tour guests had been dropped off and the establishment's palms had been properly greased, Bernie took the shuttle over to Hellsa's building. It was a gas station with only one pump, a garage behind it and restricted views on the other three sides. From the road, only the right side of the shuttle was visible.

Bernie took her time getting out, going inside the tiny front store of the garage, looking for a snack. She did the same on her way out too, sauntering back to the pump, only squeezing the trigger on the gas handle halfway, so she could slowly fill up the shuttle with fuel. All the women did this. They played into the restrained speed of their perceived age, putting on a believable show, all while Hellsa's men worked their magic on the left side of the shuttle. Out of the eyes on the street, while Bernie dripped gas into the shuttle's big tank, Hellsa's men opened the side hatches that ran along the full length of the shuttle. The doors of the hatches were magnetic, they sat flush with the lower wall of the bus, so they were unnoticeable unless they were opened. The men stuffed the compartments full of plastic wrapped packages of white powder. Each package had been pre-sized to fit perfectly in the hold, flat, side by each, like a huge puzzle, distributing the weight evenly and making sure there was no movement in the cargo at all. The gas pump was even controlled from inside the station, making the fuel flow slower, so they could lengthen the time for the shuttles if needed. It was engineered to precision. Time, space, distance and risk. The entire set up, from shuttles to diaper service, from gas stations to laundry facilities, and everyone paid in between, was expensive. Very, very expensive, but it was all paid for—in full—on the first run. That's how much was being made. This was not dope slinging. It wasn't tiny runs down the interstate any longer. It was an empire. The kingdom Bernie wanted and had promised her crew.

With only a few minutes remaining until Bernie's return, Opal had the waitress bring out the bills. She made sure to tip the server again before making her way to the facilities. All of the women made their way there. It was a prerequisite for any road trip. After all, these were the bathroom Gestapo, the mothers, the nags in every family that would pester at the threshold if 'anyone needed to use the bathroom'. They nagged, their families groaned, but inevitably, one of their reluctant kin would see the error of their ways and be begging their bothersome bladder guard for a stop just a few minutes down the asphalt.

The mussels didn't sit well with Opal. She was a strictly 'familiar food' girl, but Bernadette was experimental and insisted on the mussels. Garlic always played havoc with Opal's intestines, so Bernadette's divorce from normality had married her to the bowl. Clenching and sweating, only releasing her reaction to 'the delights of the deep' in spurts and starts, when it sounded like the bathroom was clear for a second. It was agony, having to space out what should have been a mass cleansing. Hiding behind the stall door in complete silence, buckling under the assault on her digestive track.

"Oh my God!" There was barely a creak from the bathroom door and only three words spoken, but Opal knew who it was.

She tried to pull her feet up so that Maryanne wouldn't see them, but she didn't really bend that way anymore and besides, the odor, the death hanging in the air of the powder room, was undeniable.

"Opal—Rose—Murdy, is that you?!" Maryanne danced her words out in a tango of disgust and laughter.

If Opal could have folded into herself and slipped into another dimension she would have. It was so childish and ridiculous. The shame she felt for something so natural, was unnatural, but it wasn't uncommon. While Maryanne was an absolute bully, most women did this. Do this. They perpetuate the idea that natural functions are somehow unladylike. Sure, within the confines of their closest friends they may divulge the secret that they have a functioning digestion system, but out in the wild, they hold other women to imaginary standards. They pretend and cele-brate the complete secrecy of it. As if it were a biological abnormality that should be kept from civilized culture. They are absolutely mortified by the idea that other women might know they poop. From the supermodel diet to the enduring of excruciating cramps and the unhealthy holding of air, it was and is, insane. It is the end of the cycle. The natural, human cycle of consuming energy and femininity has nothing to do with it.

"Uh, huh," Opal replied, doubled over in pain from the shellfish that were destroying her from the inside out.

Maryanne had come into the bathroom to use it, but now she was going over to the sink to wash her hands instead. No doubt a self-conscious response to having another woman in there. An act of self-preservation, even though there was a stall free, and she really needed to use it.

As she finished with the act of washing her hands, by going over to the dryer, she made sure to get in one last dig.

The button to seal the scene. "You are disgusting, Opal Rose."

The gears in Opal's head shifted and Bernadette pushed her way forward, moving Opal's sheepish self aside and took control of the entire ship. She sat straight up from the toilet seat and shot out of the stall, with her underwear still around her ankles.

"For the love of God!" Maryanne shouted before Opal threw her hand over her mouth and pushed her up against the wall.

"God has nothing to do with it." Opal was seething. "I have had it with you. I have had it with your snide comments and your judgment and your mouth!"

Maryanne struggled, managing to get her face free from Opal's hand. "You are out of your mind. This is all because of Bernie and her sister. I warned you about them. Look at you. Attacking me in the bathroom like a wild dog. Wait till I tell Cecilia and the rest of—"

Opal slapped her. She hit Maryanne hard enough to turn her head forty-five degrees, then squeezed her cheeks between her thumb and fingers, bringing it back to look her in the eye. "It's not Bernie or Ruby—I am a bad, bad woman and—I will do bad, bad things. If you say a word about my bathroom habits, I will cut your knockers off and make tit maracas out of them." It wasn't exactly the threat she wanted to make, but it was still Opal. Tit was best she could come up with, the swear word she'd learned from the trike chant and the maracas, well, that was just angry improv.

"Maracas?" Maryanne was scared and confused.

"Yes! Maracas!" Opal doubled down and grabbed Maryanne's breasts, one in each hand and shook them violently. "Cha, cha, cha!"

She let go of her victim's chest, gave her a death stare,

then returned to her stall where she closed the door and proceeded to relieve herself of all the mussels and her fear of the Bone Park bully.

The second half of January and all of February went full steam ahead and a follow up visit to Hellsa's yacht sealed the deal. The trial run Hellsa had promised was over and they had done it. The women had earned the full run of the Miami corridor and the growing notoriety as the Grand-mafia. The name was only whispered in the company of other people on the wrong side of the law, and it came with the legend that one of them had killed an FBI agent with her bare hands. No one knew their faces or names, just the lore. The mounting number of Cuban gang bodies showing up around Dade County only added to the rumors. It was of course Hellsa's people pulling the triggers, but she was a senior citizen too, so that only helped and the name stuck. It was the beginning of 1992 and the drug trade had officially gone grey.

With March well underway, MTV had begun running promos for their massive spring break concerts. The week-long celebration of youth and music would be broadcast eight hours a day, for seven straight days and be attended by thousands of college kids from all over the United States and Canada. Every kind of music would be on that stage, from hip hop to rock and all of the big names were going to be looking for what the women were moving.

Freda was not a fan of MTV, but she did like to secretly watch the men dance. She would often close the blinds and enjoy a little eye candy while she sipped a rum and coke. It was during one of these sessions that a spring break commercial came on and she got an idea. An idea she was sure that Bernie would love.

"No." Bernie heard the pitch. One sentence that provoked a one-word answer.

"No? Why not? Believe you me, we are the only people who could get the stuff in there and we could make a fortune."

"We're already making a fortune and we're not dealers. That is not what we do. In between, remember? Not boots on the ground. Leave that to the Cubans. That's their territory. We've taken almost everything else from them. Let them at least have this."

"Why? So, they can make the cash? They don't deserve it. They tried to kill you, remember?"

"Everyone kills everyone in this business, Freda. Why is the money so important to you? Don't you have enough? It's not like you've got—" Bernie caught herself, but it was too late.

"I don't. You're right. But he does." Freda was looking at Bernie the same way she did when they got rid of the wagon. "He left them high and dry. Like me. The woman —I could care less about—but his kids? It's not their fault. I'm building something for them. I don't want them to hate him. I know they must have been on his mind all the time. I want them to know that, that they were always a part of his plan. It's what he'd want."

"You are a far bigger woman than me, Freda. Those kids are lucky they have you, even if they'll never know it. Let's be honest. We all are pulling in Escobar money now, so there will be more than enough to set them up for a lifetime. For two lifetimes!"

"Not if something happens to us."

"What's going to happen to us?"

"Everyone kills everyone in this business, that's what

you said. We are no different. You had us train to carry our own pieces. Now, every day could be our last."

"At our age, Freda, it was already."

"My point exactly and believe you me, I'm going to set them up before I go."

"Freda. Let me be absolutely clear." Bernie was growing tired of the deaf ears Freda was using. "We don't deal drugs. It is a step we will not take. It puts us in a direct line of fire we do not need to be in. It puts us in people's faces. Showing our faces. We are ghosts. We don't use drugs and we don't deal them."

"Then you better tell that to Ruby's pet."

"I beg your pardon?"

"Come on, Bernie. You have to be able to see it. That girl is on something. She is strung out all the time and barely drags herself around the club when she's there."

Bernie didn't argue, she just hadn't noticed. She had been so caught up in her empire expansion that she had let it slip past her radar. Or maybe she just didn't want to see it. "I'm sure it's nothing. Ruby would know. She's no stranger to the stuff. But if you're concerned, then I'll ask."

"You should be doing more than asking. Loose lips, Bernie. Drug addicts and drunks capsize."

"I will talk to Ruby, okay? But as for this MTV nonsense, let it go."

Ruby had a lover. Natalie was out most nights, even the ones when she worked at the club, she still didn't come home. Ruby was lonely. Well, that's what she was telling herself, but the truth was that the void had returned, and it couldn't be filled by just one lover. It took many. She was rolling through the clientele like a rolodex of studs. Old, young, hot, ugly. She was wearing them like pajamas, a different pair every night. There were some frequent flyers though. Daz hadn't dared set foot in her bedroom since the event, but another had. One that was far more dangerous and damaging, but that's what made it so irresistible to her. Dangerous men were like hard drugs for Ruby. It made them more addictive, the encounter more potent and her esteem more devastated. The same cycle of self-destruction that Natalie was on, only Ruby's needle was pink.

Within a minute of her overnight guest leaving out the carport door, there was a knock at the lanai. Ruby's heart raced. Had her man been seen? Had he returned? Was she caught? These questions and the adrenaline that came with them were all part of the problem. They were all feeding the dependence. Her insatiable desire for drama.

"Poob? You home?" It was Bernie. She was jiggling the door handle. It was not her rendezvous, but Ruby still was on edge. Early morning calls weren't Bernie's thing ever since Ruby had moved out, so what had brought her to her door at the crack of dawn was worrisome.

Ruby straightened herself up quickly, then unlocked the door to the lanai. "My word, you're up early."

"I'm always up early. I'm surprised you are." Bernie was suspicious. "Your door was locked."

"I worked late last night. Had a few. Must have locked it when I came in—force of habit."

Bernie waltzed straight in and headed for the front bedroom. "Is Natalie still sleeping?"

Ruby shook her head, "No, she spent the night with her boyfriend. That surfer kid—Buck."

"Buck?" Bernie was missing something and also hating the name. "Who the hell is that?"

"The long-haired kid that came to the Christmas party.

Remember? She's been hanging out with him all the time now."

"Well, good for her. Since Christmas, huh? I guess I have been a little preoccupied."

"Why are you looking for Natalie?"

Already flustered by her ignorance of Buck, Bernie got to it. "Is she okay?"

Ruby was put a little off kilter by the concern. "Yes, as okay as an 18-year-old girl can be. Why do you ask?"

Bernie let out one of her sighs. "Freda. She's all atwitter. She seems to think Natalie is on drugs."

Ruby scoffed, "You came over here for that? Freda thinks everyone's on drugs. She thinks people are giving it away for free, hiding it in hotdogs down on the beach, trying to get people hooked."

"Well, she sounded pretty convinced. I said I'd talk to you. What little I've seen of Natalie lately is a little troublesome. She has been different. She's lost some weight and seems less energetic than she was. Withdrawn. I mean she barely said a word the whole trip to the Everglades."

"She's a young woman whose brother was murdered."

"Yes, but she was doing better, wasn't she?"

Ruby looked down. "It's me. She's been all tied up in knots because of me."

"Did you two have a fight? It was bound to happen sooner or later. You just dove into this whole thing headfirst. Not easy being a parent is it, Ruby?"

"I'm not her parent."

"I don't think she sees it that way."

Ruby paused, taking in her older sister's words, realizing that she right. "My word. Even if she does, I don't think it's that. She has—or had—a crush on Daz."

"Daz? God, he's a little old for her, isn't he? A little too one percent for her scholastic ambitions? So, it's puppy love? The weight loss, the attitude? She's moping around because of him?"

Ruby shook her head.

Bernie smiled, "Was it you? What did you do, tell her he's off limits? Look at you, laying down the law. You may not think she sees you as a parent, but you sure are acting like one. I am going to have to start calling you Mama."

Ruby paused again, even longer, then spilled her guts, "I slept with him."

Bernie took a step back. "With Daz?"

"Yes—and she caught us. But I didn't know she had a crush on him at the time or that they had—"

"Hang on. Was he with her?"

"No. It was a lot of flirting apparently and I reprimanded him for it."

"Jesus, Ruby. Finding your mother in bed with your beau, that will send a girl into a black hole."

"I am not her mother, but yes. She has been dealing with it. That's why I've been letting her run around with this surfer kid. It's just a rebound and she is an adult. Let her run the feelings through his filter, then she'll come back around."

"Well at least it's not drugs."

"You can tell Freda to back off."

"I will, but Ruby, you can't be doing that. Sleeping with our crew. Or anyone close to our interests. Let this be a lesson. It will only lead to trouble."

Ruby acknowledged the warning, but it wasn't something she hadn't already considered—and ignored.

"There's something else I want to talk with you about." Bernie was now the one taking pauses. "I—am going to be having visitors. They arrive the end of the week and I need everyone to be on their best behavior."

"Visitors? Who the hell would be visiting you? Please do not tell me it is more FBI."

"No. Nothing like that. But I've already spoken to Opal and Freda about it and Hellsa's in the loop too. In fact, for the one week the visitors are here, we won't be running anything. I need everyone to be on their best. No runs, no tricks, no problems with the park residents, nothing. Consider it a holiday for all of us. A spring break before we knuckle down for the summer season."

"What about the club?"

"No club. Absolutely no problems. Do you understand?!"

"For God's sake, Bernie, who's coming? The Queen?"

Bernie's faced changed. Her whole aura went from dark to light. Her eyes twinkled and an electric grin took over her mouth, "My grandchildren."

The round nose, full length Ford Taurus station wagon rattled its way along the interstate, packed down with luggage and bicycles like the 'family truckster' on its way to Wally World. It rode across the bridge that spanned the St. Mary's River, the watery divide between Georgia and Florida and the escape route of the Grand-mafia's product.

The cargo area behind the back seat of the wagon was filled to the headliner with luggage and toys. The bench seat in front of it was just as packed, but not with things, with little humans. Three ginger siblings, all buckled in and tuckered out. Gemma, who was 10 years old was on the left, with 6-year-old Gwen in the middle, leaning on her; 8-year-old Greg was on the other side of Gwen, passed out with his head against the right door. His orange buzzcut was so short that his scalp was wrinkling, sticking to the glass as the wagon bounced down the highway.

Marcie's blonde ponytail swayed as she turned to look back from the front passenger seat, to check on the three sleeping carrot tops. Seeing that they were all sawing logs, she reached her hand out and tapped Gemma's knee.

"Kids, wake up. We're here!" Marcie whispered in a heavy Buffalo accent filled with excitement. "Wake up or you're going to miss it."

As the kids slowly opened their road-crusted eyes, Marcie pointed forward, to the huge sign, suspended between two pillars off the right of the highway that read, Florida Welcomes You!

"3...2...1," Marcie counted down and as the Taurus passed the sign she cheered, "Woooooo!"

The back seat joined in, jumping into the celebration. "Wooohooo!"

As the cheering continued, another sign approached in the distance and this one read, 'Welcome Center 2 miles'.

"Oh, we have to stop there!" Marcie was adamant.

Behind the wheel, Brent barked back, "We are not stopping." His mustache, heavy stubble and Buffalo accent meant business. He could feel her eyes on him, so he turned to address her, "Marcie, we have been in this car for twenty hours, we are not going to make this any longer than we need to."

Marcie tilted her head. "But they have juice there. Free Florida orange juice!"

Brent looked back to the road. "I'm sure the kids' grandma has free orange juice at her place too and the sooner we get there the sooner they can drink it."

Marcie was not letting go, "Brent. It's tradition."

Brent clenched his jaw, "Whose tradition?"

Marcie suddenly went quiet. Her enthusiasm and spirit crushed under the heel of his question.

From the back seat, Gemma called out, "Mom?"

Marcie just looked forward. "We aren't stopping."

"But Mom!"

"You heard Brent. No!"

Gemma's voice got louder, "But we have to!"

Marcie turned around, ready to scold the eldest sibling. She was the ringleader of the other two and if she didn't put an end to it now, it would only become a chorus of pleading. But as Marcie turned, she saw the reason for Gemma's shouting—6-year-old Gwen was covered in vomit.

"Oh God!" Marcie exclaimed.

Spurred by Marcie's shriek, Brent tilted the rearview mirror down and saw the disaster, "Christ almighty! This is all your fault! Ya had her looking at all those signs, Marcie!"

Brent put on his signal and cranked the wheel, shooting the wagon across the other lanes and into the Welcome Center offramp.

Stan had spent the night on the couch again. He'd been spending a lot of nights out there recently. With the increased income of the new plan, Stan was getting a lot more allowance. He wasn't just the king of his pub; he'd become a regular at Moonlight and its gambling tables. Under Bernie's suggestion, Opal had given him a scripted, watered-down version of their company. A filtered disclosure of their business, just enough, but not too much, including the club and Stan barely batted an eye. The good news was that most of his allowance was going into

Moonlight's tables, which a portion of would eventually made its way back to Opal. But while his pockets were hot, her bed was cold. When this all started, she wanted an escape from him, a little break from the day-to-day babysitting, but now they barely saw each other. Part of her identity, most of it in fact, had been caring for him. Before he became dependent on the sauce, she took care of his home, his day to day and their children—and after his love of fermented things had taken over, she shifted from wife and mother, to nurse maid. She became his fixer, his handler, his lawyer—even to the detriment of her kids. She defended him and demanded respect for his disrespectful behavior, driving a wedge between her and her creations. She had chosen him over them, and they would never forgive her for it, no matter how much money she sent them.

Opal wasn't being quiet at all. Slamming cupboards, rattling pans and clanking dishes as she prepared her own breakfast. She was acting out, in the great tradition of many homemakers, turning the kitchen into a loud, psychological weapon.

"For Christ's sake, Opal! What is all the racket about?" Stan snapped at the air, like an alligator chasing a budgie.

"Oh, morning, Stan." She continued to finish preparing her food, moving the eggs and bacon to her plate, beside her toast. "Did you come in late?"

Stan did his best to stand up, scratching at his briefs with a brutish lack of humility, "Uh, yeah. Long night of cards."

"Cards again? Did you win?"

"Win, lose—it's all the same when your old lady is the house." He put on the charm, unaware of the label he'd given her. "Oh, that smells good." He walked over to the table she was sitting at, looking down at her plate with the ravenous eyes of a hung-over appetite.

"Oh, my. Are you hungry?" Opal asked. "I didn't know you'd want some." She quickly took the last mouthful of egg, followed by a bite of toast with a crispy piece of bacon on top.

"You didn't make me any?" He was disappointed and looking increasingly angry.

"Oh, no. I'm sorry," she said standing up from the table and pushing her plate towards him. "Here. You can have mine."

Before he could protest, she grabbed a few envelopes on the counter and moved to the door.

"It's a big day today! Bernie's grandchildren are arriving! Can't be late." She smiled and walked out, leaving Stan with nothing but a thick head, a yolk-smeared plate, and a half piece of toast.

Bernie was ready, dressed in a cool-white linen top and yellow palazzo pants, sitting in her high back wicker chair across from Freda, who looked like she was dying in her baby-blue polyester jumper.

"When do they arrive?" Freda fussed with the collar of the crepe material that was creeping up around her neck.

Bernie watched her friend fighting with her outfit. "If they stop for OJ? About an hour and a half or so."

Freda kept pulling on the collar of her one-piece polyester prison.

"Why don't you ever listen to me?" Bernie condemned her. "Polyester stays on the other side of the Carolina border. I threw most of mine out the window, somewhere between Pennsylvania and Maryland the first time I came down. You've got to live by the golden rule, man-made fabrics in the north, handguns in the south."

Freda let go of her collar. "Reg bought it for me."

Bernie sighed, "Well, then—sweat in peace." Bernie's sweet surrender was squashed by the figure standing outside the screen door. "Jesus, Opal! How long have you been standing there?! Just come in!"

Freda jerked around to find Opal walking in wearing her pink and white tennis outfit, complete with a matching, oversized visor.

"Oh, my, I didn't want to interrupt," Opal said, softly.

"You're not. Ever," Bernie reassured her.

"Big match, Martina?" Freda teased.

"Oh, dear, no. It's Stan's favorite outfit."

"Stan? He was at the club late last night, surprised he's up," Freda disapproved.

"He is and just in time to see his favorite girl in his favorite outfit walk out the door." She smiled.

"Oh, you devil," Freda was delighted, applauding her devious ways. "So, what's with the letters?"

"Just my monthly correspondence. With the kids," Opal said casually.

"And the Reverend?" Bernie pushed and Opal adjusted her letters to hide the addresses on them.

"A little help?" Another voice joined the group, it was Ruby calling from inside the trailer. Opal used the distraction and moved over to open the door, steadying the sprung metal 'ankle biter' for Ruby, so she could exit with the tray of drinks. "Thank you, Opal. Heaven forbid my sister ever got off her ass." Ruby set down the tray on the wicker table as she shot Bernie a look.

"I said a double," Freda barked.

Ruby handed her the highball. "It is. All rum with just a splash of coke."

Freda took a big gulp, followed by a confirming wince.

"A little early for happy hour, don't you think?" Opal was concerned.

"Nope," Freda said before taking another, disobedient sip—staring down the pink lady.

"Oh, okay. Maybe not," Opal backpedaled.

"Leave her alone, Freda. She gets enough of that crap at home," Bernie said, using her hand as a gavel on the arm of her chair.

"All Fresca for you, dear." Ruby handed Opal a fizzy, greenish drink. Opal was appreciative.

Bernie instructed, "You all know that my grandbabies are arriving today, so you will all be like mice."

"My word, I hate mice." Ruby shuddered.

"Too bad, Scarlet, you are going to be one for the next seven days." Bernie was not in a playful mood.

Opal looked lost by the rodent reference. "What exactly do you mean, Bernie. Like mice how?"

"Just be yourself, Opal."

"I can do that," Opal smiled.

"Good," Bernie commended her, then switched gears, "but you two—don't. Do not be you."

"This is going to kill our bottom line." Freda was still not completely on board. "What about Moonlight?"

"Closed. Silent. Got it? I will compensate the staff personally for the week everyone is taking a break. That includes the paid visits your suitors have been making to your trailer."

Ruby was shocked. "Bernie!"

"Don't give me that. I know you and the other women have been working horizontally. It's my job to know everything and it's Cliff's job to be very observant."

"What about personal?" Ruby pushed.

"Personal? For God's sake, Poob, can't you keep your legs closed for one week?"

"I don't know."

"Oh, I have heard it all." Freda was aghast. "You mean to tell me that you've never gone one week without it?"

Ruby winked at her.

Freda was on her. "I hope you're donating your body to science, because they are going to want to check the mileage."

"My word, if you weren't so frigid, you may just enjoy what's left of your boring life." Ruby wasn't taking it, she was swinging.

"I sure as hell wouldn't trade it for yours, you walking cold sore." Freda got up, readying herself for the fists she was making.

"Enough!" Bernie shouted. "Ruby, keep your knees together, Freda all business is closed, do not answer the phone, and Opal—just keep being you." Bernie lowered her tone, "I wouldn't ask, but I haven't seen them in very long time, Gemma was three, Greg was one, and Gwen—I haven't met her yet. I need this to go well. Please. I have made it possible for you all to help yours, so let me help mine. Don't screw this up for me. One week, that's all I ask."

Buck's room had become a flop house for them. Dirty laundry, filthy plates, soiled sheets and blankets littered the floor. The walls were covered in marker and crayon. Manic, opioid doodles and poetry, swear words and fist holes had ruined the nice drywall in this upscale home. The room was the house's dirty little secret. A reality hidden from the rest of the suburban dream. There was a padlock on the inside of the bedroom door. The latch was drilled right into the frame, to anchor the barrier between this hell and the outside world.

Natalie and Buck were lying on the dirty mattress that was on the ground, passed out, lost in their thick haze, when the door to the room shook. It was a barrage of heavy knocks and kicks. Someone outside in the hallway, really wanted in.

"Buck! Open the door," a woman's voice yelled from the other side. "I told you I wanted you out of this house!" Her voice was cracking, distressed.

Buck's eyes began to flutter, "Mom? Go away. I'm sleeping."

"Did you put a lock on this door? You are not supposed to be here! You were told when we left. The restraining order clearly states that—"

"Relax! I just came home to get a few things, take a nap and then go. Just let me rest for a bit, then I'll be gone. I promise."

The door stopped shaking. "You better not be here when I get home. I swear, if you've damaged that room anymore, if anything at all is missing from this house, I will call the police!"

Buck looked around at the trashed room and listened as his mother's footsteps moved away from the door. He reached over and gently tapped Natalie on the shoulder. "Nat, wake up. My mom's home. They must have come back from the Keys early. We gotta go. She said she would call the cops!"

Natalie stirred but struggled to open her eyes. The door shook again. Louder this time.

"Fuck, Mom! I said I was going, just give me a second!" Buck shouted.

The door flew open, blowing the lock and latch clear

across the room, kicked in by the steel-toed Dayton attached to Daz's foot. Buck stumbled to his feet, but Daz was already charging and straight armed him, knocking Buck backwards into the wall.

"Stay down," he said, his words carrying all the threat needed. He then crouched down and scooped Natalie up into his arms, like he had done the night of the Christmas party and carried her towards the door. As he reached the splintered remnants of the bedroom entrance, he turned back to Buck. "Listen to me you little fucking junkie, you stay away from her. You forget her. You forget everything about her. You don't know her anymore and you get your shit together. I know this isn't all your fault. But it ends here."

Buck didn't protest, just stayed huddled against the wall as Daz turned his back on the frightened kid and carried Natalie away.

The overburdened Ford Taurus slowly drove down the one-way road of the inner circle with all of its windows down and everyone sticking their heads out them. The wagon barely braked as it turned into the trailer with the yellow stripe and stopped just outside of the carport.

Before the engine went quiet, Brent threw open his door and jumped out "The heat makes it worse! It's like cheese and bad breath. It's under the floor mats."

Marcie got out, a lot slower and a lot less dramatic. "No, I cleaned under them at the Welcome Center."

"Well, ya definitely missed some of it!" Brent gagged. "I hope she has a hose! We can drown the mats and Gwen at the same time."

"You made it!" Bernie said warmly as she rounded the front of the trailer.

"Bernie!" Gemma shouted opening her door and running toward her.

Bernie bent down, wrapped the 10-year-old in her arms and stood up, lifting the ginger waif into the air.

"Oh, Bernie, watch your back! Gemma, don't climb all over her." Marcie was concerned.

"I'm fine," Bernie chuckled back, and she was. She was more than fine. She was elated.

Greg and Gwen took in the excitement of their older sister. At first, cautiously assessing her trust for this stranger, but after a few seconds of watching them giggle, they decided to join in, running out from the 'puke-fumed' car and latching onto Bernie's legs. The collision of two small humans against her shins caused Bernie to lose her balance and she fell backwards, down onto the thick St. Augustine grass.

"Oh my God—kids! Bernie!" Marcie was mortified.

"I'm fine, Marcie," Bernie called back from under the pile of kinder. It was an anthill of love and family and everything she had hoped for.

Brent watched the love being poured over this woman, the attention and joy the kids instantly had with her. He was jealous. Jealous that my mom and my kids were together. Not just physically, but emotionally. That even my baby girl—my baby that I never got to meet—could feel the connection with her grandma. Those babies were me, little living pieces of me. They were my children, and I was Bernie's, and Brent hated all of it.

Freda watched the kids pile on top of Bernie from the middle of the inner circle. She waited a few minutes taking in her friend's joy before she opened the gate to the pool and walked onto the deck, in her frilly blue one-piece. No one paid her any attention as she entered and made her way over to the 'bad' side of the pool. The undesirable side, where the shadow from the pool house hit and stayed for most of the day. She set her matching blue tote bag down on one of the many open lounge chairs on that side and began to dig around in the bag. After a few swipes through her sack, she pulled out her rubber swim cap—the baby-blue one with the flappy, rubber flowers on it. She turned to stare right at Maryanne and her crew, on the other side of the deck, as she stretched the cap over her tight curls and let it go with a 'snap'.

The loud noise caused the clique of old coots to look over.

"Whores," Freda said under her breath, then bent over, presenting her backside to them as she dug around in her bag once more. This time she pulled out a pack of cigarettes. A brand new, full deck of darts. She slowly unwrapped the plastic around her prize, with the reverence of Gollum, and took one of her 'precious' out of the pack. She then proceeded to light the small wizard's wand and make her way over to the edge of the pool. She sat down and hung her legs over the tiled edge, then slid into the cool blue, making sure to keep her head and her smoke above the water. It was art. The process of a pro. Someone who had worked this nicotine craft for a lifetime. Only a seasoned professional puffer could do the breaststroke like her, while keeping her cigarette in her lips and it completely dry. This legend wasn't treading water or wading, she was doing laps with a Lucky Strike stuck in her trap.

Maryanne however did not appreciate the art form. "Freda," she said, getting up abruptly from her lounge chair.

Freda paid her no mind, she just kept on with her frog kicks and respectable pace.

Maryanne pressed on, "Freda. You know there is no smoking in the pool!"

Freda reluctantly acknowledged her, pinching her coveted cigarette in her lips so she could speak out the side of her mouth. "Why? Is it going to catch fire?"

Maryanne had come to know this kind of disrespect from the four of them but was still at a loss. "Freda. I am not being unreasonable. It's not even me. Okay? It's park rules."

Freda didn't answer, just raised her middle finger up from under the water.

"Mrs. Hall, the safety of this park is all our business. If you don't want to be a team player, then maybe you and your friends should reconsider if Cicada Hollow is right for you."

"I do take safety seriously," Freda said out her side mouth. "It's safer to smoke in here but suit yourself." Freda reached up, pulled the smoke from her lips and flicked it at Maryanne, hitting her right in the forehead.

"Hey!" Maryanne patted at her head frantically.

"See? Seems more dangerous out there. Don't it?" Freda shrugged then swam back to the deep end and got out.

Maryanne and some of her group picked up their things and quickly made their way out of the pool area, while Freda dug another cigarette out from her bag and lit it.

As the women made their way across the grassy inner circle, Freda slipped back into the pool, rolled onto her back and began a leisurely backstroke, puffing the whole way, like a gruff little Mississippi steamboat.

Daz pulled the pickup truck into the clearing and parked it behind the Quonset hut. Natalie had just come around, shaken out of her near overdose by the bumps and potholes of the tire track path. Daz didn't know where else to take her. If he took her home, Ruby would know and if he took her to a hospital, the cops would know. Daz was well aware of what came next, but Natalie had no idea.

"Why the fuck am I here?" she snapped at him.

"You're here to get better," Daz said, opening her door.

Natalie took a swing at him, and connected, but her wasted body made little impact.

"You're lucky I found you. That kid would have kept filling you full of that shit until you never woke up."

"I filled myself up," she said, then spat at him.

Daz stared her straight in the eye. "Well, I hope you got your fill, 'cause you're done. This is it. This may be your last chance to get clean, before that shit's so deep inside you, you can't shake its hooks."

"Why?"

"Because this crazy shit you're doing? This is no life."

"It's the one I got."

"It's not the one your brother would have wanted for you."

"Leave him out of this."

"I can't—because I care about you. Nat, I fucked up, but that's no reason for you to do this to yourself. Hurt me. Not you. I can't let you do this to yourself. I care about you—"

"You care about me?"

Daz thought about his next words very carefully. "I do. I need you to get better. We—we can't do this—do us, if you're like this."

Natalie stepped out of the truck. "Don't you think Ruby's going find out that I'm here?'

"The place is closed for a week. Bernie's family is in town. All we need is forty-eight hours." Daz helped her up the front stairs "A hellish forty-eight hours, but I'll be here with you." As he led her inside, he pointed up to one of her brother's massive paintings on the ceiling. "And so will he."

She brought Ruby here the day after they arrived and now she brought her grandkids. Gwen, Greg and Gemma were having the time of their lives with Brent, rolling in the surf and digging in the sand, while Bernie and Marcie walked along the water's edge.

"They look like they are having a blast," Bernie said to Marcie, whose eyes were fixed on her babies.

"Thank you for getting us down here. We really needed it."

"It's the least I could do." Bernie let out one of her famous sighs. "I miss them."

"They miss you too. So do I." Marcie brought her gaze back to Bernie and then the two of them walked in silence for a few steps, just listening to the waves and the laughter of the kids. It was nice, but unfamiliar for Marcie. "So, you're full time down here now?" Marcie felt the need to fill the space between them.

"No reason to go back."

"Bernie—Brent just wanted to have a fresh start."

"I know. That's what you said. Fresh start. Sounds nice."

"We are going to pay you back for this as soon as he gets back on the site."

"Is he still not working?"

"It's hard. With the snow, everything slows down. He's been talking about finish carpentry. He'd be inside then."

"Inside or outside, it doesn't matter. He's a loser, Marcie." Bernie turned to her.

"Bernie, please. Don't start."

"It's the truth and you know it."

"He's good to me and good with the kids."

"You don't have to settle for good, just because you have kids. I didn't. Gary wouldn't want this for you."

"What? Wouldn't want what for me? To be happy?"

Bernie paused, "Are you? Come on, Marcie, fresh start? What does that mean? He just walks in and erases Gary from them? Gary is them."

Marcie went instantly quiet.

"I'm sorry," Bernie pulled back. "One moment it's seven years, then next it's seven minutes. I need them in my life."

"That's why we're here."

"Is that so? I thought it was for the free vacation?"

The two women found a giggle in the heaviness.

"That too." Marcie smiled. "I tried, Bernie. I did, but it was too hard on my own. Brent really does love me."

"Who wouldn't. You, my dear, are the unicorn. The only girl who was ever good enough for my Gary."

Marcie was overtaken by the words, tears came to her eyes. "Just try to lay off Brent, okay? For me?"

Bernie huffed, "For you? I'll try."

The screams coming from the dressing room were spine tingling. It was filled with heartache and desperation. The throat-tearing cries had gone on all night. They started as a whimper, then turned into negotiations, then begging and finally self-harm. Daz had to physically hold her, sitting on the floor behind her, keeping Natalie between his legs and wrapping his arms around her, holding her so she couldn't hit herself. He had to fight her trying to throw her head against the ground. It wasn't her; it was what comes with the lie. The promise of relief is always followed by the return of the truth and the obsession for more. Her body was in survival mode. Torn into a million pieces from withdrawal. She had only ever seen the other side of it. The watcher's point of view. The little girl inside her hated herself for becoming a statistic. The version of her bloodline she so desperately tried to avoid. This process was all about hate. Hate for the needle, hate for your sadness, hate for the fact that you have to go through this, and it is all your fault. But the real struggle was the one that kept Daz quiet as he held onto her sweat-soaked body. Wrestling her to safe positions, while saying nothing but 'You can do this'. He said nothing else because the real conversation had to be had inside her. The raging argument that every addict has. Live or die. Every needle that has gone into an arm came with the want to die a little. It has to. It is the same counter-evolutionary action as jumping off a cliff—committing suicide. Our species is hardwired to survive. To carry on, outrun the lion, outlast the drought, outfight the pack Alpha. The needle, the bottle, the glass pipe, the white lines, are all cliffs—they just take longer to reach the ground and spread the splat out into small doses. Daz had to let her find her fight. Her want to live, otherwise it would be worth nothing. Like jail or celebrity rehab, it would be a dry moment between monsoons.

Natalie's cries eventually softened back into whimpers, having tired herself out, like an infant after a tantrum. Daz laid her down on the couch in the dressing room and covered her with a blanket. He pulled a chair up and sat down watching her closely as she cried herself to sleep. He knew the rest wouldn't last, at least this first one. This was just a small crank of the jack in the box—the jester could pop out at any moment, but she had time on her side. She had only been jumping off the cliff for a few weeks, so if she could make it through until tomorrow, she'd be able to see the view, instead of the fall.

5

Sink or Swim

The trikes were out in full effect; Bernie with her Buffalo Bills' pennant flapping in the wind, Ruby flaunting her sparkling red handle grips and matching seat, and Freda on her blue trike that now had an ashtray attached to the right handlebar. As the trio approached the trailer with the pink casings around the windows, Freda laid into her bell strapped to her left grip and Opal emerged from her lanai, motioning for her to keep it down. The trio came to a stop, as did Freda's aggressive bell ringing. Opal made her way to the carport, to fetch her pink adult tricycle and quietly rolled it out to the road.

"Drunk?" Freda had no patience and no tact.

"Oh, no. I'm completely sober," Opal said, wheeling her trike out farther into the road.

"Not you, Poppins, Stan. Is he plastered?"

"Oh, I don't think so. He's just having a nap."

"He could barely stand by the end of the third game today. Fred had to forfeit the shuffleboard because of it." Freda was relentless.

Opal stopped pushing her trike, overwhelmed with embarrassment.

"I didn't hear anything about it, and I don't care. I'm just glad you could make it out tonight." Bernie put an end to Freda's prodding and a grateful Opal got onto her trike.

"It is a lovely evening, isn't it?" Opal said with a wistful sigh, going right back into her rose-colored world.

"It certainly is," Ruby affirmed her contentment and the four of them started to pedal, falling into their staggered positions, heading off down the curved inner circle road. After their group got up to speed and settled into their relaxed pace, Ruby made small talk. "Opal, did you hear about Maryanne?"

Opal's lovely spring evening was suddenly sidelined. She was immediately filled with worry about her altercation with Maryanne in the bathroom at Lulu's. It was unlike her to explode on another human being and it was probable cause for the park bully to call the police. Opal didn't want to be the one that brought their house of cards tumbling down, and all because she was poop shy.

Bernie was disappointed, "Did you have to hit her—with a butt?"

Opal's worry changed to perplexed, "I didn't hit her with my butt."

Ruby laughed at the random confession, while Freda jumped in to defend herself. "I was merely pointing out the flaw in her logic."

"I told you to lay low," Bernie said, reiterating her orders.

"I'm about as low as I can go," Ruby joked—but wasn't joking. Attention is addictive. Some would say as addictive as what Natalie was detoxing from and sometimes as destructive.

"Mary Mother of God, it has only been three days!" Freda was absolutely astounded.

"For you maybe, but then again, the desert doesn't miss the rain. The jungle however?" Ruby was aching for a fix. The rush she got from being adored, touched, wanted.

Freda broke formation and bumped her wheel into Ruby's, jerking her trike to the side, "I am not a desert."

Ruby just gave her a smirk, which did nothing to quell Freda's insulted rage. "Bernie, my phone has been ringing off the hook. People are begging to do tours. With Daytona full of bikers and half naked kids, seniors want out and they are willing to pay. We are missing so much—"

"Let it ring. Just four more days and you can answer. I don't want to hear any more about the calls, or your desires, Ruby. It's just four more days. That's it. That's all I've asked."

Opal saw the need and the window to change the subject. "So, tell us, how are those adorable babies of yours?"

Bernie's frustration became a beam of light. "Wonderful. Absolutely wonderful. When I hold them, Opal, I can feel Gary."

Opal leaned her head to the side, tilting it subconsciously in that sweet way people do when they are moved and longing. "Oh, my. I bet. So, do you think this will be a regular thing? Like every spring break?"

"I hope so. I hope Marcie can see what good it would do for the kids. Having me around. More than the money —family. I have been on my best behavior with that leech of hers too. Not said a mean word, although I'd like to take him out into the woods and make him dig his own hole."

"Oh, Bernie," Opal giggled. "I'm sure he's not all bad."

"It wouldn't matter if he were the Pope, Opal," Bernie sighed. "He's not my son."

The queen size bed looked enormous in the cramped room of the trailer, sitting under the yellow, floral curtains, with Bernie surrounded by her grandchildren. The cherubs were in that delicate space between today and tonight. Where any change in tone or cadence could disrupt their journey into tomorrow.

Bernie understood the fragility of the situation, reading slowly and monotone from the pages of the large, opened, illustrated book. "But I'm afraid those are kept on the other—Nana Scrolls."

With the last words of the fairy tale read, she sat still for a moment—just being there, with them—like she had been there with me night after night. With the babies' breaths rising and falling in deep, consistent cycles, Bernie closed the book quietly, took off her readers and pulled the three halflings in tight to her. She bent her long torso down and buried her head into their brassy manes, breathing in their essence and their love. They had my hair. My recessive gene, the same one their Great Aunt Ruby had. Bernie held them tight for as long as she could, until little Gwen started to fuss, she then slipped out from between them and gently crawled out of the bed. Tucking-in was a lost art form for Bernie, but her mastery came back easily. Muscle memory of the heart, the instinctual nurturing of a mother is never truly lost, just dormant until a needful young soul appears. After raising the blankets to rest just below their freckled chins, and gently shaping the covers around each of them, she waited at the door for a moment. This was it. The brief silence full of adoration and gratitude that makes every caregiver return in the morning to face another day of rearing. She felt normal, useful, wanted and that only made her want more.

Daz and Natalie walked up the long foot path, back to the park. This was not the same girl who was carried out of Buck's bedroom on the brink of overdose, Natalie was now on day four of being clean. The morning felt different. Familiar. The stages of waking up were less chaotic and more predictable, as was her want for coffee. The horror of the past three days was enough to keep relapse far from her mind—for now. The early detection of addiction, like tumors, creates a greater chance of survival, but that's only if the patient has the fight in them and the surgeons were able to get it all out.

"I don't know how to thank you," Natalie said as they walked through the thick Floridian jungle. The sting and slap were gone from her voice. Even her eyes were softer.

"Yes, you do," Daz said with the confidence of a wise sage. "Stay away from him and it."

"He's not a bad guy, Daz."

"He just does bad things—I've heard it before." Daz took her hand. "Nat, listen to me. This time was your cakewalk."

"Cakewalk? Daz, I puked everywhere, every nerve in my body was screaming and I shit myself in front of you."

Daz nodded. "Yeah. That was your cakewalk. You got to hold onto that hell, because if you forget what that felt like, then you're headed for the next one—and I won't be there to help you."

Natalie looked at him—it was a harsh thing to say. "I didn't ask you to be here this time."

"No, you didn't. I wanted to be. I need you to be better. But I won't do it again. You of all people know what a lost cause looks like. You are not her. You got a second chance, Nat."

She looked deep into his eyes, "We have a second chance."

Daz sighed, "Right, we do. But you can't waste it. The past two months are a blip on your life. A shitty time you can look back on and be glad you outgrew it. It's the past. And the past is something you're never meant to repeat. It's dead—and that's what happens to those who repeat it." Daz stopped walking. The edge of the park was just ahead. "This is as far as I can take you."

Daz meant geographically, but Natalie knew it had a double meaning. "I know. When will I see you again?"

Daz shook his head. "I need to work on Ruby first. Leave it to me. You just keep getting better, just stay clean and get back to classes. I'll worry about us; you worry about you."

Natalie got up on her tiptoes and kissed him—on the lips. This was the first time. All her other kisses had landed on his neck or cheek, but this one was on target, and he was there for it. The feelings moving between them were mountains, far greater than just the lust they shared on his bike. It had grown. Emotions and bonds built in the soil of her struggle and their collective rise out of the ashes. Daz was way out on a limb, going against the wishes of Ruby and the interests of his club, but he was there for her.

Natalie slowly pulled her lips away from his, their skin still tingling with the sensation of being linked. "Don't take too long," she said, both wanting and warning, then walked away from her knight in dull leather, leaving him in the cover of the jungle, heading back to the girl she was and the home she had taken for granted.

The pool was basically empty, because the three gingers were making too many waves for Maryanne and her 'Cling-ons'. There were a few of the other park residents poolside though, the ones who were there to relish the commotion, missing their own tiny lineage and delighted by all the red hair gleaming in the sunlight. It practically took a vat of sunscreen to cover all three of the melanoma magnets, but Bernie lathered it on each of them with ease and precision. She was a pioneer of the stuff, having to get a prescription for it when I was a kid. The oil they had at the pharmacy wasn't strong enough for my freckled skin, so she went straight to the professionals. The cream the kids had on smelled a lot better than the stuff she used to put on me, but doing this ritual with them took her right back to those times with me.

"Gary got so sunburned the first time Sal and I brought him down here, that he turned into one giant scab."

"Oh, poor Gary." Marcie tried to hold in her laughter.

"Poor Gary? Poor me. I had to carry around that little piece of crisp bacon."

Marcie couldn't hold it, "Bernie!"

Bernie was laughing too, "Seriously, every woman looked at me like I was the worst mother in the world. Like I'd left the roast in the oven too long and put a bathing suit on it."

"Well, you weren't the worst mother in the world, because Gary was so—good," Marcie said the words, then caught herself getting choked up.

Bernie looked to the pool with the three water-winged critters playing in it, "They're good too. Great actually. This is all great, isn't it?"

"It certainly is."

"Marcie!" Brent called over from the shuffleboard courts a few hundred feet away, "I'm shuffling!" he yelled out even louder.

"That's great honey!" Marcie called back to him.

"Mom, look at me," Bernie said under her breath.

"Pardon?" Marcie turned to her.

"Nothing." Bernie looked over to Brent. "Looks like Fred and Stan are teaching him the ropes."

"It's nice to see he's made friends."

Bernie wanted so badly to deconstruct the uselessness of Brent to Marcie, but she didn't. She restrained herself by focusing back on the kids in the pool.

"You know, Marcie, New Smyrna looks good on you," Bernie said to her daughter-in-law.

"You think?" Marcie played into it, pulling down the brim of her sun hat and lying back on the lounge chair.

"With your blonde hair and suntan, you could be a movie star." Bernie built her up.

"Well, with your compliments, and first-class treatment you've been giving us, I feel like one. You should be careful, a girl could get used to this."

"Mom!" Gemma yelled from the pool.

Before Marcie could answer, Bernie sat up, "What is it honey?"

"Is Mom coming in?" Gemma continued.

"No," Bernie said, putting her hand on Marcie's leg, telling her to stay put and enjoy the sun. "But I sure am!" Bernie got up and started to growl, "You may not want me in there though, because water makes me change into a monster."

The kids all squealed with delight as their grandma made her way around to the shallow end, pretending to transform the whole way. Marcie watched with delight as someone who loved her kids as much as she did, helped carry the load, allowing her to lie back on her chair, soak up the good times and warm rays, feeling supported and happy. Something she was not accustomed to.

Freda had never been to a yacht club before. Even though she was from Boston, she had never hobnobbed with the Nantucket crowd. Clam chowder was about as nautical as she had gotten, so walking out to the massive white ship was daunting. Hellsa was waiting for her at the top of the gangplank, dressed in all white as usual, but without the usual armed guards. She and Freda had never met face to face, but she was not threatened by her, after all, Freda was a partner and was making her a lot of money. Just like she had done with Bernie, Hellsa wanted to appeal to Freda as an equal. As an ally, so being the first face she saw as she came onto the ship was important. The guards were still there of course, but they were standing just out of sight.

"Freda," Hellsa said her name in that wonderful Scandinavian way that made everything sound like it was full of Viking lore.

Freda made her way up the ramp and extended her hand, "Pleasure to finally meet you, Hellsa."

"Yes, we should have done this long ago. I will have to speak with Bernie about it. I want to meet Ruby and Opal as well," Hellsa said, then led the way to the front deck of the ship.

"Well, don't be too eager to meet them. One's rough around the edges and the other is made of fairy dust," Freda joked, but it was lost in translation causing her to zip it for the rest of the long walk down the side of the ship.

Once they reached the front deck, Hellsa made her

way over to the white sofa and sat down, letting Freda pick her own place to land on the huge entertainment bow.

"Wow, Liberace's got nothing on you." Freda looked around a little before choosing a stool to sit on. The cylindrical, white seat was a little too far away from Hellsa for conversation, so the little old lady dragged the heavy, expensive stump closer to the boss. "What the hell is this made out of?"

"Stone," Hellsa said, motioning to the scratches Freda had made on the teak deck pulling it over.

"Oh, shit! I'm sorry," Freda said, suddenly feeling like a fish out of water and on the deck of a million-dollar yacht.

"Don't worry. The teak needs to be refinished anyways." Hellsa took a deep breath. "So, Freda, what brings you here, other than for us to have a chance to meet."

Freda was uneasy, twitching a little, shifting on top of the cold white stone stool. Hellsa noticed the signs.

"Please, feel free to smoke out here." Hellsa snapped her fingers and a man came right over with an ashtray, placing it beside Freda. "You do smoke, don't you?"

Freda was a little uneasy about Hellsa knowing her habits, but the offer and ashtray were welcome, nonetheless. Freda pulled a pack out from her purse and lit a cigarette in one swift movement, like she was a sharpshooter at a county fair. One deep, long haul on her 'grandma's little helper' and Freda was suddenly back on her game.

"I came here because I have an opportunity for us," Freda spoke confidently. "A very lucrative opportunity."

"Is that so? What does Bernie think of it?"

Freda took another drag of her courage stick. "Bernie? Yes, well she doesn't quite understand the potential of it."

Hellsa raised her brows, "You mean she isn't in favor of it?"

"You could say it that way."

"So that is why you came alone. You're going above her—over her head, are you?"

"She'll get onboard once she sees what we could do with this. The risk is higher than our current operations, but the return is higher too and it's immediate. We could build relationships that would last far beyond this one job and expand our network all over the world."

Hellsa thought for a minute. About the passion in Freda's pitch, but also about the potential of betraying Bernie. She had a hunch that Bernie was out of the loop on this get-together, and she took the meeting anyways. That was a betrayal in itself. She was already on this side of the line, so what was the worst that could happen? They were just talking. She could listen to Freda's ideas, make her feel heard and build a stronger connection with her, or she could shut her down, right here, right now and possibly create an enemy. Good bosses have big ears.

Hellsa snapped her fingers again, calling over her bartender, then said to Freda, "This sounds intriguing, tell me more."

It was the second bowl of ice cream. Neapolitan, with both strawberry and caramel syrup. A deadly combo and a return to their regular ways. This was what Ruby and Natalie did every night before the club opened, before Daz and Buck. There were never any limits on scoops or toppings. No talk about calories or guilt, just uninhibited indulgence. The transfer of addiction is real, and sugar tends to be the staple of most recovery in its early days.

Both Natalie and Ruby were trying to satiate their inner goblins and being co-dependent on homemade sundaes was working great for them.

"So, no more Buck?" Ruby was careful to tread lightly.

"No. We just weren't working." Natalie avoided her eyes.

"It happens. A lot for me. Don't worry. There will be plenty of other Bucks."

"Let's hope not." Natalie looked to Ruby. "I need to tell you something."

Ruby let go of her spoon handle, letting it rest in her bowl, taking a break from the ice cream and giving Natalie her full awareness. "Okay."

Natalie shifted a little, then, just like facing her withdrawals, she got on with it. "I haven't been going to class. Actually, I've flunked out of this semester already."

"My word, Nat. How come?"

"There was a lot of reasons."

"I hope I wasn't one of them." Ruby fished for redemption.

"You were. But just one of them and all of them were mine to deal with. And I didn't. But I'm ready to now."

"What are you going to do about school?"

"Maybe it's for the best. I know you want me to learn business, but I think I'm actually meant for something else."

"Like what?"

"Architecture?" Natalie said, still not believing it herself. "I mean, I love buildings. I think I'm pretty good at drawing them too. I think what I really want to do is design beautiful things."

Ruby nodded, "Just like Ben."

"Yeah—I guess—sort of."

"Alright then. If that's what you want, then I'm

behind it. Nat, whatever makes you excited, makes me excited. Life without passion my dear is just walking death."

"I'll have to wait till next fall to reapply, but it will give me time to work on my portfolio."

"My word. Look at you. You've thought it all out already."

"I had time to." Natalie thought of Daz. "Ruby—I forgive you, for what happened."

Ruby recoiled. "You don't have to."

"But I do. I have to. The sooner I can let go of the past, the sooner it will stop trying to take me out."

"Take you out?" Ruby's mind went to what Bernie had confronted her with. "Nat, what aren't you telling me?"

Natalie looked at her 'step-in' mother. "The way you're looking at me—I think you already know."

Ruby's eyes became pools of salt water, "Oh sweetie." She reached out for her girl and pulled her into her chest. "I am so sorry, baby." Ruby saw the faint puncture marks on Natalie's arm. The stamps on the inside of her elbow that said she had bought a ticket to the end. "Are you still—"

Natalie stopped her. "No. I kicked it. Three days of absolute hell."

"And here you are," Ruby said with disbelief and relief.

"Here I am," Natalie said, finally feeling the weight of her accomplishment and what she almost lost.

Bernie emerged from the back bedroom and walked out into the main room, where Marcie was splayed out in the La-Z-Boy—full recline with the footrest extended.

"Three down," Bernie whispered.

Marcie yawned, "One to go. Thank you for tucking them in again."

"You know, if you lived closer, this could happen all the time," Bernie said with a positive upswing to her words.

"Ready?" Brent said, getting the word out just before he belched. "Oh, excuse me. Those shrimp come right back up, don't they?"

"Do they?" Bernie was white-knuckling it.

"Brent, I'm exhausted." Marcie was looking way too comfortable to move a muscle.

"What? Oh, come on," Brent whined.

"You go. I don't know how to play poker anyway."

Bernie's ears perked up. "You're going to Tito's game at the Activity Center?"

Brent shrugged, "Yeah, I was planning on it. Stan and Fred invited me. Marcie too, said it was a lot of fun."

Bernie warned, "You be careful, Fred and Harold are sharks."

"No offense, Bernie, but it's them ya should be worrying about. I know my way around a flush," Brent said, slightly stretching as if this were a physical sport.

"Brent, just go," Marcie said plainly, tiring of the whole thing.

"Ya sure? What about you?"

"Bernie and I will have a girls night in," Marcie said turning to Bernie who instantly loved the idea.

"Alright then," Brent easily agreed, but instead of heading out, he just stood there, in front of her, like there was something left to say.

"Oh, right," Marcie groaned, sitting up and looking around the room. "There it is. On the counter by the door." Marcie pointed to her purse, that was leaning against the backsplash, by the sink.

"Yer the best," Brent responded, like he'd just gotten

his allowance and walked over to the purse. After digging around for a few seconds, he pulled out a couple of bills. "This it?" he said with the disappointment of a spoiled debutante being denied an Oompa Loompa.

"Yes, until I go to the bank, that's it. Brent, there should be more than enough there for a seniors' game. We can't drive home on fumes." Marcie was losing her patience.

Bernie went over to her own purse and pulled out a wad of cash. "Here."

"What's that?" Marcie was stunned by the thick wad of American dreams.

"Fun money," Bernie smiled.

"Fun money?" Brent was intrigued.

"Worked and saved my whole life—for this—now it's time to have some fun with it."

Marcie shook her head, "You've already done enough, we couldn't."

"You're not. He is," Bernie said, slapping the wad against Brent's chest. "Bet big, bet often and have fun."

Brent didn't wait for his wife to interject. "Thank you, Bernie."

"Call me Verna," she said, all business and he missed the warning completely, taking the cash and heading out the door. Bernie winked at Marcie as he left. "Small price to pay for a little peace and quiet, am I right?"

Marcie just shook her head but didn't disagree.

"Now, if I remember correctly, you liked sherry. I'll get us a couple of glasses and meet you out in the lanai."

Opal stood in the kitchen, in her pink nightie, over by the counter, lit only by the yellow light of the hood vent and

the blue hue of the TV. She chewed her thin sandwich—
her single-meat-slice-filled, white bread envelope—
gnashing her molars together slowly. Gnawing on the late-
night snack, staring at the sofa. Her eyes were strained, full
of tiny red spider webs. Her nose was red too. A swollen
hue of blush to its tip. She watched as Stan's chest rose and
fell. Rose and fell—passed out on the sofa beside the TV.
He was naked. His beer belly and prediabetic thighs
spilling over the side of the cushions. Opal's eyes weren't
full of love. They were full of something else. Something
she never wore outside the house. She kept taking bites of
the sandwich, getting closer and closer to the crust, until
she ran out of sandwich and nipped the end of her fingers
—hard. Not a nibble but a bite, breaking the skin. She
winced. Sucking back the pain and the blood, keeping all
sound and agony buried inside her.

The TV was on at Ruby's place as well. Natalie and Ruby
were sitting watching it, flipping through channels, not
happy with anything that was on. Ruby couldn't help but
notice how intensely Natalie was bouncing her knee. It was
about as much as Ruby was shifting in her seat. Side by
each, the two of them were the bookends of boredom.
They had gone from sugar high, to candy crash and were
climbing the walls.

Natalie turned off the TV. "Might as well just go to
bed," she said.

"Are you tired?" Ruby asked.

"No. But I can't handle this, so might as well try."

"Okay," Ruby said, and Natalie got up and went to the
front bedroom.

She didn't bother taking off her clothes, instead just

flopped down on top of her sheets and stared at the ceiling. Her mind was busy, but it was better than Dynasty or MacGyver. This was going to be the next battle. The times she was alone with her thoughts. The space in the silence where the voices came in and downplayed the risks. It's where she would picture the past through a positive lens, making the smack romantic and edgy. Convincing her that it had ultimately brought Daz to her, so it couldn't be all bad and if she danced with the devil again, he'd surely return to hold her.

There was barely even a knock before her bedroom door flew open and revealed Ruby standing in the threshold, wearing a long, red jacket. "Come on. We're busting out of this Bone Park."

Bernie topped up Marcie's little sherry glass and Marcie was all for it. The mood in the lanai was relaxed and calm, just like the evening breeze.

"He warned me about you," Marcie said, following a sip of her freshly-filled nightcap.

"Gary?" Bernie huffed.

"Oh yeah, he told me point blank that it would never work if you didn't like me."

"Marcie, I liked you the moment I saw you make him smile that way."

"Honestly, I was terrified of you—still kind of am."

"Why? I'm an old lady."

Marcie, clearly feeling the effects of the sherry and the long day, leaned towards Bernie and whispered, "I've heard things about you. Word gets around in Buffalo."

"You shouldn't believe everything you hear."

"You're a legend."

Bernie rolled her shoulders back, "Dear, you don't know the half of it."

Marcie's eyes went wide, "So tell me."

Bernie chuckled, "I'd have to kill you." She followed her words with a smile and locked eyes with Marcie, who suddenly understood the warning hiding under the grin. "I meant what I said earlier, about you and the kids living closer. I could get you a place right by the beach if you want. With a huge pool for them."

"Brent would never go for it."

"Good," Bernie said her truth, but seeing the pull back from Marcie, she laid off the gas. "You know, Gary's father was a good guy. Most of the time."

"He never talked about him. I asked but he always found a way around it."

"That's because of 'some of the time'." Bernie gave her a look. "Gary was nothing like him. He wasn't born with the same piss and vinegar in his veins. Gary didn't fit Sal's idea of what a son should be. So, he tried to beat it into him."

"My God. I had no idea."

"Whose idea was it to give Greg that buzz cut?"

Marcie was confused by the direction of the question. "Who?"

"Yes, who? Was it you? Was it Greg? Did he want to look like a prisoner? Or a recruit?"

"No—Brent took him to get it done."

"But did he want it? I remember his hair being long, wavy, like a little hippy running around in diapers. Long curly red locks just like his father."

"Brent was in the service. He has a certain way. He thinks a boy should look like a boy."

"Sal thought—" Bernie caught herself. "He thought? Christ no. That man couldn't figure out how to change a roll of toilet paper. Men think they're smart. They like it when we make them feel that way. Support them. Build the foundation for them to shine. But if we don't do that, if their world doesn't heed to their ideal, they bend it to their will."

"Bernie, Brent would never."

"You mean he hasn't—yet. He knew Gary. They weren't friends."

"I know."

"Do you? You think you know me. What do you know?"

Marcie got very quiet.

Bernie kept going, "Go on, you said you heard things. What things?" Bernie moved to the edge of her wicker throne.

"It was just rumors."

"Don't ever listen to rumors again. You hear me? You don't gossip. You shut that bullshit down right away." Bernie reached out, Marcie flinched, but Bernie took her hand and held onto it, looking her dead in the eyes. "You are family. Those three precious kids in there—are family. That is all that ever matters. If you want to know who or what I am, you ask me. You do not listen to gossip or lies, you ask me."

Marcie started to shake, her breath got short, her mouth dry with fear.

"No, no. Don't you shake. You're stronger than that. You are my family. My son's wife and the mother of my grandchildren. You do not shake," Bernie corrected her while building her up at the same time. "You are my legacy. You are my daughter and women in this family run things, they do not run from them. So, ask me. You ask me what you want to know."

Marcie fought her breath down from the edge of

panic, settling her hands and straightening her back. "Who are you?"

Bernie nodded, let go of Marcie's hand and sat back in her chair—tall and proud. "Who am I? I'm the person who couldn't be bent."

Opal was wide awake, lying in the large bed under the soft pink comforter. The sounds of the poker game going on at the Activity Center were making their way across the inner circle and in through the louvers of her bedroom window —but that's not why she was awake. Her eyes were wide, her breath constricted, trying to make the sound of the air moving in and out of her lungs even quieter.

"Opal!" Stan bellowed from somewhere in the depths of the trailer.

She jumped a little, her head twitching side to side at light speed, like she was shooing away an invisible fly.

"OPAL!" Stan yelled again, this time with weight behind it.

Opal gripped the blanket tight in her fists, pulling it up under her chin, fearing the boogie man outside the bedroom door. She lay absolutely motionless. Holding her breath, listening to the approaching, stumbling footsteps of her groom. It was an agonizing eternity, hearing her betrothed move closer to her closed door, then away, then closer again. With the slamming of the carport door, the footsteps suddenly stopped, then continued outside, slapping against the pavement, moving away from the trailer. Once the sound of inebriated foot meat and flip flops faded away, Opal loosened her grip on the covers and let out the Guinness World Record breath she had been holding in.

The turnout was respectable, four round, wooden tables full of friendly competition. Fred, Harold, George and most of the other men who were lucky enough to wake up that morning, were there. Tito was easy to pick out, he was the one sitting behind the largest stack of chips. He was the picture of retirement, post-work in the Orange State personified. Birkenstocks with socks, linen shorts, whitish tank top under an open Hawaiian shirt, with a straw fedora and a lit cigar. This was his Vegas. He was the Cuban Bugsy of the park and Brent was feeling his wrath.

Tito pushed more chips into the already large pile in the middle of the table and Brent folded, slamming his cards down in a very unsportsmanlike manner. He did however show some manners, nodding to Tito before getting up and walking over to the makeshift bar the poker club had set up over on the side. Mullet was there, leaning against the bar, sipping on a beer, watching the carnage of retirement savings going on around him.

"Hey," Brent said, happy to see someone close to his own age.

"Hey," Mullet replied. "Are ya winning?"

"Just singles and fives." He pointed to Tito's stacks. "It looks like a fortune, but I think it's a whopping forty bucks. At least the bar is free."

"Yeah, when there is a sale at Walgreens, Tito and his senior's card are all over it. It's the only reason I come."

Brent dug around the frozen water of the cooler on the floor but came up empty handed, "They're out of beer?" Brent asked.

Mullet nodded. "Yeah, sorry man, this is the last one."

Brent switched gears and went for the rum on the table, pouring a healthy amount into a plastic glass.

"Don't bother looking for mix. There isn't any. Can't tell if the old guy thinks it's fruity or he's just too cheap to buy it," Mullet said genuinely wondering.

Brent accepted the situation for what it was. Straight rum and small hands of poker. He raised his glass of budget rum to Mullet. "Cheers."

Mullet took a good swig of his malt entertainment. "So, which one is yours," he said pointing to the tables of old men as if he and Brent were dads standing by the playground.

"None. My kids' grandma lives here."

"Really? Who?"

"A Verna Hewton—Bernie."

"No shit. So, you're Bernie's son? I didn't know she had one."

Brent was quick to stop that. "Oh no. I'm not her son. Not related to her at all. My girlfriend was—her son's —wife."

"Whoa. Weird. And he's cool with you just coming down here and hanging with his mom? All my exes want me dead."

"He's—not here." Brent struggled, "He died, a few years ago. His kids came as part of the package attached to his smok'n widow."

"Oh, heavy. So you're a stepdad?"

"Yup. Three of them."

"Man, that is a huge responsibility, stepping up and taking care of another man's kids. You're a hero man."

Brent loved the praise but played it down. "No, I'm not a hero. Just doing what needs to be done. The girls are alright, but the boy works my last nerve. Bit of a sissy, ya know. I tell ya, if Marcie gains a few, I'm gone. You gotta be in tiptop to keep a guy around for all that drama." Brent took another gulp of his free rum.

Mullet was put off by Brent's harshness. "So have you met Ruby and the rest?"

"Who?" Brent was blank.

Mullet pulled back, realizing the loop he was in, was not one that Brent had been brought into. "Ah, just other park residents."

Brent paid it no mind. "So, which one is yours?"

"All of them—kind of. I work here part time—maintenance."

"Really. Good gig?"

"Oh yeah. I love 'em. They're all like family. Shit, they fought in the war. Some of them two wars. Me helping them out is the least I can do."

"I served."

"Really. Desert Storm?" Mullet was back on board with Brent.

"Ah, no. Um, reserves," Brent mumbled, and Mullet's adoration faded.

"Didn't they call most up for Iraq?" Mullet wasn't following.

"I couldn't get called up, with all the responsibilities with the kids. They need a man around, ya know." Brent tried to make both himself and Mullet feel better by sugar coating his lie.

"Right. Gotta do, what you gotta do." Mullet saw right through it. "Yeah, I'm sure all these guys had no responsibilities at home in '41."

The insult flew right over Brent's dense head, he was too busy digging around in his pocket, searching for his pack of cigarettes. As he pulled the crumpled pack out, the wad of cash that Bernie gave him fell out onto the floor.

"Shit," he said bending down to pick it up, but not before the thick wad caught Mullet's eye.

"Say, I didn't get your name," Mullet said, suddenly very friendly.

"Brent," he said standing up and offering Mullet a smoke.

"Tony!" Stan blurted out, as he stumbled in through the open sliding glass doors.

"Stan. How are you?" Mullet replied.

"Ready to take Tito down, that's how I am." Stan puffed out his chest and headed for the open seat that Brent had left.

Mullet rolled his eyes, took one of Brent's cigarettes, then headed for the sliding glass doors that Stan had just came in through.

As they stepped outside, he lowered his voice, "Thanks for the smoke, Brent. Perfect time to make our exit. Once Stan shows up, the fun usually ends. Listen, I'm not sure if you're interested, but I just heard that another game opened up. A real game. No singles or fives allowed. Just big pots and big players. I was just about to head out to it, but if you want to come, I can take you."

"Where is it?" Brent liked the sounds of it.

"Not far." Mullet pulled Brent in close and whispered in his ear, "And it's in a stripper bar."

Mullet let go of Brent, who now was smiling from ear to ear, "Well now, that sounds like a much better view."

"Hang on," Mullet instructed Brent and ran back into the Activity Center, returning a few seconds later with his hand stuffed under his shirt. He led Brent a few feet away from the sliding glass doors, then like a back-alley magician he shouted, "Ta-da!" His hocus pocus words accented the reveal of a half full bottle of rum that he'd swiped from Tito's free bar. "A little something for our travels." Mullet justified the theft and started walking across the inner field, dangling the 'rum carrot' over his shoulder for Brent to follow.

The small front door of the Quonset hut opened, and Natalie came out, closing it quickly behind her to keep the rowdy sounds in. She stepped off the landing and stood across from Daz, who was looking over his shoulder for eavesdroppers even before she opened her mouth.

"Did you talk to her?" she asked, hopeful.

"No, Nat. Not yet. This whole thing was sprung on me, last minute. I need the right time, when we aren't here."

"You haven't talked to me at all tonight."

Daz stepped up to her, looked around and gave her a kiss. Quick, but firm and on the lips. "I will talk to Ruby, maybe later, once she's had a couple. Mellowed out. But I promise—I will."

"Okay," she said and started to walk away from the front doors.

"Where are you going?"

Natalie turned back. "Home. I told Ruby. I'm tired and this is a distraction, but all the booze and—stuff—it really isn't helping. Don't think it's safe for me in there right now. I'm just going to turn in."

"Wait till Kurt gets here, will ya? He can watch the door and I'll walk you."

Natalie touched her temple. "Thanks, but my head is killing me, and I just want to lie down."

Daz saw the exhaustion in her eyes and knew first-hand what she had been through. "Alright."

Natalie turned and started walking.

Daz called to her, "I will talk to her, Nat."

Natalie nodded and waved, blowing him a kiss before disappearing into the woods.

Brent followed his new buddy all the way across the inner circle, down Gecko Drive, to the double dead-end at the far reaches of the park. The two of them kept passing the bottle, like two land pirates, swaying as they headed down the overgrown foot path into the forest.

"Is this the only way?" Brent was a little uneasy.

"There is a dirt road, but this is quicker." Mullet kept trudging along.

Brent's street senses started to kick in. He didn't really know this guy at all. He was being led out into a dark forest with a pocket full of cash, following a stranger. This had all the warning signs of a mugging.

"Maybe we should go back." Brent slowed his walk.

"Go back? We're almost there."

"What about alligators and shit?"

"Oh, no. They weren't invited." Mullet laughed.

Up ahead a figure approached them. It was dark so Brent went stiff. Tensing up, readying himself to either run or fight.

"Hey Nat!" Mullet broke the tension.

But Natalie didn't respond, she just kept walking past them.

"Okay then. Have a good night," Mullet said, handing Brent the last of the bottle.

Seeing another living soul, that didn't try to rob him and was female, calmed Brent's nerves a little, although the cold shoulder she gave didn't convince him that this guy actually knew her.

Mullet picked up the pace, almost running down the

path. Brent was having a hard time keeping up, unsure of his footing and still uneasy about where they were actually headed. It took him a bit, but he finally caught up to Mullet, just as he was pushing back the overgrown fern leaves that blocked the path from the clearing. The gates of foliage that revealed the open space in the middle of the Florida jungle, with a Quonset hut on the other side of it.

Mullet extended his arm like a 'Price Is Right' model. "Brent, I'd like to introduce you to Moonlight." While Brent took in the mirage, Mullet walked right up to the door where Daz was standing. "Daz, how are you?"

"Be better if I wasn't here," Daz huffed.

"I thought we were supposed to be down this week. What changed?"

"Don't know. Just got a call from Ruby and here we are." Daz looked past Mullet to Brent who was slowly walking up behind him. "Who's that?"

"That's Brent. He's with me," Mullet said, and Daz nodded, opening the door for them. Mullet let Brent go in first and once he was inside, he turned back to Daz. "You sure Bernie knows about this?"

Daz shrugged. "She must. But she's not my boss. Ruby is."

Moonlight was less busy than most nights, but the impromptu opening had gathered a good crowd. Brent was instantly overstimulated, shuffling his way into the wonderland. His eyes didn't know where to land, on the stage where the fully naked 50-something woman was dancing, on the three-piece blues band that was playing in the corner, on the artwork overhead and all around, or on the poker tables that were divided by stripper poles that had dancers of all ages, sizes and shapes spinning around them.

"Wow!" It was the only word he could conjure up.

"Yeah, wow." Mullet stepped up behind him. "These

women are royalty. You my friend are in the presence of greatness."

Mullet led him over to the bar, where Quincy was happy to help them. As they received their drinks, Ruby came out from the dressing room in the back, wearing a red negligee and immediately took notice of Mullet. She waved off the very eager customers waiting for table dances and headed straight for him.

Ruby took him by the arm and pulled him away from Brent, "What the hell is he doing here?"

Mullet had spilled his beer in the violent aside and was trying to wipe it off of him. "I brought him here. He has a wad of cash in his pocket, and I thought this was a good place for him to lose it."

"Do you have any idea who he is?" Ruby was beside herself.

"Yeah. He's Bernie's—daughter-in-law's—guy—thing. He said he hadn't met you. You want me to introduce you?"

"No. He can't be here."

"Why? You let me lose money here."

"My word, you are that stupid? He can't be here, because Bernie will find out."

Mullet suddenly clued in. "She's doesn't know you're open?"

Ruby shook her head.

"Okay. Um. I'm so sorry. I can fix this. I'll tell him that this is completely top secret. He can't tell a soul. We'll play a game or two, then head out. I'll get 'em so wasted he forgets the whole thing. Or at least where we were."

"And who are you?" Brent said coming up behind Ruby and putting his hand around her waist.

Ruby spun around, creeped out and startled.

"Hey, you look familiar, do I know you?" Brent

squinted, looking her up and down.

"Poker or blackjack?" she deflected.

Brent shook off the search through his mind for the matching information. The clip of one of Ruby's movies that was undoubtedly burned into his pubescent memories. "Poker," he said with a smile.

"Right this way," Ruby offered, leading the lecherous guest to the nearest table with an open chair.

Once Brent sat down, she went back to Mullet. "You keep an eye on him and you make sure he gets so sauced that he can't remember his own name. If Bernie finds out about tonight, I'll be coming for you."

Mullet understood the assignment and went right back to the bar to get a tray of shots ordered for his guest.

Ruby made her way to Nola, who was in the middle of a lap dance. "Excuse me," she said to the young man who was under the spell of the ebony goddess. "She'll be right back, and next song is on the house." Having peeled Nola off of the young man's lap, she pulled a set of keys out from her small, red clutch and handed them to her. "I need you to lock up."

"Everything alright?" Nola was concerned.

"Yes, I just need to go home. You're in charge. Just keep it small and don't let it go on too late. I'll tell Daz on my way out."

Nola accepted her orders and tucked the key into her G-string.

After going back to the dressing room, wrapping herself up in her long, red jacket, Ruby headed for the front doors.

Outside she was greeted by Kurt. "I got here as soon as I could, Ms. Ruby."

"It's alright, Kurt. It was a spur of the moment thing." Ruby looked around. "Where's Daz?"

"He asked me to watch the door. Said he'd be right back."

"Okay. I'm heading out. Nola's in charge and I told her not to go too late."

"Whatever you want, Ms. Ruby," Kurt said in his wonderful, respectful way.

He couldn't believe it. The balls on that kid. He had been warned, no mistaking, loud and clear. There was no room for misunderstanding or interpretation, but there he was. His shitty van, idling outside of the trailer with the red stripe around it. Daz crouched down and crept across the road. He made sure to get himself into the blind spot of the van. The thin strip of unseeable road, blocked by the back corner of the van. He moved fast, like a swat leader, advancing on the van, in the sliver of what couldn't be seen.

Daz ripped opened the passenger side door. "Don't you say a fucking word," he instructed, pressing the barrel of his gun into the side of Buck's nose as he climbed up and into the van. "Drive."

Buck hesitated. Daz lowered his gun, cocked it and slammed it into Buck's crotch. "Drive!"

The terrified hostage pulled down the shifter, putting the van in gear and slowly pulled away. "I—" Buck tried to speak.

"Just fucking drive," Daz cut him off, punching him in the side of the head with his free hand. "You shut the fuck up and you drive."

Buck did his best to hold it together, trying not to piss himself as he drove past the Activity Center and out of the park.

Bernie opened the bedroom door, quietly. She and Marcie stayed out in the hallway, looking at the three angels lost in their dream world. It had been a long, sherry-filled, eye-opening night, but Marcie looked better. Not on edge like she was, not afraid of Bernie, in fact quite the opposite.

"You will never tire of this," Bernie whispered to her. "Knowing they're safe. Watching them just be."

"I do it all the time," Marcie whispered back. "Brent tells me to leave them alone, so I just wait until he's asleep and do it anyway."

"This world, Marcie, is full of horrible things—that's what they are for. They are the reminder that there is good. If they exist, then so does hope. So does happiness. Brent can't keep them safe. You know that. But I can. You and I can ensure they get to do this too someday. Watch their own babies sleep."

Marcie reached out and gently pulled the door closed. "I'll think about."

The answer was major headway for Bernie. Far ahead of where they started from that night and enough to give her hope. Hope that this might continue.

"Are you sure you're alright on the couch?" Marcie slurred a little.

"Week's almost over, it's a little late to be asking me," Bernie joked.

As they made it into the main area, Marcie looked up at the clock, "Brent's still out."

"Don't worry," Bernie said. "These old guys can smell a fish a mile away and won't let him leave till his pockets are empty."

"Fish." She giggled.

"Means a bad player. A mark."

"He kind of looks like a fish, doesn't he?" Marcie giggled again.

"Grouper. Definitely grouper," Bernie laughed.

"Goodnight, Bernie," Marcie said, making her way to the front room as Bernie began pulling cushions off of the pullout couch.

"Goodnight, dear."

The door to the front bedroom opened and the light from the main room spilled in and over Natalie. She was curled up, under her covers—out like a light. Ruby did the same thing that Bernie and Marcie had just done, she stood in the doorway watching her girl sleep. She was happy knowing Natalie was safe, content watching her just be. Ruby couldn't resist, she stepped into the room, walking towards the bed, to give her a kiss. She had become the love thief in the night, the one who swoops in and smooches up all your worries and replaces them with a mother's love.

Just as she bent down, there was a knock on the trailer door. The carport side. It wasn't loud, but it was enough to possibly wake her girl, and that was not going to happen on her watch. Ruby moved back from the edge of Natalie's bed, closed her door and made her way quickly to the carport entrance, just as there was another knock thumped. Ruby looked out the small window, the one beside the door and was not pleased with who she saw outside.

As she unlocked and opened the door a crack, she was already speaking, "It's late—" A strong waft of liquor stopped her words and made her turn her head. "Jesus, you're drunk, go home." She leaned into the door, closing it, but the man stopped it with his hand.

"I'll pay triple."

Ruby paused.

"I got it on me." He followed up on the offer.

Ruby huffed and pushed the door closed—hard.

The man put his lips to the seam of the door and spoke into it, "I don't have to pay at all. You know I could always just tell her."

Ruby looked back to the closed door of Natalie's room, then opened the carport door, "She's home. You better be quiet, and you better be fast." Ruby, unlatched the chain, stepped aside and Stan stepped in.

He didn't say a word, just kissed her on the cheek and made his way down the hall, towards Ruby's bedroom, undoing his pants along the way.

Freda drove into the park like a snail. Lights off and barely rolling. It was the witching hour, the magic space between 3:00am and 4:00am, when any number of elderly insomniacs could stir. Freda was careful not to wake a soul, tapping the gas pedal with the tip of her toe, like she was teasing the engine forward. She drove the wrong way around the one-way, so she wouldn't have to pass by Bernie's or Opal's trailers. She didn't want to explain any of it, to anyone. It had been a very long night, more talking than she'd ever done in her entire life or ever wanted to do again.

She slowly pulled past her trailer, just a little, then put the car into reverse. Again, teasing the gas, she guided the car up and under the carport, gently pressing the brakes to avoid even the slightest rubbing sounds and put it into park. With the dash lights out and the engine still, she could finally let go. Unclench the millions of strands of muscle fiber she'd been squeezing tight since the dock.

After rolling her head around in semi-circles, trying to relieve the strain in her neck, she opened her door and made her way around to the back of the car. The trunk took a different key than the ignition, she forgot that, trying to use the ignition key first. She almost fully lost her shit before realizing the poor design of the rental and using the other key on the ring. She opened the trunk as gently as she could and looked down onto the old beach blankets spread out inside it. Freda pulled back the blanket and sighed. All the stealth driving made sense. It was full. Front to back and side to side. One solid layer of cocaine and marijuana bricks. Freda had done it! She had been fronted over two million dollars' worth of product. Two million dollars wholesale, which once it had been marked up, was at least ten million on the streets. Yes, she had gone behind Bernie's back, but she had a plan and once it was all said and done, she was sure Bernie would see the light—or at least the stacks of cash.

"Holy shit!" a man shouted just out of her peripheral, on her right.

Freda whipped out the semi-automatic magnum with the silencer she had gotten from Cliff—the one she had tucked into the inside lip of the trunk—she whipped it out and fired it. As she turned to her right, ready to fire again on her assailant, she found Brent standing there. His eyes were like giant saucers—frozen in shock—with a massive bullet hole in the center of his forehead.

"Brent?" she stuttered, and stepdad of the year crumpled to the ground.

The bedroom was red, lit like an Amsterdam front window. The bed was shaking, so was the glass of water on the side table with the dentures in it.

"Stop—stop." Ruby slapped Stan's back, looking up from underneath the sweaty, panting man. Her eyes darted around the room. Looking back and forth, listening. "Did you hear that?"

"Hear what?" Stan grunted.

"There was a bang."

"The only bang I'm hearing is the one I'm giving you."

Ruby was over it. "Get off of me."

"What? I'm not finished."

"Yes, you are. Get off!" she said pushing him to the side.

Ruby went straight for her robe then over to her bedroom window and looked out into the dark night.

"I'm not paying," Stan threatened, pulling on his shorts.

"I don't care. Just leave," she said, disgusted with him and herself. "This was it. I won't do this to Opal anymore."

Stan opened the bedroom door and snapped back at her, "All you bitches are the same!"

It took everything she had—and more. Freda had only been back in the park a couple of minutes and already it had all gone sideways. She grunted and groaned as she pulled the beach blanket across the grass in the dark. The blanket from the trunk of her car, the one she had Brent's body lying on. Foot, by exhausting foot, she pulled him out into the middle, stopping only to open the fence and fiddle with her nose, that was covered in cocaine. Dragging a dead body is a feat of strength for most people, but for a four foot something 60-year-old, it was superhuman and superhuman strength needed spinach. White spinach. After a hundred yards of heart pounding exertion, she got the blanket as close to the pool as she could. Looking around and seeing no one, she pulled the beach cover out from underneath Brent's lifeless body, sending his frame rolling into the water and under the thermo cover. As his body gurgled, being sucked into the chlorinated centerpiece of the park, Freda giggled. "Dear Maryanne."

Opal was asleep. Tucked in calm and still under her pink comforter. In between her peaceful breaths and heavenly coos, a large hand reached across the bed and grabbed her by the hair. Opal's eyes shot open to find Stan standing over her, drunk and angry. He said nothing, just yanked her out of the bed by her hair and threw her onto the floor. Opal screamed, at the top of her lungs, but she knew it would do nothing to stop him, so she flipped over onto her hands and knees and scurried past him, out the door, into the hallway.

Bernie came out of the bathroom, into the dark hallway with her revolver extended out in front of her. She began to make solid steps towards the main room, her gaze was laser, her demeanor one of ominous calm. She scanned the main room, through the sight of the gun, then made her way to the lanai door. She turned the knob, opened the inside door, then kicked the screen door out of her way.

Holding the ankle biter at bay with her foot, she pointed the gun left, then right, listening.

Opal was on the ground of the bathroom, huddled against the door. Holding it closed with her body. The handle on the door jiggled as Stan pounded on it from the other side. "Opal—open the door!" She kept quiet and he kept on, "Opal, open the goddamn door right now!"

Stan started hitting the door so hard that Opal's body bounced from the blows. She was beyond scared—she was crippled with fear and crying.

"Get the fuck out here! You're only making this worse!" He continued to kick the door while inside Opal covered her mouth as the tears ran down her face. "Opal, you fucking—" Suddenly he went quiet. The banging and the kicking stopped. The only thing Opal could hear was her own breath.

She wondered if he was playing with her. Trying to get her to think he was gone again, so she would open the door. Or maybe he had just passed out, like he'd done many times before?

"Opal?" That wasn't Stan's voice—it was Bernie. "You can come out now. You're safe. Trust me, you can open the door."

Opal slowly got to her feet and opened the battered bathroom door. Outside in the hallway, Bernie was standing behind Stan. Her one hand was wrenching on a tie that was strung across his mouth, gagging him and her other hand was clenched around his balls, crushing them in her abnormally large, female digits.

Bernie twisted his manhood hard and snarled, "Bend."

Stan obeyed, bending over at the waist, hunching down, struggling to breathe, engorged in testicular pain.

"Let's go for a walk," Bernie said. "Opal, could you please get the door?" Bernie motioned to the carport exit just behind her and Opal squeezed past her incapacitated husband to open it.

Bernie pulled Stan by his sack, down the steps of the trailer, out through the carport and all the way across the grass, to the thermo-blanket-covered pool in the middle of the inner circle. Opal walked right behind them, keeping up, as Bernie took him around to the shallow end. The tie across his mouth was so tight that it cut into the corners of his lips, but Bernie didn't care, she just twisted her grip on it even harder, turning the silk into a vice and dislocating his jaw.

"Get in," Bernie ordered.

Stan did his best to shake his head, that's when Bernie let go of his balls, pulled out her revolver from her tattered men's robe and put it to his head.

"Get in," she whispered, but with the intensity of a scream.

Stan looked over to Opal.

Bernie yanked his head around, pulling back on his face-cleaving gag. "Don't you look at her."

Opal turned away as Bernie moved the gun from his head to his mouth, pushing the barrel into the back of his throat, rattling the metal against the dentures of his gaping, torn maw. Terrified, Stan slowly got down into the cold pool, pushing the cover back just enough for him to slip in. Bernie, not giving him an inch, yanked back hard on the tie, slamming Stan's head back against the edge of the pool.

Bernie looked over to Opal. "It's up to you."

Opal gazed out into the darkness of the night, lost in

the insanity of the moment and the memories of a lifetime.

"Opal. This won't be on you. They will just think this drunk old senile piece-of-shit, drowned," Bernie assured her.

Opal was stone.

"Sink or swim? I can't hold him here all night."

The woman in pink, kept looking ahead, not letting her eyes fall onto the brute in the water, but began to move, slowly stepping forward, towards the edge of the pool, catatonic.

"What's it going to be? Opal, I knew he was hurting you—I just didn't know how bad. But I can't do this for you. You have to do it for yourself, just like I did. You have to put an end to this."

Opal slowly raised her pink-slipper-covered foot off the pool deck. Inside the broken Christian, Bernadette took over, moving her foot down, placing it onto the top of Stan's head. Slowly, she put all of her weight into that foot, pushing Stan down, under the water. Bernie leaned back, pulling on the gag, with everything she had, holding him against the side of the pool as he thrashed and swatted at the air, fighting for his life above the water. The more he fought the harder Bernadette pressed her foot down, until her slipper was submerged completely. Bernie's tie-gripping hand went white from blood loss as the fear in 'God's good little girl' subsided and she took a stand. Holding her weight over her abuser until the power he had—the power he had stolen from her—returned, the resistance quieted, and the nightmare ended, turning back into the stillness of the night.

6

Aftermath

So here we are. Back where we started from. The *how* has been presented to you—now you need to know the who. From up here, I can see it all. It's one of the perks of eternity. I say 'up here', because it means something to you. It fits the narrative you were sold, but it's so much more than that. It's how I have the ability to tell you about the past and take you into the present. It's how with a turn of the page, you can see the past like it were unfolding right in front of you. That moment is this moment, the one that I started you in. The one that began in between the covers of another book and led you to here. This is the morning I introduced you to. The morning that began with my mother and two dead bodies in the pool. The place where the *how* becomes *who*. The past and present moments join together and lead to a reason for it all.

Freda first, then Ruby. It was just a look to anyone watching, nothing more than a glance, but for them it held weight. It meant more than the three seconds of eye contact—it meant leave—now. Freda and Ruby immediately heeded the order, walking back towards their trailers, away from the mayhem. Ruby's trailer was closer, geographically and as Freda got close to her blue-accented single wide, she heard the screams behind her. The new ones. The ones that came from Ruby. Even though Bernie had given her the marching orders, Freda stopped and turned around. She had to, the blood curdling cries could not be ignored. She watched as Bernie ran to her hysterical sister—watched as this day got worse and worse. The screams and commotion only added to her self-induced agony, her head was killing her. The depressive hangover of sucking her own product up her nose. She hadn't slept a wink since she dumped Brent into the pool. She had just balanced her panic and the buzzing electricity shooting through her neurons with a steady stream of rum and cokes.

As Bernie and Ruby ran back towards the trailer with the red stripe, Freda's cell phone rang. She jumped a little because of her chemically heightened nerves and fumbled around in the pockets of her quilted blue polyester robe, searching for the source of the jarring sound. Finally, finding the phone in the bottom of her left pocket, she pulled it out and squinted at the screen. She didn't recognize the number on it. It was not from the state, or the states at all for that matter. It was the kind of thing she would have ignored, on a normal day. Chalked it up to a wrong number or a telemarketer. On a normal day free of dead bodies, screaming sisters and lines of cocaine, but this was not that kind of day.

"Hello?" Freda said, cautiously into the phone.

"What's happened?" The accent gave Hellsa away—right away.

"Why are you calling me?" She turned away from the inner circle, lowered her voice and walked towards her trailer.

"What's going on there?" Hellsa asked, rhetorically.

"Why are you asking me? Haven't you talked to Bernie?"

"No. I am talking to you. I do have ears everywhere and I know there is a line of police cruisers heading towards your park—but I don't know why, so please tell me what's going on?"

"Someone got in the way, and they were dealt with," Freda said, with the steely tone of an assassin. "But it *has* been dealt with."

"By you?"

"Yes."

"And the clean up?"

"Bernie's on it."

"Good. How is the product?" Hellsa asked, getting back to business.

Freda had made her way past her lanai and was rounding the front of her trailer, when she froze.

"Freda?" Hellsa repeated herself, impatient.

Freda wanted to speak, but she couldn't. Her mouth could not put into words what her eyes couldn't believe. The car was gone. The rental with millions of dollars' worth of drugs in the trunk—drugs that she had gotten on spec—was gone.

"Fine," Freda said, with her vocal cords tensed up like overtightened piano strings.

"You sure, Wilfreda? You don't sound fine."

"It's fine. Believe you me, everything is still on track." Freda was twitching, searching her head for answers, looking for signs of anything, of anyone around her trailer. "Hellsa, if you don't mind there is a lot to take care of here. Bernie needs all of us to tidy up before our uninvited guests arrive."

"Alright then. Do what you need to do. I will check

back with you later," Hellsa said, with a slight warning before hanging up on her end.

Freda was in full tizzy. The car was there minutes ago. When she heard Mullet screaming and she saw Bernie walk out into the inner circle—the car was there. She was sure of it—wait—was she? Now she was questioning her sanity. Was it there? Had she put her hand on the trunk lid as she passed by it on her way out to the inner circle? Was it ever there? Did she even drive back last night? Had she shot Brent? From tizzy to instantly dizzy. Freda walked over and grabbed onto one of the carport's wooden support beams, steadying herself, trying not to pass out. Her heart was racing. Her brow was sopping wet with sweat. Was this the heart attack? The jammer that would take her to her Reg? What the hell was she thinking, sucking those drugs up into her nasal cavities like a supermodel. She was 60 years old—snorting a pile of cocaine. Wait, drugs? She was high. Earth to Freda, it all started to make sense. Her heart was racing because she was high. She knew what was real. She was 60, not 16. She knew who she was enough to not doubt herself like this. She wasn't an idiot; she was scared, and this was not the time to question reality. She had driven back there last night, she knew it. The drugs were absolutely in the trunk of the car, and it was just here! But that meant it was really gone—stolen—and the panic returned.

Bernie stormed out of Ruby's trailer, cold and calculated. It was the switch she could turn on and off. The breaker box inside her that separated her from those who want to be her. Even though she was rocked inside by the image of Natalie laid out on the floor and the unraveling of all she

216

had built, her switch had been flicked. This is when most people broke, but not my mother, no, this was when she shines. Under pressure, like a diamond, forged in the vice of unspeakable acts.

"Tony!" Bernie shouted in midstride. "Tony!"

Mullet was kneeling down on the pool deck, hunched, with his lips spread out over Stan's. He was still trying to administer CPR to him, even though Stan was as purple and as bloated as an eggplant.

Bernie walked right onto the pool deck and grabbed Mullet by the ear, lifting him to his feet. "Tony! Take Brent through the woods to Moonlight."

Mullet wasn't really there, he was all adrenaline, unable to process. "But Brent's dead."

"Yes, Tony, he is. Now you need to pick him up and carry him, down the path to the club." Bernie was doing her best to explain it to him, but he was still glassy-eyed, so she hit him. Sometimes massaging and coddling won't cut it, so she struck him openhanded and hard, right across the face. There was no time for overexplaining, hand holding or negotiating—smartening up is necessary and the crack across his face was just the thing he needed to shatter the glass in his eyes and return the light.

"I was with him last night." Mullet started to realize the ramifications of that. Of his involvement in this dead guy's last night on earth.

"You were?"

"Yeah, I met him at Tito's game. But I swear I didn't do this!"

"I know you didn't." Bernie stopped him. "You saw him at Tito's game and that's all. That's good. That's all you know. You don't say anything else to anyone other than that. I'll protect you, Tony, but you need to do what I say. Pick him up, take him to the club and wait there."

"Okay, I'll take him. I won't tell a soul, Bernie. I promise. But what about Stan?"

"You leave him here." Bernie kept Mullet on track with a nudge. "I will deal with Stan. Now, you need to go."

Mullet scooped his arms under Brent's body, hoisting the dead weight up and staggered out of the pool deck. As the stunned and dutiful maintenance man made his way across the grass, Officer Gilroy appeared, running towards the pool with his radio in his hand.

"Bernie!" He was out of breath, too overweight and out of practice to run anywhere for any distance.

"Are you first?" Bernie questioned him right away.

"Yes. Just like you told me. Two other cruisers are down the road, but I beat them. I'm first. I heard them on the radio. They didn't see me come in, so this is mine. Who called it in?"

"I did."

"What? You put your name on this?"

"Hell no, Charlie. I said I was his wife. That I found him here. Drunk and drowned. That's the story, Charlie. Drunk and drowned."

"Okay. I got it. I can push the timeline. Say I've been here a bit and already done some of the leg work." Officer Gilroy tried to catch his breath, holding onto the hip height fence for support as he walked through the gate.

"If you're going to convince anyone that you've been here for a while, you need to get that goddamn wheezing under control, Charlie."

Gilroy leaned over, putting his hands on his knees. "Don't worry. I got it. But you shouldn't be here when the others arrive."

"What about her?" Bernie pointed to Opal who hadn't budged. "It's her husband."

"Christ. She's the one who was supposed to have called

it in? Get her home then. I'll say I already spoke to her, that she's understandably beside herself and that I'll come by and follow up later."

Bernie moved quickly over to Opal, passing through the building wall of spectators that had arrived to fill their gossip cups full. She took her by the hand, kindly, gently. "Opal, let's get you home."

Opal didn't resist, rather the opposite, she followed the gentle pull of Bernie's hand, leading her away from the inner circle, the chaos, into the space between two of the trailers, a clear path towards her home.

"What the fuck did you do?" Freda ambushed them in the alley between the two single wides.

"Move, Freda." Bernie was not having it—whatever it was.

"Where is it? I know it was you. Where is it?"

"Freda, move or I'll add your body to today's count." Bernie pushed past her, leading Opal away from her frothing partner.

Freda didn't give up. She followed them all the way back to Opal's place. As they reached the door, Bernie opened it for Opal. "Go ahead, I'll be right behind you."

Opal stepped into her trailer and Bernie immediately turned back to Freda. "You listen to me. Really listen. I told you what I thought about your plan, and I thought we had an understanding. I thought we were all in this together. But apparently not. You went behind my back."

"It wasn't yours to take."

"This place will be crawling with police. Two men are dead, Freda!"

"Men? A drunk and a loser. I did you a favor." Freda shook her head.

"So, it was you. I didn't know for sure."

"You never liked him anyway, so you're welcome."

"Jesus, Freda, listen to yourself. A favor. You killed a man in cold blood. My guest. Look at yourself. You shot an unarmed man and you're wound up like a crack head."

"Where is it?" Freda stepped forward.

"It's safe. I had Cliff take it while you were out watching the show in the pool."

"How did you know?"

"Because I knew I couldn't trust you. The moment I saw Brent in that pool and the size of the hole in his forehead, I knew you had something to do with it—that and the icing sugar under your nose this morning was a pretty big neon sign. I just didn't want to believe it."

"You have to give it back. I have a deal with Hellsa. If I don't come through, she'll—"

"It's safe. *We* will deal with it. Once these fires are out. You and I will talk and sort it out. Until then, shut your mouth and stay put. This was your freebie. Cross me again, Freda, and your exit won't be as quick as Brent's." Bernie gave her orders and turned her back on Freda, physically and figuratively, opening the door and entering Opal's trailer.

Stepping up and into the pink-decorated domicile, she almost knocked Opal down. The shell-shocked bride was standing just inside the door, just a step or two into the main room. She was looking towards the back of the trailer, down the wood paneled hall. The thin veneer walkway that just a few hours ago she'd scrambled down on her hands and knees, afraid for her life with Stan swiping at her feet.

"Are you going to be alright?" Bernie asked, knowing full well she was not. "Opal, what we did, needed doing. It was you or him. You or him! Now I need to take care of it, and I need you to stay inside here while I do it. But I can't take care of it until I know you will be alright while I'm gone." There was no response. "Opal?!"

Opal nodded. It was nonverbal, but it was a response. The most Bernie had gotten from her since she held her husband under the water with her foot. It was just a sliver away from the walking coma she was in, but it was all she was going to give, and it had to be enough, because the loose ends flapping in the wind outside were getting more tangled by the second.

"Maybe try and lie down." Bernie wanted to help her, to be with her friend at that moment, but the real help Opal needed was outside of that tin tomb. In the hands of professionals and bottles of sedatives. That would have to wait. Bernie needed to get back to the puppet strings and start pulling them before the crowd realized it was all an illusion. "Opal, I'm going to lock the door behind me. I promise I will be back. But if anyone knocks, do not answer it. You don't have to and no one who matters should be stopping by. You just try and lie down until I return."

There was so much more to say. So much more that Opal needed, but no time. Bernie went over and locked the inside door to the lanai, then took the keys from hook beside the carport door and stepped out. She put one of the keys into the lock and secured the door from the outside, hopefully keeping any unwanted guests out and her friend in. Leaving the carport, Bernie stuck to the curved road, avoiding the inner circle grass, where other police officers had now descended on.

Opal watched her go, through the window beside the door. She watched her friend leave, the one she so desperately wanted to be like, so desperately wanted to please, the only one she trusted—walk away. As Bernie faded out of sight, Opal turned back to the hallway, looking towards the back bedroom. Heeding her friend's advice, she moved down the slender passage towards the door, but got caught along the way—freezing in the middle, at the open entrance to the bathroom. Her head became an echo chamber filled with the sounds of Stan pounding on the door and his relentless yelling. She heard every hurtful word he had spewed over the last forty years. Every rough hand he'd laid on her, she felt. Every forced intimacy and every time she blamed herself, tore through her. The thin door in front of her was pitted with the marks from his knuckles and the bottom was broken with divots from his kicking feet. Opal turned slightly, away from the vandalized door, as if something was calling to her. Pulling her out from the dark memories. As her body stiffly rotated around, she was brought to the crucifix, hanging at eye level on the wall behind her. It was the large hand-painted chalkware one. The one she found at the corner store back in Halifax. The one Stan didn't want her to buy because it was tacky, and he said that "Jesus' nipples were too pink". Opal took the cross in her hand, lifting it from the single nail in the wall and held it in front of her. It was big enough for her to grab the bottom of the cross with two hands, so she did. His nipples were very pink, rosebuds, airbrushed with horrible inaccuracy. His body was off-white and his eyes—they were closed a second ago, but now were opening? Opal blinked. Her breath quickened but the statue's eyes continued to move. Just below the crown of thorns, painted poorly with cherry-red drips of blood, the Messiah opened its eyes until he was staring right at her. Judging her, condemning her, blaming her—

"Ahhhhhh!" Opal screamed, from the depths of her stomach—the place that held the first acts of abuse—she screamed, raising the cross above her head, slamming it into the bathroom door. Swinging it like an axe, chopping at the wood barrier with everything she had, causing the effigy to crumble in her hands with each psychotic blow, until there was nothing but dust left in her bloody grip.

There was no doubt that they had heard the commotion by then. The sirens for sure had woken them and she knew there was going to be questions. All she had was the distance between Opal's and hers to gather her story. To put together something believable. Something that wouldn't unravel and take her family away.

"What's going on out there?" Marcie was already standing outside in the lanai, watching the commotion around the pool, as Bernie approached.

"They found someone in the pool." Bernie played it concerned.

"Someone? Who? Brent didn't come back last night." Marcie started moving to the screen door, but Bernie got in her way.

"It's not him." Bernie put her hand on Marcie's chest. "It's Stan. Opal's husband."

Marcie's worry was instantly superseded by her empathy, "Oh my God. How?"

"Not sure, but people are saying he was pretty drunk last night. Probably fell into the pool."

It was a strong visual and it played out in Marcie's head.

Bernie could see her struggling with it, so she kept talking. "Mullet found him this morning."

"Who?" The strange name pulled Marcie out of the vision.

"Tony. He's the groundskeeper here. We call him Mullet, because of—"

"His hair?"

"Yes, that god-awful hairstyle. I'm sure it's popular with the younger crowd, but most here think it's ridiculous. I talked to him just now—actually, he said he saw Brent last night."

"Really?"

"At Tito's game."

"Did he say anything else?"

"No. He's pretty shook up about Stan, but if Brent doesn't turn up here soon, I'll double back and see if I can get any more out of him."

"I'm not waiting. I need to talk to the police."

Bernie raised her hand, stopping Marcie again. "Hey, you need to calm down. You're not talking to the cops. I understand that this business with Stan and the pool is upsetting, but I am sure Brent will turn up."

"Bernie—he's missing."

"You don't know that. He just hasn't come back yet."

Marcie picked up on the spin in Bernie's words. "What do you mean? Do you know where he is?"

These were breadcrumbs. Skillfully placed. The impromptu explanation Bernie had concocted on her way back. "Not exactly."

"Christ, Bernie, what's going on?" Marcie snapped.

This was what Bernie wanted. She needed Marcie to ask, to push her to confess. Liars spill the beans—truth is pulled out. This was how it would all appear true and how she would empower Marcie for what was next.

Bernie sighed as if she had been caught in her lie. "I told him to leave."

"You what?" Marcie was in complete disbelief. "When?"

"Last night. After you had gone to bed, he came home —and he and I had a little chat."

"A chat? What did you do?"

"It didn't take much, Marcie. I was prepared to give him more, but he took the first offer. The first amount I said, he jumped at. I don't want to hurt you, but that's the kind of man he is."

"You offered him money to leave me?'

"No. I paid him to leave. To walk away from you and the kids and he took it. Barely batted an eye."

"But his things are still here?"

"There was enough to replace the ratty old shorts and t-shirts he brought. It was a one-time offer, right there, right then and he took it. Got in the cab and headed for the airport."

"How could you?"

"How could he? I told you he was no good and it didn't take much. Gary would never have done that. There was no amount of money in the world that would have taken him away from you."

Marcie sat down at the wicker table, overwhelmed by it all. Her head swimming in a pool of emotions. "How much?"

"I beg your pardon?" Bernie wasn't expecting much out of her yet.

"How much was I worth to him?" Marcie's face changed from disbelief to anger.

It was earlier than she expected, but this was where her trail was supposed to lead. "Fifty thousand," Bernie said plainly.

"Fifty thousand. That's what I'm worth?" Her worry evaporated in the disgust of this false betrayal.

"I was prepared to go to two hundred—"

"Thousand?" The number stunned Marcie. "You have two hundred thousand dollars?"

"Yes, well, that's all I have here. The rest is—"

225

Marcie raised her hand. "My God, Bernie. I knew you were—you told me that you—"

"It's all yours and there is much more where that came from. Marcie, he was no good for you or the kids. All I did was speed up the clock. That bum would have run eventually and who knows what damage he would have done by then. I've seen him with Greg. I couldn't allow that to go on. Now you and the kids can stay here."

Marcie was swirling. She went to bed last night finding out that her mother-in-law was indeed the urban legend she had heard about and woke up to find out her man had taken off. Left her and the kids to fend for themselves. She had nothing. The house was in his name, all she had was the beat-up Ford Taurus and the shekels in her bank account. "What am I supposed to do in Florida? I don't have a job."

"You don't need a job." The corner of Bernie's mouth curled up. "You are my family. You don't need a job when you have a business—we have a family business."

"What am I going to tell the kids?"

"Doesn't matter. I bet they stop using his name by the end of the day," Bernie said, just as Gemma called from the back bedroom.

"Mom?" the little raspy voice cut into Bernie's speech.

"Marcie, this is a good thing. You are free of the dead weight now. Get the kids going. Say whatever you want to them. He's nothing but a blip in their memory. What we do now, here, will be what they remember."

"Mom!" Gemma called again, sparking Marcie to go back into the trailer, worried but putting on her 'mother's mask'. The comedy that masks all tragedies, that only a mother can wear. The one all mothers don to cover the stress that's bubbling behind it, to pull rainbows from rainstorms, to quiet monsters under the bed, all while the real ones play out in their heads. It makes simple casseroles delicious and not just the scrapings of having no food in the fridge. It makes small presents into big Christmases and absent 'child support skipping fathers' into busy weekend heroes. It is the thankless shield that protects more than any cape or army ever could.

With Marcie inside and the trailer that was quickly filling up with the joyful sounds of tiny voices, Bernie opened her cellphone and dialed. Looking out towards the yellow tape strung around the fence of the pool, her eyes changed from hopeful grandmother to 'matter of fact' as someone on the other end stopped the ringing. Bernie gave the silence a second, then ask coldly, "Where are you?"

The orange and red were mixing together with the blue, blurring the line of the horizon as Daz held his cellphone to his ear.

"I'm at the beach," he said into it. "Why?"

Daz listened, there was only a second between his question and the raising of his gun. The one he had jammed into the lap of Buck as they left the park, now had its barrel pointed forward, towards the rising orb—with Buck's head in between. The bound and gagged kid was kneeling in front of Daz on the sand, his pants were soiled, his shirt covered in sweat and his gag soaked with drool. He was weary, dirty and clearly had been on his knees for a while. That is where Daz put him when they arrived at the far end of the beach and parked behind the large dune. He tied him up and took him to the water's edge at gunpoint, to scare the kid. To send a message to him that could not be forgotten. He sat there and watched him squirm until the sun came up—until his phone just rang.

Along with the barrel of the gun that was pointing at him, Buck could see Daz's face. Had been looking at it all night, but now it had changed. Buck started to shake his head violently, side to side, pleading with the only language he had, movement. He didn't know what was being said on the phone, but whatever it was, it had caused Daz's eyes to change. From anger to sadness.

Daz pulled the phone from his ear and the sun caught the tear that had formed in the corner of his eye.

Bang.

His finger pulled the trigger and Buck was sent backwards, falling onto his heels, crumpled under the force of the bullet colliding with his skull.

Daz tucked the gun into his belt, with the soul of the lost boy somewhere between there and above, he was alone and able to release his pain-filled sobs. His lips quivered, his nostrils flared, and his eyes gushed as he grabbed Buck by the feet and dragged him back to the van. The tears were not for the boy, not for the decision he had made to pull the trigger and take away any chance Buck might have had to do better. They were far too great for someone that he had so much contempt for, so little respect for and they were unstoppable. Even as he loaded the boy into the van, turned it on, put it in drive and watched it roll down the beach, into the water, his ducts continued to spill rivers. They weren't for fear of being caught. The drop was steep at this end of the beach, a sand shelf just under the waves that led to the inlet. It was a car-swallowing envelope, dug out to accommodate boat hulls entering the manmade harbor and it sucked the vehicle down into it, to where it would eventually be found, but the tears were not for his own safety. He knew that by then, the salt water would have left no evidence that could be traced back to him. No fingerprints or fibers. This was about something else.

As the van bubbled and slipped under the waves, Daz turned around and began to run away from the water. Away from the dunes and the drowning corpse of the boy he warned to stay away. His biker boots slipped on the sand, twisting his ankles as he fought to escape what he could not escape and run towards the answers he could never find. That was where the tears were coming from and where he was trying to get to. An illusion that had shattered his heart into dust.

Bernie could see the gurney from her lanai being pulled through the thick grass towards the Activity Center as well as the cops taking statements from the residents that were gathered around to gawk. She knew it was all hot air, that the blue-hairs bugging the men in blue didn't know anything. They were just a bonus, a great distraction to the police talking to them, boring them with their useless facts and nosey questions. Noise that would confuse the situation and make the investigators all the more eager to move on.

Officer Gilroy was standing over to the side, talking to a female officer. By now there was less panic in the air, more casual conversations happening between law enforcement. Everything in the chaotic inner circle seemed to be starting to calm down. Having the body taken away, sent to the coroner that Freda's doctor's contact had arranged, made the scene stale. There was still a police officer taking pictures of the pool deck, but with no forensics team arriving, the yellow tape was coming down and the lurking seniors started to disperse.

Officer Gilroy finished up with the female officer and started to walk towards the back of Opal's trailer. He shot a look over to Bernie as he got closer, and Bernie called into the lanai door. "Marcie! I'm going over to check on Opal. I'll be right back."

The portly police officer met Bernie on the other side of Opal's trailer, around the front, out of the view of the straggling police that were still at the pool and the two conspirators went inside.

"Opal?" Bernie called out after unlocking the door, because she could see no sign of the pink lady in the main room or kitchen.

Officer Gilroy took notice of the rubble from the chalk cross spread out on the ground outside of the bathroom and brought it to Bernie's attention. Unsure of the cause of the tchotchke's destruction or what they might find, the two of them made their way down the thin hall. As they reached the pummeled open door of the rosy latrine, they found the source of their worry. Opal was standing at the sink, staring at her reflection in the mirrored backsplash. She was gently tilting her head, like a clown studying their expression, preparing for the crowd.

"There you are," Bernie said, her relief carried on the back of her breath. "I'm back, just like I promised. Everything at the pool has been taken care of. You remember Charlie? Officer Gilroy? Nothing to worry about. He's with us."

"The coroner will stick to the story, and this will all be nothing but paperwork by dinner," the cop assured her.

Opal turned her head and looked right at him. "I killed Stan," she said, matter of fact.

"Oh, Mrs. Murdy, you don't have to say anything. I know what——" Officer Gilroy stopped her confession. Trying to save her from the pain of admission and him the burden of the confession.

"He was a good man, when we were young, but the man in that pool was not my Stan. That man was mean

230

and violent and hurt me—so I hurt him. Right, Bernie? What's it going to be, right? Sink or swim?"

"Mrs. Murdy, the report will say that he drowned. All on his own, because of intoxication. You don't have to confess to me—or anyone. In fact, I strongly suggest that you never repeat this to anyone."

"Oh, my." Opal tilted her head. "That's a lie. I murdered my husband. That is the truth. He would have murdered me, so I beat him to it."

"Excuse us," Officer Gilroy said to Opal, turning to Bernie and pulling her aside, just out of the open doorway and into the hall. "I'm just here as cover, so the other officers think I'm interviewing her. She's spouting like a fountain—screw that, a geyser! You need to watch her."

"She's in shock."

"Shock? She seems pretty lucid to me, and she seems proud of it."

"Charlie, he was beating her. Probably would have killed her if I didn't show up."

"That may be, but the curtain will come crashing down on our little theater here if the wife goes around confessing."

"She won't," Bernie said, putting an end to his worst-case scenarios.

"Your word. But if she does, there will be nothing I can do." Charlie looked at his watch. "Well, this should seem like enough time for me to have written down her alibi. I'm going to head back. The other officers should be wrapped up by now. But I'll stay around the park till they're gone. That's one down, what about the other ones? You said there were three."

"This is the only one you need to know about," Bernie said, turning away from him and going back into the bathroom, where her friend was still locked in the battle that

Bernie had started. The one of guilt and punishment that survivors wage in silence. The one where the blows continue to come long after the attack has stopped. The one Bernie was a veteran of. A battle that began for my mother, when she thought she had ended it—when she took my father's life.

Ruby was sitting outside when the Harley flew into the park. Racing the wrong way around the inner circle and skidding to a stop out front. He knocked his bike over getting off it and just let it lie on the hot pavement as he ran towards what wasn't waiting for him.

"Where is she?" Daz was moving fast, up the square cement pavers heading right for Ruby.

"She's inside."

He almost ripped the lanai screen door off its hinges, racing to get to her.

"Daz. Stop." Ruby didn't stand up, but her voice did, "Stop!"

The long-haired, long-faced biker paused, turning to face Ruby.

"You don't want to see her like this," Ruby said, her voice wavering, tired from the exhaustion of the throat scraping sobs she'd wept over Natalie's body, silently, while the police were just yards away, attending to the body in the pool.

"I have to." Daz tried to settle his panting breath, put his rage aside and reveal his hurt. "I need to see her, Ruby, please."

Ruby let go of her lock on him, looking away, letting him continue on and open the solid inside door to the trailer.

The new air conditioner Ruby had bought was on high. The place felt like a walk-in cooler. Not icy, just cool, the kind of wind that should accompany a ghost. Ruby hadn't moved her since she pulled her out of her bed and laid her down on the main room floor, where she pounded on her chest until her hands went numb. Natalie's eyes were open. Still brown, but hazy. Blue had begun to settle in the white that surrounded the grainy hazel Daz loved to look into. There was a honeycomb of dried foam at the corners of her mouth, the mouth that nibbled at his neck while he drove. The one he looked forward to kissing without consequence. Ruby was right. He shouldn't have seen her like this. His *her* was in the woods still, blowing him a kiss before she turned to leave up the path, not lying on the carpet. She was gone. That goodbye—was *the* good-bye. He was too proud, too worried, too wrong and far too late.

There are no funerals for the unwanted. No last rights for those who make no impression on the living and whose faces fade quicker in minds than the sounds of their voices. Brent had no one around at his time of departure other than Cliff. He had been driven the nine hours down the coast and put onto the fan boat, taken deep into the Everglades where his body fed many alligators and what they wouldn't eat was burned down to coals. He was given to the wildlife, made into dust by flame and returned to the land that he didn't want to come to in the first place. But even before he passed by the teeth of the beast and became smoke in the air, Marcie stopped holding her breath when she thought about him. And she had stopped thinking of him by the time they had dinner that night, even taking the last piece of pizza that was normally reserved for him.

Stan was fast tracked. Pushed through the autopsy process by the paid 'less than professional' acquaintance of Dr. Noth. There was a funeral, but it was only attended by Opal. It took place at the grave's edge, where she buried his clubs with him. The Ping golf clubs he wanted so bad, but never used. No one else was there. She wouldn't even let Bernie come. She wasn't mad at Bernie, she was mortified by her family. Opal's children refused to come to Florida, and it was clear why. They were not bad kids. Spoiled and disrespectful like Bernie had originally thought. They were survivors too. Distancing themselves from the alcoholic as soon as they could, and they carried a lot of anger for Opal. They had worked through therapy for years trying to understand why their father was the way he was and why Opal had chosen him over them? Why in the world had she stayed? Well, two of them had been working through it, the other was in it, following in his father's footsteps. A lost addict, medicating his past with the poison of his oppressor.

No one mourns the villains. The hated and the forgettable—the unwanted, but Natalie could not be forgotten. She was no villain; no hate was harbored for her and if she only knew how dearly she was wanted. She was the rose in the rotting bouquet of that dreadful day. The only petal in that park. The delicate flower that no one knew how to hold or how much water she really needed. Strength is often misconstrued. It can be misinterpreted as self-sufficient and leave the strongest people aching silently for attention. Longing to be held or guided. Struggling with no knowledge of how to ask for help. Natalie wasn't processed at the local morgue; they didn't want the paper trail or the laws on burial to restrict where she was meant to rest. She wasn't processed at all.

The entire crew gathered in the woods near Moonlight. About a hundred yards from the club, in a small opening that Daz had cleared himself, by hand. He'd walked straight out to into the woods upon leaving Ruby's place and stopped at this spot. He'd spent the past three days doing it all. Trees, shrubs, rocks and even the grave itself. He sweated out the tears only stopping for water or a brief nap when it got too dark. It was his way of working through it, of showing her he cared, even though he didn't know if she could see it. There was a small rock pile placed at the head of the grave like a tombstone, he'd placed a ring of tree stumps around the rectangular hole where people could go to sit and spend time with her and the whole thing was protected under a wood beam shelter. He had constructed an open sided cabin of sorts, a tall A-frame building, a design he found in her notebook. It was to stand over her and to honor her desire to make her drawings a reality. It was to honor the flower that never got to bloom.

Opal, Bernie, Freda, Ruby, Nola, Darcy, Cathy, Daz, Cliff, Kurt, Mullet and Daryl were all there. Standing under the peaked roof, around the hole in the ground that cradled the ivory casket. There was not a dry eye or clear conscience in the forest, just guilt, weight and regret. Young souls pull at the old ones that survive them. They are the *why*, when death comes. But this *why* wasn't such a stranger, because no one in attendance was a stranger to vice. They all understood the calling that pulled this sweet girl back to the darkness, because they all can hear the sirens' call. It's a call of immense power that gathers people in shame. A shame she answered. A shame they couldn't stop her from—it's a shame that this happens too often, too easily, to everyone.

They said no eulogy, no words of love, or expressions of their regret, just flowers laid and a spot in eternity a few yards from where her brother's memory lived on in painted strokes.

Kurt and Cliff stayed back to cover the casket with soil as the rest left the spot and headed for the club. It had been three days, but the dust had not yet settled, and neither had the truth. Bernie had stayed quiet for as long as she could and pulled Freda aside as the rest walked into the club.

Once Daryl had passed them, Bernie laid into her, "We need to talk."

Freda looked around. "Now?"

"Yes now. Those souls have been put to rest, but yours hasn't. You went over my head, Freda."

"You wouldn't listen to me." Freda didn't back down.

"Because I knew something like that would happen."

"Something like that? He was drunk and snuck up on me with a trunk full of dope. You knew that was going to happen? Alright, Nostradamus, what number am I thinking of?"

"You think this is a time for jokes?"

"No, I think it's time for you to give me back the product so I can move it. I've already missed the first weekend of the MTV concerts, if I miss the one coming up—just give it back so I can take care of business."

Bernie placated her, "Tell me, what's your next move? You going to get us all killed?"

"The next move is to move the product like I said. It's a huge opportunity, Hellsa could see it, why can't you?"

"I'm not Hellsa, so tell me. How? How are you—a 60-year-old woman—going to move millions in powder and weed at a venue that's swarming with security and law enforcement?"

"Daz said he had a contact with the show. A guy who works backstage. He's going to act like our waitress. We will be the kitchen. He will take the orders, we'll fill them, then he will deliver it. Once the product is in the hands of our future buyers, we will make the rounds. Introducing ourselves, like the chef at a Five Star. Making our famous and very well-connected new clients, our biggest fans."

"That's what you sold to Hellsa?"

"More or less." Freda lit a cigarette, nervous about Bernie's lack of enthusiasm.

"Give it back." Bernie had heard enough.

"We can't give it back, Bernie. You know that's not how this works. But once we pull this off, we will have our own, high profile, distribution network."

"It won't work. Freda, you were a secretary, not a drug lord, you have no idea how this works, but I do. We have a good thing going. Low profile. Our runs are tight, the money is good—"

"Good—yes, it's good. But Bernie, you brought me in saying you wanted to do something big. We are on the backside of the mountain. Our climb happened years ago and now we are on a one-way slide down to the bottom and it is coming up fast."

"We are on the down slope, but we aren't dead. You're taking it back to Hellsa. You are going to explain that you got in over your head and you're going to give it back."

"Why won't you try?"

"Because she set you up! Can't you see it? She gave you all that dope knowing you would fail, or worse get arrested."

Freda was hit by a wave of doubt. The signs she had been so blind to because of her need to prove Bernie wrong. "I can't give it back to Hellsa—because I didn't get it from Hellsa."

Bernie paused, taking in the new information, processing it through her lifetime of dealing with the shady side of humanity. "You said you talked to Hellsa, that she agreed with your plan."

"Believe you me, I did. And she did, but she wouldn't front me."

"Then whose drugs are in that trunk?"

Freda looked scared. "The Russians. Hellsa said she believed in my plan, but that she couldn't help me because of your deal with her, so she put in a call and sent me to the Russians. Bernie, if I don't come through—"

"Jesus, Freda, she didn't just set you up, she put you in the crosshairs and built us all a coffin."

"Why?"

"I don't know. I don't know what games those kinds of people play with people like us, but she's not the only one who knows how to move their chips around."

Freda shook her head. "This isn't Tiddlywinks. It's not some game, like the one you're playing with Marcie?"

"Excuse me?"

"She thinks he's on the lamb, doesn't she? That you gave him some cash and he split town. Left her and the kids here, with dear old Grandma."

"Freda, watch your step."

"You watch yours. What's done is done. You're right, I was a secretary for my husband my whole life, but the slope only goes down, Bernie. I need to fix this. To move that product. I don't want to die a secretary. I want to die a boss. The boss of it all. Don't you?"

Bernie let Freda's words sink in. The truth behind all the insanity. The need for her invisible friend to be seen. It wasn't part of her game. This move Freda had made was adding a whole new handful of players to a board that was already crowded. But Bernie's mind had a great way of sorting through things that crippled others. In fact, the worse things got, the faster her mind worked and, in the silence, staring at Freda, she thought of something. A way to still see her plan through and give Freda what she wanted.

"Freda, if you listen to me, I think there might be a way. But only if you stop going rogue and work with me. If you do, I promise you, that we will not only fix this—when we reach the bottom of the hill, we will go out as the biggest bosses this country has ever known."

The runs were back on their feet the following week. Freda was getting caught up on all the voice messages from eager elderly ladies looking for a day out and Mullet had returned to his diaper route. The drugs were moving again and so was the money. Freda had bought herself some time with Hellsa and the Russians, citing the deaths of the past week as her setback. She was onboard with Bernie, but she had no idea what she was planning or how this was going to pan out.

Still uneasy about leaving Opal alone for too long, Bernie made sure they did their tours together. She knew it was good to get her out of that trailer, back on the road around her peers and she brought Marcie along for the ride too. Marcie couldn't remember that last time she had a moment alone since the kids were born so she jumped at the chance. Great thing about an old folks park is that there is never a shortage of babysitters. Bernie had hand-picked three seniors to do the job, three of them so they could rotate, a few hours at a time, to avoid the inevitable burn out that comes with the rigors of minding three ginger spark plugs.

As the shuttle headed into Miami, Opal fell right back into her routine, playing up to the bus, with her corny jokes and happy-go-lucky attitude. Marcie was enjoying the trip. She had never been to Miami or away from the kids for this long, so it was a dream. After weaving the bus through the usual hot spots, Bernie pulled up to Lulu's, to unload the geriatrics for their food and beverage. Marcie, being polite, let the elderly ladies get off first, then followed behind them.

"I'd like you to stay," Bernie said, as Marcie was going down the steps of the shuttle.

"Oh, aren't you going in for lunch too?" Marcie asked.

"No. I want to show you something," Bernie said, and Marcie smiled, turning around and taking the seat behind her.

With Opal and the guests safely unloaded, Bernie closed the folding door of the shuttle and drove off from the restaurant. The gas station wasn't far from the lunch spot, that was part of the design, as was the way in which they pulled in, left side facing the building.

"You wanted to show me the gas station?" Marcie was a little disappointed and hungry. "I've seen plenty of them, Bernie. I hope this one has a vending machine inside."

Bernie got up out of the driver's seat and opened the door. She led Marcie around the back of the shuttle, to the left side of the vehicle, where three guys who were busy stuffing the secret compartments with dope. The men stopped suddenly.

"It's alright guys, she's with me," Bernie said, and after a moment of sizing Marcie up, they suspiciously returned to their work.

"What are they doing?" Marcie asked, clearly seeing

that this was not a typical gas station and what they were filling the shuttle with, was not gas.

"Our business. This is what I wanted to show you. Those plastic wrapped bricks are——"

"Drugs?" Marcie was a little stunned.

"Yes."

"That is a lot of drugs." Marcie was counting the bales that kept being stuffed inside the shuttle's underbelly.

"It is and it pays us a lot as well."

"Why are you showing me this?" Marcie turned away from the men and started to walk away, back around the other side of the shuttle.

"Because this is all yours."

Marcie stopped. "I don't want it. Bernie, I have three children that depend on me. I can't be arrested or worse?"

"You won't be. I'm showing you this so that you know. So, that there are no secrets. This is how I make my money, the money I am saving for you and the kids."

"How are we supposed to use drug money? What does that even look like?"

"It looks like this. We stay humble, small means and small disbursement. Freda has helped us set up some small cash businesses around New Smyrna that we process our money through. By the time it comes back to us, it is clean. This is our business, but on paper it is a laundry service, a restaurant, a surfboard rental place and a bunch of offshore accounts."

"What about Buffalo? This is a risky gamble. I heard about the FBI."

"Good, then you know they found nothing on me. That's how good I am, Marcie, and you can be better. I don't gamble—I win."

Marcie was stern. "How can you do this after what happened?"

"I am doing this because of what happened. It's all part of the long game."

"I don't understand."

"You will, but I need you onboard. Trust me, nothing will ever happen to you or the kids and they will have the means to make all their dreams come true."

Marcie didn't answer, but the guys did. "All done, Bernie!"

With the shuttle packed and refueled, they got in and made their way back to the restaurant. Bernie let her stew. Gave her time to sort out her thoughts and that's exactly what Marcie did. She knew Bernie was 'big time', just not what she was 'big time' in exactly. She was disgusted by the means—the way Bernie made her money, but something about Bernie's confidence and inclusion of her played with her convictions. It made no sense. Marcie could never work with these people—the ones that moved the drugs that hurt so many others. The bad guys that broke up homes, destroyed lives and left bodies lying on the ground for the evening news. But was Bernie one of them—the bad guys? She wasn't a guy at all, and she had a plan. She was strong and smart and had laid out her intentions in a simple manner. She was so calm in her revealing the workings of something so illegal. She said she had a vision, and it was one that promised so much more than Marcie could ever provide for the kids alone. She was also the one who made Brent leave. In her heart, she had wanted him to go long before, but was trapped. Marcie, like so many other women, was held in hopelessness by the bars of dollars. Dollar bills she didn't have. It was illegal. It was morally wrong, but she never wanted to be a prisoner of finance ever again.

"Count me in," Marcie said from the seat behind Bernie.

Bernie kept her eyes on the road and nodded, cool and calm as usual, but inside she was elated. Now the pieces had fallen into place. Her family was cemented and now they could really start to make moves. Build the legacy she wanted and see her plan to fruition—but that plan did not include what was waiting for them outside the restaurant.

Bernie pulled up to the curb in front of Lulu's, where a wobbling Opal was waiting with the tour group. She wasn't standing on her own, she was using the maître d' as a walker.

Bernie opened the folding door and got out. "Opal, you're drunk?"

Opal traded supports, flopping from the unimpressed greeter into Bernie's arms. Marcie was quick to help, grabbing a piece of Opal and helping her into the shuttle.

"You don't drink," Bernie pointed out a very obvious truth.

"Bernadette does," Opal said, slurring and indignant.

"Who?"

"Me," Opal snapped.

Bernie turned to Marcie. "I need you to sit with her till we get home." As Marcie sat down in the seat beside Opal, Bernie addressed the tour group. "My apologies everyone. It seems that our guide enjoyed our Girls' Day Out a little too much."

The women giggled, but no one seemed to be bothered by it. No one but the maître d' who was definitely not seeing the humor in it. To make matters worse, inside the shuttle Opal started leading the tour group in a dirty version of 'Old Macdonald'. Once the last of the guests were onboard, Bernie made her way over to the snooty figurehead and slid a folded wad of cash into his hand.

The maître d' took the money, but he accepted it with

the following remarks. "I think you fossils should find a different place to lunch."

The tours weren't the only thing back on its feet, Moonlight had officially reopened its doors. Bernie had been none the wiser about the impromptu opening as far as Ruby knew and just as well, because Ruby couldn't take much more. She was having trouble handling it all including the club. It's not that Moonlight was struggling, the new girls were working great, so were the gambling tables and the place was packed. It was that Moonlight was also packed with memories. Old memories that were overshadowed by new ones. Dark ones and the secrets attached to them.

Ruby wasn't mingling like she used to, not making the rounds as the Madame of Moonlight, since Natalie she spent most of the night in the back with her girls.

"I have tests on Tuesday," Darcy said, holding in a cough.

"Is it that bad?" Nola asked.

"Bad enough," Darcy said then seeing the women's worry, tried to play it down. "Come on ladies, I've been hauling on the fags for almost fifty years. It was going to catch up with me sooner or later."

"Don't talk like that." Cathy was upset.

"It's a plant meant for ceremonial purposes. To be used once in a while, not sucked on all day, every day. I did it, I knew what I was doing, so whatever they say, I'm ready."

'Don't talk like that!" Cathy couldn't take it. "You're not going to die."

"We're all going to die," Ruby stated.

Cathy bit her tongue. "Oh, Ruby. I'm sorry. I'm just so worried—"

"My word, it's alright. But it's the truth. We do what we do knowingly, and we have to face the consequences of those choices."

"Consequences yes, but do we have to be negative?" Cathy tried to find the light in it.

"She's right," Nola backed her up. "We are all going to go eventually, but there's no need to speed it up or talk about it until it happens." She turned to Darcy, "I think you should skip the tests."

"Skip them? Why?" Darcy scoffed, not liking the bend in logic.

"Because, what's the point? If they do come back as cancer, what the hell are you going to do about it?"

"There's chemo and radiation and other things." Cathy did not like the turn this conversation was taking either.

Nola faced Cathy. "To what end? Darcy is meant to be on the stage, not in some hospital bed." She turned back to Darcy. "Is that what you want? Spend the last—what—five, ten, maybe fifteen years running around to doctors, or do you want to shake those big ol' titties around and have sex with younger men?"

Darcy was laughing so hard she started coughing again. "Sex and shaking!"

"That's my girl!" Nola shouted and even Cathy lightened up.

"Sex and shaking!" Cathy laughed.

Just then, Kurt popped his head in the door, making sure to cover his eyes. "Ms. Ruby?"

"Kurt, we're all dressed, you can look," Ruby responded and just as he lowered his hands from his face, Nola pulled down Darcy's bra, letting her naturals loose.

"Oh, man!" Kurt yelled and the girls erupted.

"Sorry Kurt," Ruby called out to him.

"I'm not." Nola was on fire.

"What did you need?" Ruby asked.

The big, shy bouncer answered with his eyes covered again. "I came back to tell you that you're up next." He barely got the words out before he pulled his huge head out of the crack in doorway and slammed it closed behind him.

Ruby turned to Darcy. "Can you do it? You're already topless."

Darcy laughed. "Whatever you want."

Ruby stood up and went for her long jacket. "I'm just not into it tonight."

Cathy walked over to her. "We understand. Hey, when we said we were going to do this, we promised it was on our own terms. If you don't want to dance tonight, don't. That's why we made this place. Our stage on our own terms."

Ruby found comfort in the support of her friends, but she still needed the solace of silence. The space needed to come to terms with the losses she'd suffered and her involvement in them. But the Belles of Burlesque weren't the only ones on her side. She also had Kurt.

He walked her to the end of the path, refusing to let her walk through the woods alone. Ruby of course protested so they compromised, he'd walk with her for the length of the path but stop at the end, and staying at the edge, where the forest met the park grounds. It wasn't just Ruby's stubbornness—Bernie had told them all to keep the visitors to a minimum since the deaths. She wanted to let things settle down without arousing more suspicion and an almost seven-foot-tall, African American man walking through a flan-cake-white retirement community at night would have caused pandemonium.

As Ruby walked down the double dead-end road and rounded the corner that led to the inner circle lane, she could hear the clicking of trikes. It was late. Too late for geezers to hit the road and cruise around the park. Ruby, Opal and Bernie were the late crew, the last ones to make the rounds in the park, but they hadn't done that in a while. She missed those rides. She missed the comfort of things being somewhat normal. She had moved out of Bernie's trailer to find peace, but her red striped home was anything but, the main room was now a grave. She couldn't sit in there without seeing Natalie's image lying on the carpet. The bedroom wasn't much better. She couldn't fall asleep without hearing the grunts of Stan on top of her. Thinking about what she had done with him and what he had done to Opal.

As she got closer to her trailer, she could see that her mailbox flag was up. Ruby's mailbox was decorated like a rocket and the little red flag on the back had been turned up, telling her that she had mail. She thought it must be a mistake because those things never got used except for party invitations, and there hadn't been a party in the Bone Park for a while. Ruby walked up to the folk-art rocket and opened the tip, lifting the hinged point back on itself. Inside, to her surprise, there was indeed a letter. An invitation sized envelope leaned up against the tubular wall. She pulled it out. It had no name on it, no address either, so she opened it. Inside there was a simple card. The kind you get at the drugstore with little flowers on it and the words, 'thinking of you' across the front in cheesy script. Ruby felt warm. She wondered which one of her girls had done it. Who had snuck up the path and put this in her box to brighten her day. She paused, filled with warmth and gratitude for her clan. Darcy, Nola, Cathy? Maybe it was Kurt? It could be. He was so adamant about walking her home, maybe the gentle giant wanted to see this smile on her face. It must have been him. What a sweetheart, she thought. He was one of the only men in her life that she didn't know biblically. The only one she hadn't screwed things up with—yet. Ever since she met him, he had always been on her side.

Ruby opened the card, so appreciative for the warm regards on a night when she really needed them, but the regards inside the card were anything but warm. Ruby closed the card fast, looking around for someone, anyone who could have left it. But there was no one. She had been at the club for hours, so it could have been left anytime. She rushed from the road to her trailer and went inside throwing the card down on the counter. In less than a minute, she had opened a beer and started to pace. Her mind was rolling over the faces of the players in the park, the people at the club. This was a pointed card, an attack on her directly. Ruby couldn't focus on any one culprit, so she went back to the card, opening it in the kitchen light, trying to recognize the handwriting. It wasn't Bernie's, that much she knew, but that was all she knew and whoever wrote it, knew too much. They were threatening her. The words were clear, no timeline but a clear threat that threatened to tear the crew apart, even more than their tattered ranks were already. Words that left Ruby with one of two options.

The card asked, "Are you going to tell Opal, or am I?"

7

Care Packages

A fully detached rancher. It even had a pool that the kids were going bonkers over. Marcie couldn't stay in the park forever. Even though Natalie had pushed the boundaries of the park rules, Bernie knew that a retirement community wasn't the best place for rambunctious kids. She had used Ruby's realtor—the 'pervy' purveyor of her red striped trailer and Moonlight, Barry Montrose—to acquire the property using funneled money, so it could be put in Marcie's name. This was the first place Marcie had ever owned. The house she had with Gary—me—was rented and after I died, she couldn't make the payments. But this was hers. All in her name, with nothing left owing but taxes and utilities and the kids were over the moon. Each brass-crowned kid got their own room, it was only a few blocks from the beach and a few minutes away from Bernie. The look on their faces made Marcie's new day job worth it. Just like Bernie said, Marcie was providing for her kids in a way she could only have dreamed of before. And just to make things even better, to put the cherry on this dream sundae, Bernie hired a nanny. A wonderful older woman, a recent widow from the park who was moved into the spare bedroom. Delilah was only 58 and she was 'The Sound of Music' from Ohio, she loved kids and clicked immediately with Marcie. This arrangement provided Marcie with a steady, safe person to leave the kids with once a week when she was on runs and whenever she went out. It made sure she wasn't alone, giving her another adult close by and it gave the kids more love. Bernie was a little jealous at first, but she knew it was for the best. Bernie spent every moment she could with her little ones, every spare second of her waking life, but those spare seconds were sparse—she was, after all, running an empire.

After one of her visits, that were always cut shorter than she wanted, Bernie made her way back from Marcie's house and headed straight for Freda's. She'd called Opal and Ruby on her way so there would be no lag time when she arrived. Freda was chomping at the bit, having kept her trap shut waiting for Bernie's promised plan to unfold, while giving Hellsa and the Russians the run around. It was now long past the MTV weekend, the event that her proposed venture hinged on, and she needed to provide her perturbed suppliers with the earnings from it or they were going to come and collect.

"So?" Freda didn't even wait for Bernie to sit down. "Please tell me this is what I think it is."

"Yes, Freda. That is why I called you all here."

"My word, am I missing something?" Ruby was trying to catch up, as was Opal.

"You are." Bernie sighed and started her speech, "As you both know, a few weeks back our dear friend Freda did something off the cuff."

"Off the cuff?" Ruby scoffed. "She shot a man in the head."

Bernie waved her sister down. "Alright. Enough. It was a startled response to what she thought was a threat."

Freda nodded, pleased by Bernie's recounting of the situation.

"What threat did your son-in-law pose?" Opal asked.

Bernie glared at her. "He was not related to me—at all —and you know that."

"Oh, my." Opal retreated. "I'm sorry."

"But Marcie's boyfriend was a threat. Freda had made a very bad decision and went behind my back and made a deal. A deal that put millions of dollars' worth of dope into her trunk. Millions of dollars of drugs that belong to the Russians. That is what Brent stumbled upon, that was the threat and that is why she did what she did."

Ruby went pale, "The Russians? Freda, have you lost your mind? You don't deal with the Russians. Only Russians deal with Russians and even then, they hold no loyalties."

Bernie interjected again, "Freda didn't know that. She isn't us. She hasn't run in the circles we have."

"How the hell did she end up with them then?" Ruby wanted answers.

"Hellsa sent me," Freda spoke for herself.

"Hellsa?" Ruby turned to Bernie.

"She said she didn't want to deal behind my back, but she liked Freda's plan, so she was helping her by putting in a word with Artyom and his crew. That was weeks ago and now they want to collect."

"Collect? Oh my, well then, just give it back," Opal said with the purest of intentions.

"Opal, it doesn't work that way. Gangs are in the business of selling drugs, not storing them. Once they leave their hands, they are expected to turn into money," Bernie said slowly, like she was teaching Opal basic capitalism.

"I thought we could move them all at the MTV concert, make contacts and expand our business," Freda confessed humbly to Ruby and Opal. This face, this humility, wasn't a look she wore easily.

"So, what now? Are we going to go out and sell them ourselves?" Ruby was livid. "Work the corners and alleys? I'm 55, Opal is 60, we can't be out slinging drugs on the street."

"We aren't going to be slinging drugs." Bernie pulled the reins in. "But I do need all of you to help move it."

Freda perked up a little in anticipation of what she hoped would be the way out of this, the brilliant plan that Bernie had promised.

"Ruby, do you remember those women you met at the hair salon? That day I sold the Lincoln, you made friends with a couple of old birds there." Bernie was nodding, subconsciously egging on Ruby's memory.

Ruby thought for a second, then nodded back, "My word, yes. How the hell do you remember them?"

"I remember everything," Bernie said with a dash of warning to it. "I'm going to need you to get in touch with those ladies—and Opal, when you went to visit that TV show, did you happen to make nice with any of his staff?"

Opal searched her memory, "Well, the only other person that paid me any mind there was a

young woman named Paula."

"Paula, alright," Bernie said with a rewarding tone. "That's good, Opal. I'm going to need you to talk with her."

Freda was trying to see the plan here, but the vision wasn't getting clearer. This wasn't the D-Day invasion she was counting on. It was a couple of questions and weird requests. Freda was beside herself—not just astonished at the lack of vison but crushed by the sheer impotence of it all. "Hang on, that's the plan? That's how we are going to avoid ending up in Artyom's borscht? You're going to get some old ladies from a salon and a TV evangelist's assistant to move our drugs for us?"

Bernie walked over and put her hand on Freda's shoulder. "You got it."

Ruby couldn't remember where they said they lived, she knew it was in a trailer park like theirs, but there were a few in the New Smyrna area and they didn't have the time to go door to door. There was however one way to find the women. A logical gamble when looking for ladies who love gossip, eavesdropping and attention. One place they were likely to go more religiously than church—and that was— the salon.

The hair parlor was buzzing. Hair dryers, clippers, energetic chatter and Harry Belafonte's Greatest Hits coming from the round speakers mounted in the yellowing ceiling tiles, created a unique, estrogen frequency that was repellant to most hetero men. But it wasn't just the testosterone team that was feeling an aversion to the place, it was hard for Ruby to be there too. The last time she was in this salon, she had thought it was all over. That her sister had abandoned her, and she was going to take herself out. A lot had changed since that day, but also, a lot had not. She had more money now than she did then, she had her own house and her own club, but she was still on the edge.

It's still surprising to me, how many beings return to the eternity of all things because of money and how so many souls still in carbon form, think it will solve everything. Even the power that financial tokens can provide is fragile, making the powerful vulnerable to those who wish to take it. No amount of money had ever made Ruby happy, or any spirit living the human experience for that matter. So there Ruby was, in the salon once again, so much richer, but just as broke.

She hadn't exchanged numbers with the women she met that day, sitting between them under the hair dryers in 'rumor row'. In fact, she didn't even know their names. Left and Right is what she had called them in her head. After Bernie arrived and saved the day, she had forgotten all about the two old broads until her sister forced her power of recall—but there they were. Sitting under the warm air domes, in the same seats they were in months ago, soaking up the gossip and living their best, retired lives.

Once she spotted the two birds from the vantage point of the reception desk, Ruby did like she had done the last time she was here. She requested the works and hinted at the compensations she was willing to provide for such a request on such short notice. She asked that the rest of the package, the nails and facial be left to the end and that they started with her cut and color. Started with the process that included the visit to the dryers on 'rumor row'.

With her hair up and wet, Ruby sat down between the two women and began her performance.

"My word! I believe we have met before." Ruby made sure to speak loud enough so that she'd get both of their attention at the same time.

The two women turned in to look at her in unison. "Well, I'll be—it is you!" Left celebrated, reaching across Ruby's lap to tap Right on the thigh. "I told you it was her."

"Ruby. My name is Ruby," she jumped in. "I'm so embarrassed, but I can't remember your names."

"Oh, it's alright darlin', I can't remember what day it is most of the time. I'm Lena and that's Trudy," Left said.

"It is so nice to see you both again," Ruby gushed. "Say, we never did get to have that drink together."

Trudy laughed, "Don't you worry, we've had plenty to make up for it."

"Cicada Hollow, wasn't it?" Lena pulled from her recall.

"My word, your memory is working just fine," Ruby marveled, "and where was it you said you were?"

"Quail's Hollow," Trudy smiled.

"That's right." Ruby raised her hands as if she'd remembered the answer to a thousand-dollar question on Jeopardy.

"Where have you been, Ruby? We haven't seen you in here at all," Trudy continued.

"Oh, I've been busy. Got caught up in a business that my sister started," Ruby opened up.

"A business?" Lena was surprised. "I thought folks came down here when they were done with business."

"Me too. But it's not a normal kind of business." Ruby cast her fishing line. "My sister—I don't know if you remember her, but she was the tall woman that came in when I was here."

"A giant!" Trudy exaggerated. "Of course, we remember. She has to be the tallest senior in the state."

"Well, she's not a giant, but her heart is. She's always trying to find a way to help people. A few days after we were here, she got an idea in her bonnet, and I have been helping her make the business happen ever since."

"What's the business?" Trudy was nibbling at the line.

"She calls it a business but it's more of a charity, a nonprofit that helps our community."

Lena's ears liked the sounds of it now. "Charity is my middle name. Go on."

"It's a service. A way for us retirees down here to send things home without paying the ridiculous fees that the postal service charges. Care packages for their loved ones, sent back home, free of charge. As you both well know, a lot of us are year rounders, down here for all four seasons, but there is another group of us that come and go."

"Snowbirds?" Trudy added, with enthusiasm, joining in the Jeopardy spirit.

"Yes, Snow Birds. That's actually what we are calling it. Our neighbors and friends that are traveling home in the spring are our angels. We organize care packages that the year rounders want to send home, then pair them up with a Snow Bird that will be driving back. The Snow Bird was already making the trip, so there is no cost incurred by them, so there is no charge for the sender."

"What happens when they get there? Do they have to deliver it too?" Trudy was eager to piece it all together.

"Oh no. One of our volunteers on that end picks it up from the Snow Bird and takes it to the sender's family." Ruby buttoned it all up for them.

"Heavens, that sounds like a great service. I bet you are up to your ears with packages," Lena said.

"We are." Ruby rubbed her hands, nervously. "We just need to find more Snow Birds."

Lena took the bait. "We're year rounders from Louisiana, but we can help! We know all sorts of folks from up north and most of them are Snow Birds."

"Really?"

Trudy got excited too, "Absolutely, we've been looking for something to do. And we know everybody, not just in the parks, but in the homes too. Played cards against most of them."

"Well, it's kind of crunch time for us right now. It's April and most of the seasonal people are heading home soon."

"That sounds like a challenge." Lena pushed her hair dryer up, freeing herself from the plastic dome. "I love a challenge. You best get your hair done quick, Ruby, because it sounds to me like the three of us have got a lot of work to do!"

Opal paced around the lot, hovering by the doors with the word 'studio' stenciled on them. This was a revisit for her too and like Ruby, it carried baggage. Opal was nervous, looking over her shoulder constantly, afraid that she might bump into the Reverend, and he would ask her where it was. She had kept her land line unplugged ever since Stan. She had been watching the inner circle road daily, worried that his long white car would come round it and she'd be pelted with guilt and questions—and threats.

She heard a click. The metal door to the studio was opening and she was exposed, out in the open, with nowhere to run if the Reverend came out—but it was Paula. The officious assistant who buzzed like an embroidery machine. She was intense, she was paperwork and clocks and she was not there to mince words.

"Opal Murdy. Good—you're here," Paula said, pulling the bendable microphone attached to her headset away from her mouth as she spoke.

Opal nervously smiled and handed Paula an envelope. "That should catch me up."

Paula squeezed the thick, sealed manila package and there was little to no give in it, "He will be very pleased," she said, then remembered her lines. "Oh, right—Bless you."

Paula went to step back inside but Opal stopped her, putting her hand on Paula's arm. "Don't you have something for me?"

Paula looked down at the wrinkled hand holding onto her, then around the lot. Opal let go of her arm and Paula depressed the large spring clip at the top of the clipboard, sliding out a stack of papers from underneath the lined schedule on top. "Donation Outreach?"

"Yes. I'm going to reach out to as many as I can and try to inspire them to contribute more. Just like me."

Paula didn't look convinced. "That will please him too. But you didn't get this from me." Paula made sure that Opal got the message she was sending with her pointed look.

"Yes, right—of course," Opal agreed.

Paula held up the envelope. "This, and only this, is why you were here, and this is the only thing that will keep him off both of our backs." Paula looked away, grasping the earpiece on her headset. She bent the microphone back down in front of her mouth. "Am I not allowed to use the bathroom? Jesus—sorry. I'm on my way," she said into the roach-sized, foam-covered ball perched at her lips, slamming the studio door shut.

Opal walked back to her champagne-colored Corolla and got in. As soon as she sat down, she pulled out a pen from her purse and started to circle names on the lists Paula gave her. She didn't circle all the names, just the names that had addresses in northern states.

Cliff, Kurt and Mullet had taken over a room at the Motel 6 and Mullet was dressed up like a scientist ready to do an autopsy on ET. He was in a full hazmat suit, goggles and respirator and was quarantined in the bathroom, where he was pouring all of the packages of cocaine into the tub along with containers of baby laxative. They could have cut the cocaine more and with more things, but they had no desire to hurt anyone, just stretch the base product out, while trying to maintain some quality. A death from someone snorting their blow was not the kind of karma or reputation they wanted. While Mullet mixed his dry ingredients together and repackaged the cut mix into ten-gram bags, then placed those bags into empty talcum containers, Kurt and Cliff got to stretching the weed. It was a very simple process, unpackaging the bricks and mixing the marijuana with dried hops clippings, the same buds used in beer making. They then sprayed the mixture of buds and hops with Lysol to make the scent of the cut weed more unison and make it smell more potent. They repackaged the weed in vacuum sealed baggies and put them into boxes with a collection of other packaged spices. Beside the bags of dried basil, sage, oregano and rosemary, the marijuana looked like just another additive for the spaghetti sauce. Once both the cocaine and the marijuana were repackaged, they cleaned up the rented room and sent Mullet back to Cicada Hollow with the cut Russian product stuffed into the underbelly of his diaper truck.

Freda worked the phones, contacting tour guests who were seasonal travelers to Florida and contacting the circled names that Opal had gotten. Lena and Trudy from the salon did not only rise to the challenge, they were superstars. They were able to line up an army of Snow Birds that were more than happy to carry 'care packages' home with them in just a few days, but the community involvement didn't end there. After two, very long days and nights of 'care package' making, Bernie, Opal and Ruby organized a team of do-gooders from Cicada Hollow to join them in the Activity Center. The large multipurpose space that overnight, had been turned into a corrupt Martha Stewart wrapping room. The boxes that the ladies had been preparing were already full and taped shut. Each packed a little differently, with different cardboard and different sizes, but all stuffed with drugs inside them, and all without the knowledge of the do-gooders. With the clock ticking, the workshop wrapped the boxes in colorful paper and ribbon, a springtime Christmas wrap-off of sorts, then carefully labeled the packages with addresses—fake addresses.

After the packages were picked up from the Activity Center, all the transporting Snow Birds had to do was go home, like they would normally, and a nice 'volunteer' would drop by their home and take the 'care package' to its final, desired destination. This was Bernie's department. She still had her contacts back home in Buffalo and those contacts had their contacts all over the northern United States. It was easy money for them. All they had to do, was send a clean-cut member of their organization to pick up the 'care package' from the nice old person and take it to their already established dealers.

The entire lot, millions of dollars' worth of drugs went out in just two days. It was sent driving across the USA, landing in respectable homes from Washington State all the way over to New York. The two million dollars wholesale more than quadrupled by the time it reached the streets and everyone from the dealers to the union contacts and finally the Grand-mafia, were more than pleased. Bernie and the ladies had solved an impossible problem. One that Hellsa had made that way. But it was more than that. Through solving the unsolvable, they had effectively established their own distribution network. Yes, it wasn't a daily pipeline, it ran infrequently, mostly in a mass migration once a year, but the amount that could be moved in that time was unlimited. They had established a clean line from the south to the north. The middlemen were out of the loop and the Good Samaritans who carried the product cluelessly would never be stopped or questioned by authorities. There were too many of them and they didn't stick out. They were supposed to be on those highways, expected to be traveling at that time of year and encouraged to do so. They didn't board planes or cross borders, they just went to and from their 'golden year retreats' in their full-sized, gas-guzzling luxury domestic sedans. Bernie had not just saved Freda from the Russians, she had outsmarted the Norwegian, and the Norwegian had no idea.

Freda put the bags of cash into the trunk of her car. The same one she used to pick up the drugs in the first place with and headed to the drop. It had been over a month since she was given the product and her lenders were very, very anxious to get paid. There would be no meeting, just a dedicated spot to leave the three bags of cash and a panicked wait for her cell phone to ring. That was the worst part of it. It was not the pulling over on the side of road in the middle of the night and humping the heavy bags of cash down into a ditch. It wasn't that she was leaving a small fortune out where anyone could have found it. It was the waiting. It was the ride back to the Hollow, the sitting in the lanai with the rest of the anxious women, waiting for her phone to light up and break the silence.

Freda had barely put out the last one, before she lit the next and Ruby couldn't resist. "My word, Freda, I understand you're worried, we all are, but you need to lay off those."

"Zip it," Freda said, breathing in the stimulant that in truth was only making her worry worse.

Ruby pressed on, "Darcy smokes like you and they think she may have the cancer."

"Lucky her," Freda snarled. "I'd take the big C over this any day. This is worse."

"Bite your tongue." Opal was not in favor of this kind of talk. "Have some faith."

The phone suddenly came to life, like a message from above, buzzing and ringing in Freda's hand. She dropped her smoke on the ground and answered it. "Hello."

Opal rushed over and stepped onto the burning cigarette, that had already made a black, melted hole in the AstroTurf. As the orange heater of the cigarette smoldered into darkness, Freda hung up her phone.

"Well?" Bernie was in no mood for the dramatic pause.

"It wasn't there," Freda said, stunned, staring at her phone.

"Come again?" Bernie's mouth dropped.

"The two million dollars wasn't there," Freda said again.

"But we——" Ruby was confused.

"The two million wasn't there——but the three million was and Artyom is very, very pleased!" Freda shouted as she started to jump up and down.

Bernie stopped grabbing her heart and Opal regained her breath. Ruby got up and jumped around with Freda, pulling Opal in and Bernie took the opportunity to finally to sit down. It was over. The Russians got their money, profits that they and Hellsa believed had come from slinging it around the MTV concerts. The north was happy, and the Grand-mafia had made five million dollars in two weeks. The old cheerleaders stopped jumping eventually. It was almost morning and they were, after all, no spring chickens. With this problem finally put to bed, the ladies were ready to follow suit. Opal and Ruby shared hugs, then left the lanai, leaving Bernie and Freda to say goodnight.

"I told you," Bernie said, walking for the door.

"He said they want to do more business with me."

Bernie didn't even look back. "Over your dead body."

June arrived and so did the heat once again. The sun and oppression had first knocked Freda for a loop, but this summer she was ready for it. Her and the crew had gotten back into a routine. On Ruby's request they had been meeting for trike rides twice a week and just as frequently they were doing early morning laps of the pool.

Freda, of course, did the exercise with a smoke between her lips. Backstroke and breaststroke with a side of nicotine. Bernie was a front crawl girl while Ruby and Opal were more stationary. Treading water and talking trash. Opal was reluctant to come at first—terrified even, but Ruby pushed her, called it 'exposure therapy'. The first day it was just standing outside the fence. The next time it was sitting on a lounge. Even though the images of that night haunted her, she faced them with the support of her friends until she finally slipped into the pool.

The tours were steady again, the diapers were going

about their route undisturbed and Hellsa hadn't brought up the Russians at all. Not to Freda or Bernie. It was Bernie's thought that Hellsa would try to play one off of the other, that now with the money repaid and her sabotage thwarted, it would be the next logical move. But she made no mention of it. Bernie had kept meeting with her regularly, on her yacht at the Smyrna Club and every time it was just business as usual.

"What did she say this time?" Ruby asked, kicking her legs like eggbeaters in the corner of the deep end.

"She said that we were destined for greatness. That she thinks we could take over the Russians."

"Artyom?" Freda said in a puff of smoke.

"No, she didn't use his name. We don't know him, remember?"

"That's a bold statement from her," Ruby said, huffing a little, her heart rate increasing with her attempt to stay above the water.

"She means it. But I don't see how. She handled the Cubans, but the Cubans aren't the Russians and she doesn't have the manpower."

"Shhht," Opal hushed Bernie, looking past her to Maryanne who was a few feet away from the gate.

Bernie stopped her recap and turned to Maryanne, Cecilia and their tag-alongs. "Morning."

Maryanne raised a light wave but no words, keeping her eyes on Opal and Freda. Freda took a purposeful drag of her cigarette, blowing a series of rings into the air to accent her presence, while Opal just stared her down.

"Good morning," Cecilia said, which got an immediate disapproving look from Maryanne.

It had been tough for Cecilia, because she had been walking the line. Living between two worlds that Maryanne was unaware of. Ever since she attended

Christmas at Moonlight with her husband Fred, she and the girls had been good. They had actually been better than good, they were friendly, outside of the presence of Maryanne of course. Fred and Cecilia had gone back to the club many, many times since the Yuletide celebration. It had actually become a Saturday night thing for the two of them and she had kept it secret. Everyone from the park who had visited the club, kept it quiet. It had divided the Hollow into those who knew and those who didn't. Those who knew, saw absolutely nothing wrong with it, in fact, it reminded them of their pasts. It was a dose of freedom and fancy in their golden years. Moonlight felt like a speakeasy, a trip down memory lane, buried in the woods. The blues and jazz bands that they were bringing in to play between the main stage acts, were just the ticket for minds that spent a lot of time in the past—and so were the women. The strippers, young and old were respected and admired by the select park residents that attended the watering hole. Most of the female guests loved the dance numbers of Ruby and her girls and they supported the green ones, cheering on the young 'up and comers' as they honed their skills. They saw it as a celebration of themselves. A comradery of similar anatomy and a step forward in the fight for equality. The dancers on the poles and the stage held the forgotten wishes of the seniors' former selves. The entertainers had the courage to bare it all and had the female park guests wondering what their lives might have been like, if they had mustered the courage, to swim against the current and dared to rebel.

It was like that for most of them, but for Cecilia, there was a little more to it. Fred loved the blackjack tables and the heavy pour on the spirits, and she loved the dancers. Really loved them. Like most of the other older guests it was reminder of the past, but her past was difficult to remember. It was something she had hid for the last fifty years but inside the arched metal walls of Moonlight, she could live it. She could watch the women move on the stage without having to turn away. She could look at every part of their naked bodies and not feel ashamed. Fred had always wondered, he never said anything, but he'd wondered. They did have children together and a sex life —twice a month, every month and they got along so well —but he wondered. They were the best of friends, but that's why he wondered, best friends know things. They are extremely aware of who we really are. Fred didn't mind that she watched the stage and the dancers on the poles between the tables. He loved how excited she was to go each week and how happy she was when she came home. True friends want us to be happy. This freedom to embrace her true self, was the whole reason she kept Moonlight from Maryanne. Cecilia had followed her around like a lost puppy for years, ever since they came to the park, lusting after the nasty woman. It's the only reason she put up with Maryanne's antics, her constant gossiping, tear-conjuring bullying and damaging lies. She turned a blind eye, because her eyes were full of wanting, but there was a new secret Cecilia had. A secret that hinged on Maryanne and nothing was worth exposing it.

Over the past month or so, Cecilia had been going to Moonlight more than just on Saturday nights with Fred. She had started lying to him, saying she was going to Maryanne's for crib night on Fridays and lying to Maryanne, saying she couldn't make crib because she was going out with Fred. Two lies that were all to support one truth—Darcy. Cecilia was taken by her the first time she saw her take the stage. She was alluring. Her tantalizing feather waving and the roundness of her supple skin called Cecilia from the depths of the woods day and night. It only got worse when she finally worked up the nerve to talk to Darcy, over by the bar, when she was getting a drink, that she didn't need. Her voice sent shivers down Cecilia's spine. Darcy was a pro. She had been around the block and back again. She knew that look. The one that Cecilia was giving her, and she had a pretty good guess as to why the woman was so restrained.

When Darcy first felt it, it scared her to death too. Back then, women were sent to asylums or jail for what she was thinking about the other girls swimming in the lake. She became promiscuous, trying to screw the gay out of herself, but it did no good. She liked the men as well. Both shorts and skirts did things to her heart and there was no changing that. She had the choice. A choice that wasn't offered in her neck of the woods, so she took it on the road. On the stage circuit, there were plenty like her. Women who loved women and she dove right in. She was blessed with the community of liberals who loved to express their sexuality, but Cecilia was not so lucky. Her suburban, Christian town was not so progressive. Her thoughts and wants were a sin and criminal, and Darcy could see it.

It started with squeeze of the hand. The next time that she came in with Fred, Darcy headed right over to her and said hello. She reintroduced herself and as she took Cecilia's hand to shake it, she gave it a thumping squeeze. Like a heartbeat and looked deep into her eyes. Later that night she slipped Cecilia a note, inviting her back, but without her man and the paper was marked with a lipstick kiss.

Lovers. That is what they were now. Intertwining in the back of the club, Friday nights and yearning for it every day in between. Only her and Darcy knew. Ruby had no idea. Not because she was afraid, but because Darcy respected Cecilia's comfort and wishes. The closet is a safe storage of self and only the owner should have the key to its door.

Having their morning swim session disturbed by the sour puss of Maryanne, the ladies gathered their gear up and headed for their respective dwellings. Both Opal and Ruby were adjusting. The pool was a big step for Opal, and Ruby pushed herself to spend a little more time at the club. Baby steps. Sure, their trailers still were filled with ghosts, but their boos were getting quieter. That is how the heart heals. In whispers. In the subtle dulling of pain soothed in the adjustment to absence.

It wasn't in the mailbox this time—it was wedged into the seam of her screen door. The metal lip between mesh and aluminum, just perfect for someone to stick a letter into and make sure you saw it. Ruby hadn't forgotten about the last letter, she had just heard no more of it. She struggled with telling Opal, but kept coming back to the same spot— what good would it do? It changed nothing and had nothing to do with what had happened that night. It would only hurt Opal and destroy their trust. She was their surrogate little sister after all. She didn't need to hurt her any more than she was hurting—like she had hurt Natalie. Ruby had started to believe that the first letter was just an idle threat. It had to be. It demanded action that she didn't deliver and there was no consequence. Opal hadn't been acting any different since it came, so there was no way she knew about it. Opal was an open book and if she had caught wind of it, in any way, they all would know about it. Whoever left it for her, clearly just wanted to stir up shit. Maryanne. Ruby had thought it was her. Who else loved to stir the pot and was already up? Ruby had just endured her snotty presence at the pool. She could have easily swung by and left the letter on her way to the pool. That is, assuming it was another threatening letter.

Ruby pulled the note from the seam in the door and went inside. She opened the outer envelope and slid the card out. It was the same card as the first one. Simple drugstore card, with flowers on it and the words 'thinking of you' at the top. Ruby opened it and while the outside was the same, the inside was slightly different. It contained more threats. 'If you don't tell Opal, I will and maybe the police should know about your club in the woods.'

This was a step farther than she expected, the threats were bigger and so were the stakes. So, who was it? Had Maryanne caught wind of the club? It's possible that someone in the park had told her. In fact, it was surprising that she hadn't heard about it yet and it was totally in her wheelhouse to call the fuzz—but she hadn't—yet. So why hadn't she? Maybe Maryanne just got off on thinking that Ruby was worried. Ruby knew she was jealous of her. Harold always stared at her and not the way he stared at Maryanne. His eyes were full of desperate desires and his neck was practically made of rubber whenever she passed. This was so amateur, trying to run her out of Dodge with threatening letters. But there was only one way to put an end to it and it wasn't cowering to the threats.

Ruby set down her bag, put on her sunglasses and headed back out the door. This was where this bullshit was going to end. She marched out into the inner circle and straight towards the pool deck. Bernie and the others had left, but Maryanne and Cecilia were still there.

"Maryanne," Ruby said, walking through the gate, "if you have something to say to me—say it."

Maryanne was startled, sitting up on her lounge and looking over at Ruby. "I beg your pardon?"

"My word, Maryanne—do not play coy with me. I know it was you." Ruby stopped at the foot of Maryanne's chair, blocking the sun, towering over her with her shadow.

Maryanne removed her sunglasses. "Not only do I have nothing to say to you, I want nothing to do with you or your sister or your friends. Trust me when I tell you that," Maryanne stated as if it were part of an agreement she had signed.

Ruby wasn't buying it, but she was clearly not going to get anywhere yelling at the woman on the pool deck. If this blabbermouth was going to talk, it would have to be one on one. Ruby would have to come up with something for bargaining, something to threaten Maryanne with, because right now her hand was not in the cookie jar. At a loss and getting nowhere, Ruby huffed and walked away from the 'stunned sun tanner' and as she did, Maryanne turned to Cecilia and remarked, "You know syphilis makes people go insane."

Bernie made her rounds after washing off the sunscreen and changing into a loose yellow kaftan. She swung by Daryl's lot to make her payments and check in with him, then circled back to stop in at Marcie's. Gemma and Greg were already at school, which just left little Gwen at home. Delilah was out at the grocery store, so it was just the three of them.

"I swear she is half fish," Marcie said watching the 6-year-old splash around in the pool.

"So was Gary," Bernie said, "he would fight tooth and nail to stay in, by the time I would drag him out, he would be one giant prune. A collection of wrinkles from the neck down."

Marcy smiled, "It's so crazy how he's here—but not. That he's in them."

"The good is," Bernie said, then changed the subject quickly. "So, the tour went well?"

Marcie nodded, "Yeah. Not a problem at all. I like it. If it weren't for the brief stop at the gas station, I'd think I was actually a tour guide."

"That's exactly what it should feel like. And how is Nola doing?"

"Good. She is a great driver, just a little spicy in traffic. That woman is no stranger to the bird."

"I like a woman with attitude—thought the two of you would make a good team. Yin and yang, sweet and spicy."

"Yeah, spicy and a little paranoid."

Bernie's ears perked up, "Paranoid?"

Marcie looked off. "It's probably nothing, but yesterday she kept pointing out black cars."

"Why?"

"She thought one was following us."

"Was it?" Bernie did her best to downplay her concern.

"I don't think so. I did see black cars, lots of them, but they all look the same, don't they? I didn't see anyone in particular that stayed behind us for long."

"Well, it's part of her job to keep an eye out."

"I know, just wanted to mention it."

"I'll talk to her, she's supposed to keep watch, not make you panic. Our routes are clean and they're protected. It's not like when we first started."

Marcie smiled, "That's what you do isn't it—make things right? I know I was mad about what you did with Brent at first, but you made things right. This has all worked out so well. The kids love their new school, the job is great, the house is too and Delilah is an absolute joy. It wasn't yours to fix, Bernie, but you made it right."

"So, it was worth it?" Bernie asked, still afraid of the risk she had taken. The lie she had told and was still holding onto.

"Yes—every penny," Marcie said. "By the way, I want to pay you back for it."

This relationship was growing. This bond with Marcie was getting stronger and stronger, as was her connection with the kids. Marcie had taken to the business like Gwen to water and it all was balancing on a lie. A big lie. One that Bernie needed to keep buried.

"Oh, no. Consider it my gift." Bernie shrugged it off, while inside she was dying.

Opal sat at the small, round kitchen table all alone. It had been dinner for one for months now. Her plate was pushed to the side, untouched. The full glass of milk had lost its condensation, having sat out on the table long after she had lost her appetite. The humid late June nights were not friendly to dairy products or the elderly without air-conditioning. Ruby had sprung for central air as soon as she got her place, but Opal hadn't even considered it. She had the money. They all had the money. More than enough to give everyone in the park air a few times over, but she hadn't given herself that comfort. The money wasn't gone. She hadn't sent it all to the Reverend. That gravy train dried up a while back. The only money that silver fox had gotten was in the lump sum she'd passed on to Paula, in exchange for the donation list. Other than that, she hadn't given him a cent. It was piling up. She'd filled all the OJ containers she had and moved on to her closet, which by then had a three-foot-tall ledge of cash in the bottom of it. It was all clean money too, having passed through the shells that

Freda had set up. It was usable, but she wasn't using it. Well, except for the three stacks that were sitting on the table, beside her ruined meal.

She had pen in hand, paper under her palm and a blank look in her eye. It was a case of writer's block. The kind that sits in the white noise of your head waiting for the voice to speak up. There were three pieces of paper on the table. Each one started the same, just with a different name. They were letters to her three children. Letters with opening salutations and nothing else. Opal didn't know what to say. She was searching for the words—how to address why they hadn't come down to Florida. She wasn't upset that they hadn't paid their respects to Stan, she was upset that they hadn't come for her. They hadn't come to see her, to make sure she was alright. None of them had even called to follow up, so that's why there were three stacks of money. It had been the only way to get their attention, so she was going to go with what worked, but this letter wasn't to say hi—or to chastise them for neglecting her.

As she stared at the paper, she realized it wasn't the words she was searching for, it was the courage to write them. The guts she never had, that had led her to be alone at this time in her life. The reason those kids saw her as an accomplice, not as a victim. She was trying to find a way to say she was sorry, so she finally put pen to paper. She wrote on the first piece, then the next and the next. She then folded the paper up and put each one into a separate envelope accompanied by a stack of cash. All three letters, with the same thing written on them. Three words, one way to apologize for the lifetime of torment they endured. One sentence for each of them—I killed him.

Friday nights were Ruby's nights off, which meant getting done up for Darcy. Her preparation was in layers. Her best undergarments, under a modest pant and blouse, with slightly stepped-up makeup. It was the illusion of normality that made it work and gave her the ability to kiss Fred on the cheek and head out the door without suspicion. A little eyeshadow and lipstick weren't alarming with the plain pants and top. It was perfect for cards with Maryanne, but what was underneath was all for Darcy.

The path through the woods was always where the butterflies kicked in. It was the rabbit hole for Cecilia, the leaving of one world for the wonderland on the other side. But in this fairy tale, there were no Mad Hatters, no Red Queens or smoking caterpillars, just a dream that became real, once a week. By the time she got to the doors of the club, she felt like herself—this self that had been in storage was finally able to stretch its legs and it was taking over. Walking into the club alone was like walking into herself and seeing the smile on Darcy's face from across the room was everything. Yes, there was want and lust, but it was more than that. It was being seen. Really seen for who she was and appreciating it without hiding it. The touching and kissing was wonderful, but only part of the sex. The intimacy started with that smile.

Sitting in the back room, the two of them were like teenagers in the backseat of an Edsel. They were hands and lips, panting and looking, squeezing and caressing, and talking. They were rolled up together and words that were unsaid for years were pouring out of Cecilia—the dam had been busted.

"If I said I love you, what would you say?" Cecilia asked, avoiding Darcy's eyes, making swirls on Darcy's naked chest with her index finger.

"I'd say that that's an odd way of saying it?" Darcy answered, reaching for a cigarette.

Cecilia looked up at her. "But what would you say?"

Darcy saw the need in her eyes. "I'd say that love is a very big word and that I don't think it should be thrown around."

Cecilia pulled back from Darcy. "I wouldn't be throwing it—I'd be saying it."

Darcy took a drag of her smoke. "Do you love Fred?"

This was not where Cecilia thought this would go, because none of this ever went there. "Why yes—I do, but that's not what I am saying."

"It is what I'm saying. You have been with him for years. You love him. That takes time and we are still crawling. This is fresh and exciting—"

"But it's not love?" Cecilia sat up, moving away from Darcy and the couch that was still warm from their bodies.

"Butterfly, calm down. We are too old to be going around in circles about this. This is great because it is happening. When we were younger everything was rushed. Don't you remember, school, jobs, sex, love, moving in, getting married..." She tilted her head. "Having children? We were all in a race to nowhere. Now we can stop running. We are too old to be sprinting towards the next step. That's what we are, Butterfly, we have stopped running and are living. I love to kiss you, I love to hold you and talk with you and think of you. That's a lot of love. Let's be here, someone else won that other race."

Cecilia softened. Age and wisdom, when they go hand in hand, is magical, and she was experiencing that spell. What was the rush? What was this need to have this become something else? Here. That beautiful, curvaceous woman with the dimpled face and dimpled thighs was lying naked in front of her, like a Botticelli model—she was here. Here, Cecilia could be herself. Darcy embraced who she was, and that was here. Not somewhere else, something else, here. She could be gay here, so she was.

"I love you," Cecilia said, as she lay back down beside Darcy on the couch and snuggled her head into her. She let go of needing any response from Darcy, because saying it was her truth and that was what mattered.

Bernie had barely poured the hot water into her mug, making the dark Sanka pebbles into a mud puddle, when Freda barged in, already highly caffeinated.

"I got another call," she said, not even looking at Bernie, just wound up and walking in circles on the main room carpet.

"Another one? When?"

"Right now," Freda said, holding up her cellphone as if the caller was inside it.

"What did they say?"

"They didn't say anything—this time it was the man himself, Artyom. He said he won't take no for an answer."

"What did you say?"

Freda raised her hands in the air. "No. I said no. What else was I supposed to say? You said, in no uncertain terms, that we were done doing business with the Russians so, believe you me, that's what I said." Freda lowered her dramatic posture. "He's not going to stop."

"Yes, he will. Every time you tell a man no, his penis shrinks a little. For some men, it makes them violent, right away they see you as a threat, so they act out. For others, they persist, only to have it shrink more, so they insult you, try and ruin your name—and the rest eventually see their little best friend disappearing and decide to cut their losses.

They move on to other targets that won't say no. If Artyom was a part of group one or two, we'd already know it, so that puts him into group three. Once he no longer can see his business between his legs, he'll move on."

"I hope to hell you're right, because he didn't sound like he had a small set on him."

"Try and put him on the back burner, okay? We have another opportunity coming up and we need to start to prepare for it."

"Oh, Christ, what's that?" Freda was not in the mood for more of anything.

"Hey," Bernie said questioning her partner. "You're the one who preached wanting to be a boss remember? We need to keep making moves to do that."

"Right. I did say that—what do you got?"

"In two months our Snow Birds will be returning." Bernie sat down at the kitchen table.

"I don't follow."

"We have an army of free transport heading back from the north, but with no cargo. I have a solution for that."

"Of course you do."

"Listen. Some of my former people, the ones who arranged the pickups of our 'care packages', have got a pipeline in Washington State. High up in the mountains, working with Canadian grow ops in British Columbia and have a safe route over the border. Their stuff is a hundred times better than the crap that the Russians gave you and we could be the exclusive suppliers to the entire south. All we have to do is reverse the 'care package' program. Get our team of Good Samaritans to bring packages back down south with them, from 'families' up north to their 'loved ones'—us—down here. It's a complete cycle and all the parts are already in place."

"Marijuana? Really?"

"This stuff is so high quality, so in demand, that they are willing to trade pound for pound for cocaine."

"So, we'll trade it then?"

Bernie took a sip of her Sanka. "No, we'll sell it."

"What? You said we don't sell drugs. You made that very clear."

"We won't be, but our people will."

"What people?"

"Don't you worry about that part, what we need to do now is reconnect with all the contacts you set up going down and establish how many of them are coming back and how many can carry a package for us."

"That's a lot of phone calls," Freda said, suddenly exhausted by the daunting workload.

"I know, that's why you have two months. Opal can help you. But I need numbers and names by the start of August. That way our northern friends can prepare the 'care packages' and get them out."

"An empire. To and from. All us," Freda stated, with trepidation.

Bernie sighed, "That's how you go out as a boss."

July came in hot and heavy as usual, and the tours were sold out every day. The ladies had their sights set on the Snow Birds' return and were working hard to confirm their unsuspecting drug mules, but the business was not the only thing in full swing. There was a growing subculture within the retirement park communities, one that stretched from parks to homes and everywhere that the elderly were living in south Florida. It was an underworld of necessity, of supply and demand and it came to Ruby's attention via the least likely of suspects.

Cards and cocktails, that was what was promised, and it was what Trudy and Lena had been pestering Ruby with ever since they reconnected. It was the least she could do, and she needed to keep them in her good books with the planning of the Snow Birds' return imminent. Cards were not Ruby's thing, well at least not the way these women played, she was more of a poker player, both strip and clothed, but a poker player. The occasional euchre was okay, but bridge, pinochle and canasta were not on her dance card, so she brought Opal. Trudy and Lena were both widows, so Ruby hoped that they might be good connections for Opal. Friends with former fellas. She said it was time that Opal started socializing, but honestly, she just really needed a wing woman to help her get through the arduous obligation and explain the rules to these complicated parlor games.

The night went as expected, a few boring hands of cribbage accompanied by some frugally spirited cocktails. Ruby wasn't feeling much from the cheap mixers, just a light buzz, enough to make the 'polite' evening manageable. Everything seemed basically benign except that Opal started dabbling in the liquid ghost again. Bernie had told Ruby what had happened in Miami, so Ruby was watching the pink widow like a hawk.

"I understand that you lost your husband not that long ago, Opal?" Trudy said, out of nowhere and completely out of context with the conversation of 'summer frocks' the table was having.

Opal swallowed the sip of margarita she had in her mouth and answered, "Oh, my. Yes. Stan died in March."

"My Henry left three years ago and Trudy's Bob just over a year," Lena added.

"Oh, dear, I'm sorry for your loss." Opal did the normal pleasantries.

As out of the blue as it was, it was what Ruby had hoped might happen. That these women might bond and maybe they could give Opal the kind of support that Ruby couldn't. Yes, Ruby had lost Ben, but it was not a forty-year marriage. She had no idea what it was like for these women, even though Stan was abusive, they had been together almost her whole life and these Quail's Hollow girls were from that world. The world of 'barefoot and pregnant', of 'man of the house' and 'obey your husband'.

"So, have you dipped your toe yet?" Lena asked, as she shuffled the cards in her hand.

"Oh, yes, I go swimming with the ladies a few times a week now," Opal said proud of her commitment to fitness.

Trudy and Lena laughed.

"Oh, darlin'— no. Not dipped into that pool, I meant the other pool," Lena raised her eyebrows, "the pool of the opposite sex?"

Opal looked to Ruby, dumbfounded, then back to their hosts. "Our pool is co-ed, is yours not?"

Trudy reached across the table and grabbed Opal's hand. "Honey, we mean sex. Have you had sex since your man died?"

Opal was instantly sober. Mortified by both the question and the interest of these two women into the affairs of her bedroom.

Lena could see the horror on Opal's face. "It's just what the doctor ordered, darlin'. They're gone but we aren't and there is still a lot of fun left to be had."

Ruby started to laugh, "I agree there is a lot of fun left."

"So, you swing too?" Trudy was delighted by Ruby's enthusiasm.

"Swing?" Ruby's giggle stopped as she clued in. "Swingers? You and Lena are swingers?"

Trudy nodded and smiled, "Yes Ma'am, we're Pineapple Pals. Lena introduced me to it shortly after my Bob passed. Opal, it changed my whole world."

Ruby was surprised and interested in this very unexpected nugget. The night of boring cards had just got less boring. "So there's a swinger community here?"

"Here, there and everywhere," Trudy laughed. "Your park is one of the biggest. That's why we keep playing 'cards' there," she said making the quotations with her fingers around the word 'cards'.

"Fellas in our age group are in high demand, I'm sure you've noticed," Lena lectured. "So, they like to spread themselves around, and why not, I've taken to like a vast variety in my later years too. We always have a good time, and the community is full of good people."

Ruby turned to Opal whose mouth was collecting flies, "So, what do you think, Opal?"

"Think about what?" Opal's brain had gone to static long ago.

"Are you interested in dipping your toe?" Ruby teased.

"Don't listen to her." Lena broke the lighthearted ribbing. "Opal, when my Henry reached 40 it all started to slow down. I stopped making myself available and he eventually stopped asking. Sure, there were the holidays and birthdays, but we didn't roll in the hay like we did when we were courting. And as 'the change' really set in, I thought it was just normal to not want it anymore. By the time he died, I couldn't tell you when the last time we had sex was, but it was long enough that I couldn't remember. I thought it was me. But it wasn't. It was us. We lost the spark. It was still inside me, it had changed, but it was still there, my tinder just needed different flint."

"Stan was a bad man," Opal blurted out.

Trudy sighed, "There are a lot of them. Bob had his

moments too. We didn't have a drought so much as I was not often a willing participant. I thought I hated it all. I think though, now, I just hated him. That man took a lot from me. All of my best years—but when Lena introduced me to this world, I was able to take something back."

Opal looked at her, glaring as if Trudy had just given her the biggest insult. She stared her down, sizing up the retiree with her unmoving eyes. Slowly, the permanent smile that was always on the God-fearing woman's face dropped, until her grin was a flat line. "You know, Trudy, I think I would like to take a dip."

It was a very busy, very hot and humid trailer. There were liver spots and body parts everywhere. Some naked, some half clothed, some in the heat of the act and others just talking, having a drink surrounded by Bacchus indulgence. Ruby felt at home here. She was no stranger to the scene; it had just been a while since she had pollenated the orchard and being surrounded by 'free love' felt good. Ruby was recognized as soon as she stepped into the trailer and was immediately propositioned by two men, two very delighted men.

Ruby leaned over and said into Opal's ear, "These boys want me to go with them, Opal, but I can stay with you if you want."

Opal waved her off, a little loose from the cocktails, but more so, tired of being babysat. Ruby shot a look to Trudy and Lena, and they nodded, knowing what she was asking, assuring that her that Opal was in good hands. Satisfied with the chaperones left to watch over the pink prude, Ruby was led away by her temporary lovers.

With Ruby gone, it was all Opal, and it was all new. No

familiar faces, but all friendly ones. After a few minutes of just being in the trailer, it was not nearly as intimidating as she thought it would be. Yes, there were men on women, women on women, men on men all around her, but they all looked so happy. So full of life and joy. There were moans and groans and screams of ecstasy, but there was also a lot of laughter. Giggles and cheers. It was the opposite of everything she had been feeling.

"You know, my first time, I just looked," Trudy said to her.

"Well, there is a lot to look at," Opal said, her smile returning to her face.

"Enjoy the view, Opal," Lena said not interested in sticking around for the voyeur corner. She then smiled, silently excusing herself and walking over to join a naked couple in the front bedroom.

"That's the Morrisons," Trudy told her. "They are into thirds. They always stick together and love to share."

"Who's he?" Opal said, motioning to a man in the kitchen. He was bald, thin framed, only wearing pajama pants and at that point he had been looking at Opal for a while.

"Oh, honey, that's Peter. He's a spring chicken too. Only started coming here this month. To be honest it's the first time I've seen him without a shirt. He's really giving you the look, isn't he? Don't be afraid, there is no pressure here. He can look all he wants."

"Or—I—could—say—hi," Opal said out of the corner of her mouth, trying to be stealthy, but looking more like she was having a small stroke.

Trudy grinned, "Or you could do that. Well, well, well. Aren't you just the badger at the ant hill. Go on then. Ain't no harm in saying hello. I'll be right here."

Opal took a very, very deep breath.

Trudy's eyes warmed, "It's okay, Opal, you're just dipping your toe."

Opal moved slowly away from Trudy and walked towards the open kitchen. There were only fifteen people in the trailer, but in a small single wide, that feels like a thousand. She kept eye contact with Peter the whole way and with every step she took, her posture and stride changed, going from shuffles and hunched, to hip swinging and chest out. By the time she made it to Peter, her hand was already out waiting for him to greet her.

Peter took her hand and kissed the back of it, awkwardly, trying to fulfill some 'Gone With the Wind' persona. "Good evening," he said, then added to the odd introduction. "You look very fetching tonight."

Opal smiled at him, keeping her eyes locked on his. "Why, thank you."

Peter swallowed, then said in a very shaky, breathy way, "I think you may be the sexiest woman I have ever seen."

Opal suddenly grabbed him by the face, pulled him in and wrapped her lips over his, practically sucking the life force right out of the man. She kissed the startled man very hard, until his surprise turned into reciprocation. Trudy watched the whole impetuous interaction from the main room in absolute awe.

Opal pulled her lips from Peter's and said, "Can we go somewhere a little more private?"

"Yes," he responded. "I would very much like that. The back bedroom's open I think."

"That'll do," Opal said, pulling the bald man behind her and heading towards the hallway.

Trailing behind her, Peter spoke up, "My name's Peter, by the way."

Opal turned back and placed her finger on his lips, quieting the shy man. "I'm Bernadette."

By August 22nd all the radio stations were abuzz with talk of Hurricane Andrew. The storm was making its way to the Bahamas, but its projected trajectory had some in southern Florida worried. It had been dancing between a tropical storm and hurricane status for a week, so while some residents were cutting their losses, Girls' Day Out was still making runs. The seasoned full timers knew that these storms change by the minute. There hadn't been a Category 5 that made landfall since 1969, so a shuttle of brave broads was making the most of it.

The roads were busy leaving Miami and Nola was as spicy as Baton Rouge jambalaya. Marcie was doing her best to cover the swears coming out of Nola's mouth, by speaking frequently and loudly over the shuttle's PA system. The tour and the talk normally ended at the city limits but now, Marcie was giving a play by play of passing road signs and even trying 'eye spy'.

"Marcie!" Nola shouted from the driver's seat, but it wasn't the first time this trip, so Marcie continued with her 'something that is blue' question.

"Marcie!!" Nola shouted again, reaching over with her right hand and tugging on the bottom edge of Marcie's shorts.

Realizing that this was not going to end until she paid her driver some attention, Marcie covered the microphone and leaned over to Nola, "Can you please stop it. Both the swearing and the constant calling of my name? I am running out of things to 'spy' and our guests are running out of patience. This is the time in our little trip when they all normally knock out. A little snooze for them on the way home and we get peace and quiet for a few hours. Can you please return us to peace and quiet?"

Nola glared at her. "Look," she said, pointing to her side mirror.

"At what?" Marcie was not into playing this game.

"Just look." Nola practically pulled her head down so that Marcie was forced to look into the left side mirror.

In the reflection, she could see the traffic behind the shuttle. "There's traffic. I understand it's busy but that's what highways are, alright? If you don't want to drive anymore, if you can't handle the Miami heat, then tell Bernie and you can stop."

"No—look." Nola was not letting this go. "It's the black car."

Looking into the reflection once again, into the mix of heavy traffic, she could see the car. A black car, but it was just one of many.

"Nola, there are plenty of black cars back there. Honestly, I love you, but I think you should take a break after this run."

"Is it the sky?" one of the elderly tour guests shouted from her seat.

"Sky?"

"Something blue!" the visibly tired woman snapped.

"No. It's not the sky, Mrs. Patterson," Marcie answered back trying to keep the game going with them while calming the increasingly agitated Nola. "Just drive. I'm sure it's nothing. Bernie said so. Our routes are safe—they're protected."

Reluctantly, Nola piped down and focused forward, allowing Marcie to return to the game and her tired passengers.

A few hours later, when the games had ended and most of the blue-hairs on board were looking at the inside of their eyelids, Nola whispered, "Look."

Marcie was startled by the whisper. It was interrupting

the hum of the shuttle, the brown noise that was causing her to drift off herself. Looking over to Nola, she found the woman calm, but concerned, motioning to her side mirror again. Marcie got out of her seat, made her way up to the front and looked over Nola to the left mirror this time. There was a black car behind them and, as far as she could remember, it looked a lot like the one that was there hours ago.

"Has it been there the whole time?" she asked.

"Uh, huh," Nola said, with an 'I told you so' look on her face.

"I'll call Bernie," Marcie said, going back to her seat and dialing her cell phone. "Hey. Sorry to trouble you—"

Nola listened intently as Marcie answered the rapid-fire questions coming at her, "No. everything's fine—it's just that there is a car. Yes—the black one. Nola said the whole way back from Miami. Okay. Will do." Marcie hung up and relayed the unheard instructions to Nola. "She says just keep on as usual. We will drop off our guests, then make our way to the depot. If it's still behind us after the drops, then she'll send Cliff out to meet us."

With a little backup now and not feeling alone in her concern, Nola pulled the shuttle off the highway and headed for the various retirement communities to begin the drop-offs.

As the short shuttle bus made its way into the first stop, the parking lot of the Cedar Oaks Retirement Home, the black car kept going, driving down the side road as they pulled in. After dropping off the three guests there, the shuttle pulled back out onto the main roads. Nola kept her eyes on both the road ahead and the road behind, checking every second or two, but there was no sign of the car. It didn't show up again at all in between any of the drop-offs or anywhere along the highway back to the depot on St.

Mary's Street. It was a welcome turn of events for Marcie, but Nola still felt uneasy. She couldn't understand why that car had stayed with them for so long. Staying behind them in the slow lane all the way back from Miami, took the same offramp and even the same road that led to Cedar Oaks. It was possible, both on a coincidental route, but it didn't sit well.

Having dropped off the shuttle at the depot, Marcie gave Nola a ride back to New Smyrna. There was no point in both of them driving to the shuttle pick-up, so they always carpooled. They talked about the strange black car most of the way back, but unlike Nola, Marcie was on the coincidence side of it. She believed that some drivers like to stay behind the same vehicle for the duration of their trip. Strangers buddying up. Matching speed with another car means they don't have to worry about tickets and there is something comforting about seeing the same car in front of you. Marcie had done it many times. On long drives it made her feel like she was safe, imaginary, but safe, like she had a friend on the road. By the time she dropped off Nola, Nola was sick of the whole thing. Ready to not hear another word about 'fairy road friends' and happy she didn't have to drive again for another week.

It was starting to get dark. It was her late night of the week, the one where she left before the sun came up, came home after it had set, and Delilah took care of the house in her absence. Her incredible nanny was in charge of pick-ups, drop-offs, breakfast, lunches and dinner. Usually, Delilah would keep the little ones up for Marcie, so she could tuck them in when she got home and that was what was on her mind. Not black cars or Nola's yelling, not even the pile of money she had made that day. All that mattered was getting in that driveway, as soon as possible, so she could kiss her babies goodnight.

Pulling up to the house, the lights were on inside and that lit up Marcie's insides. There is nothing like arriving home to lights. It's welcoming. It tells you that someone inside is waiting for you, and that is the whole reason we make homes. For the ones waiting. Marcie pulled up into the driveway and turned off the Taurus. She didn't bother locking it, because if it got stolen, then she could justify buying a new one—just like Reg had wished when Bernie borrowed the blue station wagon.

Walking up to the front door, she listened carefully, to hear the giggles and banter of her brood, but it was quiet. Gemma had been on a scaring spree lately, jumping out of cupboards and closets, reveling in her ability to make adults shake in their boots. Unlike the black car on the interstate, this was no coincidence. For sure they saw the lights as the Taurus pulled in. It was like there was a surprise party waiting inside. Marcie could just imagine them all right now—especially Gwen—the youngest. She must have been busting, trying to stay as quiet as she could, it would have been easier for the other two, they were older, but not for her. She could barely sit still to finish her fish sticks. Regardless of their plan, they were all amateurs and Marcie was ready.

She opened the front door as quietly as she could and gently pushed it the rest of the way with her foot. Nothing jumped out at her. This was good, they were either in another room or she had gotten the best of them— opening the door without them knowing. Marcie set her purse down, just inside the door and crept into the foyer. No sign of them there either, so she headed for the master-mind's bedroom. Surely Gemma, the Queen of Scream, would be waiting in there.

Marcie opened the door hard and fast. "Gotcha!"

There was no scream on the other side. No response at

all. Wow, she thought, she had underestimated the control of her daughter. She must have been honing her skills with Delilah, developing her tolerance to hold out for the big scare. She had an accomplice, a scare sensei. Alright then, Gwen's room! They must be in there. Her and Gemma's bedrooms were on this side, but the other three were on the other side of the kitchen. So, Marcie left her eldest's bedroom and moved down the hallway, towards the other side of the rancher—but she didn't make it that far.

The game stopped—her heart stopped—everything stopped.

Lying, spread eagle in the middle of kitchen floor, surrounded by a massive pool of blood, was Delilah.

"KIDS!!!!!" The scream carved out of her heart was heard all the way up to heaven.

8

Full Circle

There is nothing worse than the screams of a mother in search of her creations. The anguish tears a hole in the fabric of human love and Marcie's screams were tearing through her bungalow.

"Gemma! Greg! Gwen!" It was a cry that was set on repeat, bouncing around the walls as she raced from room to room, from front yard to back, until she found herself back where she started—in the kitchen, with her dead nanny lying on the floor. Her caregiver's cadaver only reinforced the desperation of the situation, sending Marcie running to the front foyer. Sprinting to the front entrance, her body vibrating, to find her purse, dig her phone out of it and dial. It only rang once.

"Their gone!" Marcie stuttered.

"Who?" Bernie asked on the other end, matching the panic in Marcie's voice.

Marcie struggled to find the words, "The—kids."

There was a pause, then, "Stay put, lock all the doors, stay inside. I will be right there."

Marcie didn't hang up the cell phone, she just let it fall

from her hands onto the floor as she stumbled back to the kitchen, her body beginning to process what her mind and heart could not. Tears were too far away from the fight response she was trapped in, so she yelled. Yelled and kicked and screamed, putting her feet and fists into the cupboards all around her. The wooden doors of the shelves bashed open and closed under the assault of her rage, so she broke them off their hinges, ripped the wooden rectangles from their hardware, exposing the dishes, food and—

"Gwen?" Marcie stopped—her foot cocked back, ready to take another kick at the bottom cupboard door, the one under the sink. "Honey, it's okay." Her lioness instantly ceased its roar and her mother tongue returned as she crouched down and reached out for her little, 6-year-old daughter. Gwen was wedged in tight under the sink, her little body hiding behind the elbow of the drain. She was shaking, eyes wide, fearful of everything, including her vandalistic mother.

It took a few seconds of Marcie's calming breath and gentle, encouraging nods to coax Gwen from her domestic cave. First taking her mother's hands, then being wrapped up in them.

"It's okay. It's okay, Gwen. Mama's here," Marcie said over and over, stroking the little girl's ginger hair, rushing her out of the kitchen, away from the bloody gore of her caretaker. As she calmed the tiny beating heart of her daughter, pacing around the front living room, bouncing her in her arms as if her baby girl had colic, she calmly asked, "Are Greg and Gemma hiding too?"

A small, contained headshake turned this massive miracle into a shard of hope. She had one of her babies, but not all of them. Two were missing and this one—she must have heard the whole thing. Possibly even witnessed what happened to Delilah.

Headlights shone across the sheer curtains of the front window causing Marcie to back away from the front door, retreating to the edge of the hallway on the right.

Cliff was the first to burst in the door, gun drawn, with Bernie right behind him. Bernie's eyes caught sight of Gwen right away, "Gwen?! She's alright?" Bernie said in midstride, rushing towards Marcie. "Sweep the house," she ordered Cliff, and he went left down the hallway, with his firearm held out in front of him. Bernie turned back to Marcie, "The others?"

Marcie shook her head, "You said they were safe."

"They are. This isn't about them." Bernie moved around, behind Marcie, so she could look into Gwen's face. "Gweny? Did you see the people who were here?" Gwen motioned no. "Could you hear them?"

Gwen nodded, "They sounded different. They were saying words I didn't know." Her little voice spoke up through the squeaks of being silent for so long. "All of their words were weird. They took Gemma and Greg and hurt Delilah."

Cliff emerged from the back of the house shaking his head.

Bernie walked back around to face Marcie. "Artyom. It has to be. His men are all fresh off the boat. Russian sailors who stay on shore when the boats leave. Come on, we're going back to the park. Back to my trailer."

"Why are we going back there?" Marcie was being hustled to the door by Cliff.

"We're going back there so you two can be safe and I can end this," Bernie said, pulling the revolver from the back of her waistband.

It was the convergence of the Round Table, only these weren't Knights, they were Queens, their swords were guns, and the table was made of wicker. Ruby, Opal, Freda and Bernie gathered in Bernie's lanai, while Cliff and Kurt guarded the front and back of the trailer. Considering the circumstances, what was at stake and what had been lost— Bernie was holding it together.

"Where did you pick it up from?" Bernie asked Freda.

"The butcher shop, on the outskirts of Cocoa Beach," Freda said.

"Alright, you're taking Ruby and I there."

"What about me?" Opal said, less sounding like she was wanting orders and more like she was missing out.

"I need you to stay here with Marcie and Gwen. Kurt will keep watch outside, but she needs a woman around. Only another mother knows what she's going through," Bernie instructed, and Opal felt needed.

"Just the three of us and Cliff?" Freda halted the momentum. "There were a handful of guys there when I went and Artyom is a beast."

"So am I," Bernie said. "Grab all your ammo, put comfortable shoes on, and meet at my place in an hour."

"What's the plan?" Ruby was a little hesitant as well.

"I'll know it when I see it." Bernie was already halfway out the screen door when she filled the lanai with even more uncertainty.

Ruby chased after her, catching up to Bernie's long stride a ways down the road. "Bernie, I know what we've always said about cops, but this is our family. It's time we called them. They have Greg and Gemma. Kids! This has gone way too far."

Bernie dead eyed her, "Too far? This is when you think it's gone too far? Not with Ben or Natalie or the Club or Stan or Brent—this? This is not too far, it's on par. It is definitely not what I expected, but it's in the ballpark. We handle it because that's what we do. That's how this side of things run. If we get the police involved, those local chuckle heads in their pressed uniforms will screw this up and my kids won't make it out alive. This hasn't gone too far, Artyom has gone too far! And he is going to pay for it —but not the cops—he's going to pay me."

Bernie walked right up to Cliff who was standing on the front lawn. "Get one of the shuttles and come back here. ASAP." Cliff walked straight to the car in the driveway without a second thought and Bernie kept on moving into the lanai. "Kurt!" she called out to the huge bouncer standing at the back corner of the trailer. "You're on full perimeter now."

Opening the door to the trailer, Marcie raised a finger to her lips. She was sitting on the sofa, beside Gwen who was curled up like a cat underneath the handmade Afghan blanket.

Bernie's energy immediately changed, "She's sleeping?"

Marcie whispered, "Yes. Just went out." She carefully got up and moved over to Bernie. "So what now?"

"You're both safe. You're going to stay put, while we go get the others back."

"Oh, no. I'm coming." Marcie was full of revenge.

"No. You can't. Listen, that little girl needs you. When her eyes open the only thing she should see is her mother. She has seen enough and heard enough and that's over. She needs you here. I am going to get our family. Gemma and Greg are tough kids. This isn't something they're going to forget, but they can handle it."

"Can they? A Russian gang killed their nanny and took them hostage. Is that something kids can handle?"

"Yes. They can. Gary was beaten every day by Sal.

Every time he looked at him, he got his fists. He handled it and so did I."

"He's dead," Marcie glared at her.

"That wasn't his fault."

"I don't want my children to have to handle anything."

"I don't either, but it's happened and now our job is to control the amount they have to handle. I am going to get our babies back and when I'm done, we will never have to handle anything ever again."

The parking lot was filling up just as the shuttle pulled into it. It was a strip mall on the edge of Cocoa Beach, one that was built to make a full square around the parking lot. There were plenty of stores in it, stores that were already open and doing business. The butcher shop was one of those stores. There were all sorts of patrons, coming and going from the small, Russian deli. It didn't look anything like the gang headquarters Bernie had imagined in her mind. Cliff, Bernie, Ruby and Freda sat and watched the store front from the shuttle for a while, looking for any signs of the kids, but there were none. The only people they saw were shoppers—and Artyom.

"That's him," Freda said, pointing to the man in a bloody butcher's apron who'd come out the front entrance of the shop to light a smoke. He was a beast. Pale, bald, with hairy arms that were as thick as most men's thighs. His gold chains were cliché, as was the way he held his cigarette, pinched between his thumb and index finger with his massive palm facing up underneath it.

"Ruby, go and buy some things from the other stores," Bernie said.

"Things? What things?" Ruby was looking for a little more instruction than that.

"Doesn't matter, just make sure you get lots of bags," Bernie clarified, kind of, as she motioned for Ruby to go.

"My word," Ruby said, setting down her gun and opening the shuttle's folding doors, "if I knew I was shopping, I wouldn't have worn sneakers."

Bernie ignored Ruby's debutante routine and turned to Cliff, "Take a walk around the back of the store. Keep to the sidewalk but see what you can find out."

Unlike Ruby, Cliff was up and out of the shuttle with no qualms. With two of the four gone, Freda and Bernie moved up to the front seats to keep an eye on the white gorilla smoking outside the meat shop. Freda was all lightning, ready to strike. She kept tapping her toe and bouncing her knee. Sitting and waiting was not what she was expecting. She had put her surveillance time in at the window, months ago watching Bernie. But that was the appetizer, since then she'd become a killer. A woman of action and this stakeout pace was not sitting well with her.

"Stop it," Bernie said, pointing to Freda's jack hammering knee.

"I'm anxious."

"Well, stop it. Hunting is about the stalk, not the kill. By the time the lion sets its teeth into the gazelle, it's setting them into itself, because it knows its prey that well."

"We know all we need to know about this asshole."

"No, we don't, but we don't have time to, so we are going to learn what we can, all we can, while we can."

"Why do you think they're here?"

"Because of what Gwen said. About what the men who took her brother and sister sounded like, that and the fact that this man has been pestering you to do business again. You said yourself that you didn't think he was going to take no for an answer."

"He seems too calm," Freda said. "Too calm for having kidnapped kids and killing a woman."

"They always seem calm. It's a sickness," Bernie said. "Just like serial killers, they are only settled in the midst of the storm. When most people are terrified, they're at peace."

"What about you?" Freda turned to Bernie, "You're calm."

"I am." Bernie looked back at her, and a wave of ice ran through Freda's veins. She could see it in Bernie's eyes.

"Empty!" Cliff said, opening the shuttle door. "The back alley is empty. No one watching the back door at all."

"Here comes Ruby," Freda said, seeing the bag-laden lady walking up to the door.

"It's all I could carry. I don't even know what I bought or how much it cost, I just threw a wad on the counter and left."

Bernie took some of the bags from her arms. "Artyom knows your face, Freda, so you and Cliff go around the back. Take the shuttle. Ruby, you and I are going in the front."

"What? Just like that?"

"No," Bernie said, hiding the handle of her gun between the plastic handles of one of the shopping bags, "One in each hand, barrels pointing down. Fingers on the trigger. If my bags drop, so do yours and you shoot anyone in sight."

Bernie walked out first, followed by Ruby, with shopping bags dangling from their hands, they looked just like all the other elderly shoppers moving around the mall. As they made their way to the sidewalk that ran around the front of the stores, the shuttle started up and drove away, heading for the back of the store. The bags weren't heavy, but Ruby's were slipping from her grip. It was her nerves and the sweaty palms that went along with them. She did her best to hold onto the handles, to keep the sandwich of materials in her grip, keep the gun hidden in the middle out of sight from the passersby. This was just the opening act; the real show was behind that glass door, and she prayed that she could keep it up when they walked in.

Seeing that their hands were full, a woman opened the door for them as they approached. It's a good thing she did, because opening doors with guns in your hands was overlooked in Bernie's improved plan. They all smiled at each other as they passed and the friendly lady walked out into the lot, none the wiser, leaving the vengeful Buffalo Girls inside.

"I will be with you in a hot minute," Artyom said from behind the counter in his thick Russian accent, turning his back to the women and heading for the sink. "Pigs and cows don't kiss so I must wash hands."

It was a very small shop. A long rectangle with deli counter and displays on one of the long walls and shelves full of Russian dry goods on the other. The back of the shop had walk-in coolers and the front was one big window, with cured meat hanging in it and the glass door they just passed through. The ladies moved up and stood a few feet away from the counter.

"There is a great special on Darnitsky today, but our Yubileynaya is awesome dude," Artyom said, drying his hands on the cloth towel dangling from the apron string around his waist as he walked back to the counter. He looked Bernie and Ruby up and down, then continued, "Wait, don't tell me. Fried kielbasa sandwiches for you two young ladies?"

If him killing Delilah and taking her grandkids weren't

enough, that did it. Bernie absolutely hated that common nicety. It was an insult, calling mature women young ladies, or making any mention of their age being less than it was. It was fine for them to call each other girl, but not strangers. It made fun of them. Like they were so stupid that they might believe the speaker of the compliment. That they were so horrified by their actual age, pretending they were girls was welcome. It fell in line with, 'you must be her sister' and 'can I see some ID'. It always came from men who thought that poor old women were drooling for the flirtations of a creep.

Ruby was waiting for Bernie's move, and she made none, she just kept looking at the Russian. He in turn stopped his chatter and latched onto her gaze. It was a moment of assessment. He, not sure what was going on, and them not sure if they were alone.

"Bernie?" Artyom said, tilting his head, questioning.

That was the cue.

The bags fell to the floor and the Buffalo Girls raised their guns in unison, having Artyom dead to rights before he could even think of reaching for the cleaver on the block behind him. There was a series of clicks that came from the back cooler area, where two men emerged with their guns pointed at the women.

"Shit my balls. It is you. It has to be! No other person would walk right into my shop and pull a gun. So, does this mean you want to do more business finally?"

"Where are they?" Bernie was not playing and not bothered at all by the guns pointed at her from the back.

"What? The sandwiches? I can make them to go, once we are done our business. But please put the guns away. We are in a mall."

More clicks came from the back of the shop, "Put the gun down or I will—"

"Freda!" Artyom chuckled, waving his hand at his guys to lower their guns. "How are you, you dope fiend?" His men lowered their guns and he continued, "I made her do a line before she left and I have to tell you, this woman is a Hoover!"

Bernie kept her gun pointed at him while Ruby went to the front door and locked it.

"My grandchildren. Where are they?" Bernie cocked the hammer back.

Artyom raised his hands, "Hey, lady. Ease down. I have no idea what you talk about. I want you to move my powder, that's all."

"I know. Is this your way of persuading me?"

"Bernie. I am big fan of yours. I know all about your work up north. I just want to deal with you. I'm starstruck, honestly."

Bernie nodded to Cliff, who moved behind the counter and grabbed ahold of Artyom. His two henchmen stepped forward—

Bang. Bang. Bernie put a hole in each of them.

Ruby and Freda were shocked. Their ears were ringing with the sound bouncing around the small shop, but Bernie was ice, pointed her gun right back at Artyom. "Where are they?"

"Those men were good men, Bernie! There was no need of that!" He was upset, being forced over to the left by Cliff, who had his hand on the back of Artyom's neck.

"Watch the door," Bernie said to Ruby as she made her way around behind the counter.

Cliff reached over and turned on the deli slicer. The high pitched 'ting' of the spinning blade was ominous enough when salami was heading for it, but it was horrifying when it was your face that was getting closer to the speeding razor. Cliff had the large Russian's hands behind his back and was forcing his cheek down towards the slicer.

"Tell me now, or I will take you down, slice by slice until you do," Bernie's voice was as steel as the machine she was threatening with. "Where are my grandchildren?

"Grandchildren? Bernie. I swear. That is not how I do business. I do not threaten kids."

Bernie motioned to Cliff, and he pushed Artyom closer to the blade.

"Hey, hey, hey!!!! Some of my comrades might do things like that, but not me. I am a family man. I respect you. You clearly do not respect me, but I do you. So what? You think I took them to bargain with? How? What kind of deal would that be? No trust. No respect. Where is bargain now? Huh? I don't want to work with you. There! So why would I keep kids if I had them? You have the wrong guy."

It didn't just make sense, his eyes were honest. Bernie dealt with eyes. They never lied, even at gunpoint. You could see the soul through them and Artyom was not lying. He hadn't raised the stakes at all. Never mentioned the kids once or even tried to save his own flesh by saying he knew where they were.

"Let him go," Bernie said to Cliff, who released the Baltic giant, making sure to step away quickly, so as not to catch one of the butcher's fists on his release.

Artyom rolled his neck, stretching out the kink caused by being inches away from becoming deli meat. Bernie motioned for the others to head for the back door, to the shuttle waiting outside.

"I don't know who crossed you, Bernie, but whoever did—heaven help them." Artyom said to her, both a kudos and curse.

"Heaven can't help them," she said and pulled the trigger, tapping him in the right eye and dropping the juggernaut behind his counter.

"Bernie—why?" Freda was stunned.

Bernie pushed Freda out the back door and into the shuttle. "Loose ends," she responded to her stunned partner. "They always end up tripping you—and we're done falling."

Cliff turned the shuttle engine over and started to drive away.

"Jesus, Bern. If it wasn't him then who? The Cubans?" Ruby's heart was racing.

"No. Delilah was teaching the kids Spanish. Gwen would have recognized it." Bernie was searching her mind for answers.

"Where to?" Cliff asked, pulling out of the alley behind the mall and onto the road.

"The Smyrna Yacht Club," Bernie told him.

"Hellsa?" Freda gasped.

"Has to be. Her men are all Norwegian, they speak it, and only it." Bernie sighed, the battle had just become a war and the goliath had become a God.

Kurt and Opal had taken up seats outside in the lanai, letting Marcie and Gwen rest inside. It was odd to see Opal holding her sawed-off shotgun. The pink track suit and matching runners really didn't go with it at all, but her attitude did. She was on lookout and was taking it very seriously.

"You can take a break if you want, Mrs. Murdy," Kurt said kindly.

Opal shrugged it off, "No, I don't need a break." She

turned to the humble bear beside her, "But I could use some coffee. How about you?"

"I can make it," Kurt said, getting up.

"I am sure you can. But let me. It's been a while since I got to make a cup of joe for a fella," Opal smiled, and Kurt backed down.

She set the shotgun on the ground beside Kurt. "Best we keep these from the little one," Opal winked, then quietly went inside.

Marcie and Gwen had moved to the back bedroom hours ago, so it wasn't all eggshells inside. Opal still only opened the kitchen tap a little to fill the kettle because the above ground pipes in these trailers tended to squeak a lot. Once the kettle was filled, she plugged it in and began searching the cupboards for the brown gold of retirement. The freeze-dried decaf of high blood pressure, Sanka.

"Top left," Marcie instructed, coming around the corner.

"Oh, my. Marcie, I am sorry. Did I wake you?"

"No. Just been lying there watching Gwen. Any word from Bernie?"

"Soon," she said, not wanting to say no. "We will soon."

"How are you so positive, Opal? All the time you're smiling. Even now."

Opal opened the top left cupboard and brought down the powdered coffee. "What else is there? Growing up, my father was a fisherman. We didn't have much money, but we had laughs. Lots of laughs. He always said that the pot of gold at the end of the rainbow was full of smiles. That the stripes of color across the sky was God saying, 'see, you made it through another storm, so smile'. I can frown, Marcie. I can be mean and hurtful, but it only hurts me, so

304

I smile. When this storm ends, and it will end, it too will end with a rainbow."

Marcie stepped right up to her and hugged her. Tight. At first Opal was shocked, but then gave in. It took her back to what it was like to hug her own when they needed it.

"I hope you're right," Marcie said from the comfort of her much-needed support.

"I am. Your mother-in-law is the most powerful woman I have ever met."

"This is all her fault."

"Oh, dear, no it's not. She loves your babies so much. This was someone else's plan. Not hers. But it will be over because of her—that is for certain."

"Mrs. Murdy?" Kurt gently called from outside.

Opal released Marcie and poked her head out of the door, "Kurtis, could you please keep it down?"

Kurt looked to the road, "We have company."

Opal stepped down one step so she could see around the door and there was company. On the road there was a long, white car driving slowly past Bernie's trailer. Kurt reached for his gun and Opal motioned for him to stop.

"Put that away," she said.

"Who is it?" Marcie was immediately on guard.

Opal turned back to her, "Everything's fine. It's for me." She gave Marcie a bright smile then stepped down into the lanai. "The kettle has almost boiled, Kurtis. Don't let it reach a whistle. Marcie's awake inside, but the baby isn't. Go in and pour us all a cup. I will be right back." Once the skeptical Kurt went inside, she grabbed her sawed-off that was leaning against the leg of her chair, tucked it into her pink track jacket and headed out the door.

The long white car had stopped right out front of the

trailer with the pink window surrounds—her trailer. She watched the Reverend himself get out, walk right up to her carport door and lay into it with his knuckles. Knocking on the thin metal door violently, like she owed him money.

"Reverend?" she said, walking up the foot of the driveway towards him.

"Opal Rose? We need to talk!" he snapped at her.

"Opal! Is that the Reverend Kind?" Maryanne called out from the road, walking by with Cecilia at her side.

"Why yes, Maryanne, it is."

"Well, why is the good Reverend at your house?" Maryanne was confused and jealous.

"Because he's a personal friend of mine," Opal replied. "Isn't that right, Reverend?"

The Reverend turned to the two ladies on the road and waved to them, "Yes, Mrs. Murdy is a dear friend of mine and the Ministry's."

"Really." Maryanne put her hand on her hip.

Opal was losing her angelic patience, "Say Maryanne, I'd sure like to play the maracas with you."

The word maraca, and the visual that went along with it, triggered her like the subliminal message of a sleeper cell, making the town crier stop her inquest instantly and start walking away.

Opal smiled at the Reverend, "She's a black sheep." She then pointed to the door, "It's open. Shall we go inside?"

The Reverend turned the knob and stepped up into the home. He was barely a foot inside the door, before he turned around and started in on Opal. "What kind of game do you think you are playing?"

"Oh, my. I'm not sure what you're getting at, Reverend."

"Don't you pretend with me, Jezebel. I thought I had

made our donation arrangement crystal clear with you. But you seem to think you can just stop."

"I gave a very generous donation to Paula. Did you not get it?"

"Yes, I got it. But you and I are on a payment plan. One that comes from outside the law and ends when I say it does. I could have just gone straight to the police, Opal, but I thought I would give you one last chance. God is, after all, about second chances." The Reverend noticed the odd way Opal was standing. With her hand tucked into her track jacket, like she was holding onto her kidney. "What's wrong with you? Are you not well? The Lord rewards and punishes, Opal. Have you found yourself out of his favor because of your reluctance to help his word? Smite. That's what happens!"

Opal whipped out the stubby shotgun and pointed it at the man of God. "Oh no! I am very much in his favor, Reverend. I have dipped my toe in Sodom and Gomorrah, I have broken the 6th, 8th, 9th and 10th commandments and I have never felt closer to him."

"Jesus Christ, Opal, put that down!"

"Oh, dear, Reverend, you just broke the 3rd commandment. I believe that means you need to go to confession."

"What are talking about?"

"Your heart is heavy. You need to unburden it. You drive." She wasn't asking, she was telling, with a smile, but telling, nonetheless. She put the barrels of the gun into his back and moved him out the door and towards his car. "Open the passenger side, Reverend. You can slide across."

The Reverend opened the passenger door and did what he was told. There was no courage in this crusader, just whimpering, compliance and wet, white pants. A complete fall from grace.

"Drive," Opal said, and he obeyed, turning the car on and heading out of the park.

It had been a while since Opal left, so Kurt came out to check on Opal. He walked out of the lanai, holding two cups of Sanka in his hands, hoping to disguise his concern with a ready cup of coffee. He rounded the corner of Bernie's trailer just as the white car pulled away—Opal was gone.

The shuttle arrived at the Smyrna Yacht Club and right away they could see that they were too late. Hellsa's ship was enormous, it towered over the others, and it was not there. Her ship was gone but the docks were a hive of activity. The skies had been steadily greying and the winds were picking up. The Club's two cranes were working nonstop, pulling boats out of the water while crews from other boats scurried around their moored ships, tying down sails, stacking deck furniture and sealing openings, readying for the hurricane that had throttled the Bahamas and was now heading for them.

Bernie ran out of the shuttle as soon as it stopped and headed for the docks. She ignored the questions of the security guard and cautions of the other boaters, telling her to watch her step as the waves were picking up, rocking the docks from side to side. She headed straight for the boat that was closest to where Hellsa's yacht had been moored, shouting at the man on the bow of it, when she was still a hundred feet away.

"Where did it go?" Bernie yelled and the man packing away cushions on the open front deck of his pleasure cruiser stood up. He looked around, unsure who this crazy old woman was yelling at, so she continued to yell, "Yes you! Where did the goddamn cruise ship that was parked right there go?"

The man shrugged, "Hell if I know. They never talked to me, and I never talked to them."

"What did you hear? Did they say anything?"

"They said a lot of things, in some crazy accent, but I don't speak Greek."

"It was Norwegian." Bernie stopped on the dock, just in front of the bow of the man's boat. "Do you know at least when they left?"

"Yeah, 'bout an hour ago."

"God damn it! They could be anywhere."

The man stepped to the edge of his bow and spoke kindly, "Hey, I'm sorry you missed your boat, lady. But it's probably a good thing. They headed south. But there is no way they're getting too far, Andrew's coming in hot, even for a ship that size, doesn't matter where they're headed, they'll have to dock somewhere close and soon."

Bernie went from defeated to determined in a heartbeat. "Thank you!" she said to the man and moved quickly back towards the shore, navigating the rocking dock under her feet.

As soon as the folding doors to the shuttle opened, Bernie started barking orders, "Ruby, call Nola, Cathy and Darcy—Freda call Daz, get them all to meet us at the Hollow—now."

Cliff closed the door and once again asked for directions, "So we're heading to the park?"

Bernie sat down, head spinning with thoughts, "Yes, park first, then Miami!"

Darcy was hunched over the toilet, coughing. It had been going on for an hour this time. Blood. It was easier this way, to just spit it straight into the toilet, rather than into tissues, that she would have to dispose of anyway. She hadn't been dancing at all for a couple of weeks, coming up with different excuses and plausible return-to-work dates. She did skip her doctor's test like Nola suggested, but she couldn't skip symptoms. No tests were necessary now. The proof was in the red drops floating around her toilet.

There was a loud banging at her apartment door. Darcy turned to acknowledge it but didn't move from the floor. She picked up her cell phone and looked at it, but there was no one calling. The loud knocking continued in spurts, just enough to let the knuckles of whoever was doing it, rest between sets.

"Ruby! Go away! I can't help. You and the girls will have to do it without me," Darcy shouted from her bathroom—but the knocking continued.

Exhausted, pale and pajama ridden, she got to her feet and headed for the door.

"Go away!" she ordered, stumbling down her hallway, using the walls for support. "Ruby, no!" Her plea sent her into a coughing fit, with no tissue in hand, she resorted to the sleeve of her pajama top, coating the cuff in maroon phlegm.

The knocking continued. Darcy unlocked the deadbolt and opened it, unable to speak through her coughs, but ready to kill with her eyes.

"Oh my God!" Cecilia gasped, seeing Darcy's face so gaunt, pale and withdrawn.

Darcy tried to close the door, but she was spent, and Cecilia easily forced her way in.

"Where have you been?" Cecilia's first question was followed by noticing the coughing her lover was trapped in

the middle of. "Hey, come on. Sit down." She guided
Darcy over to the nearest seat, a sofa just beyond the island
of the open kitchen.

Darcy worked hard to catch her breath, "How did you
know where I lived?"

"Nola told me. I've been going to the club, but you
haven't been there. I thought—maybe you'd changed your
mind or—"

Darcy took Cecilia's hand. "No. Nothing's changed
about how I feel. Just me. I'm not doing well."

Cecilia saw the blood spots on the cuff of Darcy's shirt.
"Cancer? Nola told me that too."

"For fuck sakes." Darcy pulled her hand away. "This is
exactly what I wanted to avoid, she had no right."

"I have a right, don't I? I love you, so don't I have a
right to know?"

Darcy softened a little, "Well, I don't know exactly
what it is—is it cancer or heart or what—but it's this, that's
all I know and before you ask your next question, the
answer is no. I am not going to the hospital or doctor. I
don't want to spend a single second of what I've got left, in
a place that reeks of death."

"Nola told me that too," Cecilia said. "But that's not
what I was going to ask you. I came here to ask you if you
wanted to leave."

"Leave?" Darcy was still spinning from the coughing,
unsure if she was missing something. "I said I'm not going
to the hospital or anywhere."

"Not even with me?" Cecilia tilted her head. "I told
Fred about you. About us—I told him everything. He's a
wonderful man. He understood. He said he'd always
known. He's hurt but he wasn't mad. He was actually
happy I found someone. That I was finally being me. I
know it broke his heart, but he gave me his blessing."

"For what?"

"To run away with you. I want us to just take off, leave everything that reminds us of anything that isn't us and just be together. From now until there is no more now."

Darcy teared up, "You're out of your mind."

"But I'm in my heart. Let's go. Fred gave me open access to the cards, we can stay in hotels until we find a spot we want to settle, if we want to settle."

"Butterfly, I may not make it past the hotel phase."

"Then at least we will have that. I am not asking for anything other than to let me love you, to share my first with your last."

The raging surge of feelings inside Darcy were as strong and powerful as the winds building up just off the Florida coast.

Cecilia urged her, "I don't know if you've looked outside, but there is a storm coming. So, we need to get going, if we're going."

Darcy kissed Cecilia's cheek. "We're going."

The sky was even darker, the rain was getting stronger, and the park residents were hunkering down inside their twister targets. August storms were not rare, but this one was turning towards land, and it had everyone on edge. That was before Bernie started talking and now, they were well past the edge, they were off the cliff, balls of raw nerves.

"You all have your marching orders—" Bernie stopped herself, she had been barking orders and plans from the moment they walked into the trailer, and she just noticed that there were people missing. "Where's Opal?" Bernie asked Kurt.

"She left," he said, honestly but worried about the response. "I thought you knew."

"Left? Left for where?"

"I don't know. A white Cadillac pulled up to her house. She seemed to know who it was, so she went over to talk to them. By the time I got our coffee ready, she was leaving with him."

"Him who?" Freda was alarmed.

"He had white hair, a tan. Nice white suit," Kurt relayed. "Bernie, you told me to watch Marcie, I didn't know Mrs. Murdy was going to leave."

Bernie looked around the trailer again, "And Darcy? Where is she?"

"She's not well." Nola stepped forward. "Trust me, she'd be here if she was."

Bernie counted heads, silently. "Jesus! These things are measured, people, time, variables and I can't measure if I don't know the numbers, is there anyone else missing?"

Freda looked around too, "No, Bernie, the rest are all here."

"Alright then, it's going to take a little adjustment, but I think it will still work. Marcie, you and Gwen are going to hunker down in the Activity Center, this storm looks like it might make landfall and the center is the only solid structure here."

"Still work? You said you'd have them back by now," Marcie was afraid and doubtful.

"That was when we thought it was the Russians—we adjust, Marcie. That's all we're doing, this would work better with all of us, if we had the numbers, but we adjust."

Ruby started to move to the door.

"Where do you think you're going?" Bernie snapped.

"Adjusting. I'm going to go find Opal. Kurt said it was

a white car—I think we both know where she went. If she is there, I'll get her, and we'll meet you at the spot. My word, she needs us, and we need her. Numbers, right?"

She let Ruby leave, because at this point, Ruby was right—they needed all the help they could get. "That's it then, the rest of you round up and get ready to go. Cliff, I'll be going with you—I just need to make a call."

Bernie walked out the carport door, catching Ruby who was making her way back to her trailer, "Poob!" She ran up to her, "I don't know what Opal and that Sunday shyster are up to, but if she's had a change of heart or gone to the cops?" Bernie pulled back a little and gave the order, "If you do find her, she either comes back with you or—"

Ruby stopped her, "If Opal has run on us—then she and Stan will be reunited."

The studio lot was empty. The broadcast was long over, and everyone had gone home. The Reverend had put in his day's work of fleecing his flock, before heading over to Opal's. She instructed him to pull right up to the studio doors. The metal ones on the side that she was familiar with. Opal made him get out, holding him at gunpoint the whole way. Making him crawl back over the seats towards her and out through her passenger door. She forced him over to the studio door, like a seasoned kidnapper and had him unlock it, before pushing him inside with the barrels of her sawed-off.

"Lights!" she shouted at him, which just like this whole affair, was out of character for her, but the Reverend obeyed and flicked a switch, turning on some sporadic house lights above them. The pot lights made the giant space feel intimate, creating donuts of light around the room, one of which landed perfectly onto the leather chair. The high back chair that the Reverend always sat in when taking calls from viewers on the show. The one where he heard confessions from and took donations in. He was in this chair when Opal first saw him on TV. It's from this 'hide-covered pulpit' that his pleas to free her heart of guilt, touched her heart and kept her coming back to be cleansed over and over.

"Sit down," she snapped at him, pointing to the chair with the barrels of the shotgun.

"If you're going to shoot me, just do it." He was becoming more and more agitated by her demands. Clearly not a huge fan of taking orders from women.

"I want you to confess. Sit down and confess," she said, a little more calmly.

"Then you'll let me go?" he asked.

"Reverend, once you have lightened your heart, you will be free to go," she said with a partial smile.

The Reverend moved over to the chair and sat down. "What do you want me to say? That I took money from you?" He looked up at the ceiling, "Dear Lord, forgive me for taking money from her." He looked back to Opal, "There. I confessed."

"That's all that's weighing on your heart?" she asked him sweetly.

"Yes. I took money from you, knowing it was the wages of sin, I have asked for forgiveness—that's it." The Reverend stood up.

Opal pulled the trigger. Bang. Sending buckshot right through the Reverend's right leg, blowing his kneecap apart and he fell back into the chair, screaming.

"That is not all your sins, Reverend. You have more. So many more," Opal encouraged.

He was writhing in pain, yelling out obscenities and pleas for his life, mixed together. Opal walked over to the tiered stand of candle offerings, just beside his chair. She picked up one of the boxes of long matches, pulled one out and lit it.

"Your sins, Reverend, are far greater than me. You used me to get to others. And used them to get more. This whole place is sin. It's a tool used by you to buy your way into heaven, while making us all feel like hell." She placed the box of matches at the bottom of one of the long set of curtains and opened it, then laid the lit match down into it. Within a second, the box was ablaze, its flames climbing up the curtains.

"This Ministry is the wages of sin, Reverend, not my money." She picked up another box of matches and repeated the process, only this time lighting it at the base of the wooden set behind the Reverend's chair.

He tried to get up again, and she shot him again, taking away his other leg and leaving him in a lump on the seat of his chair. Opal walked over and sat down on the floor in front of him, putting her shotgun down and crossing her legs like she was sitting on the church floor in Sunday school. "I have something weighing on my heart, Reverend. Something that Opal thinks we need to burn for. You see, I killed her husband—Stan. He deserved it and I liked it, but she feels bad about it, so here we are. You're going to burn for your sins and so are we."

The flames licked at the back of his chair, and he cried in pain and fear, slobbering, foaming, burning as he watched Opal close her eyes and wait for her turn to come.

"Get up!" Suddenly, through the smoke, Ruby appeared, running towards Opal.

Opal spun around and fired. The blast mostly missed

Ruby, but an edge of the spray caught her left arm, scraping it with hot pieces of small round lead.

"Opal! Put the gun down! It's me! Ruby!" the red-haired hero shouted, recoiling a little and grabbing her arm.

Opal squared up with her. "I know," she said, as cold as death and pumped the shotgun.

Ruby froze, stopped running towards her pink pal. The smoke from the curtains was filling the sound stage, making a wall of grey between the two women.

"Have you lost your goddamn mind?" Ruby shouted.

"Have you forgotten the 10th commandment?!" Opal shouted back, with even more fire.

Ruby scoffed, "Yes! I've forgotten all of that malarkey, not just the 10th! What the hell is wrong with you?"

"Thou shalt not covet thy neighbor's house, wife, servant, ox, donkey, anything!"

"You don't have a donkey!"

"Stan!" Opal screamed, raising the barrels up. "Stan! You whore! You coveted thy neighbor!"

Ruby raised her hands. "Maryanne told you."

"No. I knew. I could smell you on him, every time. That sweet smell of vanilla and sin. I smelled you on my husband—while he was on me or beating on me. I could even smell you the night I killed him!"

The smoke was so thick, the two could barely see each other, only for the light spilling down from the ceiling could they see the outline of each other's faces.

Ruby lowered her hands, "You wrote the letters?"

"All I needed was for you to tell me yourself. We don't lie to each other—sisters! You said I was your little sister! The least you could have done was give me the respect. I gave you the chance. Wrote it out for you! Even tried to spur you on, with the club threat, but you don't care. You don't care about me at all!"

"Yes, I do, Opal. I do! You are my little sister. I'm just a shitty person. I do care about you. I love you, with all of my heart, I just always fuck things up. I should have never bed down with him, but I did. I should have told you, but I didn't. I am that broken. I kicked him out the night you killed him. I told him it was over, but it was too late, and I am sorry. Opal, you might as well shoot me, because I don't think I can change. I've tried, but all I do is hurt everyone. Ben, Natalie, you—just do it. It's only a matter of time until I do something horrible again. So, do it. DO IT!" Ruby closed her eyes, leaned her head back and spread her arms, begging for the salvation of the gun.

"Forgiveness," Opal said, lowering her firearm.

Ruby opened her eyes, "No, do it, Opal!"

Opal's face softened, her eyes became rounder, "No. You confessed. You confessed and I offer forgiveness."

As a small, angelic smile came to her face, a flaming piece of the set behind the convulsing Reverend broke off and fell onto Opal.

"Opal!" Ruby cried. All selfish, fatal wishes for herself, extinguished in the panicked concern for her friend, pinned under the burning wood. She ran to her, through the blackening smoke and grabbed her by the arm. She struggled, pulling on Opal with both hands, desperately trying to free her, begging unseen powers to protect her. Not all prayers are conscious, silent cries for help from the voice of our hearts, but all love is answered. Suddenly, Opal's body became free, and Ruby didn't stop pulling, she dragged her towards the open studio door, coughing and wheezing, scrambling to save both their lives.

The two women stumbled out into the parking lot, with flames and smoke billowing from the building behind them. Ruby didn't stop there, she moved them both over to Opal's champagne-colored Corolla, that was still running a few yards from the door, right where Ruby had left it. Ruby put her stunned friend into the car then got in herself and hit the gas.

As the car peeled out of the lot, Opal looked into the side mirror and saw that the Reverend's Ministry was completely engulfed in flames.

"A second later and we'd still be in there!" Ruby said, realizing the graves they'd left in their wake.

"They still are," Opal mumbled.

"Who are?"

Opal closed her eyes, "People I don't need anymore."

"Hey, are you okay? Stay with me," Ruby said concerned, spooked by the cryptic response.

"Oh, my, yes. I'm alright, and I'm here," Opal said clearly, making her life signs and sanity known.

"I am so sorry," Ruby said, tears bursting from her eyes. "Opal, I never meant to hurt you. I hate myself for it—"

"You know, I never had a sister until you and Bernie," Opal said, lightly, as if Ruby weren't falling apart behind the wheel, she hadn't just had her at gunpoint and the world wasn't burning in the rearview mirror. "Sisters fight, I think. They fight, but they never turn their backs on each other, right?"

Ruby wiped tears from her cheek, "Right."

"Yeah, that's what he said. She said pull the trigger, but he said don't." Opal put her hand on her heart. "He said we were meant to confess our sins, they were meant to burn, and we were meant to start anew."

"Who said that, the Reverend?"

Opal giggled, "Oh, my, no. Why, it was the Lord of course. He works in mysterious ways, doesn't he?"

Even though the yacht was the length of a football field, it still found itself in trouble and had to seek shelter. Moored up against the cement pier, behind the old buildings in the Miami shipyard. It was the home port for the vessel, but it had never seen waters this rough. Hurricane Andrew was only a few miles offshore and was bearing down on the Miami-Dade coast. The ship rose and fell with the surging of the waves, pushing the limits of the car-sized, air-filled bumpers that were keeping it from bashing into the pier. The gangplank was down and was slapping on the cement with every fall, like a long, aluminum beaver tail.

The large guards were stationed at the bottom of the ramp, dressed in raincoats, fighting the wind and pelting rain, trying to stay alert and ready. This was not the destination they were headed for, but it was the safest port they had, given the circumstances.

The guard on the left raised his automatic rifle suddenly, pointing it out into the blowing wind, down the pier in front of him, between the two old, factory buildings. The guard on the right followed suit, both of them searching the rain and fog in the distance for the source of the sound. It was a rumble. A deep thunderous rumble, that could have just as well been the echo of the thunder above, bouncing around in between the two warehouses in front. They couldn't see anything. Between the blowing debris and rain, they were blind. But the sound got louder. And louder.

The guard on the left fired blindly out into the storm in front of him. Sending bullets through the tiny panes of glass in the empty warehouse and soon the two of them were showering the ghost buildings with lead. Behind them, up on the stern of the ship, at the end of the gangplank, another small group of guards appeared, alarmed by the sudden barrage of gunfire. These men were not in raincoats and with the onslaught of the storm, could see even less than the two below wasting brass.

Out of the darkness between the buildings, a light appeared. It was bright and yellow. Static at first but then it got bigger as it was charged towards the ramp. The guards fired again, as did the ones on the back deck, but the light kept coming towards them. There were two loud bangs, louder than the spray of the guards' shots and the two guards at the bottom of the ramp fell like dominoes, one right after the other. The growing light shot out from between the buildings, out into the open—it was a huge Harley Davidson, with plastic-wrapped bricks strapped all over it. As the roaring bike reached the bottom of the ramp, the driver dove off, launching it up the ramp and into the cluster of guards on the back deck.

Boooooom! The explosion was so huge, it blew out all of the remaining glass panes in the old buildings and took half of the ship's back decks with it.

The driver of the motorcycle got to his feet, swung the machine gun on his back around to his front and started firing. That was the next cue. The one that was to follow the sniper shots from Cliff, the loud bangs that took the guards at the bottom of the ramp down. After the bike bomb had been detonated, Daz's machine gun fire was the cue for the third wave.

Out from either side of the old shipyard buildings, the women appeared, locked, loaded and opening fire. Bernie, Ruby and Nola on the left, Freda, Opal and Cathy on the right, covering the emerging guards on the outside decks of the ship in a hail of bullets as they converged in the middle with Daz. Loading and reloading, the wall of women stormed through the downpour of the approaching hurricane, up the ramp, bringing the full storm of their power onto the ship.

At the top of the ramp, Donnie was waiting. He had his hands in the air and a smile on his face. "Impressive," he shouted over the howling winds, "but the party's over if you want the kids alive."

Bernie lowered her weapon and the rest of the crew stayed put as she stepped forward. "Bring them here, now."

"No, no, no. That is not how this goes. You and you alone—inside." Donnie opened the thick marine door behind him, still smoldering from the blast of Daz's explosion.

Bernie looked back at her girls. "Keep watch," she said, then stepped towards the door.

"Whoa," Donnie said. "That stays out here." He pointed to her assault rifle.

She reluctantly unstrapped it from her shoulder and Donnie motioned for her to raise her arms. Bernie complied and the smart dressed gangster had to stand on his tiptoes to pat the tall, senior down. His hands ran along her shoulders, arms, upper back and even chest, then stopped at the back of her waistband, to pull out her snub-nosed revolver. He tossed it on the deck then motioned for her to go inside. As Bernie stepped into the doorway, she waved back at her crew—fourth cue!

Bang.

Donnie fell. Another clean snipe by Cliff, through the storm and right through the head of the cocky 'yes man'.

Bernie could see her from the doorway. She was sitting in a room, in the middle of the ship, wearing all white and looking extremely pissed. It was Hellsa. Gemma and Greg were sitting on the couch beside her. Mouths gagged but looking unharmed.

"You owe me a new boat," Hellsa snarled. "Lucky for you this inside room was made to withstand such nonsense."

"It's me you wanted, so here I am. Let them go."

"Yes, here you are. I had planned to do this so much cleaner. Nicer. Over the phone, a little negotiating and then they would have been sent home, first class. But this weather? Hurricane? Only in America. I swear God sends these storms through the islands to here as a cleansing. To mop up the third world, jean shorts and inbreeds once a year."

"Best laid plans, Hellsa. We adjust. Now, let them go."

"No. Now, you have bitten through your leash."

"What the hell are you talking about? You said you don't hurt children, family, remember?"

"I do what I need to do to get where I've gotten. We adjust. The move you've made. The packages north and now moving product south? This is what I had to adjust to. You've gone out on your own."

"I only moved that because you set up Freda with it. WE had to sell it, or those Russians would have come down hard on us."

"Yes! She was supposed to fail. Die preferably. You were also supposed to fail."

"Then you don't know me as well as you say you do, because I have never been very good at that—failing. I thought we were partners?"

"Verna, do I look like someone who needs partners? You were competition."

"We were moving bodies."

"Were. But eventually? You were making friends. I know your history; it was just a matter of time." Hellsa started to reach inside her white jacket.

Bernie took off like a sprinter, her long legs closing the

gap between her and the white boss. She dove at her—throwing herself into Hellsa, knocking her down and fighting for control of her hands.

Hellsa's gun went off.

From the back of the boat, there was a sudden burst of gunfire as well.

"Run kids! Run!" Bernie yelled.

Gemma and Greg took off, heading deeper into the ship, away from the stern where the blasts of gunfire were coming from.

Bernie got her right hand free and drove her fist, the one with Vergil's golden bison ring on it, into Hellsa's face. She made three hard, fast crosses over the white woman's nose, stunning her long enough to get off her and run after the kids.

As Bernie ran down the center hallway, a bullet flew past her head. Then another past her shoulder. Hellsa was running after her, shooting wildly in the chaotic pursuit. There was a doorway up ahead, so Bernie ran for it and as she passed through it, she slammed the door closed behind her. It was a very decorative door, but it was thick enough to be watertight and was able to stop the next bullet that was meant for her.

Gemma and Greg looked out from the room on the left. Seeing their grandmother, they called to her, and Bernie ran to them, securing the door once inside.

"Come here," she urged them, getting them to come to her, spinning Gemma around and undoing her gag. "Now, I need you to undo Greg's, hurry!"

Hellsa had made it to the door and was firing into it. The bullets weren't making it through the door, but that would not last for long.

Bernie looked across the room to the balcony at the other end. "This way," she said, hustling the kids over to

324

the sliding glass door. She opened it and the wind from the violent storm outside tore into the room.

"Jump!" she said to the kids who looked at her as if she was nuts. "Trust me, you have to jump!" Bernie looked up at the sky. "We are still in the eye. It's our only shot!"

Then Gemma looked over the side. It was three stories up and the water below was all white caps.

"Go!" Bernie pleaded, but the kids were frozen in fear. They had a maniac firing bullets at the door on one side and a suicidal jump on the other.

Bang. A bullet shot through the door and hit the railing right beside Gemma's head.

Bernie grabbed the girl by the shoulders, picked her up and tossed her overboard. She immediately grabbed Greg and did the same, tossing the little boy out into the ocean.

Bang. Another bullet came through the door, shattering the sliding glass door to the balcony, but Bernie didn't flinch, her focus was on her grandkids. She looked over the edge, and in the surging white caps she could see the two of them being hoisted out of the water by Kurt and Daryl, pulled up out of the peaking water and into a hefty, rescue zodiac.

Bang. That one hit—not the wall or door or the glass this time. It hit Bernie. In the hip and she went down. As soon as she hit the ground, she pulled herself up onto her butt, leaning her torso against the balcony rail, in pain, getting soaked by the storm that had reached the other side of its eye and was opening the heavens above them. Through the space in the balcony posts, she could see the zodiac had reached the cement pier. The kids were being unloaded. They were safe.

"Was it all worth it?" Hellsa asked, spitting her words out through the blood pouring from her nose.

"You tell me?" Bernie answered defiantly.

"You mean this?" Hellsa laughed raising her arms, looking around, "I will get another boat. A bigger boat. But you will be dead, and I will have wiped out your family and friends by the time the storm has passed. So yes, it was well worth it. I really should thank you. I haven't had this much fun in years."

Bernie pressed her hand into her hip, trying to stop the bleeding coming from the bullet hole that Hellsa gave her. The pain was staggering, shooting bolts of crippling agony up her spine and down her leg.

"Look at you—dying on a sinking boat? The Union Queen of Buffalo, going down with the ship. It's a wonderful irony, isn't it?"

"You killed Vergil. I know it was you. The Cubans had nothing to do with it."

"It's about time you figured that out. I can't believe that you bought that? Honestly, it was sloppy. Not my best work. You've gotten too trusting in your old age."

"That wasn't supposed to happen—he was not supposed to die—but this? This is pretty much how I thought it would end. I have imagined this moment for years and I always knew it would come down to the two of us."

Hellsa took a step back. "Years? You're dying, Bernie, you're starting to talk the gibberish of the angels."

"Oh no. I'm here. I have worked very hard to get here. I been looking for you for a very long time, Hellsa Brünthberg. I knew it was you who killed Vergil, because it's been you all along. Your obsession with me didn't start in Miami, did it? You were in Buffalo. It was you who got me ousted from my union—from the family and business I had built. My men, my crew who depended on me. That would have died for me. For some reason, overnight they suddenly wanted me to retire. That was you. It was your mole. He was my right-hand man. I spent years teaching him, and all that time he was in your pocket. You had him snitch on me to the Feds after I stepped down too."

"Bravo Bernie! Why couldn't you have just rolled over then? If you had just gone quietly, rolled over for the Feds, all of those old women outside on the deck of my boat would be retiring in the sun, not shooting at pawns and your grandchildren would still have a future."

Bernie shouted, "You already destroyed that! They had a future, with their father! But you took him from them!"

Hellsa lowered her gun, spreading her arms wide, confused, "Your son? I assure you I did not stop his heart. I am flattered that you think so highly of me. But I am not a God, Verna. I wish I could deal out heart attacks with a flick of my fingers—would make this a lot easier—but I cannot."

"It was you who killed him. It was your shit he stuck into his veins. I found out who he bought the tainted junk from and followed it all the way up the chain. I followed it here—to Florida. I bought a house here and everything, so I could watch you. Study you. But then you had to go and put me out of my job and get the Feds up my ass. It was a setback, but I adjusted. The first of many caused by you. Vergil, Benny, the Russians, I adjust. But when I saw that girl laying on the floor of my sister's house, just like Gary, I knew it was time to end this. So here we are."

Hellsa laughed, "That is an incredible story, Verna. Your son was a junkie? Well, at least your white trash stays on brand. Fitting. But why didn't you just kill me when we first met? If you've spent the last, what is it—seven years—hunting me down, why not just put a bullet in my head then?"

"Drop it, Hellsa!" a man shouted from behind the white silk woman.

Hellsa spun her gun around to find three government agents standing in the doorway, guns drawn. Two with DEA patches on their jackets and one in the middle with FBI on his bulletproof vest.

"Agent Wallace—took you long enough, I'm bleeding out here," Bernie announced.

"Agent Wallace?" Hellsa's voice shook. "But you're dead?"

"Not dead, just another adjustment," Bernie said, proudly.

"Put the gun down, Hellsa, it's over," Agent Wallace shouted again, louder.

With death as the only other option, Hellsa dropped the gun from her hand. The two DEA agents ran up, turned her around and swiftly put her in cuffs.

Agent Wallace holstered his sidearm and ran over to Bernie, helping her up off the ground, "We need to get you off of this boat, while we still can."

He put Bernie's arm around his shoulder, and they staggered away from the open deck and the back end of the hurricane that was about to batter the Florida coast like no other in history.

There was no parade. No marching band, streamers or fanfare. Just Cliff driving a borrowed car from Daryl's lot and Bernie riding shotgun. It had been weeks since the hurricane. Since they saved Gemma and Greg, took Hellsa down and sunk her yacht on the edge of the pier in Miami. It was a full hip replacement for Bernie and a lot of Agent Wallace's questions. A lot of paperwork to sign and promises to keep. Under oath, Bernie came clean on everything she was asked to, but only what she was asked to and now, there was one last question to answer.

Cliff helped Bernie out of the car and into the lanai. He guided her down, gently into her wicker throne, holding her hands, helping her find the least aggravating position for her hip. Marcie had watched her pull up, anxious about her return, but she wanted to give her a moment. Giving Bernie the space she needed, for her pride to adjust to this new reliance on help. But she wasn't the one who needed space.

Once Cliff left the lanai, and she heard Bernie let out one of her big sighs, Marcie came out from the trailer, with a small bouquet of flowers.

"Are those from Opal's garden?" Bernie squinted, studying the wild bunch of colors in Marcie's grip.

"Ah, yes. They are." Marcie was embarrassed.

Bernie took the flowers graciously, "How did you know that these were my favorite last-minute gift?"

"I'm glad you're home, but maybe I should come back when you're settled."

"Settled? Well now that is a word I would not associate with myself. Settled. No, please sit down," Bernie insisted.

Marcie was not planning on sticking around. Her plan was flowers and an appearance, that's it.

"Please," Bernie said again, her tone soft, her eyes sullen, "I don't think I could ever be settled unless this is."

Marcie was reluctant, but compassionate to a fault and she found herself taking a seat at the wicker table anyway.

Bernie winced a little from the post-operative pain as she shifted in her chair. "I know you're angry with me, but I promise you that the kids were never a part of the plan. I did and I do want you here, but none of this was ever supposed to involve them. If you hate me——" Bernie caught herself. "I understand you're leaving Florida."

"You have an ear everywhere, don't you."

"No, I just figured you would be. I would."

"We are. Now, can we please stop with the fake friend-liness. You asked me to come here and trust me, I did not want to. But I'm here so——"

"You may not be in a moment," Bernie cleared her throat.

"Say what you need to say." Marcie was angry and antsy.

"Brent didn't leave because I asked him to. Freda shot him——"

"I know. She told me, while you were gone. She did a really good job of pleading your case. He wasn't right for me, but he didn't deserve that."

Marcie's face was stone. But that was just the opening act for Bernie, the rest—it would destroy any hope she had of keeping this relationship with her. I could feel my mother asking for my strength. Speaking to me in her head, asking for my forgiveness, so I gave her both. "Marcie, Gary didn't die of a heart attack. He died of an overdose."

Marcie looked at Bernie sideways and sat back into her chair, bowled over by the weight of the words. "Why the hell would you say that. No. The autopsy——"

Bernie shook her head, "My coroner. My words. Gary died on my carpet, with a needle in his arm."

Marcie's disbelief turned into anger. "How dare you!"

"I did it because he didn't want you to know or the kids to know. He wasn't that man. You know that. He didn't want you to see him that way. That's why I kept it a secret from you. I let him come to my house when he was all hopped up on that junk, because I could keep an eye on him and keep it away from your kids."

Marcie looked down at the ground, "I knew he was

into something, I just didn't know it was that. I thought it was booze."

"It was that too. Sal did a real number on him. I wished I'd been stronger, but when I finally found the courage, I put a bullet in the back of Sal's head. It was the night he'd hit Gary so hard that his little ears were bleeding. I was able to stop the beatings, but not Gary's hurt. I couldn't make that go away. So, I helped him—any way I could. I tried to get him clean, but it failed. Time and time again and then I failed him by letting him continue to do it. Until—that batch. The one he put in his arm that night that had the shit in it. The mix of crap that killed him. He was an addict. On again off again, but he was alive until that batch, and it came from her. Hellsa. The woman who took your kids."

"So that's why you came down here?"

"Not at first. At first, this was where Sal and I came with Gary. Then you and him and the babies. But when he died and I traced the drugs back to that woman, it became all about her. It's been dominoes ever since. First my crew 'helped me' retire. Then the Feds pulled me in for questioning. When they released me, I didn't know if I would get another chance, so I grabbed Ruby, the only person I could trust and I came here. I started this group of women as a way in. The runs with the bodies were just a foot in the door to the underworld down here. Vergil knew, and he held that secret all the way to the grave. Then she came to me, but so did Agent Wallace. He nearly destroyed everything. There was no way I could keep working with her, if the Feds were sniffing around. She'd never trust me."

"Freda killed him," Marcie stated.

"No, she killed an agent that Wallace had tailing her. That's when Wallace and I made a deal. He would cover it. He got to the scene and left all the necessary pieces to turn

the man that Freda killed into him. Then he went under-
ground—off the radar—and told his superiors it was Hellsa's men who killed the agent and he did it, in exchange for
her. I had to agree to not kill her. To give her and her
whole operation to him, as well as everything up north.
Dominoes. The deal Freda made, opened a line of
communication with the crew in Buffalo again, gave me a
line of crime to tie them to. Perfect for Wallace and the
probable cause necessary for the search warrants that went
out the moment we stormed her ship. They're all done. All
the crew across the north, the Russians and the Cubans,
and Hellsa."

"What about you? Freda, Opal, Ruby, me? Are we
chips you bargained with too? My kids?"

"No. We all are invisible, as is all the cash and holdings
we have, Ruby's club and this park. We made a lot of
money, Marcie, and that last weed deal we set up with the
northern crew? I had them pay us upfront. It's all ours to
keep. The Snow Birds have been kept out of it too. The
Feds are happy with my end of the bargain, so it's over. It's
all over. We are invisible."

"I wish Gary had told me. If I knew he was doing that,
maybe I could have helped him." Marcie finally let the
truth about my addiction set in.

"No, you couldn't. That thought is something you need
to leave right here, right now. Trust me, I have tasted the
cold barrel of a gun too many times trying to deal with
that exact same thought. That's why he didn't tell you and
why I didn't either. Those babies need him to have left this
world because of a heart that was too big for it, and they
need you to not carry the blame."

There was a light tapping on the metal frame of the
lanai door. "Oh, hi. Sorry, I hope we aren't interrupting,"

Opal said, standing outside the door, with Ruby and Freda in tow.

Marcie turned to them, "No, we're done—come on in."

The three women practically ran into the lanai, like players on a baseball team, celebrating a home run. There were hugs and squeals of joy smothering Bernie as Marcie got up and headed for the door.

"They wouldn't tell us where you were. What hospital or if you were even okay," Ruby was speaking fast, overcome with excitement.

"Wallace wanted it that way. Until everyone back north and down here had been rounded up," Bernie informed her, she then looked to Freda, "Did you do it?"

Freda smiled, "Done and buried."

Marcie stopped at the screened entrance. She was not happy with the vague, murderous conversation. "What are you two talking about? Who's buried now? What have you done?"

Freda was quick to respond, "Done and buried—meaning finished. We are all now the proud owners of Cicada Hollow!"

Marcie was less than enthused, "Oh, congratulations."

"Congratulations to you too," Freda said. "You're one fifth owner as well."

"And not just this park," Opal added. "Quail's Hollow, Cedar Oaks and a dozen more up the coast."

Ruby handed a newspaper to Bernie, "I bet you haven't seen this."

Bernie looked down at the full, front-page article with a picture of Hellsa in cuffs and the headline that said, 'Grand-mafia retired'. Bernie quietly stared at the exposé, marveling internally at the finality of it all. The devil was done. She had outwitted Satan herself. Made a deal with the serpent, walked the thinnest of lines alone, kept it hidden from her forked tongue and beat her. Hell-sa had been out-fiddled.

"Oh, my. I almost forgot. We have a gift for you!" Opal ran up into Bernie's trailer. "Close your eyes," she said, and Bernie went along with her game. "Put out your hands," Opal said, and Bernie did.

It had weight to it but wasn't too heavy. It was long and sat in both of her palms. It wasn't a cake or more flowers, that was for sure.

"Open your eyes," Opal instructed, and Bernie followed the orders.

Held across the span of her curled palms was a dark-wood cane, with a gold end and large, golden topper. Bernie raised the cane top up towards her and was suddenly overcome with emotion. There were four buffalo heads, all in gold, squaring off the topper, one on each of the four sides. They looked out in each direction, each a little different from the other. Their horned heads all met at the top, where a scripted, embossed, capital B sat as a crown for them all.

"Buffalo Girls," Ruby said with reverence.

"I thought the B was for Bernie?" Opal asked, thrown by Ruby's announcement.

"No, I thought it was for Boss," Freda corrected.

"Can't be boss. We own everything together now, Freda, not just me," Bernie said humbly.

Freda looked back to Bernie, "So that would make me a boss too?"

"I told you we would be," Bernie nodded.

"What about me?" Marcie piped up from behind the scrum of broads.

Bernie answered stoically, "One fifth."

"So, if I'm one fifth owner, does that make me a boss as well?" Marcie fell slowly into the energy of the room.

"If you want to be," Bernie said, surprised by the question, but grabbing onto the glimmer. "You will be taken care of no matter what. One fifth of it all, forever, wherever you want to go."

"Wherever I want to go? You know, if Cicada Hollow wasn't 55+ then I wouldn't have to go anywhere," Marcie said, staring straight at Bernie.

Bernie didn't even take a breath, she just shot her hand into the air, "All in favor?"

Ruby, Opal and Freda raised their hands without a second thought and saying in unison, "Aye!"

As a smile came to Marcie's face and all their hands came down, Freda then chimed in, "I didn't know this was going to be an official meeting, but if we're tabling motions, then the second order of business is—Maryanne has to go! All in favor?"

THE END

ACKNOWLEDGMENTS

Thank you, to my Bernie and my Ruby.

Thank you to my Nicole.

And as always…
Thank you to my Nanners. The original.

ABOUT THE AUTHOR

Sandy Robson is a Canadian author/writer/filmmaker/actor/artist and ginger. He strives to create worlds around characters, not the other way around, stories that put us in their shoes and let us take a moment out of our own realities, to run away in theirs.

For a deeper dive into Sandy Robson's writing, The Trine Trilogy, The Grand-Mafia series, Sandy's weekly blog, release dates, other books and more visit: www.sandyrobsonbooks.com

Scan the QR code below for more:

Books by
Sandy Robson

Made in the USA
Monee, IL
24 March 2024

55670575R00204